HOME WITH YOU

Center Point
Large Print

Also by Liza Kendall and available from
Center Point Large Print:

Walk Me Home

**This Large Print Book carries the
Seal of Approval of N.A.V.H.**

HOME WITH YOU

Liza Kendall

CENTER POINT LARGE PRINT
THORNDIKE, MAINE

This Center Point Large Print edition
is published in the year 2020 by arrangement with
Berkley, an imprint of Penguin Publishing Group,
a divsion of Penguin Random House LLC.

The text of this Large Print edition is unabridged.
In other aspects, this book may vary
from the original edition.
Printed in the United States of America
on permanent paper.
Set in 16-point Times New Roman type.

ISBN: 978-1-64358-638-0

The Library of Congress has cataloged this record
under Library of Congress Control Number: 2020932890

HOME WITH YOU

For our families . . .
the people in the real world who tolerate us
when we're living in our fictional ones.
And to our readers,
always and forever.
We hope you will visit Silverlake often
and enjoy all of our mutual friends there!

CHAPTER 1

Everett "Rhett" Braddock was not the type to hear voices in his head, especially not over the smooth, steady purr of Scarlett, his unapologetically red Porsche. Scarlett always sounded like she ran on single-malt Scotch and sex, not gasoline. But hear voices he did, on the afternoon that he pulled into Silverlake, Texas. His hometown had changed.

Silverlake still retained the charm of a small Texas Hill Country town, but it had gotten spit shined, become more picturesque.

He couldn't argue with the changes from a business point of view. Clearly, the town was doing better than it had been when he'd been unceremoniously booted out of it. But it just wasn't the same.

Rhett took in all the storefronts as he cruised down Main Street. Piece A Cake. Obviously a bakery. Amelie. Looked like a fancy dress shop. Sunny's Side Up—at least something was the same, besides Griggs' Grocers. The Tooth Fairies? A dentist. Schweitz's . . . he sighed with relief. Schweitz's had a new coat of paint and an awful garden gnome outside with a pint in his hand, but it was still there.

Oh, and something else was familiar:

Silverlake's famous sparkling Fool Fest garlands. He couldn't help grinning. The garlands were a bonus for April Fool's, strung between lampposts lining the main drag. *Better watch out,* Pop used to say with a chuckle, *Silverlake fools are fair game all month.* Practical jokes were a given.

Mama had been a glue gun–carrying member of the town's holiday committee, and before everything changed, each spring the living room down at the ranch was festooned with tinsel, ribbon, fake flowers, and crepe-paper jesters. The good folk keeping up the tradition of hanging the awful decorations used to say the neighboring towns that mocked them were jealous.

That last year in Silverlake, Rhett had been telling his family about his rodeo dreams for the New Year. They'd been telling him something else.

As he idled in front of a florist called Petal Pushers, which hadn't existed in his time, he heard, quite clearly, Pop's voice ricochet through his brain. *Son, I ain't gonna tell you again. You get your butt back in that desk chair and fill out those applications.*

So he had.

He heard Mama's voice say, *Rhett, you're special. The places you are gonna go . . .*

So he had.

Colonel Akers, his high school algebra teacher:

10

Sure, you stay here at Silverlake High, you'll be valedictorian by a mile. But life isn't about the easy choices, son. I can't teach you any more than I know myself. Full scholarship? Go. Go to Deerville Academy and push your own envelope. Strain that crazy-smart brain of yours.

So he had.

Declan's voice came to him, too, booming over all the others after their parents had died. Stoic, acerbic, an older brother learning on the fly how to be a father. *You'll get on that plane to Connecticut if I have to knock you out, hog-tie you, and toss you in the luggage hold. The horses will always be here. That scholarship won't. Go to Deerville. Go to Harvard or Yale. Go to Wharton. And go to Wall Street.*

So he had.

Except not all of the horses are still here, are they, Deck?

Not at Silverlake Ranch. When he'd found out Declan now kept only a few horses on the property, it felt like a slap in the face. That wasn't the hardest slap, though. Rhett's mouth twisted as he remembered one particular conversation. His brother had dropped it casually into a discussion about interest rates. Deck had had the unmitigated gall to give Rhett's old rodeo horse away to the Holt family—without even talking to him about it!

At least the new deal Rhett had just struck with

Mr. Holt would allow him to ride Frost whenever he wanted.

Rhett allowed himself a small smile at the thought of Declan's face when he told him what he'd gone and bought this time.

Still idling in front of the ridiculously named florist, Rhett leaned back in his seat and closed his eyes. The leather interior suddenly smelled all wrong. It was buttery and processed, a cologne and not a hide. It wasn't something he thought about in Dallas, but in Silverlake, the difference was notable.

Real leather smelled like a well-worn saddle, a bridle or a harness soaked in a horse's sweat. Real leather wasn't a pale cream color; it was dark and chocolaty and rough in places where a man's calloused hands hadn't buffed it to a working shine.

He clenched the stitched, cushioned steering wheel. German engineers didn't know about what reins felt like between a rider's fingers, and probably didn't care.

Scarlett cost upwards of $300,000 and there were plenty of days Rhett thought she was worth it; he certainly enjoyed her company more than any woman he'd dated in recent memory, and she was nothing if not loyal. Still, he'd trade her in half a second just to be home before the accident, fifteen again, and back on Frost, his silvery Appaloosa. He couldn't wait to see the old boy.

He'd rather see him, in fact, than his brother Declan, though he was worried about him after the devastating loss of the Old Barn. What did that say about Rhett, exactly?

His mouth twisted as he glanced at the passenger seat next to him. Three Red Delicious apples knocked heads in a plastic bag. A bunch of carrots roped together eagerly stared up at him. In the footwell, a six-pack of Shiner Bocks had turned on its side, condensation from the bottles staining the top of his crocodile-hide briefcase, which lay outraged on the floor.

The beer was for Frost, who loved it. Pour that dark, fizzy liquid into a bowl and Frost would slurp it right down, twitching his velvety muzzle when the bubbles popped on his tongue. Then he'd show his teeth in a big horsey grin.

Damn, Rhett had missed him.

But you didn't trailer a horse and a western saddle the size of an armchair up to Deerville Academy in Connecticut. And you sure didn't talk to anyone about 4-H or rodeos—especially when they'd already started mocking the fact that he went by Rhett.

Where's Scarlett, Rhett?

I got her right here, boys. He smiled and gave the dashboard a pat.

Of course, if he wanted to see Frost, he'd have to see Julianna Holt, too. A blessing or a curse? Rhett's smile faded at the thought of her. He'd messed that situation up but good. You didn't screw around with your best friend's little sister, and he'd gone and done just that—only weeks ago in Dallas. He'd bolted from her bed in the morning. And ever since then, he'd been trying to come up with any acceptable explanation to give Grady. Problem: There *was* no explaining to Grady, who'd kill him if he ever found out—and worse, Rhett couldn't stop thinking about Jules. He needed to erase her from his mind.

"You're leaving?" Jules had mumbled, still half-asleep. She opened her hazel eyes and peered at him, the sleepiness chased away by hurt.

"Yeah," Rhett had said, trying not to look at her. He hadn't intended for anything like this to happen, but seeing Julianna Holt all grown up had done something to him that he never could have anticipated, so he went with it. And now he had to make it stop. For even though these last few hours felt about as right as anything Rhett could remember, reality had shown up with the morning sun. And reality was, Rhett had just had a one-night stand with the one person he should have never, ever touched. "You're Grady's little sister! What was I thinking?"

"Grady's little sister," Jules repeated mechanically. Her face was blank as the white sheet over her hot, curvy, delicious little body.

"You can't tell him, Jules. Promise me. You

14

won't say a word. To anybody. If he finds out, he'll never forgive me."

She lay there, frozen under that sheet.

He almost said something then, knowing how he looked, like a careless man who broke hearts as a habit. But that's what he needed her to think.

"Right," she finally said. There was a pause. "Don't you worry 'bout a thing, Rhett." She said the words slowly, steeped in some emotion that he still couldn't read, no matter how he angled it, how many times he mentally replayed that sentence or her expression. *"I won't give your little secret away to anyone—not even my brother."*

Rhett stared out the car window at the riot of flowers in the Petal Pushers window.

That night had been one of the best nights of his life. He should have left differently, though.

Wish I'd never done it . . .

Nah. I'd do it all over again. Twice. At least.

Stop it!

Rhett turned off the ignition and stepped out of the car, letting the door close on its own.

He shoved his hands into his pockets, looked up and down Main Street, and then headed into the florist shop. He owed Julianna Holt one big apology, and he'd better do it before he set foot on her family property.

Inside the florist, a gal was arranging a huge bouquet of yellow roses with some fancy

15

greenery. He couldn't help but stare at her bare arms, which sported full sleeves of tattoos: flowers of every imaginable variety. The tats were works of art and though he wasn't usually a fan of them, they suited her. She raised her eyebrows at him, taking in his custom-tailored suit, white shirt, and gold cuff links. "Can I help you?"

A bouquet. He'd send Jules a bouquet. The one he should have sent a lot earlier, if he'd been thinking of anyone but himself and what Grady might do to him for getting naked with his baby sister.

"Yes." He smiled his megawatt *let's close this deal already* smile at her. "I think you can."

She waited.

"I need . . . I need the most beautiful, the most special arrangement you've ever done in your life."

Her eyebrows shot up to her hairline. Her eyes themselves focused on his pricey watch. "Do you, now."

"I want the best."

"Looks like you're used to it," she drawled.

He should have left the watch in his glove box. "What's your name?" he asked, trying to decide how best to win her over. *Charm Offensive Boosters activated.*

"You don't remember me?" She said it too casually.

Oh no. "Uh . . ." Nobody he'd known in high

16

school had those distinctive tattoos. "Sorry."

"Maggie," she said, her gaze shifting from his watch to Scarlett, which she could see through the storefront window. That wasn't exactly admiration in Maggie's eyes. "And you are Jake and Declan's brother Rhett. I heard you'd become some kind of banker . . . you've been busy, huh?"

"Maggie Cooper? Of course . . . sorry. It's just that you've changed a lot."

"So have you." She looked him up and down.

Rhett Braddock, Some Kind of Banker. Managing partner of my own venture capital firm, actually. I turn millionaires into billionaires—myself included, thanks to getting in on some wildly successful high-tech IPOs. But we can go with banker. "Yeah, guess I have." *Note to self: Consider borrowing clothes from Jake.* But why should he hide his money? The money that "made" him—even though he'd made *it*.

"Well, Rhett, what kind of bouquet can I do you for?" she asked.

He stared at her blankly. "I don't have a clue."

"What kind of flowers?"

"I don't know. The best."

"Yeah. You told me." She waited.

He shrugged.

"Okay. So what exactly are you trying to say with these flowers?"

"I . . . uh . . ." Rhett stumbled over this. "That . . . hello . . . and I'm sorry?"

17

"Hello and I'm sorry. And it's got to be the most spectacular, beautiful arrangement I've ever made."

"Yes." It wasn't what he really wanted to say, but it was all he could give.

If Rhett could tell Maggie to write what he *really* wanted to say . . . *You have no idea how sorry I am that our one-night stand will never be more than one night.*

Because it never would.

Grady was family. Closer than his own. Grady had been there for him when Rhett's parents' died, when Declan sent him away, and during all those tough years back East. Grady had gotten him through the bad times, and messing around with his little sister was *not* how to repay the debt.

And so, Jules? Well, Jules wasn't allowed to matter. Jules couldn't matter.

"Done," Maggie said, finishing up the order description on her pad. "Who's it for?"

"Julianna Holt, out at—"

Maggie's hand froze. She looked up from the pad, and whatever nice she had left after considering his watch and car and clothes, well, it all just drained away. "I'm familiar with the address." She dropped the order pad on the counter and then crossed her arms over her chest. "I don't think Jules knows, yet."

Rhett studied Maggie's aggressive tapping of the pen against her biceps. "Knows what?"

18

"That you're taking over her place."

Aw, jeez. Small towns. No secrets . . . Rhett cleared his throat. "That's not exactly how I'd put it. Word travels fast."

"Yeah," Maggie said coldly. "So what's your budget for the flowers?"

"Whatever it takes."

She gave him a too-sweet smile. "Mmm. If it were me? It would take *a lot.*"

They stared each other down for a moment before Rhett shook his head, letting loose a bark of laughter. He fished out his wallet and forked over his black Amex. "Obviously, I need it delivered today."

"Obviously. Women *love* flowers," Maggie said in saccharine tones as she processed the transaction and handed back his credit card. "I'm *sure* this will make *everything* all right."

CHAPTER 2

Julianna Holt had no idea that her calm, peaceful, ordered world would shatter in ninety-seven seconds flat. She whistled as she took the familiar flagstone path from her cabin on the Holt family property to the stables, enjoying the chill in the March morning air. Woodsmoke drifted on the breeze; the sun lit the cedar and mesquite trees golden and dappled the grass underneath them with intriguing shadows. A small animal scurried in the underbrush. White clouds puffed and chugged across a sky bluer than Rhett Braddock's eyes.

Ugh.

Jules shook her head to clear his image out of her mind yet again, and refocused her thoughts on her morning chores: feed and water Don Quixote—the donkey—and the horses, let them out to graze in the paddock while she dug out their stalls, and then groom them as necessary. She'd need to change the bandage on Curly's right-rear fetlock and check the cut over Shiner's left eye . . .

She needed to pick up more saddle soap and clean the tack this afternoon, too. Jules rolled up the sleeves on her oversized flannel shirt as she walked. Goose bumps erupted on her bare

20

arms, but they would fade as soon as she began work.

She fished a plain rubber band out of her pocket and secured her hair in a messy knot, then kicked a branch out of her way with the toe of one rubber riding boot. Chico the squirrel chattered at her from the same tree branch he occupied most mornings, and she tossed him the usual pecan. A cautious creature, he waited until she'd gone a few steps before he skittered down and pounced on it.

Her fanny pack held a bag of baby carrots and another Ziploc of apple slices for the horses. Dad would fuss at her for spoiling them, as usual. And as usual, she'd smile, nod, and ignore him.

He'd seemed tired and grim yesterday, his John Deere hat tugged low on his forehead and his shoulders uncharacteristically slumped as he sat on the mounting block, staring at nothing. But he'd denied anything was wrong when she asked.

Jules walked into the cool, dim barn and inhaled the loamy, musky, overpowering scent of the horses stabled there: twenty-three of them—plus Don Qui, who worked to calm them when necessary and was everyone's buddy—in adjacent stalls on each side. The stalls, like the rest of the property, had seen better days.

The once-glossy dark green paint was peeling from the old-fashioned oak enclosures, and generations of horses had gnawed or rubbed or otherwise made their marks, like kids writing on the wall that *Johnny was here.*

How she'd love to replace the old, dingy stalls with new prefab ones: iron grills and sliding doors. Better drainage in the cement floors . . .

Out of habit, she went straight to Don Quixote's stall, dropping a kiss onto his furry forehead and rubbing his brown ears. Don Qui wore a colorful Mexican halter embroidered with flowers and beads. His eyes were rimmed with the same white that adorned his muzzle. It looked almost like eyeliner. The rest of him was a lovely reddish chocolate brown. He had a tuft that stuck up between his ears.

"Hi, you funny old thing. Did you keep all the horses in line overnight? Any incidents to report?" The donkey evaluated her with his wise old eyes and rubbed his muzzle on her shoulder. He took her affection as his due and chewed phlegmatically on his hay.

Don Qui was the only creature she'd told about what had happened in Dallas. Otherwise, it had stayed in Dallas. Pure humiliation. The biggest mistake of her life. She hadn't told her friends or her aunt Sue. Jules just wanted to forget about it.

"You stink," she told him affectionately. "You need a bath."

He backed away from her, looking woebegone. A bath was an inexplicable tragedy in his life.

Jules laughed and moved on, waving hello

to Midnight, Dusty, Frost, and Blossom, who nickered as she made her way to the tack room and office. Frost. The old sweetie. Much nicer than his former owner. She banished Rhett Braddock from her mind yet *again*. What a jackass. And how she'd idolized him as a young girl. Disgusting.

Her dad was seated in the tack room, at the corner desk that was always a chaos of papers and scrawled-upon envelopes and Post-it notes. Behind him, on the wall, looking completely out of place, was a large abstract painting done up in blacks and blues. But Grady had painted it himself and given it to Dad for Father's Day one year, and Dad insisted on giving it a place of honor.

Maybe it was the blue streaks next to Dad's skin that made him look so odd.

He was staring at the cement floor, pale under his farmer's tan, his hands clasped loosely between his denim-clad knees. She'd never seen so much gray in his sandy hair, and the creases that radiated from both eyes had deepened.

"Dad?"

He raised his head and nodded at her, his hazel eyes bloodshot.

"Dad, is something wrong?"

He sighed, nodded, and cleared a bunch of feed and equipment catalogs off the folding metal chair next to his. "Siddown, Jules."

"O-kaaay." She sank into the chair, narrowing her eyes on him.

With a *thunk,* Dad dropped the stack of catalogs under his desk.

"What's going on?" she asked.

He took a deep breath. "Well, baby doll, a number of things."

Baby doll. He'd called her that ever since she could remember. It was sweet, it was endearing, and yet it kept her infantilized. Kept her forever a toddler in his eyes.

"First . . . I'm not well."

"What? What does that mean?" She searched his eyes for reassurance, and sure enough, he dredged some up for her in the form of a tired smile. It wasn't convincing.

"It means Doc found a lump in my neck . . . that sore throat wasn't a cold. Doc's thinking it's a tumor in my thyroid . . ." His gaze stayed locked with hers, but his voice trailed off.

"Are you talking about . . . ?" *Cancer?* Jules shook her head, refusing to allow the words into her ears or her mind.

Dad coughed and looked down at his hands.

"No. No, no, no . . . that can't be right. You're the healthiest guy I know. You've been active all your life. You don't even have any vices! Who's telling you this? Doc Hernandez? Maybe he's wrong."

Dad nodded. "He's not wrong, though we're

still figuring things out. Taking appointments, figuring out what stage it's at so we can figure out how to handle it." His voice caught, and for the first time that hoarseness he'd been battling for months had real meaning. "I'm real sorry, darlin'." The anguish on his face was for her. Jules forced herself not to break as she watched him work hard to keep his composure. *Oh, Dad, say you're kidding me.* But he didn't say that. He didn't say anything. Jules jumped to her feet. "Get a second opinion!"

"I have, honey. And I'll be heading down to MD Anderson next week."

The name hit her like a blow. MD Anderson: the cancer treatment center in Houston.

"Does Mom know?" she managed, through a clogged throat.

"She does."

"Since when?" Jules realized that her mother had been carefully avoiding her, and felt utterly betrayed.

"Couple of weeks. I asked her to let me tell you."

Weeks? Jules tamped down utter panic and disbelief. "What about Grady? Does he know, too?"

"Yes, honey. Same story."

"Why wouldn't you tell us all together?" Jules tried to bend her mind around it. Her dad swallowed hard. He appeared to search for words that wouldn't come.

"How bad is it?" Jules asked. *There's more to this than he's saying.*

"Well, like I said, we're gonna get me some more tests and some more consults, you know . . ." Dad shifted uncomfortably. "But that's not the whole of it."

Jules pressed her hand to her heart. "Tell me. Dad." *Tell me there is zero chance it's terminal.*

"Jules. Honey, I've sold the stables—"

"What?" Jules couldn't even process the statement.

"—but you don't have to worry about a thing, all right? The deal is that you get to keep your job here. That way—"

"What are you *talking* about? *Sold the stables to whom?*" Jules couldn't stop her voice from rising and then cracking.

"Braddock. Calm down, baby doll. Your job is safe. That is inked into the contract. You stay on as manager here, all right?"

Braddock? He'd sold to Declan? *Dad is sick with cancer and the stables are gone, sold to the Braddocks?* She couldn't breathe, couldn't think. Her entire life was turning upside down. "None of this is all right, Dad! None of this makes any sense at all! How is this even—"

She stopped.

Her dad was struggling with his emotions, his mouth a grim slash. "It gives me some peace to know that if things go south—I don't expect that, but it's all got me thinkin'—that you'll be taken care of. Far's I know, what I got—it's completely treatable."

She got up and put her arms around him, forcing the ugly feelings of betrayal to the back of her mind. "I'm sorry. I'm sorry—I'm more upset about your health than anything else."

He squeezed her tightly and stroked her hair. "I know, honey. I'm gonna be just fine, you hear? But I won't be able to work round here like I used to. Not just because of this, but also because even though I've tried to ignore it, I just don't have the stamina to run an operation like this anymore. Truth to tell, I haven't been able to make ends meet for a while, now, and it's only going to get worse while I'm taking care of my health. The doctor visits, the treatment, medication after—it's expensive. But more than that, this is a wake-up call. Your mom and I are getting older and this isn't going to be the only medical emergency we ever have. That is the hard, ugly truth. Your mom and I—we're gonna have some real tough times ahead financially."

Jules's bitterness grew. Her mother and brother—*Really, Grady? How could you?*—had known all of this while she'd gone blithely about her work, whistling while the blue Texas sky was falling in the west, along with the sun.

They'd known that Dad was sick. They'd known that the business was in trouble. And they'd known that he was selling it out from under her without giving her a chance to manage it to profitability herself. If they'd given her the control she'd been asking for, maybe they'd have the money to easily pay for her dad's treatments.

And she had so many ideas! An indoor riding ring. More boarders. More lessons—they could take on another instructor for a percentage of the fees. She'd been talking to her dad about these concepts for the last two years . . . and he'd nodded and said he'd take this and that under advisement, or that he'd think on it. He'd flapped her away like a mosquito.

This wasn't just about her being the baby of the family. It was about her lack of a college degree. Because she lacked some piece of paper and a few hours in a classroom, they thought she was helpless to fend for herself. And that was just plain bullcrap.

Get over yourself, Jules. This isn't about you— it's about Dad!

She wondered, again, what kind of a daughter she was. To be resentful about the stables instead of being more freaked out about Dad's condition. What was wrong with her?

Grady would smirk and ask if she wanted a list or pictures of everything "off" about his little sister. The big jerk. How could he not have said anything about all of this? It broke the sibling code. He also knew how much her life revolved around the stables and the horses.

She realized that he'd been avoiding her, too. She was going to kick his butt! She had a mind to go right down to the fire station and do it immediately.

Then Jules realized she was lapsing again: thinking about everything *but* her father's cancer. She took his hand, traced one of his weather-beaten cheeks with her other hand; brushing over the bristles that were now gray. She'd been fascinated with their texture as a child. His eyes, hazel like her own, watered, and he averted his gaze. He cleared his throat. "Love you, honey."

"I love you, too, Dad. So much."

"You all right?" he asked.

No. Not by a long shot. But she didn't say the words aloud. She gave him another hug, nodded that she was okay, and sprinted to the feed room to call her friend Mia, a nurse at Mercy Hospital. She needed to hear her voice, calm and soothing with just a bit of huskiness.

Mia was with a patient, but called her back within five minutes. "Hey, Jules. What's up?"

"I . . ." Her throat clogged with tears. "Mia, look, I know how busy you are. But can I swing by? Just for a few?"

"Of course," Mia said without hesitation. "Come on over. Just have one of the nurses at the station page me if I'm not with them, okay?"

• • •

Our Lady of Mercy Hospital had seen better days, but Silverlake hadn't yet started its planned renovation of the facility. It was a boring, blocky building, six stories high, with groaning elevators, uninspired artwork, and sickly green walls. Even floral arrangements delivered to the hospital seemed eager to check out and escape.

Old Kingston Nash had paid for a wing of Mercy, back in the day, but he'd recently—and inexplicably, to most of the townsfolk—switched his charitable allegiance to the firehouse, of all things. Since he'd had a war going on with Silverlake Fire and Rescue for more than a decade, people wondered if he was in his right mind . . . but the old man was so crotchety that nobody had the nerve to ask him. The town council just thanked the good Lord that he'd stopped ranting at their meetings.

Jules found Mia at the nurses' station, inputting patient records into a computer. Her red hair was in a messy French braid, strands pulling loose everywhere. Her face was drawn, she had blue shadows under her eyes, and her freckles stood out in stark relief against her pale skin. She looked as if she hadn't slept properly in weeks, and she was thinner than usual, too.

"Mia?" Jules touched her shoulder. "You okay?" She'd been through an ugly divorce from her ex, Rob Bayes, recently . . . and Rob had left

Silverlake, leaving her in debt, childless after too many heartbreaking attempts, and harboring a secret that Jules wasn't allowed to share with a single soul.

"Fine, why?" The faraway look in her friend's eyes faded as she focused on Jules. "You, however, are not. What's going on?"

Jules cast her eyes toward the other nurses.

"Yeah . . . come on." Mia led her to an empty patient room, where they sat on a couple of hard guest chairs, and Jules couldn't help spilling everything. "My dad . . . he looks so old and sad . . ."

"Tumors are often highly treatable, hon. He's probably going to be just fine."

"He looks exhausted—"

"Totally normal, under the circumstances."

"—and he sold the property out from under me, and I'm so, so, so, *angry* . . . and that makes me feel so *bad*. Because obviously he wouldn't have done that unless he felt that he had to . . . he says he just can't keep up with it any longer . . . and I'll still be manager . . . but I wanted to take over one day. I wanted it to stay in the family. I wanted it to be, well, mine . . . and—" A wave of nausea threatened to overwhelm her. "Oh, man, I do *not* feel good."

Her friend nodded and slipped an arm around her, squeezed her shoulder.

"Mia, what is *wrong* with me?" Jules wailed.

"How can I be so selfish; thinking about the stables and myself, and not my dad, during a time like this?"

"Nothing's wrong with you," Mia said crisply. "You're stressed. You're in denial. It's very common to think about everything but the elephant in the room. It's okay."

"It is? I feel like a horrible, terrible, no-good person . . . a shallow, little . . . *baby doll*." She spat out the term.

"You are not a horrible, terrible, no-good person. You're a very good person, Jules. You're like the patron saint of animals in Silverlake," Mia said soothingly.

That's when Jules realized that Mia hadn't sounded all that surprised at the news. "Did *you* know? Before me?"

Mia hesitated. "Jules, I do work at the hospital. There's a grapevine. I'm sorry."

"And you didn't tell me immediately?"

"I couldn't, Jules. I'm bound by patient confidentiality, HIPAA, all of it. You know that."

Jules struggled with a mixed bag of emotions. "I do know," she said after a long pause. "But I want to be mad at you. I want friendship to kick HIPAA's butt. Do you get that?"

"Yes," Mia said. "I'll understand if you're mad. And I'm sorry." She waited. Her rock. Her friend.

"I don't want to be mad at you. I love you. You've been my best friend since forever."

"I love you, too."

And that's when Jules let out a long, anguished wail and burst into a storm of tears. "Is my dad going to be okay?"

CHAPTER 3

Once she'd recovered, Jules went back to the stables and checked the tack room, but Dad was gone. Grady's painting reflected her mood: somber and bruised. She was staring at the desk that would now never really be hers when a bouquet the size of a sofa appeared in the doorway. And it apparently had legs of its own. The bouquet staggered toward her. It was a little alarming.

"Where would you like these?" said a male teenage voice.

She blinked at them. Roses, hyacinth, lilies, and an assortment of exotic blooms, most of which Jules couldn't even name. Gorgeous greenery woven throughout. The scent of the flowers was so strong that it overwhelmed the powerful smells of the barn: old wood, saddle leather, sawdust, hay, horse hide, and animal by-product.

"Are you sure those are for me?"

"Yes, Jules. They're for you." The sofa-sized arrangement filled her entire desk as Sam, the youngest brother of Grady's firehouse teammate Tommy, set it down.

"Who could these be from?"

"Read the card?" Sam suggested.

She rescued her laptop from underneath the monster bouquet and set it in her chair before locating and opening the small white card from Petal Pushers. " 'Hello,' " she read. " 'I'm sorry. XO, Rhett.' "

All the blood drained from her head and her knees went weak; she sat down, right on top of the computer she'd just dropped into her chair.

"So?" Sam asked. "Who're they from?" With Grady at the firehouse, Jules knew everyone on the squad almost as well as her own family. Tommy and his two younger brothers were carbon copies in looks, and it seemed that nosiness also ran in the family.

"Thank you for bringing them, Sammy, and not to be harsh, buddy, but it's none of your beeswax." She dredged up a smile to soften the words, fished out a five-dollar bill, and gave it to him. Then she eyed the stunning bouquet as if it held toxic waste—because it did.

"I'll just ask Maggie."

"You do that, bud."

Sighing, Sam slouched out of the barn, as Jules's fury grew.

Who the hell did Rhett Braddock think he was? He'd almost chewed off his own arm to get out from under her that morning in Dallas. He'd used her like a Kleenex. He'd never even called her afterward. And now this? This was supposed to make up for his behavior? Not even close.

With a silent apology to Maggie at Petal Pushers, who'd clearly put in untold hours of work on the thing, she heaved the flower arrangement into her arms. It was as heavy as a sofa, too . . . and there was only one place for it.

Dad stepped out of the small bathroom. His eyes widened. "Good Lord! Those are absolutely the most beautiful flowers I have ever laid eyes on. Who're they from?"

Jules emitted a growl.

"Pardon?"

She couldn't speak.

"Ah. They're from Braddock. They gotta be. Well, now—what a class act. He's sent them as a gesture of goodwill, has he? To seal the deal. And get on your good side, huh?" Dad laughed.

Wrong Braddock, Dad. But she had no intention of explaining to her father that she'd accidentally had a sleazy one-night stand with Rhett, the guy she'd been dreaming about forever. Well, now she didn't have to dream; reality had bitten her on the butt like a summer mosquito. Jules spied the wheelbarrow she used for mucking out stalls and lurched toward it.

"Honey? What're you doing?"

She dumped the flowers in, headfirst.

"What has got into you, girl?" Dad called after her.

"Please leave me alone, Dad. I'm sorry."

"I understand you're not happy about the sale, but . . ."

Jules trundled the arrangement the whole length

of the barn, past the gently nickering and snorting inmates who eyed her curiously, and all the way to Frost's stall at the other end. His once-white muzzle had gone gray, his lower lip drooped, and his eye sockets had sunk. But Frost was still beautiful; still had one blue eye and one brown.

She set down the wheelbarrow, kissed him on the muzzle, and then opened the half door that kept him inside. She gestured to the offensive arrangement. "What in the Sam Hill does your owner think I'm gonna do with these? Huh?"

Frost tossed his head in the air and snorted.

"Exactly. They are *obnoxious!*"

Frost eyed them dubiously.

"Does he really think I'm this easy to manipulate? Send her flowers and that'll solve everything?"

The old rodeo horse thoughtfully stuck out his tongue, as if to say, *Dummy*.

"What should I do with them, boy?"

Frost whinnied.

"Does he think flowers make up for him being an *epic* jerk?"

The horse blinked.

"Yeah, no. They do not. So do you like the taste of fern? How about tiger lilies? Roses?"

Frost nosed them gently, and then snorted pollen out of his nose, shaking his head.

"I agree. I'm sure hay tastes much better. And it's prettier, too, than these . . . this . . . fake, pretentious, overblown, sickeningly expensive, and freakin' WAY-TOO-LATE bouquet!"

Jules picked up the handles of the wheelbarrow and tipped the whole thing into Frost's stall. Then she stepped out, shut the door, and glowered down at the flowers.

Frost shifted his weight from side to side. He snorted again. Sidled around, not used to having something that size on the floor of his stall. And then, completely unself-conscious as horses are, he relieved himself upon them, blinking lazily as he did so.

Jules laughed so hard she choked. "Good boy! Great idea. That's *exactly* how they should be watered. Wish I'd thought of that myself." She unzipped her fanny pack and fumbled out a couple of apple slices. She held them flat in her palm, and Frost accepted them with appreciation, munching away.

"He likes beer better," said a deep male voice that she'd hoped to never, ever hear again. "I brought him some."

She whirled so fast that she stumbled and fell— not gracefully—into the wheelbarrow.

"Good to see you, Jules." Rhett Braddock's blue eyes danced as he extended a hand to help her out.

She eyed it as if it were a python. "What are you doing here? *Get out of my barn.*"

Rhett pursed his lips and shoved his hands into the pockets of his suit trousers—which looked as though they were custom-tailored, out of fabric she couldn't have afforded one square inch of. "Get out of your barn, huh?" He looked over his shoulder, where to further her mortification, her father stood, his brow furrowed.

"Well," said Satan Incarnate, turning back to face her. "As a gentleman, I would truly like to oblige you, Miss Braddock. But there's one small problem: It's now *my* barn. So maybe, honey, you should take my hand and get out of my wheelbarrow?" He smiled the most gentle, apologetic smile to take anything vicious out of his words.

Rhett? *Rhett* Braddock had bought their property? Not Declan?

Impossible. Unacceptable. Worse than the worst nightmare . . .

"Julianna Holt," said her father sternly, as she lay sprawled on her butt in the wheelbarrow, legs splayed. "I brought you up with more manners than this. You stand up now, you say a proper hello to Rhett, here, and then you will say a heartfelt thank-you to him, for bailing us all out of a jam."

Rage, pure rage, built within her. Thank you? Say a proper hello? How about Rhett Braddock learned to say a proper *goodbye* after his wham-bam-thank-you-ma'am routine?

Rhett felt bad for Jules, he really did. The situation was tough enough on her without Billy

Holt demanding that she make nice to him. But he could hardly explain to her father what had gone down between them. Without a doubt, he'd get a fist in the face instead of the deed to the Holt property.

He shot her a sympathetic glance, which she rejected by simply not acknowledging it at all. Nobody, not even sexy, smudged, mad-as-a-wet-cat Jules, should look that good sprawled in a wheelbarrow in dirty work clothes—but she did. Rhett's heart skipped a beat, even though she'd dumped his flowers into Frost's stall and watched him piss on them.

A classic move—even if it was, quite literally, at his expense. But it also was a move that told him something. If she was this angry, then she had feelings for him—and he wasn't quite sure how to feel about that.

Methinks the lady doth protest too much.

He was confident now that his apology bouquet had worked even better than he'd expected. She was just royally pissed at her father for selling the Holt place to him—and at him for buying it.

She was a sight for sore eyes . . . and so was Frost, after all these years, chomping on some hay. Frost looked surreal, standing in a field of pissed-on flowers.

Jules still refused to take Rhett's hand. She climbed out of the wheelbarrow on her own.

So he moved forward and stroked Frost's

40

muzzle. "Hey, buddy. Do you even remember me, after all this time?"

Frost pushed against his hand, inhaled deeply, then snorted.

"Yeah. I'm sorry. But I've missed you."

Frost nuzzled his neck, which almost brought tears to Rhett's eyes. And then he nipped him smartly on the shoulder.

"Ow! Okay, I guess I deserve that." Rhett rubbed the injury.

Jules grinned and then gestured to the remnants of the bouquet in Frost's stall. "So sorry, Big Shot. I brought the flowers to your horse to show him what a great guy you are. I set 'em on top of the door so he could get a good look. Then they kind of slipped and fell."

Billy coughed and scuffed the cement floor with the toe of his roper.

Rhett raised an eyebrow at Jules. "Sure they did. A shame, isn't it?"

"A *damn* shame." She rocked back on the heels of those filthy rubber riding boots. Then she went into the stall, plucked a lily from the sawdust inside, stood on her tiptoes, and stuck it behind Rhett's ear.

He struggled to keep a straight face.

"Jules," said her father. He shook his head, disgusted, and walked away.

"I was just being gracious, Dad. Sayin' thank you to our savior, like you asked."

"No, baby doll, you weren't. And we all know it," he called over his shoulder.

Rhett looked down at Jules, noting that she didn't seem to like being called *baby doll*. "Well, now. Thank you. That's better than a lei any day."

Her face flamed at the double entendre; the reference to what they'd had in Dallas. She looked as though she wanted to disembowel him.

Rhett chuckled, reaching out to scratch behind Frost's ear. His horse nuzzled him again and Rhett splayed his fingers against Frost's neck, looking through them at the gray sprinkled throughout the old boy's coat. Funny how he hadn't expected him to age. He'd thought Frost would look exactly the same. "Good to see ya, boy. Looking forward to riding you," he murmured.

"He can't take your weight for long," Jules told him. "Not now."

"You're the expert," he murmured, under his breath.

Her face flushed redder than Scarlett, parked outside on the gravel.

Rhett pictured her the last time he'd seen her: long brown hair mussed from her pillow and sex, her eyes hazy with sleep, her soft, parted lips. Her smooth tanned neck and arms against the twisted, white hotel sheets. She'd looked sweet and yet sultry, a dream girl.

But then the light had gone out of her eyes as he'd told her it could never happen again. Which it couldn't—no matter how much he might fantasize about it. Because Grady really *would* disembowel him. He was the dark, creative, vengeful type. And when it came to someone taking advantage of his sister, Rhett couldn't blame him.

"Get out of my barn," she repeated in a deadly undertone.

Rhett sighed and nodded. "It'll take you some time to get used to this," he said. "I understand."

"You understand nothing," Jules told him, with a sidelong glance at her father, who was staying at a safe distance and checking that cut over Shiner's eye—she'd meant to get to it earlier, but it had been quite a morning.

"I'm just trying to help you folks out." Rhett stroked Frost's muzzle again and then reached into his back pocket and pulled out a bottle of the beer he'd brought. He knocked the cap off on the door of the stall with practiced ease while Jules blinked rapidly in irritation.

"You think you're some kind of white knight," she said. "Well, you're not! You're a night*mare.*"

He tipped some of the beer into his palm and held it out for Frost, who slurped it right up. "Jules, darlin', if there's anything I am *not,* it's any kind of mare." He grinned. "And you know it. You saw the equipment—"

"If you ever refer to what happened between us in Dallas again," she said through gritted teeth, "I will *cut off* 'the equipment.' You hear me? And then I will toss it into a pan, fry it, and serve it to you for breakfast with hash browns."

The lady was nothing if not direct. "You threatening me, Jules?"

"You bet your fancy ass I am," she snapped. "Now, for the love of God, will you get out of my barn? Do I really have to turn the hose on you?"

Rhett saw that it would take some time to overcome her objection to his presence. It was no different from the hoops he'd had to jump through to recruit the marquee investors for his first fund. But he'd not only gotten them to take a meeting, he'd had them eating out of his hand by the end of it.

He'd have Julianna Holt eating out of his hand soon, too. He didn't doubt it for a second. But the secret? The secret was letting her win a minor battle or two. So he'd cede her this one.

"Okay, I'll leave now. But we're gonna have to talk at some point, Jules."

"I have nothing to say to you. Not now. Not ever."

"Don't be that way, honey. It's real good to see you. I mean that."

In answer, Jules extended her arm and pointed to the open door of the barn.

"Oh, is that the way out?" Rhett asked innocently. "Thanks for showing me."

Outside, he stood by Scarlett—who looked out of place there—and took a moment to appreciate the cool, dry, cedar-and-mesquite-scented Texas air. The crunch of gravel under his delicate Italian dress shoes. The whinny of a horse from the depths of the barn. The tension in him uncoiled, eased, dissipated. This part of Silverlake felt like home.

Then Jules followed him outside, clearly still outraged. She took in Scarlett in one sweeping, contemptuous glance and curled her lip—not the reaction he was used to in Dallas.

"You think you can show up in Silverlake and buy your way out of anything, don't you?" she shot at him.

"What? No . . ."

"Buy my silence to my brother. You're worried that a word from me would destroy the friendship. So you write a check, put us in your debt, and expect me to fall all over you—like Dad and Grady."

"No!" She was taking this all wrong. "That's not how this is, Jules. Not at all."

"Then, how is it?"

"Grady told me about your dad's medical issues. And that running the place was too much for him. He said your family was hoping to sell."

"Running the place *was* too much for him. I've been telling him that for years. In the very same conversations where I also told him I was ready, willing, and excited to take over and make the place my own!"

"You still get to run things," Rhett said.

Wrong thing to say.

"But it's never going to be mine." It looked like Jules was blinking back tears for a moment. *Aw, hell.* Rhett wanted to take her into his arms, but that was definitely not on the menu here.

"It *is* still yours," he said helplessly. "You're the manager. For life."

"Thanks so much for making that decision for me—you and my dad. Hellooooo, I'm a whole person over here! I'm not some property to be bundled into your contract along with the rest of the business."

Rhett cocked his head. Wait a minute. This wasn't just about the business. "We weren't trying to make a decision for you. We were giving you an option," he clarified.

"An option. Gee, thanks."

"Taking care of you."

"I don't need to be taken care of! This isn't the '50s."

Rhett sighed and threw up his hands. "What can I say to make things right?"

She shook her head, and they stood in an awkward silence for a while.

"Look, I'm sorry that I left the way I did," Rhett said at last. "That night was . . ." He released a breath in lieu of words.

She raised her head. "Yes?" she prompted.

Rhett cleared his throat as if that would help

clear the sexy memories from his mind. Nope. No help at all. "Very . . ." he growled. He shrugged, raising his eyebrows, biting his lower lip.

A slow blush crawled up her neck as he stared straight into her eyes. "Well, you know how it was," he said, in a low tone. "Can't buy that, or fake that . . ."

She nodded, her lips parted.

"But Grady's my best friend," Rhett said.

Her mouth shut with a snap.

"I should never have touched you, Jules. But worse, after I did, I should never have left you thinking it didn't mean anything to me. It . . . it . . ."

Her eyes widened. "Yes?" she asked in a breathy voice. "Finish your sentence."

His brain was muddled. He couldn't find a verb to save his life. And *it* hardly worked as a noun for what they'd shared. "It's never going to happen again. I promise. Obviously. I mean, it can't."

She raised her chin. "Of course not. There are two people involved in that decision, Rhett. And I'm one of them, by the way. I'm a *person,* not just someone's little sister. And as a person in my own right, I have *zero* interest in being your little side of country fun."

"Little side of . . . ? What are you talking about?"

"It was a mistake," she said flatly.

47

He nodded, even though at this point, he felt like denying it . . .

Damnation: That was Grady's dusty black Ford F-150 rolling down the gravel drive. He *would* choose this extremely inopportune moment to interrupt them.

Jules rolled her eyes and stomped back into the barn without another word.

Rhett had no choice but to wait for Grady, who decided to put on his best Texas guy show.

"Well, if it ain't old Rhett Braddock, home for Fool Fest," he boomed out the window. He took in Scarlett and whistled. "You steal your mama's egg money to buy that pickle wagon?"

"And my granny's, too." Rhett's grin was so wide that the back of his head almost fell off.

Grady swung down out of the truck, looking even more massive in person than he did on video call. His muscular frame was wrapped in jeans and a black fire department T-shirt, and the nonregulation flop of hair in front of his eyes and silver thumb ring hinted at his dark, rebellious streak. He wrapped Rhett in a dusty bear hug and clapped him hard on the back. "How ya doin', man? Look at these glad rags of yours . . . gold cuff links?" He whooped. "Gonna pick your teeth out here with those?"

"Something like that," Rhett agreed.

"Well, kick off the fancy shoes—really, WTF, man?—put on your sittin' britches and stay awhile. Never thought I'd see the day. Or the week. Or the year, for that matter."

" 'Sittin' britches'? Really? Nobody talks like that, and especially not you."

Grady smirked. "Just playin' up my local yokel for you. Seriously, you came home to Silverlake in that getup? Who're you trying to impress?"

Rhett shrugged. "Look at it as armor. And *coming home* is a relative term."

"You got all citied up just to put Deck's back up, didn't you?"

Rhett's lips twitched. " 'All citied up'?"

"You bring your golf clubs, too?"

"Screw you. You're just jealous."

"Maybe a little," Grady said.

"It could have been you, too," Rhett pointed out. "You could be crunching numbers right next to me in Dallas during the week and painting that crap nobody else understands on the weekends."

Grady shrugged. "I like playing the market for fun, but I never had your talent. I'm okay where I'm at. As long as you keep sending me that good bourbon."

Rhett smiled. They both knew the truth. That it was Rhett who was jealous, not Grady.

Grady laughed, then sobered up. "You seen Jules yet? Because—"

"Yeah." Rhett nodded.

"—she's gonna be in a horn-tossin' mood when she finds out that you bought—"

"Yeah."

"—the property, thanks be to Jesus that you did. Really, man, I cannot thank you enough for bailing out my dad."

"*De nada*. But as for horn-tossing . . . I sent flowers to your sister to, uh, pave my way, so to speak. She tossed those instead of her horns. Tossed the bouquet right into Frost's stall."

Grady chuckled. "She did not."

"Oh yes, she sure as hell did."

"That is such a Jules thing to do. Sorry. She'll get over it in time. She wanted to run the stables, you know . . . make it her own."

"She *will* run it. I'll just give her some business advice here and there."

"Can't thank you enough for that, either, man. This place is her life."

Rhett couldn't help feeling gratified. Jules wasn't seeing it yet, but he was trying to make up for being such a heel. He'd helped out her dad, saved her job, and addressed his guilt toward Grady all in one fell swoop. It was a win-win situation. But he couldn't—and wouldn't—strut about it. Not cool.

"Stop," he told his friend. "It's an investment, and that's all."

Grady nodded and punched him gently in the shoulder. "An investment in getting into the good place upstairs, maybe. If it weren't for you I'd be cashing in my retirement. And if it weren't for your stock tips, my retirement wouldn't be what it is."

If Jules has her way, I'll go straight to the bad place. "Oh, shut it, Grady. I'm no saint." *Little do you know just how unsaintly I am. Or what I did with your baby sister. And what I'd like to do again . . . and again.*

"Eyes of the beholder, bud."

Rhett averted his eyes from Grady the Beholder, before Grady beheld the guilt and shame that racked him. Before he sniffed out the betrayal. And the lust that he still had for Jules. How had he gotten himself into this mess?

CHAPTER 4

Jules squinted at the two oafs outside her stables: Rhett subtly self-congratulatory and Grady unsubtly grateful. She couldn't stand it. She kicked the nearest hay bale, hard. Then she kicked it again.

Men. Thought they could just run her world. "Save" her—poor little girl with no college degree, baby sister. Helpless. It set her teeth on edge.

She grabbed a pitchfork—feeling that she needed horns and a tail to accessorize it—and went for the wheelbarrow again. It was conveniently still outside Frost's stall. She unlatched the half door and led him out, then secured his halter and lead to a ring outside. She dug out the flowers and the now-pungent damp sawdust, filling the entire wheelbarrow, and almost growled at the sight of her brother and Rhett, casually walking back into the barn. She wheeled out her load to meet them.

"Hey, Grady. I'm pissed at you for withholding information."

He loomed over her from his six-foot-six-inch height. "I'm doin' just great today, thanks, sis. How 'bout you?"

She ignored that. "Thought I showed you the

way out," she said to Rhett, her tone overly polite. "You get lost already?"

"You know, Jules, we can hire that done," he told her, gesturing at the wheelbarrow.

"Oh, 'we' can, can we? With what funds?"

Grady whistled. "Easy, now, girl."

Rhett blew out a breath. "You know I'm going to inject some capital into the business . . ."

"No, I didn't. See, nobody has discussed any of this with me," she reminded him sweetly. "And I'm as capable of digging out a stall as anyone."

"It's not a question of your capability; it's whether you enjoy it or not."

"It's part of my job," she said flatly.

"And I'm saying we can get you a hand—"

Jules glared at him. "Unlike some people, I don't consider myself too good for manual labor."

"That's a cheap shot."

"Is it? I can't afford any other kind, right now."

"Just because I've done well does not mean I think I'm better than anyone. Here, give me that." Rhett strode forward, suit, cuff links, and all, and tried to wrest the handles of the wheelbarrow away from her.

"Let. Go," she said between her teeth.

Grady unwisely stepped in. "What is up with you, Jules?"

"What's up with me? My temper is what's up!"

"No kidding."

"You and Mom and Dad have been sneaking

around me, keeping secrets, and treating me as if I'm a toddler. Dad—all of you—know I've always wanted this place, and you conspire to sell it out from under me to this—this—*city slicker,* here, without telling me!"

"City slicker," Rhett repeated, looking amused.

She shot him a dark look, then turned back to her brother. "I'm not five, Grady. I'm twenty-five!"

"Then you're old enough to know that this is the best possible solution for everyone. Dad's off the hook and can focus on getting better. Mom can look after him. You keep your job with no stress, and Rhett'll turn this place around and make it profitable."

"I had plans! I had dreams! Nobody even asked me . . ."

"Dad didn't need to ask you," Grady said, a bit brutally. "Now, I'm sorry that you feel this way, but it's time to grow up and deal gracefully with the situation. Why don't you say 'thank you' to Rhett, instead of being so rude?"

Beyond furious at being told a *second* time by the men in her life to thank Rhett, Jules dropped the wheelbarrow and flipped Grady the double bird. Not so classy, maybe. Not so ladylike. But it made her feel better.

"What is wrong with you?"

"Nothing! Everything!" Jules shouted at them both.

Grady looked at Rhett.

Rhett looked back at Grady.

"You on your *period,* or something?" Grady asked.

That did it. She officially lost her temper. Jules picked up the wheelbarrow again and tipped the mess of stinky wet sawdust and drooping flowers right onto their feet before stomping away, back inside the barn.

How dare her brother say that to her? And it wasn't even true!

"Jules!"

It was a heartfelt—if somewhat sodden—welcoming chorus from the Schweitz's Tavern Friday-night regulars. The tension of the day began to slip away immediately; nothing quite like a mess of friendly faces when you're feeling low.

Schweitz's was a Silverlake landmark, one of the oldest German businesses in the Texas Hill Country. The interior was lined with repurposed barn wood. The tables were either old whiskey barrels topped with hammered copper or picnic tables flanked by benches. The walls were hung with not just the obligatory beer signs, but also wagon wheels, mirrors lined with horseshoes, and black-and-white historical photos of the town. Every Monday night at Schweitz's was polka night, but this evening the sound system played a mix of rockabilly, country, and rock. A track by Two Tons of Steel played as Jules made her way to the bar.

At the table by the door, Old George and Rafael, off duty from the firehouse, hoisted bottles in the air by way of greeting. Behind the bar, Otto saluted her with a towel. Rhett's little sister, Lila, and her roommate, Amelie, looked up and smiled before turning back to discuss what looked like a plan for world domination. Maggie gave a wave from the bar, where she sat next to town attorney Perfect Bridget, who was pressing a black and silver glitter sticker onto the nail of Maggie's pinky finger.

Jules raised her palms and gave a double wave to her hometown crowd before hopping up on the vacant barstool next to Bridget.

Bridget's perfect, classic Louis Vuitton bag hung from the back of her stool, and her auburn hair fell in perfect waves over her shoulders. Her makeup looked as if it had been applied by a professional for a photo shoot. She wore her signature pink cowboy boots with a barely-there denim mini and a fluffy angora cap-sleeved T-shirt that would have made Jules look like a bear. It somehow accentuated Bridget's curves and contrasted with her bare, perfectly tanned legs. Jules wondered whether she was cold in the March chill—no sign of goose bumps—or if she was just permanently, annoyingly hot.

"Is it true?" Bridget asked her.

Jules gave her a dark look. "Yup."

Bridget's jaw set. That prosecutorial look she'd perfected in law school made her eyes glitter. "I think it's bullcrap, Jules, I really do. You could have done so much with that place. If you were the sort to sue your own father, I swear I'd help you."

"I'm not suing my own father," Jules said with a laugh. "I don't suppose I could sue Rhett?"

"Aww, sue a Braddock?" Bridget said, making a hilarious sad puppy face. "That'd be like spitting on the historical marker at the end of Main Street. I wouldn't do it, and I have as much of an excuse to wanna make a Braddock cry as you do." Bridget—the girl who seemed to effortlessly get whatever she wanted—hadn't been able to keep Rhett's brother Jake, though she'd been his girlfriend for a time.

"You should definitely try to make Rhett Braddock cry," Maggie said cheerfully. "You get those flowers?"

"Oh, I should have said right away. I swear I took a moment to appreciate the time and effort you put into that. They were gorgeous . . ." Jules winced.

Maggie looked amused. "But?"

"But I'm sorry to say that they did not survive the day."

Maggie finished the dregs of her beer and

57

waved for another. "Given that his credit card payment went through, I choose to be neither upset nor surprised."

Jules shot her a rueful smile. "Thanks. For understanding."

Maggie shrugged. "I'd say the gang's all here, except no Mia. A-*gain*. Did she find better friends or something?"

Jules tensed, not about to give anything private away. "Oh, you know. She's got her side business going . . . it's a lot of work."

"I don't understand why she works so hard. That house of hers is spectacular. Bigger than the old Nash place . . . and Rob let her keep it."

Otto saved Jules from having to answer when he slid a beer bottle each to Maggie and Jules and poured a third beer into a glass that he slid to Bridget. "Prost," he said, lifting the empty bottle before heading to the opposite end of the bar to take another order.

"I really want to kill Rhett," Jules muttered after taking a tiny sip and suddenly realizing she didn't want the beer after all. Her head hurt and beer wasn't going to fix that. The only thing that could fix the stress she was under would be the quick departure of Rhett Braddock from this town, her stables, and that place she'd like to excavate in her heart.

"Kill him with *kindness*," Bridget said. "He's not going to be around for long anyway. He's a city boy now. I'm more likely to see him when I'm in Dallas on business than you are to see him here in Silverlake."

Jules shook off an unwelcome wave of jealousy.

Bridget looked Jules straight in the eyes. "Obviously, you're not sitting in my law office paying me gobs of money to solve your problems, but I can tell you this. The best way to handle Rhett and still maintain some control over your situation is to make friends with him. So if you're butting heads with him, back off." Bridget leaned in close and gave a sly grin. "Better yet, try cultivating *closeness*. Might make it more . . . tolerable."

Jules cocked her head, trying to read between the lines of Bridget's statement.

"Okay, well, that sounds more fun than suing somebody," Maggie said, wiggling her fingers and examining the stick-on nail polish that now graced all ten digits. "He may be a snotty rich boy, but he *is* hot."

"And exactly how is Rhett's hotness relevant to this conversation? It's not like I'm going to sleep with him." *Er, well, not* again.

"He's actually more than just a snotty rich boy," Bridget said, suddenly a little prickly.

Maggie and Jules quieted. *Snotty rich girl* was something people said about Bridget, too. "I didn't mean—" Maggie began.

"I've gotten to know Rhett better in Dallas,"

Bridget said, pulling a hot-pink lip gloss from her bag. "Well, whatever you think about him, Jules, it doesn't change the situation. Keep your friends close and your enemies closer. Okay, who's gonna go to the powder room with me?"

Maggie did the honors, and the two women headed to the ladies' room.

Alone on her end of the bar, Jules took a moment to admire the new mechanical bull that Otto had talked Schweitzie into installing. He was a handsome fellow, a Longhorn, of course. But someone had stuck an aluminum pail under it and taped a sign to his butt for Fool Fest. It read, MILK ME.

She laughed. Even old Tom Fullery himself would have applauded.

Tom Fullery, a wool merchant by trade and one of Silverlake's first settlers, was immortalized in bronze at the east end of Main Street. He had created Fool Fest, which had originated as a bastardization of his name into Tom Foolery, because he liked to play practical jokes on his employees, friends, and neighbors.

Tom's most legendary prank had been to ensure that the local priest, Father O'Donnell, had gotten well into his cups on the last night of March 1887. And on April 1, 1887, the same priest had woken up on the roof of the Catholic church, his bed roped to the steeple. He'd rung the bell repeatedly in order to be helped down . . . and when he was, he'd tried to ring Tom Fullery's bell, too.

The priest had been crowned Silverlake's very first King of Fools, and was roasted at the town's very first Feast of Fools. The tradition had grown from there into a monthlong celebration of good humor (for those playing the jokes) and good sportsmanship (for those on the receiving end).

Jules had fished her phone out of her bag to see if Mia had texted to cancel when the tavern door swung open again. Just as with her own entrance, everybody swiveled to see who it was, beers raised high. But this time there was a tiny pause, a moment of stunned surprise, as none other than Rhett Braddock came through the door in his city duds.

Acid burned in her stomach at the sight of him, while a silent question hung in the air: *Is he still part of this town or not?*

And then Lila Braddock looked up from her conversation with Amelie and saw her brother. She leaped up, knocking her chair to the floor. With a sheaf of cocktail napkins fluttering in the air around her she yelled, "Frankly, I *do* give a damn!"

Rhett—and the entire bar—busted out laughing as Lila launched herself at him. "My brother's finally home!"

And, just like that, any awkwardness disappeared.

Jules couldn't help but be moved by the reunion. Rhett looked so genuinely pleased, as if he was actually surprised by his sister's enthusiasm. Being so close to her own brother, Jules couldn't imagine things any other way, and it made her sad how things had gone so wrong for such a nice family.

Doesn't mean he has to stampede into the middle of things with your *family,* said the angry voice still there in the back of her head. But when Rhett's gaze finally tore away from his sister and met Jules's own, she had Bridget's advice in the back of her mind.

And truth be told, it wasn't the worst thing in the world to have an excuse to keep Rhett Braddock closer. She cast a guilty look at his soiled shoes. She should probably apologize for dumping that muck on them. Grady had deserved it far more than Rhett.

Jules felt, more than saw, several pairs of eyes swivel to her, then to Rhett, then back to her. It really was a small town. Word had gotten out about the Holt sale, and people wanted to see how she was dealing with it. *Ugh.*

No matter what she'd done out at the stables, no matter how soiled Rhett's shoes might be at the moment, she wouldn't add to the gossip. She'd hold her head high if it killed her.

"Otto!" she called. "I'd like to buy that man a beer."

Rhett's eyebrows shot up almost comically. "You would?"

"Absolutely," she said, pasting a delighted expression on her face. "We're celebrating your purchase of my dad's property."

"We are?"

"This guy is a hero!" Jules said to everyone within earshot. "He is helping my family out of a jam."

Lila cocked her head and squinted at her, as if she saw right through the charade.

Next to her, Bridget swallowed a chuckle and said under her breath, "You learn fast, don't you?"

"That I do, Bridge. That I do." Then she shut up as Rhett, a local IPA in hand, made his way over to say thank you.

"About five hours ago you wanted to kill me, Jules," he said, clinking her own beer bottle with his and eyeing her quizzically.

"Sorry about your shoes," she muttered into the vicinity of his chest, while trying not to remember what it looked like shirtless.

"What's that? Oh, no worries. They'll clean up fine."

"I sort of doubt that . . ."

"There are more where I found these. So, can I ask what's brought on your change of heart?"

She shrugged. "I guess it just took me a day to, um, get used to the situation."

"A whole day."

"Yeah." Her chin came up on its own to challenge his skepticism. "And now, I'm having, you know—grace about things."

"Grace," he repeated, his eyes filling with amusement, at her expense.

She thought of her fall into the wheelbarrow and flushed. "Would you stop that?"

"Stop what?"

"Laughing at me."

"Not a chuckle passed my lips."

"It's silent mocking. You're worse than Grady!"

"I'm filled with the utmost admiration for you, I swear."

"Liar."

"I actually mean that," Rhett said quietly. "I'll admit that I didn't stop to think about whether you'd be unhappy about me buying the stables. I just listened to my friend's problem and came up with a way to solve it. You know: x plus y equals z. That's the way my brain works—in equations."

"If we're at z," Jules said, "then it doesn't leave us far to go in the alphabet."

There was a pause while Rhett cast her an unfathomable look. "Maybe it means that we need to start over with a."

"Huh." Jules gazed down at her beer bottle, her eyes unaccountably landing on every a on the label. "I think you should maybe go back to mocking me, after all. I'm not sure how to deal with you when you're nice."

That slow, lazy grin of his made her stomach roll over like a dog exposing its belly to be scratched . . . or kicked. "I'm always nice."

"Oh yeah?" She deliberately dragged up the memory of him leaving her without so much as a dawn goodbye kiss, back in Dallas. "I guess you're just not a *morning* person, then."

She had the pleasure of seeing his face fall.

"Jules—" Rhett set his beer down on the bar with a snap. "I—"

But she interrupted him. "So you own the Holt Stables now. Does that mean you own all of the horses, too?"

"What? Oh. Yes. Land, buildings, livestock."

"You don't get Don Quixote."

He shot her a mystified look. "Who?"

"My donkey. He was a rescue. *My* rescue. He was just a little, tiny, starved, and abandoned colt when I found him. And he's mine."

"O-kaaay," agreed Rhett. "Where'd you find him?"

"Way out past the Lundgrens'. He was trapped in some barbed wire and all cut up. Hadn't eaten in days, was totally dehydrated. Would have died if I hadn't loaded him into my truck and brought him to the vet. She put him on an IV immediately. I woke up every four hours to feed him once he was off it."

Rhett picked up his beer again and evaluated her. "That was very sweet of you."

Jules snorted. "I'm a lot of things, Braddock. But sweet ain't one of 'em."

"You sure about that?"

"Yes."

He leaned forward and brought his lips to her ear. "Because you sure tasted sweet to me, that night."

Her face flash-fried and her heart rate sped up. Jules pressed one hand to the pounding in her temple. She wished he didn't still have the power to affect her so much. She sighed. Her brain might know exactly who Rhett Braddock really was deep inside, but her body sure wasn't getting the message.

She pushed the neck of her bottle into his chest to push him away, ignored his wicked grin, and slid off her barstool. "Excuse me, Rhett," she said coolly. "You enjoy that beer. I'll see you around."

"Yes, you will," he promised. "Tomorrow at eight A.M. out at the stables. So we can take a look at the books."

Ugh. There was no avoiding him. Her stomach flipped as she exited Schweitz's. What fresh hell would Rotten Rhett put her through then?

CHAPTER 5

With regret, Rhett watched her go. What other girl could demand a donkey with a straight face and look that good without even dragging a comb through her hair? It looked like the feathers of an angry rooster, tied up in that rubber band. She'd ditched the rubber barn boots for scuffed western mules, but other than that she hadn't changed clothes before coming to Schweitz's. She still smelled of physical exertion and outrage and horse. And she didn't give a rat's ass.

Rhett did admire that about her. She was who she was, with no apology. With Jules, there was no cover-up and no varnish. Her face was bare of makeup, her nails free of polish and clipped short. But she couldn't disguise that rockin' little body of hers, even when she draped it in what looked like one of Grady's old flannel shirts. The shirt hung down almost to her knees, for chrissakes, and yet he could still discern her curves as she strode away.

As she disappeared through the door of Schweitz's, Rhett suddenly became aware that everyone in the bar seemed to be studying him, whether overtly or covertly. He felt . . . as if he no longer belonged—even though Lila had broken the ice for him, bless her.

Rhett found himself threading his way back

through the bar to his sister, where she held court. Good Lord, had she changed in the last decade or so. She'd gone from a scrawny and rebellious teenager, frankly a pain in the neck, to . . . wow. Dark hair like his. Sky blue eyes like his. Dressed like some kind of rock star, which was entertaining. Purple, spike-heeled boots in a python print. Where she'd found those, he didn't know. Wasn't sure he wanted to know, frankly.

She'd paired them with skinny jeans, way too much cleavage, and a dark green, cropped leather jacket. None of it was in style . . . but it wasn't out of style, either, because it was so unusual. Somehow, the getup came across as creative.

The peacock feather earrings made him laugh. Lila had morphed from an annoying little blue jay into a peacock. When did that happen?

She looked up as he approached. Appraised him frankly. "Ever-Rhett, honey. Ditch the cuff links, roll up your sleeves, and stay awhile." She slid an arm around him and gave him a squeeze.

His breath caught at the unexpected affection. The understanding, compassion, and tenderness in her voice.

"Otherwise people're gonna think you're a right 'rageous a-hole." Lila grinned.

Rhett stared down at her. She was trying to rescue him. A parade of memories went through his mind: him and Jake and Ace stuffing her into the sofa, piling cushions on top of her, and sitting on her while she screeched. The time they'd dug a hole and buried her to the neck in dirt, telling her they'd pay her a dollar if she stood for it. And then stood around laughing at her when she couldn't get free.

Deck had grounded them for a month for that—not that they'd paid any attention. What was Deck going to do when he came home and found them gone, anyway? Take away their Dinty Moore stew, or their sloppy joes or SpaghettiOs fresh from the can? Maybe threaten not to buy any more TV dinners? "A: I don't care what other people think." *Anymore.* "B: I *am* a right 'rageous a-hole."

She looked up at him, somehow wise to him. When had she gotten wise? "No. I don't think so. You just have the act down, real good."

Rhett sighed. "What exactly is my crime?"

Lila wrinkled her nose. "Oh, you know. Outside money buying up the town?"

Rhett stiffened. "I'm still Rhett Braddock from Silverlake, Texas."

His sister cocked her head. "Are ya?" And with those words, she set down her beer and proceeded to remove his cuff links.

"What do you think you're doing?" he said mildly, trying, and failing, to manufacture some outrage.

"Making you real again."

"I *am* real."

She examined the cuff links in the dim light of Schweitz's. "Tiffany?"

"Maybe. Why?"

"Meh."

"I don't recall asking you for your opinion. Besides, I think you're a little jealous, Peacock."

Lila grinned. "Maybe of how much they're worth. How about I hock them, split the proceeds?"

"Excuse me?" He couldn't help laughing. "You don't have my permission to do that."

She dropped the cuff links into her crazy-colored handbag. Then she slid both arms around him this time and hugged him as if she'd never let him go. "Yeah? Well, you didn't have my permission to leave for over a decade and not come home to visit us. I missed you, you butthead."

Something cracked open inside Rhett. While he tried to sweep up the broken shards and piece them back together, Lila rolled up his sleeves, French cuffs and all, until they lay folded just below his elbows.

"There," she said with satisfaction. "Now you look somewhat normal."

"You done bossin' me around, little sis?"

"No."

Rhett shook his head with a smile. "Well, hit me."

"Call Jake."

"I will. That all?"

"Go see Declan," Lila said. "He's the first one of us you should have seen. Don't make him the last."

Rhett didn't feel so much like smiling anymore. "Why do you think I'm here? It's not just the Holt place. I've been worried about him since we FaceTimed the day of the fire."

"You should be. He's not himself. I know he's always kept his feelings locked down, but ever since the ranch fire . . . Maybe it's denial. I don't know, but he's *down*."

Rhett glanced away, suppressing the unwelcome worry building within him; Declan was supposed to be the strongest of all of the Braddocks. This new version of his brother made him uncomfortable. Of course, there seemed to be a new version of all of them. He looked back at Lila. "What are you doing with yourself now that you can't plan events out there in the Old Barn?"

"I haven't really had a choice: I've been expanding my outside events business. And I got a major new client."

"Oh yeah?"

Lila took a large gulp of her drink. "Uh-huh. Silverlake's town council. You haven't heard, bro?"

He shook his head.

His little sister grinned. "I'm producing all of Fool Fest! And since you're here, you can stay for the extravaganza."

Rhett stared at her. "Lila, I haven't been to Fool Fest since I was thirteen."

"Well, welcome home, fool. Welcome home."

Rhett laughed. "You can't really say that until I step foot on the ranch."

Lila arched an eyebrow. "You're not *scared* to go and see Deck, are you?"

"What the—?" Rhett gave her a cocky grin. A cocky, Dallas boardroom, *I've got this* grin. "Let it go, Lila. I am not scared of my own brother. I was planning to head out there tomorrow. I want to take a look in person at the damage on the Old Barn, see if I missed any opportunities with the insurance. But, far as I know, we're ready for a good old-fashioned barn raising."

Lila's face didn't light up the way Rhett expected it to. "What?" he asked.

"Declan doesn't want to rebuild. That's what I'm trying to tell you."

Rhett stared at his sister. "Since when? He loved that barn."

Lila stared at the toes of her purple pointy boots for a minute and then looked up. "I guess he finally learned the same lesson you did, Rhett."

"And what's that?" he asked.

"How to walk away without looking back."

Jules slouched out of Schweitz's, a scowl threatening to overtake her face. There was only one person who would understand her in this mood, and that was Aunt Sue.

I'm trying to have grace, she'd said to Rhett. Or something like that. And he'd laughed.

Because she was mostly graceless: That was true. She embraced her gracelessness mostly because Aunt Sue had taught her that being a lady, like Mom, was overrated.

Being a lady meant relying upon men to be gentlemen—and that was a dangerous position to take in this chaotic world. Rhett had certainly been no gentleman the morning after their . . . whatever it was. He'd been a prize pig.

She rattled and squeaked in her Chevy over to Aunt Sue's tiny two-bedroom place about fifteen minutes away. In defiance of her neighbors, Sue had painted it periwinkle, with the front door and shutters a pale aqua color. A stone hedgehog guarded the door, flanked on the other side by a pot of geraniums that spilled to the wooden floorboards—also aqua.

In the flower beds out front stood not rose-bushes or something equally feminine, but a variety of cactus and succulents.

Jules knocked and yelled, "It's me!" Then she let herself in with her key.

Inside the tiny house, it was cool and dark, the shades drawn against the insistent Texas sun. Two apartment-sized, brown leather couches wearing quilts faced off on either side of a little stone fireplace, an oval oak coffee table between them. It was piled with magazines and books. Sue's fluffy gray cat, Stinky, snoozed under the table, barely opening one yellow eye to acknowledge her presence.

"Hi, hon," Aunt Sue called from the kitchen. "C'mon in."

"Did you know?" Jules asked, stomping in. The kitchen was painted a cheerful butter yellow and sported decorative Mexican tiles. A dream catcher hung in the one tiny window that faced out over the back garden, where Sue grew her own vegetables.

Sue turned from the sink, where she was washing some radishes, tomatoes, and peppers. Her white hair was twisted up on top of her head and secured with two wooden chopsticks, the ends permanently stained with soy sauce. She wore long turquoise earrings, a tie-dyed dress with a gray sweatshirt slung over it, and no shoes. Her toenails were painted sparkly turquoise. "Your father only just called me. You all right, hon?"

"Oh sure," Jules said. Then, "No."

Sue shook water off her hands and reached for a dish towel. She surged toward her niece and enveloped her in her arms. "It's all gonna be okay, baby girl. Gonna be fine."

She smelled of organic rosemary shampoo and homespun sunshine. "When?" Jules accepted her embrace, the tight squeeze of reassurance. "And on what planet?"

Sue rubbed her back.

"And couldn't Dad have just talked to me before he sold the place out from under me? Given me a heads-up?"

Her aunt sighed. "It's not Billy's way. He avoids conflict at all costs. He wouldn't have wanted to hear what you had to say or have wanted to override it. He knew it would upset you."

"But finding out this way upsets me so much more!"

"Yes, but he can now stick his head in the sand and not hear you," Sue said, more than a little bitterness in her tone.

"And he sold it to *Rhett Braddock,* of all people."

"You've had a crush on him since you were a kid."

"That's ridiculous, Aunt Sue."

"But true."

"No, it's not! And if I ever did, believe me, that is not the case now. He is a . . . a . . . *oh!* I don't even have a word bad enough to describe him."

"You saw him in Dallas, right? When you took that hunter-jumper up? And you came back in a terrible mood."

Jules shrugged. "Let's just say he's changed. And now he's *here.* Ugh."

"So you've already run into him?"

"You could say that. He's sent me flowers, and I've bought him a beer."

Aunt Sue's brow wrinkled. "But you don't have a word bad enough to describe him."

"No!"

"You always buy beers for people you hate?"

"Aunt Sue, don't you see? I cannot let him know that I hate him. And like Bridget says, 'Keep your friends close and your enemies closer.' So yeah, I bought the jerk a beer," she said gloomily.

"Coffee, hon? With a nip of something stronger in it?"

Jules looked into her aunt's pewter-gray eyes and nodded. "The worst of it all is that I'm so worried about Dad, and I feel guilty for being so mad at him—because he's sick."

"Guilt," Aunt Sue said, moving toward the coffeepot, "is a downright useless emotion. Kick it to the curb." The bitterness came back into her tone as she said the last words. "I spent too many years feeling guilty. Second-guessing."

Jules fell silent. The tragedy in her aunt's past had shaped not only her outlook, but her entire life.

"I don't feel guilty anymore," Sue said as she set up the coffee. "Anyway. The two emotions are different things. And you can be worried and mad at your father at the same time. Need permission? I give it to you." She pulled a bottle of

Baileys out of a cupboard and set it down with a snap on the counter. "Billy will be just fine. The sale of the property will give him the funds to get treatment. And there are mighty fine doctors at MD Anderson, hon. He'll be in good hands."

Jules nodded. "I just can't believe that they all knew—Mom and Grady, too—and nobody told me. They've treated me like a child. I'm really mad at them, too."

"Your mother does what Billy tells her to do. You know that. And Grady's his boy . . ." Aunt Sue walked over and set her hands on Jules's shoulders, looking into her eyes. "Listen. I don't—" She bit her chapped bottom lip. "I don't have kids of my own, hon. And I don't have much. Just this little place, here. But I want you to know that it'll be yours, one day. That no matter what Billy's done with the land, you'll have a house of your own, a place to go. All right?" She squeezed her niece's shoulders.

A lump rose in Jules's throat, and tears welled in her eyes. "Th-thank you, Aunt Sue," she whispered. Then she hugged her tightly, molding her own body to her aunt's warm, pillowy one. "I love you."

"I love you, too, hon. Now, how about some Irish coffee?"

"Sounds great."

Jules settled into one of Sue's padded kitchen chairs and accepted the coffee. She always felt

77

so comfortable with her aunt—unjudged, loved. Whereas her carefully made up mother set her teeth on edge. Her mother . . . who must be sick with worry over her husband's health. She needed to go check on her. But not now. In the morning.

"You look exhausted," Aunt Sue said, her eyes searching Jules's face.

"Rhett Braddock'll do that to a girl," Jules grumped. And then flushed when she caught the double meaning in what she'd said.

If Aunt Sue noticed, she didn't comment on it other than to add, "Sofa's always yours. You know that."

"Thanks, but I'll sleep at home tonight."

Sue nodded, seeming a bit disappointed. Then she clinked her mug against Jules's and took a big gulp. With a wry smile, she added more Baileys. "Why do I have a feeling that things are gonna get complicated around here?"

CHAPTER 6

The Hotel Saint-Denis didn't exist in Silverlake when Rhett was a kid. It looked a little like someone built a castle in a cattle pasture. The thread count was high. The temperature carefully modulated. The bottled water gratis, according to the small card with the fancy script. The soap smelled like French lavender.

It was awesome. The stuff of dreams, if you weren't used to it. He was used to it, what with the money he'd been able to splash out throughout his career, and, in that way, it shouldn't have made much of an impression.

Maybe what made the impression was the sense of contrast. Rhett thought about his brother waking up in the family house out at Silverlake Ranch. Even if the two of them never saw eye to eye again, there was something nice about the idea that they were probably up at the same awful hour. It would be chilly there; Declan probably had a fire going. Well, after he did a round of chores. Maybe he was using the same cozy-but-lumpy quilts. Maybe he was using the same cast-iron skillet to burn eggs for breakfast. Maybe the rooms still smelled more like cedar and hard work than lavender.

Jules, too. Jules would be getting up in a little to start work at the stables.

A flash of Jules waking in the morning mixed up in the sheets knocked him sideways. Sexy hair tangled more from his own hands running through it than from sleep. Flawless skin and a second of a sweet, shy smile before she realized he was bolting.

Loneliness coursed through him; Rhett sat up on the side of the bed and hung his head in his hands for a moment. *Why am I here?*

To make sure Silverlake Ranch and his family were okay. To make sure Grady was okay. To make sure Frost was okay. He paused when he thought of Jules. He hadn't asked her about her dad. Not the way he should have. He'd gone straight to work on the business. These were people he'd known his whole life. Thing was, he was used to putting feelings like that in a box with a lock and shutting it all away. He hadn't really discussed it with Grady, either. He'd offered to buy the Holt operation and figured everyone could read between the lines: *I do care.*

Their dad had thyroid cancer with a good prognosis but no guarantees. That's pretty much all Grady had said.

No guarantees.

You can do better, Rhett.

So as he'd done a million times before in prep school, in graduate school, and as a rookie in the cutthroat world of high-stakes finance, with the weight of expectations on his shoulders and nobody to help him carry the load, he took a deep breath, muttered, "You got this," and seized the day.

He made quick work of his Dallas projects, eager to head out into town and then over to Jules's—*well, his . . . maybe a little of both? Weird*—at a more reasonable hour.

He checked the markets. He sent e-mails to his team back at the firm, which was more than capable of operating in his absence. And then he put on sweats and running shoes and took an early-morning jog through Silverlake, observing as the town shook off sleep and embraced the slow dawn.

The rich orange, pink, and gold sunrise unfurled east of town, spreading its glow over fields of wildflowers (despite the March chill in the air), pecan, peach, and apple orchards, and placid livestock intent on grazing. It lit the local vineyard that produced peach wine, a quite passable chardonnay, and a cabernet that he enjoyed greatly. Not that he'd been there . . . but even from Dallas, he ordered from the locals here as much as possible, to support them.

As the rising sun began to bathe the local businesses, Rhett fought a rising tide of sentiment that he had absolutely no use for. He sloughed it off like the sweat beading on his forehead, with a casual swipe of his sleeve.

Rhett jogged past the local storefronts again, noting that Sunny's Side Up was already open and serving at six A.M. Sunny caught sight of him as she poured coffee for a customer, hesitated for a split second, and then waved with her order pad.

He found himself absurdly touched, wiped his face with his sleeve again, and decided he needed a good old-fashioned country breakfast before he tackled things with Jules and the Holt books.

He opened the door and went in. There were old-fashioned wooden booths lined up like open arms, with waxed, red gingham tablecloths. Old farm implements served as decor on the walls, and ceramic rooster planters held napkins and silverware in the center of the tables.

"Why, hello there, darlin'," Sunny said. She was a handsome woman in her mid- to late forties, with crow's feet around her eyes that emphasized her good humor. She stared at his face and shook her head.

Instantly Rhett stiffened. He changed his mind about breakfast.

"Why, you are the spittin' image of your mama," she said. "It just caught me off guard for a sec. C'mon and sit, Ever-Rhett. Right here in the corner."

Rhett felt himself relax again, and let her lead him to the booth she indicated. "You knew her? My mother?"

"Sure did. She was a wonderful lady. What can I get you, hon? Coffee? Specials are right here." She pointed at the laminated plastic menu she slid in front of him.

"Coffee," he said gratefully. "A big ice water. And"—he scanned the menu quickly—"omelet with cheddar, turkey sausage, onion, and spinach."

"Biscuits on the side? Hash browns?"

He almost choked as Jules's words echoed in his head. *I'll fry up "the equipment" and serve it to you with a side of hash browns . . .*

"Biscuits," he said. "Thank you, Sunny. Been a while, huh?"

"You haven't been in here since you were, what, thirteen? Since before you went back East, Rhett."

"I'm surprised you recognize me."

"I'm not, honey. Anybody would peg you for a Braddock, but I'd know your face anywhere, and that's the truth. Don't be a stranger." She looked at her watch. "And if you take your time, you'll meet up with your brother Deck, right here at seven. This same booth."

Meet up with Deck. Nah, he'd take a pass on that for today. Tomorrow was good enough. What the hell would they say to each other, anyway? How would they begin when it had been so long? There was so much water under that bridge, but they'd sailed in opposite directions.

"Sure," he said. "If I have time."

Sunny's eyebrows shot up, but she said nothing and went to get the coffeepot and his ice water. When she returned, she assessed him shrewdly as she poured. "Pride," she said succinctly. "It goeth before a fall."

And that was the only thing she said until she came back with an overflowing plate of food, ruffled his hair as if he were ten, and said, "Eat up, darlin'."

Jules woke early around four thirty A.M. instead of five thirty A.M. She lay in the dark of her tiny cabin on the property, random thoughts hitting her consciousness like heavy raindrops before a storm.

Mom . . . need to talk to her. How is she holding up? How does she feel about this whole sale-to-Rhett business?

Doesn't matter how she feels . . . she always agrees with what Dad thinks is best. It's how she was raised. To be a good, traditional wife: supportive, sweet, and a fantastic country cook.

Poor woman. How did she get me as a daughter?

Where can I get a humane mousetrap? There's that squeaking overhead again.

Darn. I have no milk for cereal.

She needed to start eating better. The same queasy feeling from yesterday was back, and as much as she'd like to blame everything on Rhett, this might be more than stress.

Do not get the flu. You can't work the stables with the flu, and Rhett will take over everything!

With that thought as inspiration, Jules slipped out of bed, shivering in the slight March chill. She turned on her tiny electric faux fireplace and streaked through the shower before realizing that both of her two towels were still in the dryer of the Holts' outdoor laundry facility—in another shed.

Her choices for drying off were the plastic shower curtain (not promising), a hand towel, or paper towels. She grabbed a faded blue hand towel embroidered with daisies, which had been her grandmother's, and mopped at herself.

The tiny towel was useless for her hair. So she twisted the water out of it and stuck it in a clip on top of her head. She'd run out of conditioner, too, so it was going to be impossible to comb through it . . . might be easier after it dried. She didn't much care.

She dug through the trunk she kept her clothes in and produced another flannel shirt, an old Silverlake High T-shirt, and a battered, paint-speckled pair of jeans with holes in the knees. She didn't bother with a bra, yet. Not as if the horses cared, and the darn things were so uncomfortable . . . she'd go back and get one before she met up with Rhett or gave any lessons.

It was five A.M. now, so her mom would be awake. It seemed to be the single thing that she'd inherited from the woman who'd given birth to her: a tendency to pop out of bed before dawn like a slice of toast.

Jules made her way along the winding flagstone path that led from her little cabin past the laundry and storage shed to the back patio area and its fire pit with outdoor seating. The wind chimes tinkled; her mother had hung them from the pergola along with various baskets of flowers and a birdhouse that looked like a tiny red barn.

Another birdhouse, made by her dad and painted the same shade of blue as the house, stood atop a big branch that her father had nailed to a square wooden platform.

Jules went up the back steps, opened the screen door, and knocked lightly. Then she pushed open the main door and entered the tiny back porch that led into her mother's blue and white kitchen.

Bacon was already slowly frying in a plug-in, nonstick skillet. It was turkey bacon, these days, much to her father's disgust, but it still smelled good. Her nose detected biscuits in the oven . . . yum. A full pot of coffee stood ready to invigorate anyone who needed invigorating. And her mother was pouring milk into a little steel pitcher to set on the table, which was set for three—as if she knew Jules was about to walk through the door. Uncanny.

"Mornin', sweetheart," Mom said with a gentle smile. It faded a bit as she scanned her daughter's appearance.

Jules groaned inwardly. "Good morning, Mom." She kissed her cheek and slid an arm around her. "How are you doing?"

"Well. All right, I suppose. All things considered."

"How's Dad?"

Her mom grimaced. "He had a rough night. He's still sleeping. I made him take a pill." Then she changed the subject, staring pointedly at Jules's chest.

"Honey, no daughter of mine is going to walk around without a bra. It's not decent."

"I just came to borrow some milk. And the horses don't care."

"Julianna Holt."

"Okay, okay. Fine."

"And what on earth is going on with your hair?"

"Ran out of conditioner. Can't comb it right now."

Helen Holt compressed her lips and silently poured Jules a cup of coffee.

"Thanks." Jules added liberal amounts of milk and sugar.

"Do you want sweetener instead, sweetheart?"

Subtle. "No, thanks. I prefer the real thing."

Helen turned to check the bacon, turning each piece carefully.

Her mother's blond hair was cut in a neat bob and turned under at the ends. She wore pressed dark jeans, a starched white shirt with a collar, small pearl stud earrings, and her own mother's cameo necklace. Her nails were painted the palest pink and her simple wedding band glinted under the rustic kitchen lighting.

Jules didn't know any other woman who'd be fully pressed and dressed by this hour of the morning. Good Lord—she had her makeup on, too. Very understated, as usual. But flawless.

Jules sprawled into one of the chairs her father had made, plopping her behind onto the cushion her mother had made, and sipped at her coffee.

"Are you wearing the sunscreen I gave you?" her mother asked.

Jules rubbed at the freckles on her nose and mumbled something indistinguishable into her mug.

"If you don't, you'll look like a leather bag at my age."

To this, she said nothing. Aunt Sue had never worn sunscreen, and she was still gorgeous. Jules liked the crinkles at her eyes and the brackets around her mouth. They gave her character.

"I heard you were quite rude to Rhett Braddock, honey," her mom said next.

Jules tried not to growl, she really did. She failed.

"Good Lord, what was that noise?"

"My stomach, Mom."

"Well, the bacon's almost done . . . and the biscuits are ready. I'll do the eggs next. Unless you want pancakes? Though you should probably avoid carbs . . ."

"Mom. Stop. Why didn't you and Dad and Grady tell me anything about what was going on?"

Helen opened the oven door, slid out the biscuits, and placed them on the stovetop. She set down her oven mitts and then turned around. "We didn't want to worry you. And we . . . we all needed time to think about things."

Jules let her silence express her outrage.

"I mean . . . your father wanted to talk to Grady. About whether he wanted to take over the stables—"

"Grady? Whether *Grady* wanted to take over?"

"Well, he is your father's son."

"And I'm his daughter. Grady wants to bachelor it up at the firehouse and throw paint at canvases. He has no interest in the horses; never has."

"Your father wanted to make sure of that— whether or not he took an interest in his heritage."

"Dad knows he doesn't!"

"Honey, when a man gets to thinkin' about the end of his life, he entertains dreams of having his son carry on in his footsteps."

Why does it have to be his son?

"Keep his name alive, you know."

"Last time I checked," Jules said carefully, "my last name was Holt, too."

"But your name will change when you get married—"

"Maybe. *If* I ever get married. And I'm sorry, Mom, but why would Dad assume that anyone needs a . . . a . . . *dick* to run a stables?"

"Julianna! I will not have that kind of vulgarity in my house."

"A penis, then."

"You stop it, you hear? Just stop."

"Stop what? Telling the truth?"

"You're not truth-telling. You're rubbing our noses in the fact that we are traditional folks. And we refuse to apologize for that, young lady!"

"Mom, I never asked you to apologize. But I *am* asking you to consider the fact that I am just as capable as a guy, I love the horses, and I'm really hurt that you and Dad didn't ask *me* if I wanted the property."

"You're our daughter, and you will always have a place here. But you are not a businessperson, Jules. You couldn't even stay in a junior college."

And there it was. The insult she'd known was coming. Her mom had just verbalized the unspoken undercurrents that flowed through the family. And triggered the shame that Jules felt.

"Mom, that's unfair. I hated college—it wasn't that I couldn't stay in it."

"But you didn't have the discipline to do so."

90

You're lazy and irresponsible. Those were the words Helen didn't say, but they reverberated around the kitchen, just the same. They hurt so much. And they weren't true. She just wasn't a mini-Helen. She couldn't be, no matter how hard she tried. And she didn't want to be.

Jules squirmed, despite herself. "Mom, I have plenty of discipline to do things I actually care about. I'm in my midtwenties and you still treat me like a child. I'm sick of it." Seething, she set down her empty coffee cup and got up. She grabbed the jelly jar of milk her mother had poured for her.

"You're sick of it?" Helen asked. "And yet you seem just fine with living for free in a cabin on our property. You can't remember to buy yourself basic necessities or even comb your hair. You don't seem to give any thought to your future and you're not even seeing a nice man who could give you one."

Jules's mouth fell open in shock.

"So please *do* excuse your family," her mother continued inexorably, "for being annoying enough to worry about you. For treating you like the child that you seem *all too comfortable* still being." Her mother's face was set in creases that Jules didn't recognize, and her eyes conveyed something tough and cold. It was a rude shock.

"What's going on, here?" her father said sleepily, appearing in the kitchen doorway in

91

his pajamas. His hair stuck up in tufts, and there were sheet wrinkles on his face.

The two women sprang apart. "Nothing," Helen said, shooting her daughter a nervous look that warned Jules not to upset her father in his condition.

"Just talking," Jules mumbled.

Dad grunted and went on through to the refrigerator.

Jules managed to give her mother a wan smile and then she shut her mouth and picked up her jelly jar of milk, sidling toward the door.

"Breakfast is almost ready, Julianna." Mom gestured with her spatula.

"I'm sorry, but I'm not as hungry as I thought."

"But I made enough for three." She narrowed her eyes and suddenly the spatula became a scepter, wielded by the queen of the household.

"I—" She cast a look of mute appeal toward her father.

"C'mon, baby doll. Break a biscuit with your old man," he said, utterly failing to rescue her from Mom and her relentless expression of unhappiness with who Jules was.

Miserably, she put the jelly jar in the fridge, pulled out a chair, and sat down.

Mom produced a smile and served her some eggs with only one piece of turkey bacon; no biscuit.

After she'd served Dad two biscuits and two

slices of turkey bacon; then herself the same, Jules got up and snagged what she considered to be her biscuit and the leftover two pieces of bacon.

"Carbs," murmured Mom.

Jules took a breath and reached for the butter.

"Fat," Mom whispered.

Jules scooped out extra, politely ignoring her.

"She looks just fine, Helen," Dad observed.

"Yes, but she's got my frame, which means it's never too early to watch her weight. Remember that I had to take drastic measures . . ."

Jules stuffed half a biscuit slathered with butter and jam into her mouth. "Mom," she said through it, "I never sit down all day. I'm on my feet, digging out stalls and riding and training and giving lessons."

"Don't talk with your mouth full," Helen reprimanded her.

Back in her cabin, Jules stewed. She'd eaten too much because she'd been outraged, and now she felt sick. She shoved the stupid jelly jar of milk into her mini fridge. Was it true? *Had* she contributed to her family's treating her like a baby? She didn't like to think about it. What was wrong with living here, in a perfectly good cabin near her parents?

Or was her mother simply so upset about her father's illness that she was getting mean?

Jules dug a bra out of her trunk and holstered

the girls. She glared at her wet hair in the tiny bathroom mirror. It was just fine in its clump on top of her head. She didn't need to look like some Stepford wife. And she didn't need a Stepford husband to "give her" a future, either.

She would create her own future, as Aunt Sue had taught her.

CHAPTER 7

Jules heard Rhett before she saw him. As she sat at the corner desk in the tack room, the floorboards directly behind her creaked, and she shot out of her chair, doing a half turn in midair. She landed facing him.

"Paranoid?" he asked mildly. "Or too many cups of coffee?"

He had no right to look—or smell—that good. His dark hair was still damp from a shower, and his aftershave spoke of luxury travel: private jets and polo matches and five-star hotels. He wore pressed khakis and a blue button-down with driving moccasins, no socks. A watch that could probably pay someone's mortgage for a year.

"Neither," she said stiffly. "Good morning."

"Mornin'." Rhett gestured at the desk. "You got another chair? Or you want to pull up your wheelbarrow?" His eyes twinkled with mischief.

Jules fought a losing battle not to laugh. "I have another chair."

"Tell me where to find it, and I'll be happy to bring it in."

"Oh no. You only get to carry your gentleman act so far."

"My gentleman *act*? How do you figure it's an act, Jules?"

All her mirth disappeared. "I judge from recent history."

He sighed. "Look, I've explained to you why I reacted the way I did."

And I can't explain to you that I've been in love with you since fifth grade. Even if I could, I wouldn't . . . it makes what you did so, so much worse. And I refuse to give you the satisfaction.

"Yup," she said. "So. How can I help you, Rhett?"

"I think *I* can help *you,* if you'd care to let me see the books for the stables."

She fetched the chair, unfolded it next to the desk, and reached for her laptop. "My dad went from an old-fashioned ledger to an Excel spreadsheet. Which worked okay. But I converted everything to QuickBooks three years ago." She typed in her password, tried not to think about how good he smelled, and tried to ignore his . . . toxic . . . masculinity. Toxic. That was exactly the right word. He might smell good, but he was rotten inside.

She frowned as she pulled up the software. Not rotten. Not exactly. Just not for her. Rhett was her childish fantasy that had finally been put to rest.

He was a man's man. Grady's man. Not hers. He'd made it totally clear where she stood in the order of things.

"Jules?" Rhett prompted. "Hello? Jules."

She blinked. Snapped out of her reverie. "Sorry. Back to business."

"Yes, but first . . ." He frowned.

Jules rolled her eyes. "*What,* Rhett?"

"You get any new info about your dad?"

"No, but I'm going to join him at his next consult. I'll let you know his status after that. I don't see that it will affect anything we're trying to do here," she said briskly.

"That's not why I asked."

She paused and looked him in the eye. "Why did you ask?"

"I just wanted to say that I'm sorry you're having this scare. And if you need . . ."

She raised her eyebrows, waiting for him to finish. "If I need?"

"If you need anything, I guess. Related to . . . that. Just let me know." He cleared his throat, looking a little lost.

"Thanks," she said awkwardly.

"Of course. Anyway. The books."

Jules stared at Rhett for a moment and then shook herself out of it. "Yeah. The books. Here. I'll let you get acquainted with things." She reluctantly turned the screen to face him. "Do you know QuickBooks?"

He quickly repressed a smile. "Yeah, I think I can handle it."

No doubt he was used to far more sophisticated programs, high math and derivatives and algorithms. She'd forgotten. Boy genius had gone back East to boarding school, then college at what, seventeen? And straight to Wall Street after graduating—to some hedge fund thing. Whatever that was. She wouldn't know a hedge fund from a hedge apple.

Grady had told her that Rhett's employers had been so taken with their hire that they'd paid in full for his MBA. He had two degrees, and she had none.

Jules got up and paced the tack room a few times, trying not to resent him for it. She was perfectly happy with who she was. She didn't need letters after her name to make her whole or justify her existence. She was just fine, being Julianna Holt the barn manager.

"Hmm," said Rhett, tracing a column of numbers with his index finger.

Or was she?

Was he about to tell her that she was terrible at her job? That she couldn't add up or subtract figures? Resentment began to build in her again. She could just kill Dad for putting her in this position, having to justify her business decisions and expenditures to this guy, of all the guys on the planet.

Stop it, Jules. Dad did what he thought was best. And he's sick enough to head out to MD Anderson, so don't even joke about that . . .

"Got a notepad?" asked Rhett. "A pen?"

She silently produced both. "I can't just stand around doing nothing, Ever-Rhett. I'm going to go groom some horses, 'kay?"

He nodded. "Let's meet up here in an hour or two."

"I have until three P.M.," she said. "Then I'm giving a trial lesson to a potential client, and after that, I have a meeting with the city council about starting up a Silverlake horse show."

"Fine."

She grabbed the caddy that held her horse brushes, comb, currycomb, and hoof-pick, along with hoof oil, clean rags, and rubber bands. She trudged with it to Blossom's stall, first. Blossom was a sweet old mare, a chestnut with white markings and a bloom of white that looked like a full-flowering rose across her forehead.

"Good morning, girl." Jules fed her a couple of baby carrots before entering her stall and brushing the sawdust and dirt off her back. It took the rubber currycomb to loosen the patches of dried mud here and there. "Had yourself a good roll, did you?"

Blossom tossed her head up and down.

"Bet that felt good."

The chestnut snorted her pleasure at the circular contact of the currycomb, which offered up a pretty good back-and-body scratch, as well as the benefits of grooming.

Jules brushed her and picked her hooves, next,

removing all of the packed dirt and tiny rocks that could bruise the mare's feet. Then she slipped a halter and lead on her, led her out of the stall and into a fresh one that she'd already dug out. Some of Jules's former students rented time with the Holt horses for trail-riding on the paths that zigzagged a little farther out of town. Blossom was ready to be taken out later by less experienced riders. The others could ride Curly and Frost.

Blossom began to drink a truckload of water.

"Really?" Jules said to her. "Gonna make me dig out that stall, too?"

Blossom eyed her, blinked lazily, and resumed drinking water from the bucket that hung in the corner.

"Thanks," Jules said with a rueful grin. "I know you do it on purpose." She moved on to Curly, so named because he was a North American Bashkir, dun in color, with curly hair. It was impossible not to hug Curly, stroke his dark muzzle, and run her fingers through his funny, textured coat as she brushed him. She could swear he hugged her back. She checked his fetlock, which was healing better, now, and rebandaged it.

And she thought about what it would take to heal her dad. Surgery, certainly. But then, maybe more treatments that would make him feel sick. Probably medication and monitoring for life, if all that worked. It was bound to be a long, exhausting, expensive road, whichever route he went.

As she finished up with Curly, she checked her watch and reluctantly forced herself to go meet Rhett again in the tack room, where he sat with *her* laptop, poking his nose into *her* business. Reviewing *her* decisions. It was just plain galling.

Jules smelled of horse liniment as she stepped back into the tack room with her plastic caddy of grooming items. The stuff was like Bengay on steroids—eye-watering—but it was as familiar to him as his own aftershave and it knocked him back over a decade, to when he'd groomed Frost and soaped his own saddle; applied Fiebing's oil to keep it supple. He'd been a pro at roping steer—won rodeo awards. How a woman could reek of horse liniment, sport a smudge of dirt across her left cheek, and look that good in a filthy Austin Lone Stars baseball cap, he didn't know. Her hair trailed out the back of the cap in an uncombed ponytail—did she even own a brush? He wanted to put down the laptop, stand up, and wrap her hair around his hand. Pull her close . . .

"So. How bad are my books?" she said, interrupting the fantasy he'd been about to indulge in.

"Your books are perfect," he said. "Why would you assume I'm here to criticize?"

"Aren't you?"

"No. I'm here to . . . encourage best business practices."

"Meaning what?"

"I'm looking for ways to economize, but I'm also looking for ways to maximize profits."

"You won't find any. There are none. But you knew that."

Rhett sighed. "You want to sit down? And this will be a lot easier if you lose the attitude and stop being defensive."

Jules set her grooming caddy down with a *snap* on its shelf. "Lose the attitude. Okay, Mr. Fancy Pants. Let's you and me do a . . . what're they called in the corporate world? A groundbreaking exercise? You know, so that we can feel what it's like to step into each other's . . ." She cast a pointed look at his expensive shoes. "Loafers.

"How would you react, Ever-Rhett, if I sashayed all bowlegged into *your* office and announced that I'd somehow bought your business out from under you? And that you had to open up every aspect of it to me, an outsider, so that I could wreak havoc on everything you'd done or planned to do? Would you have an attitude? Would you be defensive?"

"Not at all," he said calmly.

Her eyebrows shot up to heights hidden by the Lone Stars cap. "Bullcrap."

"I wouldn't ever be in that position, Jules.

Simple as that. Because I'm down in the weeds of every aspect of my business. I run queries in the data all day long to find patterns and answer questions that I haven't even thought of, yet . . ."

Her face flushed. "Oh, I'm not down in the weeds? Down in the manure doesn't count?"

"Cut it out," he said. "C'mon. Sit down. Face the facts: This isn't about me being 'better' than you for any reason. This is about me having a different perspective and different training. That's all, okay?"

Jules folded her arms across her chest and stared at him, refusing to sit.

"We can work together, Jules. Or we can work at cross-purposes and I'll make decisions without even consulting you. Is that what you want?"

"No. Of course not."

"We have a common goal, here: to make a profit for this place and to help your dad recoup some losses."

She squinted at him. "You've already bought it out from under him, so how exactly are you going to do that?"

"First of all, I don't like the implications of *bought it out from under him*. I gave him a much fairer price than he'd have gotten from anyone else. You should know that. And if you'll kick off your boots and stay awhile, I'll give you some possible answers to that question."

Looking as though she'd rather eat her boots

than spend any time with him, Jules blew out a truculent breath, dropped into the other folding chair, and waited.

Rhett took one look at that raised, stubborn chin and repressed a smile. She was going to be one helluva management challenge. It probably served him right—he hadn't been easy himself. He'd been called a cowboy on more than one occasion. Headstrong and bullheaded. Without humility.

"So?" she prompted him.

"So. You've got a few different income streams here."

"Tell me something I don't know."

"Jules, with all due respect, shut your way-too-pretty face and let me talk."

She blinked at that, and he fought the urge to wipe the smear of dirt off her face.

Don't treat her like a kid. Clue in. That's what she's pissed about.

"Income streams," he repeated. "One: You're boarding horses for other people. Two: You're giving group riding lessons to kids, letting riders sponsor horses, and doing weekend trail rides for adults. Three: You're training and selling high-end hunter-jumpers. Four: You lease land for grazing. And five: You've got the saddlery in town."

"Uh-huh."

"So all of that brings in money. But let's look at your expenses and your ROI."

"My what?"

"Return on investment."

"O-kaaay." Jules eyed him cautiously.

"What do you enjoy doing the most?" Rhett asked her.

Jules's face lit up. "Giving lessons to the kids. Teaching them to love and respect horses. Come by Sunday afternoon and see it in action," she said. "I'd love to expand the school."

"I'll do that. What else?"

"Training the horses."

"How much does that bring in?"

She told him.

He nodded. "That's not bad . . . especially when you make a good sale."

"Like I did in Dallas."

The tension between them ratcheted up again. But he nodded.

"What's your capital outlay when you purchase a horse like that?"

"It's all there in the books."

"Okay. But my point is, the horse costs quite a bit and then you have to put months into training it before you recoup your purchase price or make any kind of profit. What do you charge for your time? How do you build that in?"

She stared at him. "I don't."

"Mistake," he said. "Your time and expertise is worth a lot of money."

"But I make that on the back end."

"After all the expenses of feeding and training, you personally aren't making squat. Let's find a way to change that. You need a better salary."

News to her, clearly. But she wasn't arguing, for a change.

"Let's talk overhead. You've got maintenance, feed and equipment, veterinary bills . . . insurance and taxes. It makes sense on this property, though I think you could lose the grazing land."

"But—"

"Hear me out, Jules. You can think about it. But the single biggest expense you have—and the greatest capital outlay on inventory, which doesn't move much, by the way—is the saddlery in town. That, my girl, has got to go. Sell it. Yesterday."

Jules stared at him. Then she laughed. "Oh no. No way. You're out of your mind. Holt Saddlery has been part of this family for decades. It's . . . it's a tradition. Not to mention that my aunt Sue would be out of a job if we sold it! And that is one hundred percent not cool."

"Aunt Sue?" Aunt Sue . . . Rhett vaguely remembered her. Kind of a gypsy-looking woman, loose, flowing clothes. Head scarf. And some kind of scandal attached to her name . . . it had rocked the town, years back. What had Sue Holt done in her misspent youth to shock the church ladies? He couldn't remember.

"My dad's older sister." Jules looked at him sideways, probably trying to gauge whether he remembered anything about her. She grabbed a rubber band off the desk and started messing with it, doing a cat's cradle–type of thing with the elastic stretched over her fingers. She seemed to be struggling internally with something.

"So your aunt works at the saddlery?" Rhett nudged her.

"Yeah."

"Full-time or part-time?"

"Sue works when it suits her. But her cell phone number is always on the door, inviting people to call her if they need something and the shop is closed."

"Works when it suits her . . ." Rhett digested this.

"Dad's always been a little, you know, afraid of her."

He lifted an eyebrow while Jules rushed on.

"She'll go after hours to sell an item as small as a tin of saddle soap. So it adds up to over forty hours, I'm sure. Everyone knows she's happy to go in."

"What's your top-dollar item there, Jules?"

"Saddles. Boots."

"And how many saddles has Aunt Sue sold in the last six months?"

She swallowed. "Um. One?"

Rhett closed the laptop and looked at her while the silence between them stretched on. "And pairs of boots?" he asked, at last.

"Two?" she ventured. "But she does repairs. Makes small leather goods, like holsters and canteens."

He folded his arms on top of the computer and continued to gaze steadily at her. Waiting for her to reach the right conclusion: that Holt Saddlery, Aunt Sue or not, had to go.

"Heh," she said. She started messing with the rubber band again. Stretched it to breaking point. It snapped and flew to the floor between them.

Rhett picked up the tiny rubber snake and handed it back to her, along with his unwelcome logic.

"Look," she said with a note of desperation in her voice. "I know how it looks on paper. But maybe you should see the place . . . talk to Aunt Sue, you know . . . before you—uh, we?—decide. We could go this afternoon after I finish up with my to-do list and you . . . do . . . whatever it is you do when you're not looking over my shoulder." She gave him a sugary smile.

Rhett snorted. "Sure," he said. "There's something I've been putting off." He could swing out to Silverlake Ranch and pay homage to his older brother for a few minutes, to ease his own worry about Declan, as well as to get Lila off his back. Then he could meet Jules at the saddlery after lunch. Not that he anticipated changing his mind. It was just that his earlier thought was sticking with him—*I'm not in Dallas anymore.* He figured he ought to give Jules every opportunity to state her case, though numbers, unlike people, didn't lie. A business was not a charity. Aunt Sue, who worked *when it suits her,* could find another job.

Because if Rhett was in the business of letting himself and the people who worked for him do whatever they *felt* like, he'd have Julianna Holt up against a wall with his mouth pressed to hers.

CHAPTER 8

Clods of dirt and small pebbles dinged against Scarlett's rims as Rhett eased down the winding road to a place he'd once loved more than anything. He wondered if he'd recognize what he'd find. Or maybe too much time had passed, and especially with the Old Barn destroyed, he'd remember none of it.

He rolled down the window and let the cool March air sweep through the car as he drove. By late April the Texas heat would start to slither in; by late May the humidity would coil and rise. And by summer? Even the water in garden hoses would be steaming hot.

The blurry outpost in the distance began to take shape as he neared. And when he finally stopped the car at the entrance and looked his fill, Silverlake Ranch took Rhett's breath away.

There were the familiar black iron gates with their bucking bronco silhouette, its rider a testament to everything stubborn. The bronc was a metaphor for life. Sometimes a man stuck in the saddle like a son of a gun. And sometimes he got bucked off and lay in the dirt with the wind knocked out of him. Maybe got up with some broken bones.

Beyond the gates, the pale gold and green

vista of the Braddock family land stretched for miles until it greeted the sky. The place was a patchwork of different pastures and crops.

There were picturesque fenced paddocks with horses grazing peacefully in them. There were neat rows of crops marching in orderly lines like obedient soldiers. There was a gully that fed a stock pond, to water the animals and cool off kids on a hot summer's day. And in the orchard, there were rows of apple trees, soon to be bursting with fruit. The edge of the lake was visible, too, along with the silhouette of the fishing shack that Pop had built out there, his version of a man cave.

Rhett had been away for a long, long time. Long enough to think he'd hardened his heart to any sentiment that a little waving grain and some well-placed wood beams could stir up. Early bluebonnets greeted him, waving hello to the long-lost stranger. By late April, they'd be everywhere, fields of glorious, heartbreaking, true blue. He remembered how they could almost count time by when they pushed through the soil in the beds on both sides of the front steps. He used to pluck handfuls of them and run them back to Mama just to make her smile.

I should've sent bluebonnets *to Jules* . . .

Before that thought could take further shape, Rhett quickly stepped out of the car and pushed the door shut. Then he leaned against Scarlett and stared up at his childhood home. It wasn't so different; it also wasn't the same. Declan had done some fine work on the house. Modern work, with a lot of glass, but he'd managed to blend old with new. The glass brought the live oaks almost inside of the house; gave the sensation that interior and exterior were one and the same. Truly, it was beautiful.

"Can I help y—"

Rhett turned to find his brother coming round the side of the main house, walking in the direction of the paddocks.

Declan's face remained neutral, but he nearly dropped the pails he was carrying before he set them down. A smattering of oats spilled over the sides and scattered in the dirt. "Everett."

Rhett's heart caught in this throat. Video wasn't the same, and seeing his older brother after that fire last fall didn't compare with reality. It wasn't just that Declan looked every inch the Silverlake rancher he was—every inch the Silverlake rancher Rhett once imagined himself.

It was that Deck looked like a shell of his former self. A stoic, hardened, muscular shell. His face wasn't just neutral—it was blank. There was no joy, no drive, no energy present beneath his rugged Braddock good looks. It wasn't how Rhett remembered his brother at all, and it suddenly occurred to him that Declan must have had dreams just for himself, just as Rhett had once. Maybe his older brother had also stopped hoping they were going to come true.

The loss of the Old Barn had clearly hit Declan harder than any of them. And if he and Declan still had anything in common, what was bothering his brother wasn't just the smoldering eyesore in the ground that Rhett had seen on video. It wasn't only the loss of income, though that weighed on him heavily, too. It was the loss of the memories . . . all the boys in the barn, working on old cars with Pop. The sense of brotherhood, of family, of love and normality. All gone up in smoke because of an idiot girl who couldn't follow basic rules of safety. And hadn't even bothered to send so much as a letter of apology.

Rhett himself had so many personal memories he'd blocked out. Declan had been his closest friend, his most beloved sibling. Mama used to say they were two peas in a pod, except that Rhett had too much in his mind and Declan had too much in his heart. Somehow in all of the jealousy and the anger of being sent on a life path Rhett hadn't wanted, he'd forgotten so much of the good.

For a moment Rhett was a teenager again, the smell of fresh-turned cemetery earth still on his jacket, standing on the curb at the Austin airport. A battered suitcase lay at his feet. Declan was standing by the idling truck with a determined look on his face . . .

Rhett didn't know what to do to say goodbye, so he just raised a palm in an awkward wave and then picked up his bag and walked away.

"Wait!" Declan called.

Rhett turned slowly, because he'd already started crying and he didn't want Declan to know.

"Gimme a hug," Declan said gruffly.

Tears tracked down Rhett's face as he shuffled back, immediately sinking into the utter comfort of being wrapped in his big brother's arms.

"It's gonna be okay," Declan whispered. "It's gonna be okay."

Well, he was right. And he was wrong. When Rhett called from boarding school a week later with a blackened eye and begged to come home, Declan said no. When Rhett called a month later with water from the dorm toilet bowl stinging in his nose and begged to come home, Declan said no. And when Rhett called six months later with a cut lip and blood in his mouth, Declan still said no.

Rhett never asked again.

And now here they were nearly toe to toe and yet a gulf a mile wide between them. Part of Rhett wanted to punch his brother's lights out, but most of him wanted that feeling of being hugged in his big brother's arms.

Neither of them did a thing until Declan wiped the sleeve of his work shirt across his sweaty brow. "Well," he said. His gaze slid to where

Scarlett was parked and back again to Rhett's face.

"Hey," Rhett said, not really sure how all this should go. Declan didn't look pleased so much as uncertain. "So, you probably heard I'm in town. Wanted to see for myself that you didn't get smoked like a ham when the Old Barn burned down."

"You saw me on video."

"Yeah, well . . . maybe I want to see your ass in person for the first time in more than a decade. Would that be so wrong?"

"Just a little shocking, is all."

Silence reigned for a long moment.

Fine. His brother didn't want him here? He'd leave again.

"Look, Deck. Cut the crap," Rhett said, stepping backward toward his car. "You don't want to see me, that's fine—"

"I didn't say that." Declan looked down and swore. Then he raised his chin again, the chin so like Rhett's own. He whipped off his work gloves and held out his right hand, the intensity in his eyes catching Rhett by surprise. "It's good to see you. In person. I'm glad you're here."

The words were right and the grip was firm, but old wounds cut deep.

Rhett studied Declan's face like a cop trying to catch someone lying, and went back to what he knew, what was comfortable—sticking it to his brother: "I also came back to make sure Frost was okay," he said, knowing how this conversation was going to go.

Declan's eyes narrowed. "You think I'd put any horse in a bad situation? You know how much I love horses, and you have to know how hard it was to decide to stop keeping extras on the ranch."

"This isn't any *extra* horse. This is *my* horse," Rhett said, the challenge in his voice coming through loud and clear.

"What the hell are you saying?" Declan asked, so quietly it was unnerving. Rhett felt off-balance. His brother's energy was intense. This wasn't like arguing about a business matter over the phone.

"You never thought to ask me how I might feel about giving Frost away?" Rhett asked.

"No. Seeing as how you haven't been home in forever and riding horses never came up once when we talked on the phone, Rhett, I did not." His older brother's voice was cool, dry, and detached.

Rhett stared at him.

Declan stared back. "How was I supposed to know you cared?" he finally asked, a slight crack in his tone this time.

For a moment Rhett wasn't sure they were talking about a horse. But he didn't want to talk at all, if it wasn't about his horse. *Of course this is about a horse.* Rhett knew he was being a jerk when he made a show of straightening the gold knots on his French cuffs. Lila had nabbed the monogrammed set, but he still had these. In a bored tone he added, "Well, I guess we both know it doesn't matter now. Solved that problem when I bought the entire Holt operation, so Frost is mine again."

His brother reared back in surprise, amusement warring with disgust. "So you really did buy an entire business just to take title on a geriatric horse. I'd managed to convince myself there was a really good reason to drop that kind of cash."

"Geriatric?" Rhett snapped.

But Declan kept going, the corner of his mouth now curled in . . . yeah, he'd settled on disgust. "You could have bought Frost from Jules. She probably would've given him back for free. But you had to go and *buy the Holt operation?* For what?"

"Grady called me. Told me his dad had a thyroid tumor. And that the stables and property were mortgaged to the hilt. He was going to go under."

Deck grunted. "I guess that makes you a hero."

"I didn't say that. But I did want to help. And unlike some people, Billy *took* my help."

"You can't just throw money at certain problems, Ever-Rhett."

"I never 'threw' money at you!"

"Didn't you? Then what the hell was that monster check in the mail?"

"The one you tore up? That was to help rebuild the Old Barn, and you know it."

"We all know there were strings attached; you'd want to do it your own way and control it all."

"No," Rhett said, working to keep his voice even. "I just want it rebuilt exactly the way it was."

"Not possible. Lila and I . . ." Deck broke off, clenching his jaw. "Pop—his essence was in there. It'll never be the same again. Ever."

"I disagree."

They faced off against each other, neither budging an inch.

Then Deck had to go there. "The Holt property . . ." he muttered, shaking his head. "Silverlake wasn't enough for you to bother coming home?"

"Silverlake—as you've made clear to me—isn't home," Rhett said.

The cold silence felt like a door slamming shut in his face.

Declan looked out over the range. "Nah, I guess not. Listen, I've got a lot of things on my list, and apparently, you have your own place to run." He gave Rhett a long look. "Lemme know if you need any advice on that."

And he picked up the feed buckets and stalked off, close enough to cause a shower of sweet feed and oats to drop all over Rhett's wingtips.

CHAPTER 9

Jules was outside rinsing out pails when that curvy, red sex symbol on wheels came into view. She'd had enough trouble not thinking about things she shouldn't have been thinking about, and, oh, look. Here came that smooth operator Rhett Braddock now—with his ridiculous car. She could see him literally a mile away from where she stood on the property and had plenty of time to run a hand over her hair and lick her dry lips for absolutely no good reason at all.

Her own car keys were in her pocket, and when he finally pulled up and leaned out the window, saying, "Y'all ready to go?" she was even more compelled to just walk on by. They were not going to pull up to see Aunt Sue in *that* thing. She pulled her keys from her pocket and jingled them in the air.

"You don't want to take a ride in Scarlett?" Rhett asked.

"Scarlett." She groaned. "Really?"

He grinned. "Really."

To avoid Trouble, to specifically look Trouble in the eye and then ignore it, Jules marched right past Rhett's Porsche and headed toward her own ride. "Let's take my truck." It was a 1994 blue Chevy Tahoe, perfect in every way. Her doors creaked, her seats squeaked, and she rattled with gusto in various places that Jules didn't care to identify.

She crunched over the gravel toward it, without waiting for an answer from Rhett.

They sat in their respective cars for a moment in what, to Jules's mind, had to be the world's least exciting game of chicken, when, finally, Rhett got out of his fancy car, shaking his head, and headed over.

He opened the passenger side door, *creeaaaak,* and got in without comment. Shifted a Whataburger wrapper and a crumpled napkin with the toe of his driving shoe. Tried to stretch the seat belt across his chest, but it stuck.

"It's broken," she said without apology.

"You might want to get it fixed—just for the sake of anyone who rides with you."

"That never happens—most people are afraid of what's in this truck." She laughed.

"Should I be?" Rhett plucked a wadded-up Taco Bell bag off the dashboard and tossed it onto the floor with the other garbage.

"Probably. I've hauled everything from hay and feed and dirty tack to dogs to miniature goats to a baby donkey in this thing."

"That would explain the smell." Rhett rolled down his window. "And the fact that it's impossible to see out the back windows, through all the smears of slobber."

"I like the smell," Jules said.

Rhett grinned and shook his head. "Of course you do. So can I ask why you had goats in the back?"

"They are annoying and destructive. So I gave them to your sister when she was setting up the petting zoo out at Silverlake. Deck wasn't too happy." She laughed. "I gave her a feral chicken, too."

"I didn't know chickens came in that flavor."

She cast him a glance to see if he was joking. "It's not a—"

"I know. Where did you get a feral chicken?"

"Bastrop. There's a whole gaggle of feral chickens ruling the roost on Farm Street there. I was trying to make a sale when one of them walked right up to my truck and sort of hissed at me. I had some sweet feed in the back, so I gave him some. Next thing I know, he's flapped up inside and refuses to come out. So I took him home with me, and that's when things started getting funny."

"How's that?"

"Well." Jules took a hard left out of the stables and headed for Main Street. "I have absolutely no idea how he got there, you understand? But he somehow made his way into the firehouse shower."

"Somehow." Rhett's lips twitched.

"Yeah. Crazy, right? And *somehow* all the other

guys except for Grady knew about it. So it scared the daylights out of my brother when he climbed in."

Rhett hooted. "Oh, hey—why? I mean, I shower with feral chickens on a daily basis."

"Grady, after a lot of cussing, declined ownership. Go figure. Dad refused 'that bastage redheaded rooster,' too. Told me to get rid of the 'son of a gun.' So, since I didn't feel like driving him back to Bastrop, I drove him out to the Old Barn instead."

Rhett's laughter fell away.

"I'm sorry," she said. "I can't believe it's gone, and all because of that crazy Bridezilla girl."

"We'll rebuild. Don't you worry."

"That's not the word . . . but that's also not my business."

Rhett stared out the window without comment.

"Anyway. So I pull up to the Old Barn, stuff the rooster under my arm, and crash a Garden Club luncheon that Lila'd orchestrated. Told them I'd arrived with their entrée . . . but it was a little undercooked, still."

Rhett's mirth returned. Shoulders shaking, he turned to face her again. "Jules."

She cackled. "I'm not sure who was more petrified, the chicken or the Garden Club ladies."

"And what did my sister do?" he inquired.

"Grabs the chicken from me, says she ordered coq au vin, if you please, and stuffs it into an empty cupboard for the next couple of hours."

"Priceless."

"Then she kicks me out."

"My guess is that you weren't dressed for the Garden Club luncheon?"

Jules bit her lower lip. "Well, no. Not exactly."

They'd pulled up in front of Holt Saddlery by this time, and she took a deep breath.

The bells on the knob jingled as Rhett opened the door for her, and they walked into the shop. It looked and smelled like a peculiar combo of Wild West meets *Arabian Nights*.

Aunt Sue had incense burning from hanging, hammered-tin containers, large beeswax candles—Mia's—burned in colorful glass holders, and strings of porch lights (in cactus, cowboy boot, and chili pepper shapes) glimmered from almost every molding.

Some of the English saddles were slung on their stands over exotic fabrics. The western ones sat atop woven Mexican and Indian blankets. Bridles, halters, martingales, and leads hung on one wall. Rows and rows of hand-tooled western boots sat on another wall, waiting to walk out with their lucky new owners.

Aunt Sue did shoe, boot, and bag repairs in a back room, and in addition to holsters and canteens, made leather jewelry with semiprecious stones and feathers.

Folk art, homespun Texas crafts, and turned-wood objects nestled in every corner and crevice . . . Aunt Sue liked to help out other local craftspeople. Mia's other beeswax products sat showcased in their own shelf near the cash register. The shelf itself was made by a local furniture-maker, handcrafted of polished driftwood and glass. It was a two-tiered affair that held a few items of Southwest jewelry on the higher shelf.

"Y'all come on in," Sue's husky voice called from the back room. "Be with you in two shakes."

"Chocolate or vanilla?" Jules called.

Rhett groaned.

"What? Is that you, Jules?" Aunt Sue stuck her white head out of the back, her pewter-gray eyes leveling on first Jules and then Rhett. "Ah. Wondered when the new owner'd be stoppin' by." Soon the rest of her emerged, too—wielding what looked like a small sledgehammer.

No flies on Aunt Sue. She didn't miss a trick. She was a handsome, comfortably padded lady of about fifty-five, dressed in a leather apron over an artistic, flowy silk top. That was draped over a long, swirly skirt and cowboy boots with flowers embroidered on them. Her white hair was pulled back in a turquoise-studded clip, and beaded, feather earrings dangled almost to her shoulders.

"How do you know who I am?" Rhett asked, a touch awkwardly.

She smiled. "Easy. You look like your mother, rumors run amok, and you're with Jules . . . who looks as if she'd rather not be here, introducing you. That tells me that she's touring you around the business and you're looking for . . . should we call them . . . inefficiencies?"

Jules winced, but Rhett seemed to respect her logic. "I don't think I'd dare call you an inefficiency, ma'am. You might hit me with that hammer."

She considered him coolly and bared her teeth in what just passed for a smile. "I might."

"Be nice, Aunt Sue," Jules said.

"Sure, sure. I'll be just as nice as you were, doll. Tossed Maggie's flowers into a stall out at the barn . . ."

"Dad is a gossip," Jules said. "Like everyone else in this town."

"It was your mother who told me."

"Oh. How is it that the entire family has been treating me like I'm two years old?"

"Don't feel discriminated against. Billy only just told *me*." Aunt Sue's eyes went cloudy. "I am worried about him. Your mother's a wreck."

"I'm worried about both of them."

"Well. We don't want to suffocate Ever-Rhett, here, by airing our family laundry. How can I help you, sir?"

"Oh, just wanted to see the place," Rhett said, a shade too casually.

"Sure." Aunt Sue shot him a caustic glance. "Well, come on in. Check out our horse community photos—over there, see? On the wall opposite the ribbons and trophies."

It was a deliberate move by her aunt: show Rhett that the Holt Saddlery was a Silverlake fixture, almost a museum as well as an odd, artsy general store. The community photo wall was one of Jules's favorite spots in the hodgepodge of the saddlery.

Aunt Sue had inexplicably slung a beat-up suede couch and a trunk for a coffee table across two glass-paned double doors that opened inward. When questioned about this furniture placement, she flapped a dismissive hand. "Aw, nobody uses that entrance, anyway. So why not?"

On the adjacent walls hung a wealth of town horse history: trophies and ribbons on one wall, and on the other, photos of local kids and adults in rodeos, horse shows, special equestrian competitions and at the annual Black Tie & Boots Soiree, which raised money to rescue wild horses—mostly mustangs—from kill lots.

There stood Aunt Sue, MC at the 2003 soiree, blazing in bright red lipstick, a rhinestone collar and matching earrings, a long black velvet dress slit up to the thigh, and black cowboy boots with skulls on the toes; red and white roses climbing the shanks.

"Lookin' good," said Rhett.

"I held my own, back in the day." Aunt Sue nodded.

There was Jules, in riding breeches, coat, and black velvet helmet, on the back of Lancelot, a massive bay gelding. They were hurtling over a fence that was six feet high. She had perfect form—heels down in the stirrups, leaning forward, shoulders back. She was proud of that—though what the photo didn't show was Lancelot balking at the next fence and her flying over it to land in a heap on the ground. She remembered Dad's white face, bending over her. Then Sue shoving him out of the way, getting down on her knees to do CPR if necessary. But Jules'd just had the breath knocked out of her. It returned, along with a nice dose of public humiliation.

And there . . . Jules chuckled. There, in fact, was Rhett himself: flying through the air after getting unseated by a pissed-off bull.

He winced. "Not my best event," he said.

"I think you were dumb to even get near that animal," Jules told him. "Stick with the mechanical kind. Did you see Schweitz's finally got one?"

"I did not."

"Otto finally wore down Schweitzie. It should make for some good evening entertainment."

"Good Lord," Aunt Sue said. "I'll have to take that in, a night or two."

"You always were a wild child, Auntie."

Sue snorted. "And now I'm a wild old woman."

"Still a beauty," Rhett said.

He got a squint for that. "Puh-lease. Save your charm for someone else, boy."

"You'll never be old," Jules said. And she meant it.

"All right, you two. Why don't you cut bait and tell me why you're here, for real. Don't like my profit margins, is that it?" She leveled her gaze on Rhett.

"They were fine," he said carefully, "when all you had to pay was taxes. What you may not know is that Billy refinanced everything. Including taking out a big mortgage on your shop building, here."

Jules swallowed hard. "He did not."

Rhett nodded. "He did. He needed the cash."

Aunt Sue's face drained of color. "Oh, *Billy*." She sat down hard on the suede couch. "Darn it." Then her expression changed to one of puzzlement. "But you—you bought the whole operation, didn't you?"

"I bought the operation, Sue," he said. "But I haven't paid off the mortgage on this particular building. First of all, I need an interest write-off. And second, I don't know that the numbers justify doing that."

Her chin came up and she did her best to stare him down.

He didn't blink. "So for example . . . when

you take people's work on consignment"—Rhett gestured around to various items—"you may want to start taking the normal fifty percent cut, instead of only fifteen percent."

"Why should they do all the work and only get paid half," Sue murmured, "while the only thing I do is display their items?"

"I hear you," Rhett said. "And I applaud the sentiment. But times have changed, and every square inch in here needs to start paying for itself."

Aunt Sue patted her padded hip. "Every square inch, you say?"

Jules could practically see the cogs turning in Rhett's head. *How to handle a woman like Aunt Sue?* And he chose well.

Rhett nodded. "Every square, beautiful inch."

One side of Aunt Sue's generous mouth quirked up. She wasn't completely immune to flattery. Then she wiped any vestige of a smile off her face. "I don't like change," she said flatly.

"Neither do I," he shot back. "But you bring in enough change, you'll find yourself looking at a stack of dollar bills."

Rhett rubbed the back of his neck as he and Jules headed back out to her goat-and-chicken-scented wreck on wheels. Aunt Sue had been running the saddlery as part charity for other artists, and part hobby shop. It was so far in the red, it wasn't funny. This would be a tough call; everything in there called out to the kid who'd once loved rodeo. But just because you loved something didn't mean it worked.

"Well?" Jules said when they were back in the truck.

He sighed. "I don't know what you expect me to say. I get that Holt Saddlery is important to you. I get that your Aunt Sue is *really* important to you. But this is a business."

"You could've been a little nicer," she said. "I mean, who doesn't like Aunt Sue? Except you, I mean."

"I didn't dislike her!"

"You were . . . hard on her."

"It's not being hard, Jules. It's *business*. And she had an opinion about me before I'd even opened my mouth. She could've given me the benefit of the doubt."

"But you didn't change your position, did you? You still want to close down the shop."

"Look, yes, I still think the best thing would be to close it down and find your aunt something else to do—something she'd really like. But like I said, I'm willing to consider alternatives. I think that's pretty reasonable."

Jules looked out the window. "Do you have *any* feelings for Silverlake, Rhett?"

He watched her push her ponytail off her neck. That same spot he'd had his mouth on in Dallas.

Yeah, I've got feelings for Silverlake. Feelings I need to ignore.

"Something's got to give, Jules," Rhett said. "You can't have it all and there are other areas where you've got to make changes."

"What areas?"

Rhett hadn't wanted to dump this on her all at once, but if Jules wanted a straightforward approach, that's what she was going to get. "You've been overpaying for feed and supplies. You can place bulk orders much more cheaply with a big national chain," he told her.

Jules folded her arms and shook her head. "We support local. We have always done business with Fred's Feed and Supply. Always."

"Well, maybe it's time for a change."

"Fred and my dad went to A&M together."

"Uh . . . Jules, that's great. They can still hoist a beer or two now and then for old times' sake. But this is business."

"Rhett, I know you're a big-city guy. But you did grow up around here, and I'd hope you'd remember the way things are done in small-town Texas. We support our neighbors, through thick and thin."

"And that's a fine sentiment and an admirable way to be, but—"

"During the Great Depression, Fred's dad, old Mr. Comstock, kept on delivering to the ranches around here, even when the owners couldn't pay him, or couldn't come up with quite enough. He fed half the county's animals on credit, knowing that the ranchers would make good when they could. On a handshake. And they did."

"I love the story, but it was a different day and age, Jules."

"Old Comstock supplied feed to Silverlake Ranch, too," she continued, as if she hadn't heard him or didn't care what he was saying. "*Braddock* livestock would have starved if not for him."

Rhett fell silent at this and sighed.

"In return, when the Big-Box Boys came around offering better prices to all the local ranchers on their feed, they—and we—stuck by Fred's Feed and Supply. We still do. And that will change," Jules gritted her teeth, "over my dead body."

"Over your dead body, huh?" Rhett said. He dragged a hand down his face in frustration. "That's very helpful, Jules. I'm trying to come up with business solutions for you. Get this place into the black."

She stared stubbornly back at him. "Well, you're not going to do it by cutting out Fred's."

"All right. What would you rather do? Look at cutting out your salary?"

"*Pardon?*"

"Well, you said it yourself: You live for free in the cabin out here. Even your utilities are paid. So maybe we could just call that enough."

"Rhett Braddock, the contract you signed with my dad guarantees me my job here, and you know it."

"Sure," he said. "And I will always honor that. However, the contract does not guarantee a specific salary. Read it."

She gaped at him.

"Aw, close your mouth, Jules, before a horsefly swoops in and takes a seat on one of your molars. Decides to kick back and stay awhile."

"Gross," she said.

"I'm not going to cut your salary," Rhett said irritably. "I was just making a point. In fact, as I told you, I'm trying to find ways to increase what we pay you! But I can't find those ways if you won't at least try to work with me."

"I *am* working with you, unfortunately. But we'll have to look at something else. Not Fred's. My dad would have a conniption fit."

Rhett didn't point out that he didn't have to ask her permission—or her father's. But he was sure it was written all over his face—even if one Julianna Holt refused to read it.

"Fine. We'll revisit the idea later."

"Or not," she said sweetly.

"How much do you order from Fred's at a time, and when?"

She told him.

Rhett leaned back and thought about it. "So what if you ordered six months' worth at a time and paid up front for it? Might be worth Fred's while to give you a better price if he gets a big chunk of money all at once."

"I can't pay all at once. I don't have the cash. Besides, the sweet feed has to be stored in a climate-controlled environment, or it will rot. And it starts deteriorating after a month."

"But oats—they'll last up to a year, if stored right. So what if we did a combo? And you *can* now afford it. Remember? You've got an injection of capital, via yours truly."

"Okay, Yours Truly." Jules somehow made it sound as though there was an *Up* before the *Yours*. She was talented at that. "Then you tell me: Can we afford a year's worth of oats at one time? How about hay?"

He nodded. "Yes, and yes."

"Huh," she said.

"That's eloquent. So may I please, Miss Holt, have your royal permission to petition Fred for a better price? Make a win-win deal for everyone concerned?"

"I guess so," she muttered.

"How can I express my undying gratitude to you?"

She made a graceful hand gesture and rolled her eyes. "Sit and spin."

"Wow, Helen and Billy invested in charm school for you, did they? And you graduated with top honors."

"Absolutely. Now, could you and all of your brilliant ideas just . . . get out of my face for a while?"

"There's no need to growl at me," Rhett said.

"That was my stomach," Jules said. "I'm hungry."

"Maybe that explains the 'tude," Rhett muttered, mostly under his breath.

"*Excuse* me?"

He grinned at her.

She blew out a breath and shook her head. "What are we going to do about Sue?" she mumbled, jamming a hand down into her boot, doing who knew what.

Rhett grew serious again. "I don't know. But I promise you I'll work on it." He'd start by getting a valuation on the building that housed Holt Saddlery. Then he'd have a better idea of how to move forward.

Jules paused, clearly thinking about his words. He added, "In any case, I'll let you know before I mess with the saddlery."

"Promise noted," she said.

"What are you digging for, anyway? Lose your toes?"

"My wallet."

Rhett began to laugh. "You keep your wallet in your *boot*?"

'Yes. Why?" Jules gave a small grunt of satisfaction as she retrieved a battered little leather rectangle. It appeared to hold exactly one bank card, her driver's license, and a few worn bills. Maybe an insurance card—he hoped. Though, come to think of it, he hadn't seen any sign that she had health insurance through the stables. Billy, his wife, Helen, and Sue did. But not Julianna Holt. What were they thinking—that she was so young, she didn't need it?

Horrible scenarios went through his mind. Jules could be knocked to the ground and stepped on by a horse. Get shocked by faulty wiring. Be hit with a pitchfork . . . bitten by that yellow-fanged donkey out there. The bite could get infected and spread toxins through her body.

"Why not keep your wallet in your fanny pack?"

She looked offended. "The fanny pack is for horse snacks. I'd never put my wallet in there. Anyways, I was digging for it because I'm starving. We're going through a drive-through. Your choice: Taco Bell or Whataburger."

"I'd be glad to take you for a decent meal somewhere," Rhett said.

"Drive-through is *very* decent. Fast. Hot. Yummy. And I don't need your charity, thanks."

Jeez, the girl is prickly. "I didn't mean it that way, and you know it. I just meant we could sit down at an actual table, maybe with a real table-cloth, and real vegetables."

"Pickles and onions are vegetables. So are fries."

He ignored this logic. "We could discuss new angles for making money at the saddlery."

"I don't have time for a restaurant meal. Too much to do. Thanks, though," she said grudgingly. "So, which fast-food flavor do you want?"

Rhett sighed. "Whataburger. Best fast food in Texas."

She grinned. "Finally, we agree on something! Onion rings?"

"Of course. With the bold barbecue sauce."

"No way! *Honey* barbecue sauce." She gulped some of the disgusting cold coffee in her console—

"Honey? You gettin' sweet on me, Jules?" he teased.

—and blew it out her nose, sputtering. "That," she promised darkly, "is never going to happen."

Without even thinking about it, Rhett resented that. Even though he'd said so himself, in regards to Jules. Even though he'd deliberately engineered things so that there were no complications from their one-night stand. And even though he kept fixating on the annoying things about her: gruesome, mud-caked rubber riding boots, fanny pack, apparent lack of a comb, garbage truck on wheels. *Sister of his best friend.* He wasn't used to being dismissed so readily. With such gusto and . . . and . . . amused indifference.

He was quite a catch, after all. Not the ugliest man alive. Hot car. Billionaire.

But she'd pretty much blown the very idea of him out of her nose, along with that crap advertised as coffee. And it was downright offensive—really, it was.

Never going to happen, huh?

Correct. You copy, numbskull? Grady's. Little. Sister. Never going to happen.

He stared at the hideous, sparkling Fool Fest jesters strung along the garlands on Main Street as Jules made a beeline for the Fredericksburg Whataburger. He felt like one of them—God's own joke, a plastic fool without a soul, only here temporarily . . . for the holiday.

He'd head back to Dallas after the Fool Fest weekend. He was needed there, and he'd have a handle on the Holt business inside of three weeks, easily.

He smelled the Whataburger before they got anywhere near the famous orange *W*. He had to admit, it smelled like home.

Sure, they had them in Dallas. But for some reason, he associated the place with Silverlake. Remembered all the hijinks and high school date nights. Remembered Grady and him sinking beers into the ice of the oversized, covered soda cups. Threading the plastic straws right down into the beer. Getting drunk while looking like the picture of innocence . . .

"Sweet and Spicy Bacon Burger, please," said Jules into the speaker box. "Onion rings with honey barbecue sauce. Iced tea. And . . . ?" She turned toward Rhett. "I'm buying your lunch."

"You'll do no such thing. Patty melt, please!" he called. "Onion rings. Bold barbecue sauce. Iced tea. And her credit card is stolen! Don't take it. I'll give you cash."

"It's not stolen!" she yelled at the box.

The teenager inside gave them their total. "Drive up to the window, please."

Jules glared at Rhett. "I have cash, too. And I'm buying."

"Pull up," was his only answer.

As she did, he slipped out of the passenger side, leaving the door hanging open. He vaulted easily over the hood and stood blocking the window while Jules cussed at him.

"Hi," he said with a blinding smile at a dazed girl in an orange uniform. He handed her thirty bucks. "Keep the change, darlin'."

She nodded. "Thanks."

"*De nada.*" Rhett stiffened as a punch landed in the vicinity of his kidneys. "Hey," he said over his shoulder. "That's no way to treat a man who's buying you lunch."

"I said it was my treat!" Jules shook her fist at him.

"Uh-huh. I saw the number that constitutes your poor excuse for a salary."

"I live for free in the cabin," she protested. "I don't have any big expenses. It's fair."

He snorted and accepted the bag of food from the clerk, just as Jules banged on his kidneys again.

"I'm afraid that I'm going to have to teach you some manners," he said. He walked around to the front of her wreck, and in full sight fished not the patty melt, but her burger, out of the bag and unwrapped it. With an evil grin, he chomped down on it, taking a huge bite.

"How—what—hey!" she yelled. "You can't do that!"

"Mmmmmmm," he said. "Needs mustard."

"Don't you *dare* put mustard on my burger, you son of a—"

Rhett took another bite, waggling his eyebrows in exaggerated bliss.

Jules gunned the engine, looking mad enough to run him down.

He swallowed, took a long draught of iced tea, and didn't move. "Say 'thank you,' Jules. I know it's foreign to you. I know it's hard to pronounce. But repeat after me: 'Th-th-thank you, Rhett. You are such a gentleman . . . now I see it's no act.' "

Her rage, curiously, had faded. As he watched her expression change through the dirty windshield, he couldn't for the life of him discern what she was thinking.

"You remembered," she said. "That I hate mustard."

"Of course I remember that you hate mustard,"

he said. "You always did. Now—you gonna run me down?"

"Not if you stop eating my burger," she told him. "And give me two bites of your patty melt. Fair?"

"Fair." Rhett got back in the car, tried and failed to put on the seat belt again, set down the bag between them. He handed over his patty melt and gave her ponytail a tug.

Another fleeting, inscrutable expression crossed Jules's face at that. Then she unwrapped the patty melt and took a bite as someone behind them honked.

CHAPTER 10

Rhett was still digesting the crazy from Whataburger and the situation with the Holt Saddlery while he worked through his in-box back at the hotel. Someone pounded on his hotel door. "Hey, Fancy!" shouted a familiar voice. The pounding continued. "Fancy, are you in there? Open up." It sounded suspiciously like Rhett's brother Jake.

Rhett opened the door and, sure enough, Jake along with Grady and fellow firefighter Mick nearly toppled into his hotel room. "What the hell, guys?" Truth be told, seeing his old buddies all together warmed Rhett's heart. He shook hands with Mick, feeling a twisted nostalgia for the past when the man slapped him hard enough on the back to dislodge a major organ. Rhett remembered the big guy from grade school as a skilled practical joker; he probably considered Silverlake's Fool Fest a major holiday. Jake once mentioned Mick had developed a touch of mama hen in his time at the firehouse, but Rhett was hard pressed to reconcile how the young troublemaker in his memory could have changed that much.

Jake held his arms out from his sides. "Are you *kidding* me? *Are you kidding me?*"

Rhett just started laughing. Sometimes you

could see family expressions and mannerisms come through on video calls, but Jake, here, with his unruly dark hair and stubble looked more like his lost twin than ever. Mama used to say it was lucky Jake had that one dimple on his left side or he'd get lost in the Black Irish Braddock shuffle.

With an incredulous look on his face, Jake began to stalk the hotel room repeating his words even louder. "ARE YOU KIDDING ME? If I had a dollar for every time someone asked if I'd seen you yet, I'd be the one staying in these fancy digs."

"Weren't you on duty?" Rhett asked, grinning like a maniac.

"Yeah, so? You've seen Lila. You made a special trip out to see Deck. You've been hanging out with *Grady,* for Pete's sake." Jake's finger moved accusingly between the two of them. "You two share no DNA. It's embarrassing."

It was only when Jake's finger stalled in front of Grady that Rhett realized the boys were tossing his hotel room. "What the—?"

"This is a jailbreak," Jake said. "Gotta get your stuff."

"Get my . . . ?"

Grady elbowed him aside and went to the closet where Rhett's suits were neatly hung. He started grabbing them off the hangers and piling them on the bed. Jake took over at the drawers. "Awww, really?" He pointed to the neat rows of socks.

"Look, boys, Rhett got him some 'life-changing magic.' He pressed his hand to his heart and blinked doe eyes at Rhett. "Does lining up your socks like that really spark joy in your heart?"

"Shut up. Seriously. What are you guys doing? We're not twelve," Rhett said, trying not to smile.

Mick wrinkled his nose. "True. Grady always tells me I act like a thirteen-year-old."

"Who put him in charge?" Rhett asked.

Grady folded his arms over his chest. "Here's the deal. You can stay in this fancy hotel by your lonesome and pretend you're back at boarding school where nobody talks to you, or you can come stay with us in the bunk room at the firehouse and raise a little old-fashioned hell with a bunch of boys who won't give you a minute's peace."

"Donating what would have been your hotel costs to the firehouse fund, of course," Mick suggested with a cough.

"Doesn't seem like a difficult choice to me," Jake said, "but then again, I've been around Mick's dirty socks for so many years I can't smell 'em anymore. Besides, Hunter's on leave so you can have his bed and his locker."

"So, you guys need money, do you?" Rhett asked.

"Surprisingly, no. Grandpa Nash has turned into quite the benefactor. He's a big fan of Jake's now," Mick said.

"But we're only allowed so many of those bulk-sized boxes of candy bars a month, so consider it a personal gift," Jake said. "You can spark some joy in *me*."

Rhett grinned. "Oh, *I'll* spark some joy in you, all right!" he threatened, jumping on Jake and attempting to wrestle him to the ground.

"See, now, *this*," Grady said, not helping at all. "This is what I'm talking about. Come on over to the firehouse and stay with the boys while you're in town."

Mick called a draw on the wrestling after he and Grady finished packing up all of Rhett's things. Jake and Rhett finally stood up and backed away from each other. Clothes ripped, out of breath, both of 'em grinning ear to ear.

"So, what's it gonna be, brother o' mine? You coming with us?" Jake asked, pushing by and hoisting Rhett's suitcases. They barely closed and one sleeve was sticking out the side.

"Here's your one chance, Fancy," Mick said. "Don't let me down."

"Shut up, weirdo," Rhett said, following Jake out of the room.

Not twenty minutes later, Rhett was escorted with friendly force into the firehouse before Grady and Mick peeled off, leaving him to be greeted by a golden Labrador, who barked at him and then promptly shoved his nose into what Rhett had previously assumed were his most private parts.

"Hey!" he protested, taking a step back. The dog took two steps forward, wagged his tail manically, and kept on exploring. "This Lab is yours? Aren't you supposed to have a dalmatian? What's wrong with this fire station?"

"It'd take too long to explain." Old George, the retired fire captain, came out to greet Rhett. "Been a long time, son," he said through his bushy gray mustache. "How ya doin'?"

"Can't complain—except for being turfed out of my comfy room at the Hotel Saint-Denis and dragged here by the scruff of my neck."

Old George chuckled. "Welcome. I think the only member of the squad you don't know yet is Rafael, and he's out on a call. Oh, and this here's Not-Spot. Tommy brought him home, and we didn't have the heart to replace him. The only dalmation in town belongs to Sophia at the jewelry shop. She dresses to match it."

"O-kaaaay." Rhett dislodged Not-Spot's nose from his crotch and scratched him behind the ears. "So where am I sleeping?" he asked Jake. "Not in the dog's bed, I hope?"

"On pool noodles in the shower," Jake told him with a grin. But this turned out to be false. Soon Rhett's luggage was installed in the bunk room at the firehouse.

He followed it, taking in the seven neatly made bunks. "Which one's mine?" he asked Jake.

Jake pointed to a bed with a big, unapologetic

cowboy hat on it. A Stetson. With a laugh, Rhett stuck it on the toe of his shoe when he flopped down on his extra-long single and tucked his hands behind his head. "I gave up nine-hundred-thread-count sheets for this?"

Jake grinned and threw a pillow at his head.

"Is that even clean?" Rhett asked.

"No. Not-Spot likes to sleep there. I'm pretty sure he's drooled on it."

"Butthead."

"I thought you were the one with the fancy vocabulary. Didn't we all send you away to that snotty school to learn some better insults?"

"Thou art . . . the rankest compound of villainous smell that ever offended nostril," Rhett intoned.

"What the—?" Jake said incredulously.

"Shakespeare," Rhett said in an English accent. "And I still don't know why you all sent me away to that snotty school. It sucked."

He didn't mean to kill the mood, but Jake stared at him in awkward silence. He sat down on the bed across from Rhett's and looked at the floor.

"Yeah, well." Rhett left it at that.

"Declan always said you were doing fine. He bragged about all your awards, your GPA, all the colleges you got into."

Maybe he shouldn't have been surprised that Declan was so proud. Maybe if he'd listened a little better to his eldest brother he would've heard that pride coming through. Still, Jake couldn't understand. He didn't know. "Declan either lied or was in denial. I told him I wasn't doing fine."

Jake stared at him, his brow furrowed.

Yeah. Maybe saintly Declan Braddock lied. Chew on that, bro!

"But look at you . . . it seems that you're doing better than fine now."

Rhett picked up the cowboy hat and turned it in his hands. "I do okay," he admitted. "How are *you* getting along with Deck these days?"

"Better than ever." Jake's smile was a mile wide. "I really missed having an older brother," he said quietly. "I had two, and then I had none. Besides, I've come to feel that Declan did the best he could with us. He had some tough choices and some promises to keep to Mama and Pop. And we weren't perfect, either."

Rhett gritted his teeth together, surprised by the wave of emotion sweeping through him. "I was darn *near* perfect, Jake," he said, to lighten the mood and keep himself from acting the fool in front of his brother.

It got the laugh he expected. "Did you ever ask him if you could come home?" Jake asked after a moment. "Maybe if you'd told him—"

Rhett sat bolt upright, the cowboy hat falling to the floor. "Are you serious? Only every other

Sunday! Didn't he pass on anything I ever said?"

Jake looked stricken. "Sorry, man, I didn't mean to touch a nerve."

Rhett ruffled his hair, exasperated. "It's fine. Let's forget about it."

"I'm glad you're here, now," Jake said. "We need to get everybody together. Lila's been harping on it since she saw you at Schweitz's, and things are serious with Charlie—"

"Charlie Nash, huh? I really wasn't sure how that'd all pan out."

"Long story. Point is, it would be nice to all sit down, do a family dinner before you leave. I'd love to see you and Deck start to patch things up."

"I think that ship has sailed," Rhett said tightly.

"I thought the same thing about Charlie and me. Don't waste any more time, Rhett. Don't have regrets. Don't leave Silverlake without making up with Declan."

Rhett's stomach dropped a couple of feet. *What the—?* "Is something wrong with Declan?"

"No," Jake said quickly. "Just . . . what if. But whatever you were just feeling a second ago, imagine feeling that for the rest of your life."

"I don't think either of us has to imagine that," Rhett said grimly, and he saw from Jake's expression that his brother understood he was talking about losing their parents. He'd sure like to be talking about something else.

"I'm really glad you're getting deeply in touch with your feelings," he drawled, doing his best to get back on familiar ground with a little brotherly sarcasm. "I'll have to thank Charlie for that when I see her again. In the meantime, say hello to your Inner Child for me."

"Shut up," Jake said, but without any heat. He grinned the ridiculous grin of a man in love.

"So, it's really like that, is it? She's 'the one'? You gonna be the first of us?" Rhett asked.

He expected his brother to protest, but Jake looked Rhett square in the eyes, a slight flush on his smiling face, and said, "Yep. But keep it to yourself. I haven't said a word to anybody else about it, and I want to really surprise her."

Rhett grinned like a madman. He slapped Jake on the back by way of congratulations, unable to articulate the happiness he felt for his brother. There was something unexpectedly . . . well, *beautiful,* about sharing such a simple moment of joy with family. Face-to-face, not video call. He'd forgotten what that was like.

Jake held out his hand. "Welcome home, Fancy."

Rhett huffed a laugh and took his brother's hand, staring at their clasped fingers. "Please don't tell me that nickname's a thing around town now."

Jake told him nothing of the sort, probably because it was too late to stop the terrible nickname and because Rhett got busy trying to stuff that drooly pillow back in his brother's face. *Now who is acting like a kid?* Rhett was loving every second of it.

Jake finally wrestled the pillow back and threw it down the vintage pole hole in order to end the scuffle. "Hey!" someone downstairs called. The pillow came shooting back up through the hole.

"Listen, I've got to get back over to the Holt place," Rhett said.

"How are things going with Jules? The entire town's watching, you know. She's Silverlake royalty and you done made that girl cry," Jake said with extra twang.

"What?!"

Jake's eyes widened. "Whoa. I was just messin' around."

Rhett blinked. "I don't think so. Not really. What exactly are they saying?"

"I thought you'd laugh," his brother said. They shared an uneasy glance. *Maybe it takes more than a single handshake to be family again after such a long time.*

"Jake, what are they saying?"

Jake shifted his weight and cleared his throat. "I mean, yeah, everybody's talking about the sale and what's poor Jules going to do now that . . ."

"Uh-huh? Go on."

"Now that that rich boy bought up her future." He paused. "Everybody knows she wanted to run that place. She's never been shy about saying what she wants."

His words brought back a time in a very different place under very different circumstances where Jules Holt hadn't been at all shy to say what she wanted.

"You've got yourself in a somewhat tricky situation, is all I'm saying. Tread lightly."

Somewhat? Rhett pressed his forehead against the wall. He wanted to punch something. "That's how everybody sees me," he said, his voice a low growl. "I was born here, Jake, same as you, same as Jules."

"I thought you'd laugh," Jake repeated. "I'm sorry."

Normally, I would. Rhett took a deep breath and shrugged it all off. "To answer your question, things are going well, especially under the circumstances." *Man, if Jake only knew* all *of the circumstances.* But then Grady would find out, because to hear tell, Silverlake firefighter loyalty was some kind of supernatural force. And if Grady found out, Rhett would be six feet under before Jules had fed and watered the horses the next morning. "Jules is a great manager. You know how hard it is to find motivated people who care about what they're doing?"

"Outside the firehouse, yeah," Jake said.

Rhett chuckled. "Jules is the whole package. She's smart, she's kind, she's a doer . . ."

She's gorgeous, great in bed, a good friend, a good daughter, just a terrific all-around human being . . .

"I think I lost you there, Rhett," Jake said, the corner of his mouth curling up in a suspicious smile. "Huh. I just meant, were the books what you were expecting? But, by all means, do go on about Julianna Holt's many fine qualities."

"Now you're getting annoying again," Rhett said, lowering his voice. "Grady's going to overhear and misunderstand."

"Oh, I don't reckon Grady's gonna misunderstand a thing," Jake said, not lowering his voice a bit. And with that he tipped up the brand-new cowboy hat and plunked it right down on Rhett's head.

CHAPTER 11

Rhett had gotten his first taste of firefighter life at one of Mick's beloved sit-down meals. For the first time in a while, he felt like a part of something bigger. He could see why Jake loved being a member of the department; it was like having a second family.

Only thing was, Rhett hadn't eaten this many carbs since his sadistic trainer in Dallas had ripped a cheese Danish out of his hand, and, to add insult to injury, tossed it in his garbage can. Then the bastard had had the nerve to bill him extra for "motivation." And the balls to nod when Rhett asked him if he was for real.

He felt a little sick, truth be told, because apparently Silverlake firefighters didn't cut corners on anything, including a "housewarming" party for their new roomie the prior night. But he also felt happy and homespun and Mick's chicken and waffles specialty was perfection in a pan. Crispy, crunchy, tender inside—pure fried poetry. Bonus points for grease; it did seem to be fixing the hangover right up.

Even Mama hadn't made it quite that good.

"Sorry, Mama," he muttered as he left the station and climbed into Scarlett, fired her up, and pulled out of his spot across from the fire department. Only to find Declan coming up behind him in his Chevy Silverado. Rhett waved him forward and his brother drove up alongside him rather than passing him by.

The two stared at each other for a long moment through their respective windows. Then Deck sardonically lifted his hat, and Rhett caustically lowered his shades a notch, then nodded before shoving them up to the bridge of his nose again. Declan stared blankly at Scarlett. *Yeah, I earned this car.* Rhett gunned the motor, just to piss off his brother. *You're the one who sent me off to the big time. Wouldn't "coddle" me when I was getting the crap kicked out of me.*

Up yours, Deck.

As if he'd heard the words, Deck hit the gas and rumbled by without further acknowledgment. About five minutes later, Rhett had just gotten up to speed on the highway when he saw Jules's wreck on wheels, pulled onto the shoulder at an extremely awkward angle. An accident? Had someone hit her?

Then he registered that the wrong end of her seemed to be driving.

Rhett blinked.

No, what he'd seen was real: Jules's denim-clad buns in the air—and they were fine—behind her steering wheel. She was bent over, reaching into the back seat for something.

Dignity, thy name is Julianna Holt.

Rhett pulled over behind her and stepped out of Scarlett. He walked up and knocked on her window, whereupon two things happened.

First, some sort of disgusting, hairy monster exploded off the floor, snarling, and tried to eat him through the glass of the window. Second, Jules shrieked, hit her head on the roof of her truck, and landed sideways in a tangled heap.

She then recovered, lowered the window, and pronounced his name as if it were the most disgusting cuss word ever invented. *"Rhett Braddock."*

"Yes?" he said cautiously.

And then the disgusting, hairy monster—which looked a lot like a Saint Bernard—sprang from the back seat onto Jules, and then out the window.

"Holy—!?" Rhett took two muddy paws to the chest, four hundred decibels to the ears, and lost his vintage Ray-Bans to the slavering jaws of the creature, who crunched them in half before streaking onto the highway to escape. The stench of the animal remained on him, however. "What the—" Rhett wiped slobber off his face as he stared after it.

"Beast!" Jules yelled. "Come back here!" She wrenched open the door of her wreck and ran after the dog—straight into oncoming traffic.

Rhett swore and dove after her. She was a walking calamity.

And yet both she and the dog neatly dodged a

speeding baby blue Mini Cooper and a big yellow school bus, not to mention a navy Taurus with its front bumper held on by duct tape.

"¡*Pendejo!*" shouted the driver of the school bus. Thankfully there were no children on board.

Rhett caught up with Jules and the dog on the other side of the highway, unable to stop the stream of profanity from coming out of his mouth. "What in the hell were you thinking?!" he finished up as Jules, utterly ignoring his words, turned around and demanded his belt.

"What? Why?"

"For a leash."

"Leash . . . for all you know, that thing has rabies! Ringworm! Ugh, it smells like it's been eating roadkill."

"Belt," said Jules, inexorably.

"But—"

"It's your fault he escaped my car, so give me the darn belt, Braddock!"

"How do you figure it's my fault? You're the one who rolled down the window . . ."

First Lila had pilfered his cuff links. Then the dog had chowed on his Ray-Bans. Now Jules was stealing his belt. What was next? But Rhett reluctantly unbuckled his belt, causing a carload of teenagers to honk and shout dirty suggestions as they drove by. Next a trucker honked in appreciation. Some world.

Jules, who'd been hanging on to the dog's neck

hair with determination as she crooned to it, looped Rhett's pricey Allen Edmonds belt around its neck and told it what a good boy it was.

"It's not a boy," Rhett pointed out.

"What? Who cares? You *would* look there, you perv."

"I'm not a—oh, jeez. I give up. I'm always the bad guy, with you."

"Come on, good girl," Jules said to the dog. "Quit whining, bad guy."

Whining.

"Come on! We need to get her to the vet."

"We?"

"My truck is stalled."

"Stalled?"

"Well, it won't start again," she amended.

"Let me take a look."

"Um," Jules said, looking both ways now for traffic. Like a normal person might. "That won't be necessary."

"Of course it's necessary," Rhett said. "We need to get it rolling again."

"I'll just call Grady," she said. "He can stop by while we take Beast, here, to be looked at."

Rhett squinted at her. "You're not thinking that I'll allow that animal into my car, are you?"

She squinted right back. "Why not?"

His mouth literally dropped open. "Oh no, no, no. Not gonna happen, darlin'." He waited for a battered Chevy Impala to pass, and then crossed the highway toward her truck. "I'll get your truck fixed instead."

"You won't be able to," she called.

"I'm pretty good with cars," Rhett called back. He and Deck used to work on them in the Old Barn with Pop. Those were some good times . . . taking stuff apart and putting it back together, figuring out how things ran. The smell of clean motor oil pervading the place . . .

He was in her driver's seat before she and the growling, hairy creature wearing his belt could cross. He turned the key in the ignition, and the engine sputtered. It didn't take a particle of Rhett's much-vaunted genius to see what was wrong. "Are you kidding me?" he said to her when he got out.

Her face flamed.

"You're out of gas."

"I told you that you couldn't fix it," she muttered.

"Can I show you something, Jules?" He pointed into the vehicle. "There's a gauge, there. See? And it's like a small miracle. You can use those beautiful eyes of yours to keep track of how much fuel you have."

"I meant to . . . but then the riding lessons yesterday ran long, and I had to run out to Slater's to pick up some stuff, and I forgot . . . and I thought I could just make it to the grocery store before it ran out completely . . ." She shrugged. "If you can just drop us at the animal hospital, then Grady'll bring me some gas. He's good like that . . . Did you just say my eyes were beautiful?"

"Yes, I did. Any objective person would say so."

"Gee, that's nice. Now, open your car door, please."

Rhett put his hands on his hips and shook his head. "You clearly didn't hear me earlier. That hairy thing you have tied to my belt is *not* getting into Scarlett."

The dog lowered her head at him and growled.

"Especially," he added, "since it wants to eat me."

"She won't eat you. Will you, Beast?" Jules crooned to the creature and scratched it behind the ears while it drooled in bliss.

"Correct. Because she won't be getting into my car."

"Yes, she will. Because she really needs medical attention."

"That's as may be. But you need *psychiatric* attention if you think she's riding in Scarlett."

Jules made puppy eyes at him. "What if you were starving, lost, alone, cold? Wouldn't you smell, too? Wouldn't you eat a little roadkill?"

Rhett cast his eyes heavenward. "I'm not going to listen to this."

"Wouldn't you depend on the kindness of strangers, just like her?"

"Aaaagh."

"C'mon, Ever-Rhett . . ." Jules wheedled.

"She can depend on the kindness of a stranger who doesn't drive a seriously expensive sports car!"

"Fine, Fancy. You suck," Jules informed him.

"I *suck?*"

"We will just walk. And I'll probably be late for the first riding lesson. Might even have to cancel it. And there goes the income! Oh well, I guess. Come on, Beast." She squared her shoulders and turned her back on him.

"Why not call Grady for this, too?"

She stopped.

"Uh-huh. He's told you, *No more animal rescues,* hasn't he? He does enough of them for the town."

"Maybe," she admitted. And started walking again. Looking cold, forlorn, and alone. Dependent on the kindness of strangers.

"Help me," said Rhett to the sky. "Please, help me."

The sky didn't answer.

He got into Scarlett and pulled up beside Jules and the repulsive-smelling, filthy dog. He leaned over and opened the passenger-side door. "Get in."

He was rewarded by a brilliant smile. "I knew you'd come around!" Her hair jutted from the top of her head in a messy bun as she slid her small, curvy body inside and coaxed the dog onto her lap.

Beast whined and panted, but finally got in, smearing Rhett's cream leather seats with mud and poleaxing him with the stench of her fur and her breath. "Dear Lord." He took refuge by burying his nose in his own armpit.

Beast, being a drooly sort of dog, shook her head and sprayed slobber over every inch of his once-pristine Porsche. He looked around in disbelief, then got another whiff of the dog's breath and shoved his face back into his armpit.

"Gonna be hard to drive like that, Ever-Rhett." She squeezed his biceps affectionately.

And just like that, he felt himself falling for her.

Why? Because she'd squeezed his arm? Was he kidding himself?

Rhett gripped the steering wheel even tighter and focused on driving, not even a little sorry about the prospect of leaving Beast in the competent, compassionate care of the Silverlake Animal Hospital. Esme, the vet, wouldn't be there on a Sunday, but she was always on call.

When they got there, Rhett didn't ask who was paying the bill. While Jules explained Beast's situation, he gladly fished his wallet out and forked over the Amex Black Card again.

The girl behind the reception desk wore a smock printed with multicolored paw prints, and immediately hit him up for a donation to the Black Tie & Boots Soiree. He nodded without complaint and was rewarded with an adoring look. Leaving Beast in good hands, they headed out, stopping almost immediately again at the Grab n' Go for gas. Rhett topped up a five-gallon container that he purchased inside, and drove Jules back to her wreck on wheels. "No need to trouble Grady," he said gruffly as he filled the tank.

"Wow, thanks so much!" She rewarded him with an actual arm punch this time.

His heart rolled over and showed its belly.

For an arm punch. Really?

"You're welcome," he said gruffly. "So did you find the dog out on the highway?"

"Yeah. I couldn't leave her out there. I was afraid she'd get run over. So I stopped and got her to come to me with a piece of cheese from my Lunchables packet—"

"You eat Lunchables?"

"Sure. Don't you?"

"No." She was like a little kid with her diet of fast food and snacks.

"They're super easy. I have stacks of them . . ."

Why was he not surprised?

". . . they come in handy when I have back-to-back lessons and stuff out at the barn. Well, and then I supplement from the horse snacks in my fanny pack." She grinned.

"Someone needs to feed you a decent meal now and then."

"My mom tries. But it always comes with a lecture or a little annoying piece of advice on how I don't have my life together. She doesn't understand who I am, really. Because I'm not like her."

"I hear you." Rhett's mouth twisted. "But there are times when I'd give anything to have my mother nagging me again. Anything at all, just to have her back."

"Sorry," Jules said quickly.

"You didn't say anything wrong." He glanced wryly at the dirty claw marks in the seat leather beside her. "But I have a question for you: Who's going to give Beast a home?"

"Well," she said, stalling. It was clear that she hadn't even thought about it.

"Well?"

"Maybe Grady . . ."

"Don't they already have a dog at the fire-house?"

"Maybe my parents—oh no."

"Is there a shelter in town?"

"Not officially, no."

He waited for what he knew was coming next.

"So maybe I could, um, keep her out at the stables?"

Rhett sighed. "Just please, train her not to eat me—or any small children. The teenagers are fair game, though." He winked. "Meet you at the stables in a few?"

"Yep. Just grabbing a couple of things at the store. My first lesson is coming up."

"I'll be in the office," Rhett said, heading back to Scarlett.

"Hey, Rhett!" she called.

He turned.

"You're not half-bad sometimes." Jules gave him a blinding smile. "Too bad about the other half!"

Rhett snorted, shook his head, and got into his trashed car.

No.

He was not falling for Julianna Holt, Grady's Little Sister. Not happening.

After all, he was a genius, not an idiot.

Everybody said so.

CHAPTER 12

Rhett sat in the tack room at the desk and made quick work of catching up on some lingering Dallas responsibilities. He found himself eager to finish and get out to the riding ring. He remembered the pull of the ring from his teen rodeo days. He could hardly ever wait his turn with the barrels, or to try a few rope tricks.

The mental math of his finance job was enjoyable in its way; he'd always liked puzzles. But the feeling of solving a math problem or even making a multimillion-dollar deal couldn't compare to the pull of this life. He still felt it. He'd probably always feel it. It just wasn't his path anymore. He glanced at his watch and realized that Jules would probably be out in the riding ring by now, working with the kids.

He cast a wry look down at his ruined shoes and figured a little sand in them wasn't going to hurt any more than it helped. Next week, he'd go buy a pair of western boots from Sue. For today—screw it.

He wandered out to the ring, avoiding a pile of horse apples. He grinned, thinking back to the horse manure fights he and his brothers had gotten into. Absolutely disgusting, but the spice of life to preteen boys at the time. Especially when he and Ace ambushed Declan unawares. Ha!

Nobody would believe it of him now: that polished, urbane, wealthy Rhett had ever sullied his hands with horse manure. But he hadn't been too good to get his hands dirty back then—and he still wasn't.

Rhett leaned his elbows on the top rung of the riding ring. Jules looked radiant. She'd clearly showered, since her hair was wet and hung down over her shoulders, dripping onto the clean black sweatshirt she wore. In white block letters, it said: LIFE IS SOUP, AND I'M A FORK. He watched Jules patiently calm the little pig-tailed girl on Blossom, who'd gotten spooked and burst into tears when her mount began to trot. Jules walked over to meet horse and rider, took hold of Blossom's bridle, and brought her to a halt.

"If you squeeze her with your legs, sweetie," Jules explained, "or if you kick her in the sides like that, she thinks you want her to go faster. So just sit calmly and feel her rhythm, her gait, through your seat. Sway to the way she walks, okay? Keep your lower back loose, and sway to and fro with her. Communicate with her through your body language: your seat, your legs, and your hands. Make sure not to pop her in the mouth. If you yank on the reins like that, the bit hits her, and she hates that. So be gentle."

The little girl nodded.

"She's also very smart emotionally. When she senses that you're upset, she may get upset, too. So let's dry those tears, honey."

Little Pigtails mopped at her eyes with her sleeve.

"Awesome! See, Blossom is happier already. She likes you. She wants you to have fun. She knows you are gonna be a fantastic rider!"

Rhett's heart melted like an ice cream cone. Really, it was sort of disgusting . . .

And it got worse as Jules approached Frost and made sure the kid on him was okay.

Look at him, the former trickster imp Appaloosa, patiently plodding along with a little boy on his back. As if he knew he carried precious cargo. He was attuned to the fact that the kid didn't know what he was doing up there. But Frost wasn't taking advantage of it, as some horses would.

Huh. Frost had sure tried to take advantage of Rhett, back in the day. He'd bucked him off, tried to scrape him off on a tree, and taken the bit between his teeth and galloped hell-for-leather with a twelve-year-old Rhett clinging like a burr to his saddle.

Finally, foaming at the mouth, steaming and wet from sweat, Frost had run out of gas and had gloomily allowed himself to be steered back to the barn.

Rhett himself had gotten a round of applause.

He had a bruised and muddy backside, mesquite needles in his hair, a busted-up knee. But he'd stayed on and eventually gotten the horse under control. His first triumph of many to come. And Declan had given him a thumbs-up, awarding him respect on that long-ago day.

How times had changed.

Rhett gazed at the little coal-haired boy on Frost and envied him. He longed to feel that pure joy in his eyes, the sense of adventure and possibility that radiated off him in waves. He coveted his uncomplicated innocence and the assurance of his family's love.

What he'd give to be that kid again, to not know the heartbreak and loneliness that was heading his way. To not understand that life involved more than Tonka trucks and Tinkertoys, wrestling with brothers, or tormenting little sisters.

"Yah!" said the little kid on Frost. "Giddyup!"

Frost's ears pricked up, and he picked up speed, breaking cautiously into a trot.

"Yee-haw!" whooped the kid.

"Carlos, I need you to just walk for now, all right?" Jules called.

"But I wanna go faster," the kid whined. "Walking is boring."

"Stay with the class. We'll go faster once everyone is ready to do that, okay?"

Carlos pouted and pulled back hard on the reins, popping poor Frost in the mouth.

Rhett winced.

Frost stopped completely.

Carlos kicked him in the sides.

Frost leaped forward.

Carlos yelled, "Whoa!" and teetered in the saddle, hauling back on the reins again.

Poor Frost. He rolled his eyes and tossed his head, but slowed to a walk.

"Hey, kiddo," Rhett called. "Let me show you something."

Jules looked up and frowned, but she was busy with another kid on Shiner.

Rhett walked into the ring and approached Frost and Carlos. "Hi," he said. "I'm Rhett. Frost used to be my horse, when I was just a little older than you."

"You're super old now," Carlos informed him.

Rhett blinked. "Well, yes. That's true. How old are you?"

"Seven."

"I'm four times as old as you are."

"Close to dead!"

Rhett coughed. "Well, I hope not. Anyway, let me show you how to hold the reins. Right now you've got one in each hand, like a rope. And what you want, since you're riding western, is to take them both in one hand, like this . . . good. Now, the other thing you should remember is that the reins are *not* something to hold on to to keep you on the horse. They are only a way to communicate with the horse. What holds you on is your own balance, in your heels and in your seat. If you have to, it's okay to grab your saddle horn. But you don't hang on to the reins like they're some kind of climbing harness, okay?"

"Okay."

"Frost wants to help you be a good rider, but it totally confuses him if you tell him to giddyup and then you yank back so hard on the reins . . ."

Once he was satisfied that Carlos understood, Rhett patted Frost's neck, dropped a quick kiss on his muzzle, and went back to the sidelines.

Frost seemed grateful. And he also seemed to enjoy having a kid on his back again.

He was part of something, part of the evolution of a new generation of riders and horse lovers.

Rhett felt an ache growing in his chest. Had the old boy been bored, out at Silverlake with nothing to do? Had Declan seen that? Perhaps realized that he could have a better life and more regular exercise here at the Holt place? A purpose?

Rhett kicked idly at one of the posts that anchored the riding ring. Was he a jackass who'd misjudged his brother out of some misguided, territorial impulse?

Oh hell. Probably.

He didn't much like thinking about it.

So he focused on Jules again. At how patient

and kind and understanding she was with these little kids . . . teaching them to love and communicate with the horses. To conquer their fears and grow in confidence and skill. She had a gift for teaching. A gift for training.

As he stood there admiring her—and, okay, covertly checking out her backside—she suddenly bent, braced her hands on her knees, and took several shallow breaths.

"Jules? You okay?" he called.

She shook her head. Then she straightened and sprinted for the barn. "I need you to hold the fort for a minute!" she called over her shoulder. "Need a break."

Rhett looked around the ring at the four tiny Tater-Tots perched high on horseback. He smiled reassuringly, even though he was completely out of his element. "You're all doing just great," he said.

"I want Miss Jules," Pigtails whined.

"I'm scared," said another little girl with a short blond mess of curls.

"I want to gallop like the Lone Ranger!" Carlos whooped.

"I have to pee, real bad," said the last kid, clutching himself.

"Uh . . ." Rhett was at a loss. "Miss Jules will be back soon," he promised them. "There's no need to be scared. We are not doing any galloping, so don't even think about it. And no cowboy pees in his saddle, got it? It's just not done. So man up and hold your water, son. Because I think Miss Jules is in the restroom."

"Yessir," said the would-be little pisser. "But I could go behind a tree?"

"Keep your pants on and stay on your horse till Miss Jules gets back, señor. Got it? Won't be long."

"I'm hungry," Pigtails informed him next.

"Uh . . . well, Miss Jules has apples and carrots in her fanny pack." And probably Lunchables in the mini fridge in the tack room. "So hold your horses." *Literally.*

This was going okay. Fine, really. He could handle this.

Then Blossom got too close to Shiner, who swished his tail into her face.

Annoyed, Blossom reached out and nipped Shiner's hindquarter.

Shiner kicked out at her; Blossom sidestepped, tossing her head, and her rider shrieked in alarm. This in turn spooked Blossom, who bolted with a wailing Pigtails on her back.

Rhett vaulted clean over the railing of the ring and intercepted her.

"Hey! No fair. She got to gallop!" Carlos shouted.

"Don't even think about it," Rhett warned him as he caught hold of Blossom's bridle and brought her to a halt. "Hey, sweetheart," he crooned to

173

Pigtails. "You're fine. You're just fine. You just had yourself a little adventure, okay?"

"Whaaaaaaah! I want my mommy . . ." Tears mixed with snot trailed down her chubby little cheeks. "I want Miss Jules . . ."

"Okay, darlin', okay." He hesitated. "Here, why don't you just come down from there. I've got you—see? Right under the arms."

And just like that, Rhett had a little girl cradled to his chest, her head tucked under his chin. It was awkward. It was terrifying. And it was oh-so sweet. She smelled of Johnson's baby shampoo and watermelon Jolly Ranchers.

Blossom nuzzled her gently, as if to say she was sorry for scaring her.

That made her scream louder, so Rhett did his best to calm her down. "Blossom just wanted to give you a kiss, honey. She's not scary. She's just tall. And she didn't know what to do when you screamed like that—so she took off running. But everything's okay now. We're all friends. See?"

"I don' wanna be friends," Pigtails howled. "I want my mommy!"

"What is going on here?" Jules called, coming back through the gate.

"Just havin' our own little rodeo," Rhett said, behaving as if he held little girls in his arms every day.

Jules's eyes softened as she took in the scenario.

174

"Oh . . . you look almost comfortable with her."

"Sure, sure." Rhett fought a completely irrational urge to set down the little girl and take Jules in his arms instead. When she looked at him like that, he felt like a superhero. "Everything's fine, except we need a mommy for this one and food for that one and a restroom for . . ." He cast a questioning glance at Pee Wee.

"Justin," the kid supplied. "I gotta pee, Miss Jules!"

She nodded. "All right." She cast a sidelong glance at Rhett. "I don't suppose you could take Justin to the bathroom, while I talk to Abby, here? Abby, we don't need to call your mommy . . . she's coming in ten minutes anyway. Listen to me: You're a brave girl, and you're just fine."

So Pigtails was Abby.

Rhett hesitated. "I—uh, I don't have much experience with this."

"I know *how*," Justin said, offended. "And I don't need anyone to take me, Miss Jules. I know where it is."

"Yes, but we have a policy out here. No unaccompanied minors anywhere on the property. Sorry."

Rhett nodded. "Okay, kid, let's go." He swung him down from the saddle and handed the horse's reins to Jules. "You all right?"

She shrugged. "Yeah. Maybe something didn't

agree with me." She added quietly, "Or maybe it's just that I keep thinking about my dad. I don't know."

Rhett frowned. She looked jittery and anxious. Of course she was worried about her dad. Thanks to the Silverlake grapevine, Rhett knew Billy had made two trips to MD Anderson for consults in just the short time he'd been in town. Again, Rhett fought the urge to put his arms around her; to smooth her hair back from her forehead, and make her feel better.

He did none of those things. But he did drop a quick kiss on her forehead, which appeared to stun her. "It's all going to be okay, Jules. Your dad's going to be okay."

Jules finished the lesson, helped the kids lead their horses back to the barn and remove the saddles and bridles. She babysat them, essentially, until their parents came to pick them up. The sun was already going down.

When Rhett appeared out of the blue to help her groom the horses, she had mixed feelings. There he was, in her space again. Taking up too much oxygen. Doing things like easing her mind about Dad and then kissing her on the forehead, which was a complete and total invasion of personal space . . . besides which, it wasn't where she wanted him to kiss her.

Wait. That was a disturbing thought.

She didn't want Rhett to kiss her at all. Not even a little bit. Not on the forehead, not even on the rubber toe of her boot! Rhett could kiss her ass. That's what he could kiss . . .

Oh, but he'd been so completely disconcerted and adorable with little Abby this afternoon. Holding her in his arms and soothing her. And he'd taken Justin to the bathroom, even though he'd been uncomfortable and out of his element. And he loved Frost. That was clear.

Jules swallowed. She had to come clean with him about Frost. That the old rodeo horse had some health issues.

Rhett was in Frost's stall, brushing him from head to toe until his coat shone in the last bit of waning sunlight coming through the window. He was, in fact, giving him a special back-and-hind-end scratch by rotating the brush in circles. Frost bobbed his head up and down in appreciation and shifted the weight between his back legs to guide the brush where he enjoyed it most.

Gone were the fancy watch, the designer sunglasses, the cuff links. Rhett looked like any normal guy, standing there in old cross-trainers and Levi's, his shirtsleeves rolled to the elbows. There was a look of peace and contentment on his face, mirrored in Frost's.

"Hey," she said softly. "Doing my job?"

He glanced at her over Frost's haunches. "You mind?"

She shook her head. Then, provocatively, she said, "You know, Rhett, we can hire that done."

He laughed. "Touché, Jules."

She stood there and watched them: man and horse. So elemental. Change the contemporary clothing and they could be in any century at all . . . before the advent of the automobile. How long had human beings and horses taken care of each other? And now, in the twenty-first century, so many people barely even encountered a horse.

Rhett and Frost had been quite a team back in the day. And they clearly still were. The affection between the two was palpable. As she stood there, Frost turned his head and pushed his nose under Rhett's arm.

A lump rose in her throat. "I've been meaning to . . . trying to . . . find a way to tell you this. But—"

Rhett's hand stilled, brush and all. "He's not well, is he?"

She shook her head.

Silence.

"It's part of why Declan wanted me to take him. He wanted him to have more personal attention, Rhett. More affection. We've been keeping him active, which is good for him. He likes the kids. He likes having something to do, and . . ."

Rhett held up a hand and shook his head.

She looked at him, helplessly. Feeling pity rise

in her. It stung her eyes and seeped through every pore of her skin.

"Jules." His voice was ragged.

"I'm so sorry," she whispered.

"Can you—" He jerked his head.

She nodded.

"Just give me a minute."

Feeling awful for him, she turned and slowly walked off. She felt an odd melange of emotions. Wanted to put her arms around him. Comfort him. Yet she felt forlorn at being pushed away; dismissed. She felt that old hurt from childhood: that outsider feeling she'd gotten when Grady and Rhett hadn't wanted the pesky little sister trailing them and getting in their way. Messing up their good times.

Well, now she'd gone and done it. Messed up Rhett's good times with Frost. But how could she not tell him? She'd had to.

She heard his voice calling her back again. "Jules?"

"Yeah." She went back to the stall.

"I'm sorry," he said. "I just needed . . ."

She unlatched the low door and went inside. Stood with him in the clean sawdust next to Frost and stroked the old boy's neck. He nuzzled her. She unzipped her fanny pack and gave him an apple slice and a baby carrot to make him happy.

Rhett stood behind her, silent. Then at last he said, "Thank you."

She felt his warmth behind her, smelled the laundry detergent of his shirt and a tinge of his aftershave that reminded her of ocean breeze and yachting and single-malt Scotch. And then she shuddered as his lips brushed the back of her neck, oh-so softly. Like the wing of a butterfly. With a tenderness that made her ache.

Somehow that single touch eddied out to every nerve in her body, sending out an echoing shiver.

"Jules." He breathed, rather than said, her name into her ear.

A question drifted between them, light and soundless, as imperceptible as a single dust mote in the evening light.

She didn't know how to answer. Didn't know if she could.

And then Rhett dropped his mouth to her nape, settled it there, warm with longing.

She stood frozen as his arms slipped around her waist and tightened; pulled her to him. She did her best not to tremble.

"You're great with the kids," he said. "They adore you."

She smiled. "You did all right yourself."

"Frost adores you, too." He turned her to face him. Settled his warm hands on her shoulders and gazed down at her. He let go of one shoulder to reach up and stroke her hair.

Just then, Esme's van pulled up in a cloud of dust. Jules pulled herself away from Rhett, leaving him with the horses as she headed out to meet the vet, who'd opened the door and was half in, half out. The dog jumped out of the van, but Esme kept her close by the collar. "Hi!" she called. "Special delivery. I was heading out to the Lundgrens', so I brought her with me."

Beast had become a beauty. The Saint Bernard was clean: shampooed and brushed, with her nails trimmed and neat. "Hi, there, Gorgeous!" Jules exclaimed, when Esme set her free. "Look at you . . . just look at you." She swallowed a lump in her throat. She'd done a good thing.

"She sure cleaned up well. You must have spent all day on her."

The dog's formerly matted, soiled fur was a beautiful mix of brown and white with the characteristic of Saint Bernards. Her eyes were softer and more trusting already, and she perked up at the sight of Jules.

"When I see a dog in that condition, I just can't wait to make things right. We didn't have any major emergencies today so . . ." Esme shrugged.

"Thank you so, so much." Jules sank down onto her knees and gave the animal some love, stroking her head and scratching her behind the ears.

"Sure. So she's malnourished, as you can see," Esme said. "She went quite some time without regular meals. She's also dehydrated. But she's in surprisingly good shape for what she's probably been through. We've dewormed her, but she'll need another dose. She'll need regular heartworm medication."

"Of course," Jules said.

"We'll donate the collar and leash. Least we can do. You have food?"

"Not yet."

"Want to try her on the Science Diet? Mix of wet and dry?" Esme asked, lowering a cardboard box of supplies from the van.

"Sure." Jules fished around in her boot for her tiny wallet.

Esme waved it away. "Your, ah, friend? He said he'd take care of everything."

Her friend?

Friend: Rhett Braddock. Jules stole a glance back at the barn, where Rhett was still with the horses. Jules stared at her lone credit card and driver's license. At the exactly nineteen tattered dollars folded up behind them, cheering that they weren't about to be spent yet. And she felt a combination of grateful and guilty.

How would she have paid for the vet bill without Rhett?

She'd have put it on her card, and then would've had to pay it off slowly at 18 percent interest. It would have been worth every penny, but still . . .

He'd let her put the dog in his car. He'd paid the vet bill. He was buying food.

"We need to say thank you," she said to Beast. "Don't we?"

Beast whined and sat down, cocking her head.

"Yes, we do. Even if I'm still annoyed about that charm school comment," she muttered. "And his general sarcasm. And the incredibly off-putting way he has of coming up with really smart ideas that I wish *I'd* thought of—or could execute—myself."

"Excuse me?" said Esme. "I didn't catch that."

"Oh, nothing. Just . . . thank you. Thanks so much for taking care of Beast—and on a Sunday, too. Treating her and cleaning her up and everything."

"You're welcome. It was our pleasure. Especially after she calmed down and decided not to rip our faces off," said Esme dryly. "Understandable, though. I don't think she's been treated well. So she's wary."

"There should be a special place in hell for people who mistreat animals," Jules said darkly.

"Agreed."

"But no face-ripping," Jules said to the dog, who looked devastated by this order. "We'll get you a few toys to mangle, instead. Okay?"

Beast whined again.

"In the meantime, let's think of something nice to do for Ever-Rhett."

Beast wagged her tail.

"Here's the paperwork. I'm going to go check

on Curly and Frost while I'm here." Esme clapped Jules on the shoulder and headed toward the stables.

Jules shaded her eyes against the sun and patted Beast. She eyed Scarlett, musing. Then she brightened. "Oh, I know *exactly* how we'll say thank you, Beast!"

CHAPTER 13

Unfamiliar barking pulled Rhett out of his reverie. He ran his hand down Frost's mane once more before turning to the sound just as Jules called his name.

"Come and see," she said as he strolled through the stable door. Jules opened her arms as if she were revealing a game show prize. A beautiful Saint Bernard eyed him.

Wait a minute. "That's not the Swamp Thing that tried to eat me, is it?" he asked.

"Yes, it is. Can you believe it?"

"Is it still named Beast?"

"For now. We should probably come up with a nicer name, though."

"Hi, Beast," Rhett crooned.

She growled at him.

He sighed. "Why am I persona non grata with this animal, when I took her in high style to the vet and paid her bill?"

"She could tell you didn't think she was good enough for your Porsche."

"Good enough? That's not it at all. I just didn't want mud, mange, worms, and roadkill remnants in it. Why is that a reason to condemn me?"

"She needs unconditional love. All dogs do. That means you love her even when she's disgusting."

Rhett eyed her. "Is that right." *I let you in my Porsche. And you were disgusting, too. Not to mention exasperating. Does that mean I love you, too? No, but you are hot. Annoyingly hot.*

And you're Grady's little sister. That hasn't changed.

"Yes. That *is* right."

He chuckled. "Couldn't have said it better myself."

"So . . . can I ask you to look after Beast while I do a couple things?"

The dog eyed Rhett suspiciously. Rhett eyed the dog suspiciously.

She tilted her head. So did he.

She growled; he followed suit.

Then they both subsided.

"Will she chew off my legs?" Rhett asked.

"No, because I've got a bone right here in my bag." Jules produced an enormous, smoked one from what looked like an army surplus backpack.

"Are you kidding me? That looks like a femur."

"Yes, I believe it is," she said cheerfully.

"So how am I supposed to be filled with confidence that when she's done with it, my own femur isn't next?"

"Not to worry. This'll take her a couple of days."

"Right. That relieves me so much."

"I almost forgot . . . I also got you a bunch of carrots for Frost." Jules pulled those out of her backpack, too. "I bet he can smell them from here."

He furrowed his brow. Was she trying to get him out of the way? Why? "O-kaaay," he said. "Guess I'll go do the honors."

She nodded eagerly. "Great. I'll . . . be in the tack room."

Rhett smelled a rat, but he couldn't see what harm it would do to go give Frost a carrot. So he did, watching Esme checking out Curly's injury.

When he headed back to the tack room, Jules wasn't there but Beast had made herself comfortable on a horse blanket in the corner. She looked up from her bone and growled halfheartedly at him.

"Aw, cut it out. Only *one* femur for you. Got it?"

She seemed to understand and went back to gnawing.

Where had Jules gone?

He looked around, didn't notice anything missing, and shrugged. He sat down again at the tiny corner desk, opened up the laptop, and started scanning the figures to see where else they could cut costs or make more profits.

And that's when he heard it: the sultry purr of Scarlett as a key turned in her ignition.

Rhett jumped to his feet and ran out of the tack room as her engine gunned. "What the fu—"

He sprinted the length of the barn and out

the open door. Jules raised her hand and waved merrily at him in the rearview mirror as she sped down the gravel drive and out onto the highway. Rhett swore a blue streak. She'd gone too far. He had a good mind to call the cops. The crazy girl had stolen his car!

Rhett ran to Jules's Chevy and looked under the visor and then in the glove box and drink holders for the keys. Nothing.

At which point Esme strolled out from the barn and stood there with a grin on her face, watching him. "Well, that's Julianna Holt for ya." She paused. "Need a ride somewhere?"

It was thirty minutes before the very thorough Esme finished with the horses and had the two of them bumping down the road away from the stables. Another twenty minutes to stop and examine a tagged goat who seemed to have wandered away from home about halfway to town. The entire time, Grady's phone was busy and Jules and Jake didn't answer. Fuming, Rhett considered his next move while a call to Lila went straight to voicemail.

The vet's bemused expression didn't help matters. Didn't help at all. At least she had the decency not to laugh as Rhett sat along beside her in the van, his phone to his ear.

Finally, finally, Grady answered. "What do you mean, my sister stole your car?" he asked, his deep voice amused.

"I mean exactly that!" Rhett thundered into his cell phone. "Is she at the firehouse?"

"Give me a sec," Grady said, and then a second later: "Nope, sorry."

"Well, she swiped my key and took off in the thing. You know what they call that?"

"Grand theft auto," Grady suggested pleasantly.

"Grand theft auto!" Rhett echoed, not as pleasantly.

"Okay, Jules is a little . . . uncensored . . . sometimes. But she's no thief. You know that."

"I don't know it—my car is gone, and she's at the wheel of it. I'm tempted to call the police and report it stolen. This is insane, Grady!"

"Did you piss her off?"

Rhett was silent. "Which time?"

Grady groaned.

"She's not exactly easy to manage, and this isn't always an, ah, comfortable arrangement. If you know what I mean."

"Oh, I do."

"But I draw the line at having Scarlett ripped off. I really do."

"She'll return her."

"In what condition?! Grady, have you seen that wreck she drives?"

"Yes, I have. I've ridden in it many times. She likes it. She doesn't want a fancy car. She hauls around dirty stuff for the barn. And critters."

"Yeah, I know. She stuffed a rabid, stinking

dog into Scarlett when I found her out of gas on the highway—"

"Not again?"

"Yes. How often does she do that?"

"Oh, now and then." Grady seemed unconcerned.

"Does this mean I'm going to find Scarlett out of gas and abandoned somewhere on I-35 between Waco and Dallas?"

"Doubt it. She's better with other people's things than she is with her own. Listen, let me call Bode—"

"Bode Wells? Why?"

"He's the town sheriff, genius. You didn't know that?"

"No."

"Okay, now you do. So I'll call Bode and check if he or one of his deputies has seen Scarlett around town."

"How about I call him and report a stolen vehicle?"

"Don't do that. Please, Rhett. I'll get this taken care of. Promise."

Rhett hung up, feeling stymied. Julianna Holt had made a fool out of him. He was no better than those googly-eyed, sparkling jesters strung up all along Main Street. And he didn't like it one bit.

Esme looked over at him. And then she stared straight back through the windshield.

"What?" Rhett asked with a sigh.

"I moved here last year," Esme said, her lips

twitching slightly. "And I have to say that Fool Fest is my favorite holiday ever."

Rhett's cell phone rang.

"Yeah?" Rhett barked into it. "Grady?"

His friend was laughing. "Hold on a sec. I'm gonna put Bode on."

"What?" Rhett waited.

"Everett Braddock," Bode's voice said. "I heard you were back in town."

"I am."

"Didn't swing by to say hello."

"I'm not even sure who lives here anymore, Bode, and that's the truth."

"Well, I do. And I'm a little confused, here."

"Why's that?"

"Well, I've found your car—"

"Oh, thank God. Is it in one piece?"

"Not a scratch on it."

Rhett exhaled in relief.

"Now, Grady, here, tells me you want the driver picked up for grand theft auto," Bode said.

"Well, wait a minute—"

"The question is, would you like me to arrest her now, or wait until she's finished hanging an air freshener?"

"Excuse me?" Rhett could hear Grady hooting in the background, though Bode was doing an admirable job of keeping his tone even and serious.

"And the, uh, perp—she'd like to know if you want pine-scented or citrus?"

Rhett leaned back in the seat and began to laugh. "I'm going to kill her," he said.

"Whoa, now, sir. You cannot make statements like that to an officer of the law. That is a threat of bodily harm and must be taken as such . . ."

"Give me a break, Bode. Seriously?"

"Are you going to press charges for the Armor All and the leather conditioner?"

"Oh, you bet."

"And what about the wheel detailing?"

"That I may let slide."

"I don't know, Rhett. She's done an awful thorough job. With a toothbrush."

"A toothbrush," he repeated, his shoulders shaking.

"So. Toss her in the slammer, should I?"

"That won't be necessary, Bode. But I do appreciate the offer."

There was a commotion on the other end of the line. "There's one more thing." Grady's voice. "We don't want you to panic."

"What?" Rhett asked warily.

"We're not sure about the engine," Grady said.

Rhett's hand clenched around his phone.

"You gotta get down here!" someone shouted into the receiver. *Jake.*

"Jake?"

"Hey, bro," Jake said cheerfully.

"What's wrong with the engine?" Rhett asked.

"Well, we're not sure. So, me, Grady, Jules, and

Bode are all doing some test-driving to figure it out."

"Son of a—"

"Better get down to Sunny's and have a look-see for yourself."

"Sunny's? What the—" Rhett looked at Esme. "Change of plans," he ground out. "If you could drop me at Sunny's instead of the firehouse, I'd be much obliged."

Rhett hung up, still hearing a chorus of laughter in the background.

Sure enough, when he finally got to the diner, Grady, Jake, Jules, and Bode were tossing Rhett's keys around in front. The men gave him a fool's welcome, including catcalls and backslaps and a severe messing-up of the hair, to boot, before heading back inside Sunny's for more coffee, thus abandoning a laughing Jules to his mercy.

Rhett tried to smooth his hair down and looked at Jules. He took in his car.

Scarlett was immaculate. She looked, if possible, better than the day he'd first sat in her, on the showroom floor in Dallas. There were no smudges on the cream leather seats, no dirty claw marks. She smelled once again like premium processed leather and pine air freshener . . . not even a whiff of roadkill.

Jules tossed Rhett the keys and leaned a denim-clad hip against the Porsche as he walked around, looking for any sort of a scratch that would give him an excuse to . . . what? Throttle her? Kiss her senseless? Throw her down on the hood and have his wicked way with her?

"So," Jules said, her eyebrows raised. "Still going to have me arrested?"

"I just might."

"Oh, c'mon—it's in better condition than when I stole her. She's washed, waxed, Windexed. She's been vacuumed, wiped down, conditioned. I even shampooed the rugs and detailed the wheels!"

"It wasn't okay for you to take my car without permission," he said, looking at her from under lowered eyebrows.

She didn't apologize. "But . . . ?"

"Thank you. She looks beautiful."

"Did a good job, didn't I?"

He nodded. "I'd say professional."

"So the end justifies the means."

"Maybe."

"And I *gotcha*." She grinned, a little too pleased with herself. "Fooled for Fool Fest."

"You sure like playing with fire, Jules. Feral chickens in the firehouse shower. Grand theft auto detailing. What else do you get up to?"

She scrunched up her nose and thought about it. "Well . . . there was the time I put the pig in the teachers' break room."

"One of the Lundgrens' hogs?"

"Way too big—and mean. This was just a piglet, really . . . but the teachers didn't take it well. I would have gotten away with it, but Dolf Menges told on me. Little twerp."

"What happened?"

"Got suspended from school for three days. Then grounded for a month." She grinned. "Worth it, though. You should have heard Mrs. Fabian and Mrs. Kosinsky and Mrs. Dominguez shrieking. Jumping up on chairs, yelling for help. And skinny little Mr. Gallagher, trying to be a hero and running after it—he got stuck under a desk when his collar snagged on the armrest."

"You're a menace."

"Always. Grady was the good kid. I had to take a different route."

"So you're the bad kid?"

She shrugged, looking uncomfortable. "Not bad, exactly. Irresponsible. Disappointing."

"Disappointing?" He frowned. "To whom?"

"You know what—forget it. I need to get back to the horses."

"You're not disappointing, Jules. Not remotely."

"Yeah? Then why wasn't I given a chance on my own family's land? With the business?" She swept her hair behind her shoulder. "Nobody even considered it. Not my dad. Not my mom. Not Grady . . ." Her voice trailed off.

"Jules, it had nothing to do with them being—"

"Let's not talk about this, Ever-Rhett." She threw a too-bright smile over her shoulder as she started toward the door to Sunny's. "Oh, I meant

195

to ask you. Did you ever hear back from Fred's Feed?"

Way to change the subject. "Yeah, I forgot to tell you. We've got a deal."

She stopped in her tracks. "Oh."

"I just forgot. There's been a lot going on. It all happened quickly . . . on the phone. He's actually very happy with the new terms."

"Good. Glad to hear that," Jules said. "Guess we did need a real businessperson around here."

Oh, ouch. He hadn't meant to make her feel cut out of the loop. He'd honestly forgotten to tell her. Rhett gazed helplessly after her. Why did every good thing he did feel like a bad one, around this girl? What could he say to that?

"You are a real businessperson, Jules."

She waved a dismissive hand in the air as Grady and Jake strolled up. "I was just coming to find you," she said to Grady.

"You going to go up to dinner with the 'rents like that?" Grady asked, gesturing to her sweatshirt. "I'm fine with it, but you know how Mom gets."

"You think Mom isn't going to like my sweat-shirt?" Jules asked innocently.

"Nope."

Jules grinned an evil grin. "Guess we'll find out." She took a step forward and stopped short. "Whoa."

"You okay?" Rhett asked.

"Head rush," she said.

Rhett laughed. "You weren't sitting down."

Jules shrugged.

"You want to come up for a family supper, Rhett?" Grady asked.

"Thanks, but, uh, I'm . . ." Rhett blanked for a moment, realizing that when Mom and Dad were alive, the Braddocks had a family supper, too. And since they weren't here, he had no Sunday supper plans whatsoever even though all but one of his siblings were in town.

"I'm stealing him back for a little," Jake said from behind him. "Sunny's holding a table."

"You jealous that Rhett likes me better?" Grady said, walking backward toward his truck. He shrugged with exaggerated helplessness. "It's not my fault."

Jake rolled his eyes.

Jules gave a wave. "See you bright and early Monday morning, Sunshine."

Rhett watched her twist her hair up into the warrior's knot again as she walked to Grady's truck and hopped inside.

"See you bright and early, Sunshine," Jake whispered in his ear.

Rhett whirled around. "You looking for a beatin', Jake Braddock?" With a grin on his face, he punched his brother in the shoulder.

Jake punched him back, chasing him up the walkway, and they burst through the diner door like a couple of brawlers. Sunny came clucking down the rows of tables. "You boys behave yourselves in Sunny's diner, you hear? I've just made a fresh cinnamon-caramel-apple pie. Who's in?"

Rhett and Jake looked at each other and then back at Sunny, simultaneously saying, "Me!"

"Take a seat, boys," Sunny said with a big cheerful smile and a wave of her coffeepot. "You want anything else to eat, or just coffee and pie?"

"Just coffee and pie, please," Jake said.

Rhett nodded with a grin. "You're going to put ten pounds on me easy, while I'm here."

"That's my job," Sunny said.

Rhett looked around—the place didn't seem that busy at the moment, and most of the customers who were there already had their food. "Can we buy *you* a cup of coffee?"

"Well," said Sunny. "I'd rather that I was fifteen years younger and that it was a steak dinner and a ride in your Porsche, but that makes me feel like a dirty old woman, so sure. I'll settle for some coffee."

Rhett laughed and gestured to the seat opposite his.

"Hang on one sec, boys," she said, and turned to the room at large. "Hey! Listen up—I got a question. Which one of you jokers put the bumper sticker on my van? Huh? The one that says 'Kiss My Grits'?"

Everyone laughed. "That's a good one, Sun. I didn't do it, but I applaud whoever did."

"Hear, hear!" A few more customers chimed in. "I like it," Sunny admitted.

"Happy Fool Fest, Sun!"

Shaking her head but unable to repress a grin, Sunny grabbed two plates of pie and three coffee mugs and then took a seat next to Jake, across from Rhett. She looked between the two of them. "All you Braddock boys. Lookers. Every last one of you. Jake here, knows I was crushing on Declan until you walked in. Now I'm tossing him aside. Want to get married, Handsome?"

"Well, I'm busy this week," Rhett said. "But maybe next?"

"Sounds good. And I can see why," Sunny said, pulling a couple of napkins from the holder and sliding one each in front of the Braddock boys as a matter of habit. "Holt Stables is a busy operation and when Julianna isn't happy she can be a handful."

You could say that.

"How's it goin' with her?" Sunny asked.

Jake laughed. "You trying to bribe Rhett to spill some gossip with this here pie?" he asked.

Sunny's eyes sparkled. "Why, Jake Braddock, what a thing to say! I'm the one people *tell* things to. I been in this town as long as anyone. I'm older than dirt, darlin'."

"Not hardly. You don't look a day over twenty-nine."

"Puh-lease. You shameless fibber." But Sunny

199

fluttered her lashes, a smile playing on her lips.

"You got any questions for Sunny, Rhett?" Jake asked, trying to stop laughing long enough to take a swig of coffee.

Sunny cocked her head. "Oh, now, where to begin. Just look at your brother, Jake." She gazed straight into Rhett's eyes and told him, "You've got questions in your eyes, memories writ all over your face, and auld lang syne in the way you walk."

"You Scottish, Sunny?" Rhett asked.

"Yes, sir. My granddad was a cowboy in a kilt. He was a scandal, that man."

He chuckled at that. Sunny reached for the coffeepot and refilled the mugs. She took a sip and then added, "I think the only people in town who've ever matched him for scandal were Tom Fullery himself, the Brockhurst family in its entirety, and Sue Holt."

"Sue Holt, huh," Rhett said. "The scandal it wasn't polite to talk about when I was growing up."

"Sue . . . yes. That was some dustup," Sunny said.

"What happened?"

"She was a year ahead of me at Silverlake High. Caught the home economics kitchen on fire, did Sue. Well, she was wild, that one. She'd been sneaking out at night to meet this no-good ranch hand from the Gonzalez operation. He was a hot tamale, and he was trouble with a capital *T*.

"They couldn't be caught at any of the local watering holes, since she was underage. So he'd stop down the road from the Holt place and she'd run into the clear blue midnight to meet him, and out they'd drive to the ranch. He couldn't take her into the bunkhouse with the other hands there, o' course.

"So they'd go out onto the property, the fools. Gonzalez himself caught them skinny-dipping in the stock pond one night, of all things. They got dressed at the end of his rifle, and then he fired the hand, marched 'em both to his pickup, and drove 'em, still wet, out to see her father."

Rhett raised his eyebrows and exchanged a startled glance with Jake.

"You're beginning to get the idea," Sunny said. "Well, Bart Holt, he didn't want to see his daughter married to a half-baked ranch hand with nothing to his name, but she was already pregnant—just hadn't told anyone. He wasn't going to have his daughter disgraced in the community, and he wasn't going to have a bastard grandchild, neither.

"So all's a sudden, there's a white wedding planned! And what do you know? The ranch hand is gonna take a job managing the Phillips 66 station closer in to town, owned by a cousin of Bart's. Wild-child Sue is expected to stay at home and learn proper motherhood and wifeliness.

201

She's made her bed and now she's gonna lie in it."

Sunny had to get up to seat a couple of customers, take their orders, and pour their coffee, but she soon returned. "Now, where was I?"

"I take it things didn't work out that way?" Rhett prompted her. "With Sue being the new model for domesticity?"

"No, they did not." Sunny shook her head. "Our hero the ranch hand—"

"Did he have a name?"

"Yes, but nobody around here will say it."

"Anyways. He was a heavy drinker, mean as a snake when he wasn't having fun seducing young girls, and he didn't take kindly to being domesticated, either. So he started hittin' the bars and doing what snakes do when they slither off with their own kind. And he started comin' home and beatin' the livin' daylights out of Sue."

Rhett closed his eyes and swore.

"Sue bein' Sue, she was too proud to go and tell her father, Bart, or even her brother, Billy. And that girl learned to shoot when she was, what? Ten? So after one particularly nasty go-round, she waits until Mr. Wonderful leaves hungover for his gas station job, and she runs out to the Holt place and borrows her daddy's Remington."

"Go on . . ." Jake said.

"Snake comes home obliterated the next night, knocks her around, kicks her in the stomach—"

"Oh God." Rhett had a feeling he knew what was coming next.

"So she grabs the gun and blows him right out the side of the cabin. Silverlake's Shotgun Divorce, they call it."

Jake exhaled loudly.

"I take it he didn't survive?" Rhett asked.

"What do you think? Shotgun, close quarters, in a cabin that's twelve foot by fourteen foot, if that?"

"Yeah, no."

"So there was a trial, the whole works. Sue got off, but it was one big ugly mess."

He almost didn't have the nerve to ask. "He kicked her in the stomach . . . What happened to the baby?"

Sunny swirled the coffee in her pot, losing all expression. "Poor little mite. Didn't never have the chance to be born. Listen, darlin', I got to get back to work. But you boys, come by and see me anytime." She got to her feet, and he noticed with sympathy that her ankles were already swollen. Managing a diner and waiting tables was no picnic.

"What time do you get to work, Sunny?" Rhett asked.

"Got customers comin' in by five thirty. So I'm up by four A.M."

Jake grimaced.

"Thanks for the story," Rhett said.

Sunny paused for a moment and said gently, "It wasn't just idle tattling on my part. Sue ain't had it easy. So—"

Rhett nodded. Undoubtedly Sunny knew that he'd been thinking about what to do with the saddlery. "Cut her some slack." He filled in the blank easily. "I'll do my best."

Sunny raised her coffeepot to him and rocked back on her rubber heels. "You're all right, Ever-Rhett. I don't care what they say."

He felt himself stiffening. Who'd been talking trash about him? And why?

Jake snorted a laugh as Sunny poked Rhett in the ribs. "Relax," she said. "It's a figure of speech. I'm just teasing. But you know what?"

"What?" asked Rhett and Jake at the same time.

"I only tease the ones I like. You know what else I like? Seeing Braddocks sitting down together in my diner. You know what I don't care for? Seeing Declan left out of that." She leaned over the table. "You don't want to have any more regrets in this life than absolutely necessary, Rhett Braddock." She stood up. "And you only have so much time to figure out what's necessary. You hear me?"

"Yes, ma'am," Rhett said with a lump in his throat. Sunny patted his cheek and went to swap out her coffeepot.

Chapter 14

On Monday morning, Rhett stole a travel mug with Jake's name on it from the firehouse kitchen and grabbed two big pancakes off the stack Mick was piling up on a dalmation-shaped platter.

"They sure keep you busy," Rhett said. "I don't remember hiding in the kitchen being your style. Back in the day."

"Nobody's hiding. Nice thing about cooking here is that I don't have to clean. Besides, cooking during Fool Fest is *fun*." Mick gave him an evil grin that had Rhett double-checking the pancake he was eating. Now *that* was the Mick he remembered.

Mick leaned forward. "These are safe. Go ahead and take another for the road. Really. Go ahead."

Rhett knew a dare when he heard one. And only part of his mind actually worried that Mick had done something awful to the pancakes. The same part that suddenly remembered that they used to call him Mick the Menace. He grabbed one more pancake and pointedly took a giant bite, saying through a full mouth, "That's got to be the ugliest platter I've ever seen."

"It is. But Dottie and Libby gave it to us for Christmas one year, and nobody has the heart to get rid of it."

Rhett chuckled and turned to head out for the stables. He got to the bottom of the stairs before Mick shouted, "You cork-sucking hound from hell! Give those back!"

"Pardon?" Rhett called.

A scrabbling of claws and the thunder of boots ensued.

"Not you," Mick yelled. "Not-Spot just stole three pancakes!"

Rhett laughed.

"Dog, you'd better run . . . beware my spatula, you criminal counter-surfer . . ."

When Rhett got to the stables, Jules wasn't anywhere in sight, which was good, right? Tamping down disappointment over that, Rhett went back to the desk he'd commandeered in the tack room and started going through various files on the business. The Holt tax returns for the past decade were stacked neatly in a drawer, and though they weren't really any of Rhett's business, he followed his instinct to look at them. Grady and Jules's dad didn't have any business training, and it didn't look as though he used an accountant. Every penny mattered to Helen and Billy under the circumstances . . . Maybe Rhett could help.

The tax records were eye-opening. While Billy did regularly write off the property taxes and interest on the loan, he was missing countless opportunities to save money on his federal income tax returns. He wrote off the cost of feed, wood shavings for the stalls, and vet bills, but not repairs or maintenance or the contract labor he'd hired to do them. He wasn't depreciating the value of any of his vehicles or farm equipment. He wasn't writing off the office space. And he wasn't deducting the expense of paying his daughter for the work she did. And didn't Helen do something around here? She should take a salary of some kind, too.

All of this added up to thousands upon thousands of dollars . . . dollars that Rhett could get back for them, especially with the help of a tax accountant. His face split into a huge grin as he mentally totaled up the figure. He couldn't wait to tell Jules the good news.

Unfortunately, Jules didn't look too receptive when she appeared in the doorway, her hands on her waist and her cheeks flushed red. "Aunt Sue just told me you went and had the saddlery business and property appraised! You *promised* you would try to keep it. You *promised*. Are you going behind my back and selling the business?"

"Having something valued is about gathering information, Jules. I wouldn't sell anything without discussing my reasons with you first."

She made a sound of disgust. "Not that what I'd have to say would stop—" Her gaze shot straight to his hands on the pile of her father's tax envelopes and that shade of red in her cheeks turned a touch brighter. "What do you think you're doing, Rhett Braddock? Those are private! Who gave you permission to look at those?!"

He opened his mouth to explain, but she over-rode him.

"Unbelievable! Give me those, and get out from behind my desk."

"Jules, I figured I could take a look and maybe help—"

"You figured? How would you feel if *I* figured I should look at your private bank statements or stock portfolio?" Her voice was shaking with anger.

"There are certain deductions that your dad hasn't been taking."

"I don't want to hear it. You shouldn't have looked at his private papers."

"They pertain to this business, which I just bought, so—"

"Did you ask him first?"

"No, I didn't," Rhett admitted. "Because he's ill, and I just wanted to see if I could help."

"We don't need your help." Her tone was low and deadly. "Especially when it involves you snooping and taking advantage of the situation."

That pissed him off. "How do you figure I'm taking advantage? Please explain that one to me, Holt."

"You just showed up here and bought this place out from under me, and now you're trying to change everything and you're poking your nose in where it doesn't belong and you're making me completely crazy!"

Rhett wasn't used to being yelled at—not by anyone. He was, frankly, used to a lot of ingratiation and brownnosing because of his net worth and the fact that he was the boss. Because people wanted to "get in good" with him and take advantage of any opportunities he might be able to give them.

In fact, he wasn't sure he'd been yelled at since high school, by Declan—until recently when he'd had the pleasure via Jules in the stables. He didn't take kindly to it, and especially not when he was trying to help the individual raising her voice to him. So his next words were ice-cold.

"Number one," Rhett said, "I didn't buy the place out from under you. Number two: My nose does belong in this business, since I now own it. Number three: Consider the concept that you were already completely crazy—long before I came along."

"How dare you?"

He just raised his eyebrows.

"Get out!"

"Ejecting me from my own property again, Jules? This is getting old."

"Out!"

"Fine. When I return, I hope you'll have gotten over your tantrum. I don't want to bother your dad at the moment, so I'm going to go talk to

Grady regarding those returns, and maybe he and your dad can get with—who's the tax accountant downtown?"

"Pullman Duff."

"Get with him and get some money back from the IRS. Money that your dad needs."

Jules stood there, seething. "Admit that you didn't have the right to look at those."

Rhett sighed. "I didn't have the right to look at them."

She glared at him for a long moment. He noted with concern that she was looking pale. "You getting enough sleep?" he asked.

"I'm fine. There's a lot going on in my life, is all," she said pointedly.

"I *am* trying to help . . . Do you want to go to the accountant with me instead of Grady? I mean, I figured you'd prefer the stables by a long stretch, but I'm not trying to leave you out of it."

"Thanks," Jules said reluctantly. "But I think I might be coming down with something." Then she gasped, turned on her heel, and ran.

Rhett chuckled. "Girl's allergic to me." Sure enough, when he knocked on the bathroom door to ask if she needed any help she told him in no uncertain terms to get lost.

Pullman Duff's office was, weirdly enough, housed in the old town jail, and still had the iron bars to prove it. Even weirder was Pullman's catfish collection, which was wired onto the bars. There were painted, stuffed, wire-sculpted, and wooden catfish everywhere, in every color combination imaginable. There were also wildlife photographs of catfish, in color.

Grady had warned Rhett before they went in, but that didn't prepare anyone for quite how quirky Pullman was, either. Duff himself looked like a catfish in steel-rimmed spectacles, with wide-set eyes, a broad, thin-lipped mouth, and long gray mustachios that drifted down to embrace his chin.

Grady nudged Rhett when they encountered the bar Pullman kept under the window. It was made out of an old meat smoker and held various decanters of alcohol that Grady promised were the cheapest brands found on planet earth and would scorch a man's throat before rendering him speechless. It was rumored that Pullman was, in fact, so cheap that he poured Thunderbird into a wine decanter for dinner guests at home.

But he was a damn fine accountant and could make a nickel crap a dollar bill, according to Old Kingston Nash, a frenemy of Rhett's brother Jake—and his fiancée's grandfather.

"Hiya, folks!" said Pullman, welcoming them into his office. "Well, I'll be danged. Everett Braddock, home after all these years. Never thought I'd see the day. You coming home to settle down like your brother Jake?"

Grady snorted. "Rhett's not the settling-down type."

Rhett rolled his eyes. "Speak for yourself."

"Oh yeah?" Grady asked, a little too amused for Rhett's taste. "You got someone in mind?"

"I'm just saying I don't need you to speak for me," Rhett said, his heart pounding a little too fast. *Yeah, I have someone on my mind, and I wish I didn't.*

"Uptight much?" Grady asked.

Pullman Duff looked between the two men, clearly delighted by the building tension. "What about Julianna?" he asked.

"What about her?" Rhett and Grady asked at the same time.

"Girl's a looker, even if she's not one for a comb."

Grady choked. "She's, uh, cute, I guess," he allowed.

Rhett kept his mouth shut, unwilling to risk arguing that *cute* was selling Jules short—by a lot.

Unfortunately, Pullman didn't have any such qualms. "Cute? She's all grown up. I hear tell your Rafael at the firehouse has a thing for her—"

"What?!" Both Rhett and Grady growled at the same time.

Grady looked at Rhett in surprise.

Pullman shrugged. "Hey, hey. Don't jump down

my throat, boys. Just repeating what I overheard in Schweitz's."

Grady glared at him. "Rafi'd better stay away from my sister, or he's gonna lose a length of hose."

"You don't like Rafi, then how about Rhett?" Duff asked, ramping up Grady.

"Rhett and Jules?" Grady scoffed. "Now *that* would be a total mismatch. And Rhett knows better."

Rhett released a breath he hadn't realized he'd been holding too long.

"Well, the Braddocks are full of surprises." Duff leaned forward and slapped Grady's shoulder, a huge grin on his face. "Remember little Lila dancing on the bar at Schweitz's a few weeks back? Aw, Rhett, that was a sight; your mama woulda spun in her grave."

Rhett couldn't believe his ears. "Excuse me?"

"Ha! Didn't hear about that all the way in Dallas, didja?"

"No." Rhett frowned. "When was this?"

"A few weeks back. She led Jake and Charlie and the F and R boys on a merry chase, she did . . . cartwheeling on the bar! Had Tommy proposing before the night was over."

"Cartwheeling?" Rhett turned to Grady. "You didn't tell me about this."

Grady shrugged uncomfortably. "Yeah, no . . . they got her down. No harm, no foul."

Rhett didn't like it at all—imagining his little sis being ogled by a crowd.

Grady knew him well enough to put the kibosh on Rhett's welling fury. "How about we get down to business?" he suggested hastily.

"Yup, yup," Pullman said, clapping his hands together. "You blew back into town with some bright ideas, I hear?" He glanced at Rhett, who left the next step up to Grady.

Grady nodded. "Yes, I think so. You know Rhett's bought the stables from Dad. And"—Grady winked at Rhett—"Jules asked him to take a look at Dad's tax returns to see if, well, he's been overpaying our sainted Uncle Sam."

"That right? I've offered to do his taxes for him before, but he said he could handle 'em. Well, slide 'em over here, son, and lemme take a look."

Grady slid the pile of envelopes across Pullman's desk, which was, in fact, a massive oak door set over two sawhorses. It wasn't fancy, but it fit the old jail setting to a T, for *taxes*.

"Care for a drink, fellas? Got some mighty fine bourbon, or some genuwine Ta-Kill-Ya, ha-ha!"

"Oh, gee, thanks, Pullman," said Rhett. "But we'll take a pass. Lots to do today."

"Ya sure, now?"

"Yeah, yeah, rain check on that," Grady put in. "For sure."

Rhett had a hard time not laughing as Johnny Cash's "After Taxes" came on over the sound system, and Grady kicked him under the desk. It was all they could do not to sing the lyrics.

Duff was a classic index-finger licker, and he hummed along as he paged through the returns and glanced at Rhett's notes.

"Um-*huuum*," he said while they waited.

This was followed by a pursing of the lips and a decisive nod.

"Dag *jiggety,*" he said next.

Rhett looked at Grady, who shrugged.

"Hot dog with *relish,*" he mused, next.

He flipped through the following set, and the one after that, while Rhett decided that aside from grouper, catfish were the creepiest fish he'd ever laid eyes on. Especially when 139 of them, all at once, had their eyes laid on *him*.

Finally Pullman Duff was ready to pronounce his opinion. He stood up, took off his steel-rimmed spectacles, laid his hands flat on the desk in front of him, and winked at Rhett. "Boy, they always did make a fuss of how smart you were. I think you get it from your mama's side of the family—though she wasn't smart enough to marry me."

Rhett said a quick but silent thank-you to the good Lord for that.

"By my calculations, you are one hundred and seventeen percent co-rrect." He turned to Grady. "We got a good case here for your pop to get a six-figure refund."

Grady let out a whoop. "Six figures?!"

"Yes, indeed. And given his condition, I ain't gonna charge 'im for makin' the case to the IRS. We'll get 'er done for free."

Given his condition . . . and the fact that I did all the work for you, sir. But Rhett didn't say it aloud. "That's awfully nice of you, Mr. Duff."

"It is," agreed Grady. "I really can't thank you enough. My dad doesn't have great insurance, so this is the very best news possible—aside from total remission."

"Well, son. Molly and I will pray for that to happen, too."

They both thanked Pullman profusely, turned down another offer of "mighty fine bourbon" off the meat-smoker bar, and saluted all the squinting catfish.

Outside, Rhett asked, "So Molly is Pullman's wife?"

Grady nodded. "She teaches nursery school and is the only woman in town who owns exactly two pairs of shoes: an everyday pair and a Sunday pair. Her frugality is something of a legend, I guess. Even my sister owns more shoes than that."

Rhett laughed.

"Pullman Duff is probably richer than Kingston Nash, though, if you ask me."

"Then, where's all his money go? It's certainly not invested in his office decor."

"Couldn't tell you. There are rumors he gives a lot to charity—or is planning to."

"Kids?"

Grady shook his head. "Just catfish."

"Well, you don't have to put those through college or save for their retirement."

Grady laughed.

"I haven't participated in Fool Fest in a long time, but I think we should put white beards and Santa hats on every single one of those catfish. What d'you say?"

"Brilliant! I'll get the Fire and Rescue squad's help."

"It's a plan."

"Listen, man—thank you. I'm going to go give Dad and Mom the good news. This is much appreciated. Really. We owe you."

"You owe me nothing," Rhett said. "I'm heading to the saddlery, and then back to the barn. Maybe your sister will speak to me now that my 'snooping' paid off."

Grady shot him a sympathetic glance from his superior six-foot-six height. "Maybe. She's always been a pistol, but I've never seen her like this. Ornery as all get-out."

Rhett sighed. "She'll get over it."

"Hope so, man. I really hope so, for your sake."

CHAPTER 15

Rhett had a double motive for going to the Holt Saddlery, where he knew Jules's aunt Sue had nice boots. She was putting a hammered silver necklace into a Lucite display case when he pulled up, and she took in the sight of Scarlett without comment.

"Mr. Braddock," she said as he came into the shop with a tinkle of the bells on the door. "How's our Julianna been treatin' you?"

He gave her a tight smile. "Great. I'd like to get a decent pair of western boots. And then I've got a bone to pick with you, Miz Holt."

Sue shot him a knowing look and compressed her lips as she locked the Lucite case. "How can I help you, boss?"

"Boots first," he said.

"Sure thing. You want Lucchese? Tony Lama? Justin?"

"I'll try whatever you've got."

"What happened to your shoes?" She looked at the stains.

"Your niece happened to them."

"Ah." Her mouth worked. "She can be . . . headstrong."

"No, really?"

"I'm afraid I taught her to be that way. I taught

her not to take any crap from men." Sue led him over to the wall of boots and gestured for him to take a seat. "And I told her not to delude herself with romantic fairy tales."

"Not all romance is a fairy tale," he commented.

She ignored that. "What size are you, hon?"

"Thirteen."

"Lucky thirteen. Big feet." She smiled and raised an eyebrow as she handed him a pair of brown ostrich boots with elaborate, hand-tooled shanks.

He refused to blush. "Nice," he said as he slipped off his shoes.

"Lucchese. I happen to think they're the best in the business. A lot of folks will argue for Tony Lama, though, and Justins are a classic. Just depends on what you're looking for."

"Comfort. Style. And watertight," he added ruefully. He eased the boot on over his sock, then put on its mate and stood up. "Incredibly comfortable, just as I remembered."

Sue nodded.

"Got 'em in black?"

"I believe so. You want to try on any of the others?"

He shook his head. "No. These in black. Perfect."

"Be back in two shakes."

He didn't employ Jules's cheesy joke about chocolate or vanilla. Just waited for her to come back. As he tried on this pair, too, just to make sure, he asked casually, "So why did you teach Jules to be headstrong and not take any crap from men?"

"Let's see. You've been in town now, for what? Three days? You'll have heard my story. Don't pretend you haven't."

"Okay, I won't." He met her gaze in the shop's full-length mirror. "Any regrets?"

"Yes, of course. I wish I hadn't had to do it. But he broke my cheekbone, three of my ribs, and—"

"I'm sorry. I really am."

"I'm sorry, too. Sorry I ever met him. Sorry I blew him right out the wall of the cabin. But if I hadn't killed him, he would've killed me." She noted the question in his eyes. "Yes, the same cabin Jules lives in now. I couldn't go back to it. Never stepped foot in there again. But walls can be repaired and painted, and new lives can be lived in an old space. It's not haunted. He wouldn't dare."

"Where do you live now?"

"Got a little cottage over on Birch and Fourth. Cute place."

"By yourself?"

"Most of the time." She smiled and didn't elaborate.

"You're not . . . afraid to be on your own?"

"No, darlin', I'm not. Truth to tell, I'm more afraid to be *with* somebody." She got to her feet and put her hands on her hips. "So. You gonna take those Lucchese's, Mr. Nosy?"

"I am. How much?"

They were not cheap. Then again, Rhett wanted Holt Saddlery to start making a profit. So out came the Amex Black Card again, and in one swipe, he became the owner of the boots. "I'll wear them out," he said.

"No problem. Just don't let Jules wear *you* out." She chuckled. "I'm tellin' you, I taught her well."

Rhett sighed. "So it's you I have to blame, is it?"

"You bet your sweet ass it is. If she'd turned out like her mama, you'd be buried in casseroles and pies and cookies."

"That sounds *terrible*," said Rhett caustically.

Sue laughed evilly, sounding exactly like Jules. "Listen, if that's what you're looking for, you find yourself an adorable debutante in Dallas."

"I didn't say that was what I was looking for." He rocked back on his heels and shot her a challenging look.

"You don't need to. You go buy yourself half a dozen of 'em, all righty?" She stepped forward and smacked his black Amex against his chest. "Two blondes, two brunettes, two redheads. But you leave my Jules alone. I can feel the attraction between the two of you, and you need to forget about it. You hear me?"

"Loud and clear. My question is, Why are you warning me off?"

"She's not a toy. Not a plaything for a man like you."

"A toy . . . a man like me . . . What do those terms mean, exactly, Sue? What kind of man do you think I am?"

"You're a city slicker, Rhett Braddock."

"Am I."

She compressed her lips and squinted at him. "Sure as shootin'."

He was quite sure she'd used the phrase deliberately.

"I encountered a few in my day."

"And they were too slick for you?"

"Why, that's a rather insulting question, Ever-Rhett."

"Oh, I'm the one who's insulting? News to me. So did you get outslicked? Is that why you're trying to protect your niece from me?"

"I've brought Jules up not to need my protection. Taught her how to shoot when she was ten. Taught her how to break in a horse at fourteen. And how to smell BS from miles away."

"Gave her a signed certificate upon graduation, did you?"

"Ha. You don't belong here," she said, "and I'm not afraid to say it."

The old hurt, the old anger, ignited again and coiled, low in his gut. "Seems to me that I decide that, not you," Rhett said. "Not anybody else in Silverlake."

If she heard the dangerous undercurrent in his tone, she ignored it. "What are you doin' back here, Ever-Rhett?"

"I'm here to bail your family out of a jam, among other things. So maybe a little less hostility is in order?"

"Maybe. Maybe we can be best buddies, down the road. Just don't mess with my Jules."

Rhett slid the Amex card back into his wallet and tossed his ruined shoes into the boot box on the floor near the counter. "You should know that I don't mess with anyone, Sue. Not unless they mess with me first."

"Good to know."

"So why did you mess with me by telling Jules that I had the saddlery business and property appraised?"

"Not everything is about you, Mr. Braddock," Sue said. "If something concerns me, it concerns Jules. Simple as that. I told her because she had a right to know what was going on."

"A little out of context, don't you think?" Rhett said, not missing the slight tinge of acid in Sue's tone. It was hard to tell how much she was intentionally trying to manipulate the situation, but there was no denying she sure had Jules's back. "I would have told her myself, Sue."

"Oh sure. When it was convenient for you.

Thanks for your biz, boss man. You come back soon, ya hear?"

He spun on the heel of his new Lucchese boot and walked to the door.

"Oh, Mr. Braddock?"

He looked over his shoulder at Aunt Sue.

"I'm glad you stopped by. But you remember my words. And you remember where your loyalties lie: to your friend Grady. I can't imagine you will ever care about Julianna more than you care about Grady."

Stunned, Rhett didn't have a response for that slap in the face so he just walked out, the bells on the door jingling as he left. *Remember where your loyalties lie: to your friend Grady.*

Damn it.

City slicker. You don't belong here.

He'd been called worse, and he'd been told worse. Still, the words hurt. They reverberated through his head as his shiny new boots clipped along the pavement. Sue had a nerve. And she wasn't smart to antagonize the guy who now had the power to close down her business.

Or was she?

Rhett deliberately walked through a mud puddle to take some of the shine off the boots.

She'd read him like a book, actually. By accusing him of being a city slicker, she'd knocked him onto the defensive. Made him want to prove that he was no such thing.

Rhett's mouth twisted as he got into Scarlett, mud and all.

You don't belong here . . .

If not here, then where?

Maybe he should drive back to Dallas right now. Scarlett would get him there in three hours if he drove like a bullet and wasn't spotted by highway patrol.

But that felt like running.

I'm supposed to leave Jules alone. As Rhett drove back to the Holt property, his mind wandered back to that night with her in Dallas. He remembered seeing her walk through the crowded bar at Nick & Sam's Grill. It was a place where he was a regular and he could be the shiny, city version of Rhett Braddock with maximum efficiency and style should an old college buddy or a client be passing through town. He didn't have to think too hard or care too much; he knew what to order, he knew how to impress, and he knew the evening could be wrapped up in two hours if the company didn't warrant extending the evening.

Julianna Holt pushed through that crowd, looked around the room, and smiled when her eyes found his. It was the only night in Dallas he could remember wishing would last forever.

He hadn't seen her in years. He hadn't seen her as a woman until that moment in her good jeans and a cropped velvet blazer over a T-shirt, worn cowboy boots on her feet, and her hair loose and free around a face with a minimal amount of makeup. And for a moment, when his body joined with hers later that night, it meant so much more than the act itself. In her arms it felt as if she was calling him home. Holding out her hand and saying he'd be welcome back in Silverlake. Giving permission that he didn't even know he needed to reclaim a part of himself that he'd lost. "I'm so happy to see you again," was the first thing she'd said, all sunshine and wildflowers and honesty.

And then he messed it up by spooking because of Grady. *No, Rhett. It wasn't just because of Grady. You were scared. Admit it. You were scared you didn't know how to be the person you used to be. That version of yourself as a boy in Silverlake. You missed him; you wanted to be him for a long time. And some part of you spooked because you didn't want to fail. You didn't want to show up in Silverlake and know for certain that you could never go back.*

Jules's aunt Sue didn't think he could come back, not for the long haul. She didn't want him to. Did Jules feel the same? Was she really just counting the days before he left? She'd been mad as hell that first day he'd stepped foot at Holt Stables, but it wasn't that first day anymore. Sometimes he thought he caught her looking at him like she had that night at Nick & Sam's.

Maybe Sue is looking at you all wrong. Sure, you're a city man, a money man. But everybody has different versions of themselves and maybe one of them doesn't have to be a lie for the other one to be true. Maybe you should just talk to Grady. He tested that theory out in his mind for a moment and then realized that was still a stupid idea, and 100 percent not worth it, given that Jules wasn't interested in a second chance.

At the end of the day, he was still going back to Dallas, and Jules was staying here. What was the point of telling Grady about any of it?

CHAPTER 16

Jules stood staring at Rhett, unable to believe her ears. "Six figures? Your snooping is getting my dad a tax refund of over *six figures?*"

He nodded, his blue-chip eyes bluer than the sky overhead. "I thought that might make you feel better."

He looked quite impressed with himself, proud that he was saving Billy Holt so much money. And she had to hand it to him: He had a right to be. So why did she want to punch him?

"Well, Pullman Duff helped calculate it all. He knows tax law better than I do. But I did have an instinct that your dad wasn't claiming enough."

"He can go and get treatment at MD Anderson now, without going into crazy debt."

Rhett shoved his hands into his pockets. "Yeah."

If only *she* had thought to look at the tax returns. Do some research on allowable farm deductions. Take them to Pullman. "You're a prince among men."

"Uh . . ." a flush started at his collarbone and began to rise higher.

"Which completely and utterly pisses me off."

"Wait . . . what?"

"I don't know whether to turn five cartwheels,"

Jules mused, "or get Otto to serve you a beer with ex-lax in it. I honestly cannot choose."

Rhett looked alarmed. "That's just . . . *wrong*. And anyway, Otto wouldn't do that."

Jules brought her chin up. "For me, he might."

"I'm seriously confused, here," said Rhett. "How exactly have I made you angry *this* time?"

Jules snorted. "Do you understand that I'm really, really tired of having to *thank* you? Especially after how you behaved in Dallas?"

He sighed. "I don't want you to thank me. This was for your dad. And I've explained and apologized for how I left things in Dallas."

"Yes, you have. But it doesn't change what you did or how it made me feel. Used. Tossed away without a thought."

"Believe me, I thought about you. Didn't stop, in fact."

"Nice way of showing it."

"Jules—"

Maybe it was time he knew the truth. "What you didn't get, Rhett, is that the little brat who followed you and Grady around when we were kids? That little girl you were kind to, when Grady would barely tolerate me? Well, his stupid, dorky baby sister with the buckteeth—she had a crush on you. And she pretty much never got over it. Until *Dallas*."

He stared at her, looking stricken.

"Yeah. I used to write your name in my school

notebooks. Rhett plus Julianna equals barfy hearts and flowers," she said bitterly. "So, you unbelievable marauding a-hole, Dallas was my dream come true—until you scraped me off your shoe in the morning without a second thought."

"Oh, Jules . . ."

"Because you'd messed with Grady's . . ." She struggled for the right word. "Grady's property. And that wasn't okay. Because, you know, it's all about your bestest buddy, dearest friend, your brother from another mother. And me? I was just a convenient way for you to get off that night."

"No," Rhett said. "That is not how it was!"

"You used me. And no matter how nice you are now to make up for it—"

"Stop. Would you just stop for a moment?"

She shut up and glared at him.

"For the record, I did *not* use you. I was unbelievably attracted to you."

"You were?"

"I still am!" He scrubbed a hand down his face, dark with frustration and a day of stubble. She couldn't help melting a little. "Jules, I don't view you as anyone's property . . . I view you as . . ."

"As?" She waited a little breathlessly. Couldn't help it.

Oh God, she was an idiot. Still vulnerable.

Bad idea, Jules. Toughen up. Hang on to the anger. Much safer.

"I view you as hot! And even though I knew it

was a bad idea that night, I couldn't help myself."

Rhett Braddock thinks I'm hot.

A flush climbed up her face as she waited for him to elaborate.

And I still think he's the most handsome man I've ever seen.

He shrugged. "I drank too much and lost my judgment."

She evaluated him frankly. Head to toe. Those mile-wide shoulders, the trim waist, the long, athletic legs in the snug denim. Couldn't help appreciating what she saw. Despite her best intentions, she softened toward him. Melted, in fact. What if . . . *Oh no, don't you dare even think that, much less say it . . .*

But she did. "Would you like to lose it again?" she asked, a little huskily. "I guess I could use you right back . . ."

"What? Yes. No! I can't do that. Grady would kill me."

Her oversized brother did not belong in this conversation. "Why don't we leave Grady out of this?"

"I wish," he muttered.

Irritation surged inside her. "Choose," she said, simply. "Me or him."

"I can't do that! It's not that simple."

Jules pursed her lips and nodded decisively. "Then you won't mind if I keep hating you."

"I do mind!"

A big part of her was relieved that he hadn't taken her up on her offer. Who was she kidding? Use Rhett Braddock for sex? No. She'd end up falling in love with him all over again, and being crushed all over again.

She shrugged.

"Damn it all, Jules." Rhett threw up his hands. "For a simple country girl, you are waaaaay too complicated. And as the saying goes, I don't know whether to sh—uh, crap or go blind around you."

She sighed with a satisfaction she didn't quite feel. "That makes me happy. It's poetic justice."

"It's not poetic," he growled. "And there's no justice about it, either. In fact, it's downright evil that you would be thrilled that my head is about to explode."

Jules nodded, delighted. "It is, right?! It's perfectly, one hundred percent evil." She laughed. "And right now, I'm okay with that. Go grab a beer with Grady, why don't you?"

Rhett growled again, and walked away.

CHAPTER 17

Rhett couldn't ever remember feeling like such a jerk . . . *stupid, dorky baby sister with the buckteeth . . . she had a crush on you . . . And she pretty much never got over it. Until Dallas. Dallas was my dream come true—until you scraped me off your shoe in the morning.*

Words couldn't even describe how rotten he felt. And it explained everything. Why she'd thrown the flowers into the stall. Why she'd been so hostile. Why she still couldn't get past it.

He'd not only broken her heart, he'd wiped the floor with it.

Was there any way to fix it?

When he arrived back at the firehouse that evening, sounds of raucous laughter and an old track from the Doors was spilling from the second-story window. The garage door was up, showing off Big Red, who looked like she'd been detailed recently. In keeping with the time of year, someone had stuck an enormous jester made out of glitter and tinsel on the front grille by the American flag decal.

He remembered climbing all over the vintage curves of this very fire truck as a kid, ladders and all, on parade days. A smaller, dustier city vehicle was parked on the far left of the cavernous garage and an empty spot indicated someone was out on official business. Well, it wasn't empty, per se; an inflatable pool octopus was sitting in the middle ready to annoy whoever came back from duty. Someone had strapped a Silverlake Fire and Rescue helmet on it, and it looked a little confused.

A loudspeaker in the corner crackled a bit, as if it couldn't wait to announce an emergency, and the boys were clearly ready. Against the brick wall along the floor, several sets of fireman's pants were lined up neatly, waists shoved to the floor, protective boots poking through the tops of the leg holes. A racking system held heavy jackets and helmets. An assortment of other equipment remained boxed, shelved, categorized, and otherwise neatly stowed, funny in a look-we-all-grew-up sort of way; neither Jake nor Grady could've ever been accused of being neat and orderly back in the day.

Cooking smells wafted down the stairwell as Rhett headed up the old wooden stairs to the upper floor where the action was. Not-Spot came bounding over to greet him with the customary nose to his no-longer-privates. He scratched the dog behind the ears. "Snag any more pancakes?"

A peculiar odor assaulted his nostrils, and he did his best to waft it away, eyeing Not-Spot accusingly. Not-Spot shook his head, whined, lay down, and put a paw over his nose, as if disclaiming all responsibility.

Rhett paused for a moment. This . . . this was not a good smell. No way Mick was at the stove. A few more steps proved he was correct.

It was Lila at the stove, clearly in charge as she gestured wildly with a ladle. Mick and Rafael stood on either side of her, shooting worried glances at each other over her head. She gave Rhett a wave; Rafael used his quick reflexes to avoid getting whacked with her weapon. Though Rafi's lean, muscular build probably matched most everyone, save Grady, for strength, it was clearly his dexterity that set him apart. And saved him from being brained by Rhett's sister.

"If I can just perfect this sauce, we'll be on our way to the greatest Fool Feast finale ever!" Lila said enthusiastically. Lila was a go-getter, a doer, with ambition for miles and the sort of can-do attitude that inspired others to get their asses in gear. Not only could she start things up, but she could see 'em through the middle and get every-body to the end. So, yeah, she was smart, pretty, and fun.

What she wasn't: a good cook. She'd never been a good cook, and there was a reason why it had always been either Jake, Ace, or Rhett helping their parents with the grill on Friday nights and the griddle on Sunday mornings. Declan couldn't cook, either, but at least he'd had no problem admitting it.

Rhett gave Rafael a sympathetic look and

then caught sight of his brother Jake holding a grown-up Charlotte Nash in the circle of his arms. She pulled away from Jake and came forward. "Hi! You do remember me, right, Rhett?"

He nodded, smiled, and clasped her hand. "Of course I remember you, Charlie Nash," he said warmly. Then, feeling that wasn't quite enough, he pecked her on the cheek.

Jake flashed him a grateful look, and Lila smiled.

Mick and Rafi stiffened a bit, though, and turned back to the stove. Rhett got the feeling that they weren't Charlie's biggest fans—and he knew Grady still struggled to accept her after her role in defunding Silverlake Fire and Rescue. But for Jake, he did his best, understanding that she'd been between a rock and a hard place.

He remembered how in love with Charlie Jake had been in high school. And he also remembered how heartbroken his brother had been when she'd left him behind.

Rhett evaluated her fresh, blond good looks. He had never been in love with anyone like that. And now that Jake had his girl back . . . was going to *marry* this girl, Rhett considered it all a blessing. He sure wasn't going to hold the past against her.

It should go without saying.

"With Rhett home, it's like we have a Braddock quorum for the first time since . . . since . . ." Lila looked around and her voice faltered.

Since our parents died?

"Since *forever!* Maybe Ace'll come home for the holidays this year," she finished.

Fat chance. Rhett was regularly in touch with Ace, a pro baseball player who'd gotten out of Silverlake as fast as he could. If only Ace had been the one with the supercharged brains, maybe Rhett could've stayed here in town. Anyhow, Ace wasn't coming back until he couldn't play ball anymore, and as long as he kept himself out of barroom brawls, he should be fine enjoying life with his "real" family, the Austin Lone Stars baseball team.

"I followed the recipe, I swear!" Lila was saying.

Rafael's dark brows knit together as he peered down into whatever awful concoction Lila was brewing. He sighed and shook his head. *"Me duele la cabeza,"* he muttered.

"Don't worry," Lila said, "It's a practice run." She looked up at Rhett. "Spicy Mole Gravy! It's Rafi's family recipe."

"Maybe Rafi should make it, then?" Grady asked, coming up behind the folks at the stove and peering into the saucepan. He winced and pulled back.

"It's good . . . for a . . . first try," Rafael said loudly. He started to back away from the stove, but Mick plunked his big hands on his squad mate's shoulders and held him by Lila's side.

"Don't even think about abandoning your post, man."

Rafi gave him a withering look but gamely looked back into the saucepan, blinking rapidly as the fumes made his eyes water.

Rhett rolled up his sleeves and joined the others at the stove in the firehouse kitchen. He peered into the pot at a thoroughly unappetizing brown mess. "Wow. Just . . . wow." He stepped away.

"Guys," Lila said, her face going serious. "This should be . . . *more. Bigger.*"

Rafael took the saucepan off the burner. "It really shouldn't," he said.

"I'm not talking about the mole," Lila said, putting down her ladle and untying the Mick-sized firehouse apron engulfing her body. "We should have a big, group Fool Fest Finale Feast for any off-duty firefighters and extended family. We're all working overtime to pull it off, so we deserve a wrap-up party! Silverlake Ranch can handle a lot of people. We'll ask Declan. He'll probably love the idea."

"I'm sure he won't mind," Jake said.

"Why the hell do we need Declan's permission to have a party at our parents' house?" Rhett asked. His voice sounded surprisingly bitter in his own ears. His two siblings stared at him. An awkward lull settled over the kitchen.

Then Mick—who was probably grateful for

something to do other than figure out how to dispose of the stinking mass of burned mole sauce—put a hand on Rhett's shoulder and saved the moment. "Yo, I'm about to go on duty. Just wondering if the work party up at Holt Stables is still on for next week? We can knock out painting those paddock fences in no time."

"I . . ." Rhett found himself uncharacteristically speechless. Grady had mentioned something about it, but Rhett doubted he'd get the same helpful response to the Holt Stables' call to action now that he owned it, instead of Grady's family. He figured he'd have to bring labor in from Dallas or something.

"We got a whole team of useful dudes ready to go. But we gotta work around schedules, so I kind of need to know," Mick said.

"Yeah, it's on," Rhett said, a little surprised that the squad's offer to help out at the stables was more than just an idle offer. He caught Jake's eye, and his brother smiled as if to say, *Yeah, this is what it's like here.*

"You be sure to let me and Charlie know the exact timing, too, Ever-Rhett," Lila said.

"You're planning to work out at the stables in those purple python boots?" Rhett asked. "Or do you have a pair of sparkly silver heels that's more appropriate?"

Lila grinned. "I'm going to focus on hydration and sustenance."

"Lila, hon, when you use those big words like that, it slays me," Tommy said, his hand on his heart. He was the rookie of the squad.

"Tommy, *hon,* do you even know what they mean?"

"Well, it's the *way* you say them. And I think both of them have to do with . . . using your mouth," he said a little too dreamily.

Rhett and Jake both frowned and turned toward Tommy instinctively, but Lila put a hand on Rhett's arm as if to say, *I've got this.*

"Jeez, that's so sweet. You do know that you and me are never gonna happen, right?" As Tommy's expression fell, Lila added, "That said, you're likely to have a full audience of eligible women at the work party. Can't imagine anybody who has some flexibility in her schedule would miss the opportunity to watch a bunch of sweaty, good-looking men use their muscles."

Amid a smattering of laughter, the crowd in the kitchen dispersed. Jake whispered something in Charlie's ear and she squeezed his arm and slipped out of the room. Grady left to handle a call for assistance on the community help line. Rhett was about to head out to work on his laptop but Jake and Lila looked at each other and Jake held up his hand. "Wait up, Rhett. What you said about Deck . . ." he said, "I think we need to clear the air."

Rhett sighed.

"I get how you're feeling. I've felt it, too," Jake said. "But I've made peace with the fact—and it is a fact, Rhett—that Deck did the best he could as a stand-in father, and there's nobody under the circumstances who could've done better. Back then and now. And as it turns out, Declan's best is pretty awesome. We wouldn't still have Silverlake if it weren't for him."

Rhett opened his mouth to protest, to claim some credit, though it made him feel small, but Lila chimed in first. "We also needed the money you loaned to keep it going. Nobody's saying otherwise. But a ranch as special as Silverlake doesn't keep going on cash alone. It takes hard work and heart. And it's Declan who's left his heart on the dance floor, not any us."

The three of them stared at one another and Lila smiled. "It sounded better in my brain. It sounded really clever. But you know what I mean."

Rhett nodded. He grabbed the back of his neck with his hand as he formed his next words. "There's something in me that needs you to know that he couldn't have done it without me. That he still can't . . . man, I guess I'm just still so mad at him. When all of you were running away as fast as you could, I was the one who would've given anything to stay on the ranch with him. He made me go, Lila. He sent me away."

"He never wanted it to be forever. Stay for Fool

Fest, Rhett—and our very own Feast of Fools. Promise me that," Lila said.

Julianna Holt's beautiful face suddenly flashed in Rhett's mind. "Can't promise, but I'll do my best. You just never know . . ."

CHAPTER 18

Rhett parked Scarlett and walked into the barn in his new Lucchese boots, which fit like a dream. He felt the years dropping away, felt almost like his old self again: the Rhett he'd been before he'd been sent off to school and donned camouflage for protection. Learned how to fit in with the other preppies, even though he'd never totally lost his Texas accent. He'd learned how to entertain them with it, though. And once he'd employed the right to make fun of himself before they could, they'd begun to respect him a little more. Tolerate him, any way.

With practiced ease and grace, Jules was pitching hay from the wheelbarrow into the horse stalls. Her hair this afternoon was more rooster tail than warrior knot, and tendrils of it fell around her face as she worked. Her movements were more dancer than farmer, even in those rubber boots. He was watching a . . . hay ballet.

Rhett shook off the strange thought and called out to her. "Hey, Jules. Got time for another pow-wow in the office? I have some ideas for this place."

She stilled, then turned to face him, pitchfork in hand. For a moment he thought she might use it on him. But then she blinked, smiled, and said a strangely mechanical, "Of course."

Huh. But Rhett nodded and led the way to the tack room office, where he'd kept the second chair next to the desk. He sat in it, so that she could take the main one. She seemed surprised by that.

"So what ideas do you want to discuss?" she asked, crossing her legs and bouncing her foot rapidly.

"I think we could really expand business here if we not only gave the place a face-lift, but took in more boarders. I'd like to go ahead and get an indoor riding ring built for your lessons, so that they don't have to be canceled in bad weather, and in fact . . ." He went on until he registered that her face had turned to stone. Beautiful stone, but stone, nonetheless. "Is something bothering you?"

She gritted her teeth. "Not at all."

"I don't believe you. Talk to me."

"Talk to you. Okay. I will. Rhett, these are all great ideas. But they are great ideas that I've been discussing with my dad for years! Trying to get him to listen to me. And nothing I said got through to him. I have plans and designs that I showed him. He looked at them as if I'd just given him a macaroni-and-glue project on construction paper. *That's nice, honey,* is what he said."

"You have plans and designs?" Rhett asked. "Show me."

Jules heaved a deep sigh and then dug into the beat-up old file cabinet next to the desk. She pulled out a folder with neatly drawn projects inside: one for an indoor riding ring, one with new sliding stall doors, one for adding an upstairs office space above the riding ring with a window that looked down upon it. She'd priced things out, too. Done cost projections and roughly calculated the financial benefits to the projects. She'd clipped pictures of clean, modern, brightly lit, attractive stables. She'd collected some pictures of indoor riding rings, too. And tack rooms.

Rhett took his time reviewing the papers, trying to ignore that Jules was a ball of tension behind his right shoulder. What he saw was impressive. She'd already filed for permits. She'd already gotten blueprints stamped. She'd researched materials and considered different options. From the looks of it, all she really needed was money and labor. This was more than a dream. This was an achievable goal. Rhett looked up; Jules was chewing on her lower lip. Even when she was nervous she was sexy as hell. He shook off the unbusinesslike thoughts. "This is impressive. You really have thought this through."

"Yes," she said flatly. "Fat lot of good it did for me."

"Why do you think your dad resisted your ideas?"

"For one thing, because I'm a girl. He listens to everything Grady says. And for another, because there wasn't any money and he saw it as a demand for something he couldn't provide and didn't want to take out loans for."

"Okay. So what if I can provide it?"

Her mouth worked for a moment. Then, with that weirdly careful, neutral expression, she said, "That'd be just great."

Why did Rhett feel that he'd just pissed in her Cheerios? If remodeling and expansion had been her dream and he could make it happen, how was that bad?

"You're annoyed," he said. "Why?"

She shook her head. "No, no. I'm grateful."

He narrowed his eyes on her face, which had that stony look again.

"Jules. What are you not saying? You don't look as though you *want* to be grateful. What is the undercurrent here that I'm sensing?"

"No undercurrent—besides what we talked about the other day."

He just kept his gaze on hers.

"Fine. What you're sensing is that again. These are great ideas, but I wasn't allowed to make them happen on my own terms. And now they'll happen on your terms. And I just feel like everyone's puppet!"

"You are no puppet," he said quietly. "And there are no strings attached here."

She shot him an evaluative glance.

"What?" he prompted her. "What's going through that hard head of yours?"

"Oh, I don't know. Maybe I'm a little annoyed that you, Rhett Braddock, *of all people*—that you get to control everything that I ever dreamed of controlling. My family property, my dad's gratitude and respect, my brother's gratitude and loyalty, my barn, my horses, and now my dreams."

"This was never about control," Rhett said.

"Maybe not for you."

"I don't want to control you, Jules."

"But . . . you do."

"I'm just trying to help all of you."

"Why? Why aren't you out at Silverlake Ranch, trying to help Declan?"

Rhett took the words as a punch to the gut. "*What* did you say?"

"You heard me. Why us? Why not pay off your own family property?"

"Not that it's any of your business, Jules, but Declan won't let me."

"Why not?"

Rhett gave a short, unamused bark of laughter. "Because he doesn't want to give up control of the place. He refuses to be a charity case."

Jules folded her arms across her chest and

nodded decisively. "Well, I don't want to be one, either—especially not to *you*."

"All right. Point taken. So what do you suggest we do about this situation, Julianna Holt? I've invested a good amount of money here. Am I supposed to just sign over the deed to you and walk away? I don't think so. What do you want from me?"

"What do you want from *me*?"

"Hard work. Vision. Commitment. The passion you bring to this place and the horses and the kids. That's it. I don't need your gratitude, especially since it galls you so much to be told to have it toward me. But I do need your cooperation. And less hostility."

She blew out an audible breath. "Fine. Fair enough."

"And I'd really like to use your plans to create a more picturesque and viable business out here at the Holt Stables. The boys at the station who are going to be off duty next week are clearing their own schedules to come up and work. I was assuming the planning for an indoor riding ring was going to take time, so I figured I'd just put them to work on smaller prep jobs. But we can use your plans to get the riding ring started."

"My plans. You'd use *mine*?" She seemed stunned.

"Why not? They're great. And we've got available labor. Let's get them going and make the upgraded version of Holt Stables official."

Jules swallowed. "You're going to keep the name?"

She was looking at him as if she had her heart in her throat.

"It's a small thing to me, and a big one for you. So . . ." He shrugged. "Yeah. Holt Stables."

Rhett was rewarded by sudden sunshine in her face.

"Oh, thank God. I was so afraid you would change it!"

He spun around to assure her just as she lurched toward him. Surprise hit them both. Off-balance, Jules's mouth missed his cheek and Rhett's lips brushed across hers in a streak of fire. She gripped his forearms to keep from falling against his chest, and in one swift move Rhett shoved her against the desk.

A moment of the most intense silence followed. Rhett still braced her with his arms, his body starting to close the small amount of distance that was left. It wasn't to stop her. It wasn't that at all.

The delicate *tick tick tick* of his watch only emphasized the uneven exhale of Jules's breath. Her gaze locked on his mouth. He'd only just barely tasted her in that last moment, and the primal heat building between them as he held her steady against the desk brought back the memory of holding her up against the wall in his bedroom in Dallas.

No second chances . . . Jules doesn't want that from me . . . definitely not telling Grady . . . you'll never love Jules more than Grady . . .

Rhett released Jules, indulging for one last second in the sensation of her body sliding against his arms. "Sorry, Jules, not sure what just—"

Lightning fast, she closed the distance back up and took his mouth hard in an irrefutable, scorching-hot kiss.

Everything good about that night in Dallas came flashing back into Jules's mind. A split second of *What am I doing?* followed by *He wants me just as much as I want him* followed by a complete lack of thought at all. Just touch and warmth and the extreme hotness that was everything Rhett Braddock had always been in her dreams.

"Jules, hon, you in there?"

Rhett stepped back so quickly, Jules staggered a little as her dad rounded the corner. She reflexively put her finger up to her lips. *Sssh.*

Rhett held the back of his hand pressed against his mouth. And maybe she was imagining it, but did the light in his eyes dim just a little? Confused, Jules stared at him. Was he disappointed? Disappointed . . . why? Because he didn't get another roll in the hay before heading out of town? Or because . . . Jules's heart pounded for a moment, before she forced herself to dismiss the notion that Rhett Braddock could possibly want

250

something more than a couple hours of a good time.

A throat cleared. Jules blinked and focused on her father, who was looking suspiciously between her and Rhett. "What'd I interrupt? Bad news about the books?" Dad shook his head without waiting for an answer. "I should've hired someone to help me with that. Funny, I thought that would be a stupid use of money at the time . . ."

Jules tore her gaze away from Rhett's face, her heart still pounding. "We're taking care of all that, so don't you worry 'bout a thing. How you doing, Dad?"

He gave a sheepish laugh. "Well, I'm a little bored, to be honest."

"You want to go for a drive?"

Dad didn't look too excited until he realized Rhett had the keys to the Porsche in his palm. Jules's breath caught as her dad's face broke into a wide smile; he was grinning like a teenage boy. "You know where to drive to stay clear of Bode Wells?"

"Well, I'm not the one driving, so as long as you know, we'll be fine." He held the keys out to Jules's dad, who seemed uncertain whether to laugh or swear. He was doing both when the two men walked out of the barn, Dad clapping Rhett on the back.

Jules pressed her right hand to her heart, completely confused by how much she felt for Rhett Braddock in that moment. "See you tonight at dinner, Dad!" she called. With the sound of Scarlett revving outside, Jules went back to work, the taste of Rhett still on her lips.

CHAPTER 19

It was after five when Jules finished up feeding and watering all the animals, and Dad and Rhett were still not back. She had just enough time to take a shower and change before heading to her parents' for dinner. Grady and Aunt Sue were coming, too. On the menu: Mom's Tex-Mex Macaroni, which Grady referred to as Chihuahua Pasta. It was basically chili mixed with elbow macaroni, and Billy Holt loved it.

As she stood in her tiny shower, she tried not to think about the fact that she'd kissed Rhett. *Way to complicate things, Jules.* She tried not to think about how good he'd smelled—just him, not that expensive cologne of his. He'd smelled so clean, of soap and leather and man. She wrapped her arms around herself and tried not to think about how *his* arms had felt—rock hard, dangerous, and yet safe at the same time . . .

Before she knew it, the water had gone cold. How long had she been standing there like an idiot, mooning over Rhett Braddock? Shivering, she shampooed her hair and realized that she'd forgotten yet again to replace her conditioner. At least she had a normal-sized towel to dry off with.

She jumped quickly into clean jeans and a long-sleeved tee from Schlitterbahn, shoved her feet into flip-flops, and ran up the path to her parents' house, her wet hair falling loose down her back. She flew through the back door and into the kitchen, where she pulled up short at the sight of Rhett laughing easily with Dad.

"Billy here almost wrecked Scarlett," he said to Mom, who eyed Jules and then the clock, pointedly. She was late.

"Julianna, your hair—" But Mom stopped.

"I did no such thing," Dad protested. "Just took the bend out at the lake a little fast."

"Almost took out the bait shop, you mean." Rhett winked.

Dad looked flushed, happy, and a decade younger. His hair was mussed, standing on end with no John Deere cap in sight.

Jules felt her heart roll over. Just a ride in a sports car, a simple pleasure, had done wonders for him. *Rhett* had done wonders for him.

She felt like kissing him all over again.

His gaze locked with hers; hot and intense, then slid to her lips.

She flushed, shifting her weight from one foot to the other.

He lifted an eyebrow.

And then Grady appeared, his massive shoulders filling the doorway.

Jules tensed.

So did Rhett. A muscle jumped at his jawline. Other than that, he hid it well.

"Braddock!" Grady slapped him on the back. "You're gone for over a decade. And now you're everywhere, growin' on us like black mold, man. In the firehouse, in the stables, and now here in my mom's kitchen."

"And just as sinister," Rhett said, winking again.

"Hi, honey," Mom said to Grady. "You kids are late." But she walked over and stood on tiptoe to kiss his cheek.

"Sorry." Grady picked her up, clean off the floor, and wrapped her in a bear hug until she squeaked. "We ran late on a drill. Mmm, the Chihuahua Pasta sure smells good."

"Put me down," she demanded.

"The *what?*" Rhett asked, laughing. He turned to Mom. "You got ground Chihuahua in your Crock-Pot, Mrs. H?"

"I have no such thing in my Crock-Pot, Ever-Rhett, and you know it. Staying for dinner?" Helen allowed a small smile to play around her mouth.

Jules leaned against the stove. *Don't you dare stay for dinner. Please stay for dinner.*

Rhett looked as though he could read her mind. He grinned.

She scowled.

Grady, clueless as to this byplay, lifted the lid of the Crock-Pot and inspected the contents. "Yep. Chihuahua. I see the tail."

"That is not true!" Mom swatted his butt with a kitchen towel.

"Well, ma'am, I don't know." Rhett adopted a dubious expression. "If it's not a small dog, what sort of critter you got in there? Is it tender?"

"It's possum," said Jules. "And Mom pickled the feet."

Her mother frowned. "That is disgusting, Juli-anna."

No affectionate swat with the towel for her. No kiss on the cheek, either.

Rhett observed the dynamic and stepped in easily. "Oooh, I do love me some pickled possum toes. With Tabasco."

"What can we get you all to drink?" Mom asked, ignoring this.

"Red rum, please." Grady tried to get to the Crock-Pot with a spoon, but she shooed him away.

"Beer?" Rhett suggested, though he knew better.

"Not at *my* table, young man. You may have iced tea, milk, a Coke, or water."

"I have Baileys in my purse," Aunt Sue called from the other side of the screened kitchen door.

"Where it will stay," Mom informed her evenly. "Come on in, Sue."

"You can't drink that with Chihuahua Pasta anyway," Grady pointed out, opening the door for her and wrapping her in a bear hug, too. "It's a flavor crime."

"A hanging offense," Rhett added.

"It's for my coffee," Sue clarified, utterly ignoring Helen Holt's pointed look. "It ain't against *my* religion."

And so it went.

Not-So-Rotten-Rhett did indeed stay for dinner, and Jules couldn't decide whether she was happy about it or not.

Dessert was homemade apple cobbler with vanilla ice cream, and Aunt Sue did indeed splash Baileys from a flask into her coffee while Mom was in the kitchen.

Billy shook his head, but grinned.

So did the rest of them.

Mom appeared with a tray of plastic champagne glasses and a bottle of ginger ale. "Sue, you left your purse open. And you all—y'all can wipe the smirks off of your faces, you disrespectful bunch. But we do have something to toast."

Jules stared at her. "We do?"

"Yes. You can help me pour the ginger ale. If you can keep your wet hair out of it."

Jules pulled a rubber band out of her pocket and fumbled with her hair.

Mom's lips flattened. "Not at the dinner table, Julianna. Please."

Jules sighed, got to her feet, and ducked into the hallway, where she pulled her hair back with the help of a reflection from a picture frame. By the time she got back to the table, Mom had poured all the ginger ale and set the plastic flutes down in front of everyone.

"So we got some good news from that fancy doctor on Billy's prognosis," she said.

"What fancy doctor?" Jules asked.

"The one that Rhett got in touch with on Dad's behalf," Grady said.

A lump grew in Jules's throat. Not-So-Rotten-Rhett, yet again . . .

"She thinks the tumor is treatable with just surgery and then medication," Billy told them.

Jules stared at him, tears welling in her eyes. "That's—that's—" She ran to hug her father.

"Fantastic," Rhett finished for her, raising his glass.

Grady laughed in delight and raised his, too.

"Thank the good Lord," Mom murmured, toasting Dad across the table.

"Amen," said Aunt Sue, raising her coffee cup.

Mom shot her a look of irritation.

Aunt Sue just grinned and had herself a big swig—bless her heart.

After dinner, Jules stopped by her cabin, retrieved two gallon Ziplocs of rosemary and lavender sprigs that she'd harvested from Aunt Sue's garden for Mia, and, accompanied by Beast, headed out to her friend's showplace of a house on the outskirts of town. Built of pale gray brick with white trim and double doors, Mia's ex, Rob, had spared no expense on the grand facade of the place, complete with a white columned portico that looked as though it was ready to receive the governor and first lady of Texas at any moment. It would be no surprise if the doors were opened by a butler in full uniform, parading a silver tray of iced tea.

Appearances could be as deceiving as Rob, who had borrowed too much money, run out of it, failed to pay it back, and then skipped town. A real peach of a guy, was Rob. *Good riddance.*

But Jules wasn't allowed to mention any of this to anyone, on pain of death. Rob, as far as anyone in Silverlake knew, was working in Europe. And Mia was never so much as a day late on any payment of any loan of any kind. Mia was as honest and sturdy as a live oak—and twice as proud. No tongues would wag about her business. She and Rob had just drifted apart; the divorce had been amicable; they still cared deeply for each other.

Yeah, right. What a crock. Jules wrinkled her nose as she rang the doorbell, which played— yes, really—a strain of "The Eyes of Texas" to announce visitors.

Mia opened the door with a classic eye roll, wearing yellow rubber gloves. "I swear I'm going to shoot that thing right off the wall."

Jules grinned at her. "You've been saying that for six months."

"I mean it this time."

"Hey, at least it doesn't play 'Up Against the Wall Redneck Mother,' " Jules said as Mia made a fuss over Beast and congratulated her on her choice of owner. Beast licked her face, wagged her tail, and then headed off to explore the house. " 'The Eyes of Texas' is classy."

"All the livelong day." Mia's eyes lit up at the sight of the herbs. "I could kiss you! I was just running out of lavender. And the rosemary is perfect, too."

"Aunt Sue has mint, if you want it."

"Yes! Thank you. How's your dad?"

Jules shared the good news.

"Wonderful! I'm so glad to hear that." Mia led the way into the huge kitchen, where she had three double boilers going on the stove, each with four jars submerged in the tops, full of chunks of beeswax.

In another was a mess of pinkish goo.

"What is that?" Jules asked.

"My very first batch of beeswax lip balm. It's got shea butter and coconut oil in it."

"Why's it pink?"

"Raspberry juice."

"Interesting. How are you packaging it?"

Mia heaved a sigh and pointed to five cookie sheets in the middle of the gourmet island, each one covered with at least a hundred tiny plastic jars. Next to them lay sheets and sheets of round labels, printed with her business name: You & Mia, Ltd.

"You're kidding me." Jules stared at her friend. "You have to fill each one?"

"And screw on the lid after it cools. And center the tiny little labels on each one."

"How much can you sell them for?"

"Five bucks. I test-marketed them in spas in Austin. They flew off the shelves."

"Okay." Jules settled herself on one of the kitchen island's stools. "But I am charging you margaritas for my time and chances are that I will cuss when trying to center the stickers."

"Done. You're a lifesaver."

"And I want blues music, not country."

"Hey, hey! Demanding little wench, aren't you?" But Mia put on some B.B. King and then headed for the blender. "Lay down some wax paper. And then fill that measuring cup with the melted lip gloss. I'll bring you a tiny funnel. Only one funnel-fill per jar."

"Got it." Jules inhaled the scent of the lip gloss. "I think some lavender would make it smell really nice."

"Ooooh. Good idea!"

Twenty minutes later, they were both working, margaritas at the ready. But something about the smell of the lime and tequila was off-putting to Jules. She barely touched hers.

"Any sign of Rob yet?" she ventured.

Mia compressed her lips and shook her head. She reached for her margarita and took a liberal slug of it. "So what's happening with Rhett?"

Jules cracked her neck and placed another label. She smoothed it down. "He's . . . annoying."

Mia cast her a sidelong glance. "Seems to be staying for a while."

"Yeah. Camping out at the firehouse, instead of going home to Silverlake Ranch."

"He and Declan . . . will they ever patch things up?"

"No idea. But in the meantime, he's driving me crazy."

Mia lifted a reddish eyebrow.

For some reason, Jules found herself blushing. She could feel the heat rising from her neck all the way to her forehead. "He stayed for dinner tonight at my parents' house."

"Did he?" Mia waited.

Jules outwaited her, the silence stretching.

"Uh-huh. You still have that thing for him," Mia finally said, placing three colorful polished river rocks artistically in the top of one of her candles. They would glow, adding charm and luster when it was lit.

"I do not."

"Whatever you say. You sure came back in a terrible mood after Dallas. Did your meeting fall through? Weren't you going to have dinner with him there, or something?"

"Didn't feel like it."

"When are you going to tell me what happened?" Mia could be ruthless.

"Have you tried rosemary in the candles?"

"It's for the lotion. Nice subject change."

Jules sighed. "Fine. I did have dinner with him. And . . . you know."

Mia's eyes widened. "You did not!"

"I did. It was . . . disappointing." *It's only half a lie. The morning was.*

"Bull."

"That's all I have to say."

Mia evaluated her frankly. "It may be all you have to say, but you are withholding something big. Let me guess: He pulled the Grady card."

"Aaaaaagh." Jules took a swig of the unwanted margarita and squinted balefully at her friend.

"I knew it."

The tequila burned an acid trail down her throat. "Got any munchies?"

"No. At least not the salty, fattening kind that you want—only celery, carrots, or fruit. And I'm not done asking you Rhett-orical questions, girlfriend." Mia grinned.

"Yes, you are. At least if you want my help packaging the next nine hundred of these obnoxious little lip glosses, you are."

"Fine."

"Mia, why not have a bunch of girls over to help you? We could make a party of it."

"Believe me, I've thought about it. But then word will get out about the house . . . I can't have that."

Jules shook her head. "So you'd rather that people just think you're snotty and won't invite them over?"

Mia sighed. "Yeah. The truth is too embarrassing."

"We could do it somewhere else, then. Kristina's kitchen at Piece A Cake? C'mon. You need help—more than I can give you—especially if you want your products ready for Fool Fest."

"Kristina's got her own production issues for Fool Fest. I can't ask her."

"So you're going to work your nursing shifts and take care of your in-home patients and stay up until all hours doing this . . . until you drop?"

Mia shrugged. "I don't really have a choice."

"I'll be over again tomorrow night," Jules informed her, eyeing the endless rows of tiny plastic jars. "You have to sleep sometime."

Tears welled in her friend's eyes. "Thank you."

"Stop it." Jules slid off her stool and wrapped her arms around Mia. "Shut up and drink your margarita."

Mia hugged her back. "Okay. If you insist."

CHAPTER 20

Rhett stood, hands on his hips, surveying the area that would become the new indoor riding ring at the Holt Stables. It would back right up to the barn. Massive piles of two-by-fours lay at each corner of the ring, along with extension cords, sawhorses, tarps, toolboxes, nail guns, and everything else imaginable that a construction crew might need to frame out the building. He'd gotten a work crew in a few days ago to sink the posts in cement.

Jules had avoided him as much as possible for the last several days, which was downright confusing, considering that she'd planted a kiss on him. When they had run into each other, they both ignored the tension spiraling between them.

She was busy now corralling the horses and that donkey of hers in one of the far paddocks, so that they'd be away from the noise and chaos of today's work party.

Rhett didn't know how Declan had gotten the memo, but he showed up for Saturday's work party, too, along with Jake and Grady and the rest of the Fire and Rescue squad not on shift. He'd barely acknowledged Rhett and was inspecting the French drain along the barn wall. Drainage was crucial.

Jake was reviewing the plans. Grady, Rafi, and Mick had gotten to work marking and measuring.

Lila, Charlie, and a bunch of their friends set up the "party" portion of work party.

Apparently, there was going to be quite a spread, because they already had a table containing a massive catering carafe of coffee and two boxes of pastries in addition to a series of wrapped platters and drink coolers being arranged on a second folding table.

"Hey." Lila came over to elbow Rhett and shoved a cup of coffee and a plate holding a pastry at his stomach. "Declan hasn't eaten anything yet."

Rhett stared down at the food. "Can you please stop trying to force this? Declan and I are miles apart and there is no pastry on the planet that is going to fix that right now."

"It's a raspberry Danish from Piece A Cake," Lila said. "It might."

Rhett sighed and took the food from his sister, who used her free hand to grab a second cup of coffee. Rhett growled more than sighed this time and gingerly added the second cup to his haul. Cursing under his breath as the coffee sloshed over his fingers, he made his way across the grass to his brother.

"From Lila," he said, holding out the food to Declan, who'd evidently approved the drain and was now at the compound miter saw.

Declan grunted by way of thanks. He accepted the coffee and took a sip.

The two men drank coffee in a silence that might have been halfway to okay, were it not for Rhett's memories. "Do you remember the summer Grady finally bought a dirt bike with his savings?"

Deck cracked a smile. "He called us up and told us to bring Pop's tools. The three of us were going to *clean it up a bit,* as I recall."

"Yeah. I'll never forget the look on his face when we got here. He was so excited. I think it was just about here . . ." Rhett pointed to a grassy knoll behind them. "That's where the guy unloaded this heap of scrap metal. He'd convinced Grady it was a legit fixer-upper."

"I remember standing by the stables when that guy peeled away in his truck as fast as he could, before we could stop him and get Grady's money back."

"That thing was a piece of crap," Rhett said.

"Yeah. I thought Grady was gonna cry," Deck said. The two men laughed softly.

Rhett realized they'd both finished their coffees already. He looked to where the firefighters were trooping away from Lila's refreshment stand, putting on work gloves, getting down to business.

Lila was standing next to the coffee carafe, sipping at a cup, watching her brothers. She gestured like a referee for them to *continue play.*

"Thanks for the coffee," Deck muttered. He

walked over to a pile of two-by-fours, grabbed a couple, and hauled them to the sawhorses that stood nearby the saw.

Rhett followed him and helped him clamp the wood down in preparation for making the cuts they needed. They put on safety glasses and worked in silence for a few minutes. Then he said, "Used to be, you and I couldn't stop talking."

"I remember." Declan glanced at him, then turned his attention back to the saw.

"I just don't get it," Rhett blurted, after the roar of the thing had subsided. "You'll break your back working on a piece of property that's not even yours, Deck, but you won't so much as have a conversation about rebuilding the Old Barn."

Declan didn't take the bait.

Rhett spat a bit of sawdust out of his mouth and wiped the sweat from his face. "That barn is part of our legacy. I think—"

"How 'bout you shut up or go work in the far corner, little brother," Deck said evenly, unclamping the piece of wood he'd just cut.

Rhett took it from his hands. "How 'bout we just have this out right now," he said just as quietly. "Would it make you feel better to punch the daylights out of me?" He threw down the two-by-four on a pile of others that were trimmed. "What do you *want* from me, Declan? I'm *trying*, here."

Declan turned toward him and whipped off his safety glasses. "Okay, Rhett. Sure. Let's talk. You tell me exactly what it is you're 'trying.' *Out here.* Because it looks to me like you're *out here* trying to one-up me by buying another property. It looks to me like you're out here trying to get in Julianna Holt's pants."

"*What* did you say?"

"It looks to me like you're trying to prove yourself with enough time left over to get back to Dallas for dinner. It looks to me like you're trying to send a message to me and you don't realize the message got through, and you can stop now."

Rhett stared at him, absorbing the bitterness in his tone.

He hates me. My brother hates me.

"If that's how you feel, why did you come here today?" Rhett asked, not working even a little bit to keep the hurt and trauma out of his voice.

"You just don't get it," Deck snapped. "You used to get it, and I miss that guy. It takes heart to make a place like Silverlake or Holt Stables last. It takes dedication." Declan slammed his palm against his chest. "You've got to *be* here, be part of the land. You've got to live it and work it and breathe alongside it."

"If you think I haven't got the heart or the dedication, if you think I'm going back to Dallas, I'll ask you again. Why are you helping me right now?"

Declan put on his safety glasses again, his mouth twisting. "Oh, there's definitely heart, dedication, and a love for the land here, Rhett. In Julianna Holt."

Rhett felt kicked in the stomach.

Deck's eyes narrowed behind the plastic barrier. "I'm here for *Jules*. She's Silverlake through and through. Maybe you went and bought Holt Stables, but this place will always be hers." And with that pronouncement, he turned his back on his brother and fired up the saw again.

Rhett watched his brother work for a few moments, trying to process everything he was—and wasn't—saying. "Deck. Declan!"

His older brother looked up. And when Rhett couldn't find the words immediately, Deck sighed, shook his head, and went back to work, the saw roaring into the silence of everything they couldn't say.

Rhett strode over and clapped him on the shoulder. "No, I'm serious!"

Deck switched off the saw. "*Get off me.* I'm trying to do a job here."

Then the words started pouring out of Rhett. "I don't want to do this with you anymore. I don't want you resenting me; I don't want to resent you. I want to rebuild the Old Barn with you."

Declan blinked.

Rhett saw the anger in him flare, saw his brother hold it back. It was almost comical how much of a struggle the two of them had just trying to stay adult enough not to work it out with their fists.

"Rhett, it's just too late," he said calmly. "It burnt to the ground. Everything's gone. And nobody in the family cares enough to justify rebuilding. Not really. Yeah, it feels bad that it's gone, but that's not the same thing as having a good reason to bring it back. Lila's over it and she's already getting other business for herself. Ace was never coming back anyway. Jake's heart will always be with the fire squad. And it's nice that you say you wish our family was whole again, but you're just going to turn around and go back to Dallas. We'll do the phone calls we always do. And eventually I'll kick the bucket, the rest of you will work out a deal to sell, and then nobody will have to do the phone calls, either."

No, no, no—that's not okay. Not what I want.

Rhett felt almost desperate. "I'll give you the money. For the Old Barn."

"It's not about the money!" Declan roared, his voice raw and even louder than the saw had been.

Lila shot them a worried glance.

Rhett advanced on him and shoved his brother with both hands. "*Everything* between us is about the money!"

Declan was clearly not expecting what he got. He stumbled backward, tripped over the saw-horse, and fell to the ground, staring up at Rhett.

Rhett stared down at him. "I'm sor—"

Lila's voice interrupted them. "Okay, hi, yeah, um, no, this was *not* a good idea. My fault! My bad! Everybody up . . ." Her loud stream of consciousness preceded her actual body by several seconds. "You okay, Deck?"

Declan climbed to his feet, ignoring the hand Rhett offered. "I'm fine."

Lila pushed her dark hair out of her face, then made a sound suspiciously like a sniffle. Both men froze.

Rhett stared at her in horror as her eyes got more and more watery. He looked at Declan, who looked equally petrified.

"We're just dealing with some stuff," Declan muttered.

Lila cleared her throat. "Let's not lie, okay? This"—her index finger moved between them— "isn't working at all. So, okay. Rhett was right. I shouldn't have pushed it. We should focus on what we've got, not on what we don't have. And at least we've got Jake back. That's a lot."

Deck looked at Rhett, his forehead wrinkled.

"Let's just . . ." Lila looked behind her, where her friends were all taking seats by the refreshment stand. "Could we not air our dirty laundry? I shouldn't have pushed you two together, and I'm sorry. But this is supposed to be a fun time for everyone." She looked back at Deck. "*Everyone.* Let's try, okay? Please?"

Declan nodded and finally held out his hand to Rhett. Rhett clasped it and shook, but quickly let go. "I'll go back and check on the drainage again," he muttered.

With more than a little relief, Rhett left Lila and Deck and headed toward Grady.

"Hey, Rhett," Lila called out, still struggling to end the tension. "I know what I did wrong. I should have sent the blueberry Danish!"

Rhett produced a chuckle and raised his arm in a wave of acknowledgment, but without looking back.

The ringside lawn chairs were lined up like loungers at some swanky Miami resort, not the hardscrabble Holt Stables in Silverlake, Texas. All they needed was an ocean view and a cabana boy. Scratch that: Jules would take their current view over an ocean any day. And she didn't mind getting her own iced tea, as long as that view was available, shirtless, rock-hard, and sweaty: half the Silverlake Fire and Rescue squad and a couple of off-duty cops, along with Rhett and Declan Braddock.

Yum. Just . . . yum.

Mick was in basketball shorts and nothing much else, his muscular legs taut and toned.

Tommy, in Levi's, had shoulders that were almost wider than he was tall. And the biceps of a Greek god.

Grady, in cargo shorts, didn't count to her, but the other girls followed his every move with rapt appreciation.

Rafi . . . oh my! His cycling shorts were a little revealing for her taste, but she couldn't complain.

Declan's signature red bandanna marked a very fine backside.

Bode Wells and one of his friends both wore standard-issue police department athletic shorts and tees, but the tees seemed to be coming off already . . . Yep, there'd be plenty of distraction were it not for Rhett.

Rhett, in a pair of ratty khaki shorts that were missing a button. Rhett . . . massive shoulders, chest tapering into a hard, flat, cut abdomen. Sweat running in rivulets down his bronzed back.

"This feels so wrong," Jules said, not exactly regretting the fact that she was sprawled in her lawn chair, sipping a cold drink, and watching extremely attractive men go about the business of physical labor—on her behalf. She did feel a little guilty, though.

On one side of her sat Lila. On the other side was Mia, though she had only thirty minutes before her next in-home patient appointment. Charlie and Maggie filled out the row of five lawn chairs. Lila had erected a snack table a few yards away. It was piled high with sandwiches, bags of chips, apples, an assortment of baked goods provided by Jules's mom and Aunt Sue, and three huge coolers filled with iced tea, Gatorade, and water.

They'd only just set it up twenty minutes ago and the spread was gaining longing looks from the men who were busy shoveling and moving soil around, double-checking the drainage, and making sure the ground was level in prep for laying the surface. Was there anything better to gaze upon than a lot of hot, dirty, sweaty men with tools?

And Rhett was one of them. When he looked her way, part of her hoped he was just trying to decide between ham and Swiss or pastrami. The other part of her hoped he wanted her on the menu. *Stop it, Jules.*

"I should go back to work," Jules muttered. "We all should. This is like an old Diet Coke commercial! It's not fair to sit around while they bust their butts."

Nobody moved. Lila gave her a look that said she was crazy, and took a massive bite of sandwich.

"I'm here in case somebody needs medical attention," Mia said with a grin. "So, really, I *am* working."

"I'm just here to stare at Jake," Charlie said.

"I'm equal opportunity; I'm here to stare at all of them. Mick is looking verrry nice today, without clothes," Maggie said, unapologetically. "And I mean this is the absolute first time I've ever seen Rafi with his shirt off. And in full, um, silhouette. I'm not going anywhere."

"You have a thing for Rafi?" Lila asked a little sharply.

"Whoa. I'm just appreciating the view," Maggie said, raising her palms in defense. "Not if *you* have a thing for Rafi."

"*I* don't have a thing for Rafi," Lila said.

"Well, somebody should," Maggie said, her head cocked sideways to fully appreciate everything the firefighter had to offer.

"Maybe *you* should," Charlie said, elbowing Mia.

"Maybe I should deal with my ex first," Mia said mournfully.

Charlie and Lila exchanged bummed-out glances. Jules reached over and squeezed her friend's hand.

"Holy All Things Hot and Irish!" Amelie blurted, walking up. "Declan's looking *divine*."

Lila looked around, saw that Deck was trucking a load of sand across the grass toward the ring area, and then winced. "You're drooling over my brother." She put up a palm to shield Declan Braddock's finely muscled, sweaty torso from her sight. "I can't *even*."

"I could," Maggie said.

"I wish," Mia said.

"I always wondered about you two," Lila said. "Living practically next door and all . . ."

"Just friends," Mia said, waving the idea away. "No chemistry. But I can definitely still appreciate the Braddock glory." She punched Lila lightly in the shoulder. "You okay there?"

"Actually, yeah," Lila said. "It's great he's here. I didn't expect . . . it's just that we've been arguing about rebuilding the Old Barn. I just assumed he wouldn't want to . . . I don't know, I guess I thought it would make him feel sad to come here and do this."

"I don't think your brother is one to spare his own feelings when someone else needs help," Jules pointed out.

"You sound like you know almost as much about the Braddock boys as Lila here," Maggie said, a little too suggestively.

Jules glared at her pal, but it was too late. Lila's head jerked up. "Oh yeah?"

Maggie whistled, the picture of innocence.

"So what happened back there, between Rhett and Declan? Why did Rhett push him?" Jules asked Lila.

"There's always tension between those two," Lila said. "I sort of forced them together, and it was a bad idea. Anyway."

A pause ensued.

"This is business," Lila said, as if testing the concept. Her arm swept outward, gesturing to where Rhett stood with Grady, working on drainage.

"Right," Jules said, finding it slightly difficult to meet Lila's eyes. "Just business." A strange feeling settled in the pit of her stomach when she thought of talking to Bridget and the advice she'd been given. But it wasn't like that now. It wasn't just Jules trying to be nice to stay on Rhett's good side. Truth was, she might have tried, for a hot second, to separate her emotions from the reality of losing her grip on the stables, but her feelings seemed to be just as ornery as ever; Rhett might have disappointed her, but she'd never stopped caring about him. That seemed impossible.

In a sudden panic, Jules tried to catch Maggie's eye. Maggie was the only one here who'd been at the table listening to Bridget's advice that night. *Maggie! It's not like that. It didn't turn out the way I expected. I'm not pretending to care. I don't know how it will end, but if you tell Lila what Bridget advised me to do . . . she might not understand.*

"Just business, huh?" Maggie asked with laughter in her voice. "Keep your friends—" Then she caught Jules's look of distress, because she shut her mouth.

Lila blinked. "Are you and Rhett—"

"Incoming!" hissed Charlie.

The men were coming in for a break as a team. Mick, Rafi, and Grady seemed to be comparing arm bruises. Jake and Rhett were laughing at something. Bode Wells and his buddy were walking in with Declan.

"We need some music," Amelie breathed more than said.

"We need a *breeze*," Lila said.

"And some slow-motion video," Mia added.

Jules sucked in a quick breath; Rhett looked so happy. And in his rattty khakis, he looked so much like his teenage self. Flustered, Jules got up, grabbed a stack of red party cups, and started filling them up. "Who wants water?"

"Yo," Rafi said, reaching out. "Thanks."

"I'll take a Gatorade," Mick said. Jules passed out the filled cups and then it went dead silent as the men tipped their heads back and guzzled their drinks.

Maggie released a long, considering breath of air.

Somebody actually squeaked. Mia, Lila, Charlie? Who could say?

Lila's gaze followed a drop of water as it trailed down Rafi's chest, then arrowed straight down.

"You okay?" Rafi asked, his accent a little thicker than usual.

Lila brought her head up and focused on his eyes. "Fine," she said briskly.

"Gracias," he said with a wink.

Lila swatted his chest and burst into laughter.

CHAPTER 21

Watching the most eligible men in Silverlake work half-naked on behalf of her stables was good for the soul, but Jules was eager to dig in with her own two hands. Sure, she didn't want to lose the momentum from Saturday's work party, but it was more than that. There was nothing she liked better than working outside on a crisp, blue, spring Texas day; Monday was the perfect specimen. And since Rhett had asked her to pull the "fences," or jumps, out of the old riding ring before the work party, she figured that now was as good a time as any to sand and paint them.

So she balanced a long wooden pole on two sawhorses and got to work with her electric sander. The pole had once been painted a cheery red and white, which had faded to a sad, dusty rust and mottled, dirty gray over the years. Jules took the paint completely off, sanding down to bare wood.

The sun was warm on her neck and seeped through the long-sleeved T-shirt she wore. The air was redolent with the scent of mesquite and cedar and the earth around her. Absorbed in her work, brushing away the sawdust that gathered on her plastic goggles, Jules barely noticed as

Scarlett pulled down the gravel drive with Rhett at the wheel. She'd gotten used to seeing his ridiculous car out here . . . and at least riding in it had taken the edge off her dad's cares the other day.

"Need a hand?" Rhett called over the noise of the sander.

She switched it off and raised her eyebrows. He wore a black T-shirt, snug Levi's, and his black boots. He'd settled a pale gray cowboy hat over his head. Had he just stepped out of *GQ* or *Texas Monthly*? Whichever magazine it was, he looked good. Way too good. And nothing like Rhett-the-Suit who'd initially appeared in Silverlake—not a gold cuff link in sight.

Though something inside of her sat up and begged like a dog at the dinner table, she swatted it down with a rolled newspaper to the nose. "No thanks."

Was that disappointment under the day's growth of stubble on his face? "You sure?" he asked. "You've got quite a pile, there."

"You'll get all dirty."

"I like getting dirty." He smiled.

She didn't.

"Why don't you quit fighting me and gimme the sander, Jules? You can start priming the ones you've already done, and we'll finish in half the time. Then we'll get them painted tomorrow."

She wasn't trying to be rude. In fact, the sun

was actually getting to her a little and she had the extreme urge to crawl into bed for a bit. But she just didn't want to be around him. He knocked her off-kilter. He always had, and he always would. But it was worse since that kiss the other day, the one Dad had interrupted. It was so much easier to be angry at Rhett than to be attracted to him. Desire for him led nowhere good. Nowhere good at all.

Jules slipped off the goggles and gently smacked the business end of the sander into his chest, leaving a rectangle of sawdust on his black T-shirt. She grinned.

"Nice," he said.

"Always."

"You're getting sunburnt," he told her, and dropped his cowboy hat over her head.

She was absurdly touched. Touched in the head, probably.

Half an hour later, Rhett's black T-shirt was soaked through. He switched off the sander, set it down, and grabbed the hem of the shirt with both hands, tugging it upward.

"What—what are you doing?" she asked, alarmed.

"What does it look like?" Off came the shirt, whipping over his head and sailing down to the grass next to them. "This is sweaty work."

It was one thing to watch him shirtless at a distance, but this was up close and too personal.

Jules swallowed and looked everywhere, any-where, but at Rhett Braddock's bare chest. His bare arms, bronzed by the sun and cut with muscle. She resumed applying the primer to a pole.

"Jules?"

"Hmm?"

"You've already painted that one." His voice rumbled with amusement.

"What? Oh. Well, it needed another coat," she said, flustered.

"Is there some reason why you're keeping your head down and refusing to look at me?"

"Yes. You're . . . half-naked."

"And that's a problem for you?"

"No—why would it be a problem?" Somewhat desperately, she met his gaze. And then . . . then, go figure, but her own gaze slipped south. To his chiseled lips, the stubble on his stubborn chin, and lower still to his pecs and—*dear Lord, that was more of a twelve-pack than a six-pack at the abs—and—no! Stop at the belt buckle and move up again, Jules. Eyes up. Back to his, which are crinkling at the edges in a most annoying and oh-so-sexy way . . .*

She had to speak—say something—do something—*anything*. Anything to break this unbearable tension between them. Tension that could be chased away only by—

"What changed you so much?" Jules blurted.

The crinkles around Rhett's eyes disappeared. "Huh?"

"It's you. This is the you I grew up with. Followed around, like a puppy. Who is that other guy? The one in the suit? Where'd he come from?"

Rhett shrugged and set down the sander. "He . . . evolved."

"From?"

He leaned back against the wall of the barn and folded his arms over those magnificent chest muscles, glowing with sweat. "Imagine what happens, Jules, when a kid from rural Texas trudges, in his western boots and his Wranglers and his pearl-snap-buttoned shirt and his belt buckle the size of a dinner plate, into a fancy East Coast prep school."

"I don't know."

"D'you think those kids welcome him with open arms? Ask him for a good barbecue recipe?"

His face had gone completely blank. "I'm guessing not."

"Not. Exactly. Those kids are more likely to open with a snicker, scale up to outright mocking, and finish with shoving that kid's face into a urinal. And that's just for starters, darlin'. That's just the first day or two."

"Oh, Rhett. I'm sorry . . ."

"Then they find out that he goes by 'Rhett.' And it gets nothin' but worse. Maybe they dogpile on him and pound on him until he agrees to holler, 'Scarlett, save me!' just to get them off him. Just to breathe. And then that goes round the whole school, and there's more snickering and more dog-piling."

Horrified, all she could do was stare at him.

"And next thing you know, the kid's got his head jammed into a toilet, and maybe not so clean a toilet. And he gets real, real sick of all of this, so he learns to fight back. And fight hard. Sometimes dirty. Like the day he gets some good blackmail on his rat roommate—and says he'll keep quiet if the roommate will loan him some clothes that don't make him stick out like a nerd's Adam's apple in a herd full of no-neck jocks."

"So that's how it started," she said quietly. "As camouflage."

"You bet. Couldn't have said it better myself. Camo." Rhett's blue eyes had gone hard and cold. "Now they treat me differently. Suck up to me for donations and blather on about school spirit. Ain't that grand?"

"Wasn't there any adult you could go to?" Jules ventured. "Anyone who could help?"

Rhett snorted. "The only thing worse than a redneck in a place like that is a snitch. I'd rather have died than report them."

"Did Grady know?"

"Some. My brother Declan knew—I called

him weekly to beg to come home. No dice."

"I'm sure Deck thought he was doing the right thing . . ."

Rhett's face darkened. "You know what? Let's get back to work. You got the answer to your question."

Jules fidgeted. "I'm sorry. I didn't mean to bring back bad memories."

His expression softened. "I know you didn't. None of that has anything to do with you."

She stole another look at his chest as he picked up the sander.

"Jules?"

"Yeah?"

"You'd better stop looking at me that way, honey, or I'm gonna have to take you into the barn and do some real wicked things to you." He winked.

She gaped at him. Then, mortified, she fled.

Was that soft laughter she heard from Rhett as he watched her go?

It seemed like hardly any time had passed at all before Jules stood, hands on hips, unable to believe her eyes. Her much-longed-for indoor riding ring stood before her: a simple construct of hunter green–painted steel arches with a sturdy aluminum roof laid over them.

Rhett had ordered the parts from somewhere, a massive freight truck had delivered them, and then a crane, a construction crew, and half the Silverlake Fire and Rescue squad had shown up again to erect it.

She couldn't believe how fast it had gone up— like an oversized Lego project.

It gleamed before her now in the spring sunshine, the sky above it cloudless and heartbreaker-blue. It was a testament to the power of dreams.

As she drank in the sight, she felt both giddy and annoyed. And then guilty and ungrateful for feeling annoyed. It was so beautiful, and it truly would triple her business, and . . . *Rhett* had made this happen, not her. Rhett, with his masses of money.

"Like it?" he asked from behind her right shoulder.

"How did you order a *building?*"

He shrugged. "Pretty simple, really."

"How much did it cost?"

"Does it matter?"

"Yes."

"Okay. Let's see . . . with the labor and materials, around seventy-five K. The office that's going in next will add to the total. But all said and done, less than a hundred thousand."

His tone was so casual. So matter-of-fact.

"I'm gonna have to give a lot of lessons and train a lot of hunter-jumpers to pay that back."

Rhett was quiet for a moment. "I wish you wouldn't look at things that way."

"What way? Hard? As if this is a business?"

"You know it's more than that." He caught a flyaway strand of her hair and brushed it behind her ear, sending a delicious, dangerous shiver throughout her body.

She stepped back. "What is it you want from me, Rhett?"

"Nothing."

"That's not true. I can feel the lie. So what do you want?"

A long pause ensued as he evaluated her. "To make you happy," he said at last. He set his hands on her shoulders and turned her toward the indoor arena again, where another dump truck had just pulled up, loaded with more sand for the floor. "Does that make you happy?"

She'd wanted this for so long. It was beautiful. Tears welled in her eyes, and despite her best efforts, she couldn't hold them in. They spilled down her cheeks as the sand spilled out of the dump truck and onto the packed dirt floor of the ring. She nodded. Tried to swallow the lump in her throat.

"Hey . . . oh, hey . . . what . . . ? Why are you crying?" Rhett took her face in his big, warm hands. "What have I done now?" He brushed away her tears with his thumbs.

"Everything," she managed.

"And that's bad?"

"Probably."

"I really do not understand." He stared help-lessly at her.

"I know." She dredged up a smile.

Rhett pulled her into his arms and held her tightly, despite a whistle from the dump truck driver. "Can you help me to understand?"

"It's complicated." She sniffled.

"Try me. I do complicated well."

"Fine. For example: I do not want to be in your arms right now."

He stiffened and tried to drop them, tried to pull away.

She hung on to him. "But it feels so good when I am."

He froze.

"I want to hate you, but I can't. Especially when you do things like"—she gestured at the indoor arena—"like this! How am I supposed to hate you?"

"Uh . . ."

"But then I tell myself that it's easy for you to order a building, and that to you, it actually seems inexpensive. So it really doesn't mean much, right?"

"Jules."

"But to me, it means *everything,* and I'm not okay with that!"

"With what?"

"With owing you."

"You don't. You're overthinking things."

"But—"

He lowered his head and placed his mouth firmly over hers. Warmth flooded her as she fell headlong into the kiss, and as Rhett backed her against the fence, the dump truck reversed, too, beeping as it changed course, getting ready to head back into town. The driver whistled again.

Neither Rhett nor Jules paid any attention.

"I got some champagne," he said huskily when they finally came up for air. "To celebrate. This should be pretty decent stuff."

"I wouldn't know good champagne from shampoo," Jules admitted.

"Well, then, maybe it's time you had some. C'mon." Rhett tugged her by the hand, over to where Scarlett was parked near the barn. He opened her passenger door, and there—in a silver ice bucket, no less—was a bottle chilling. Rhett grabbed it, along with two flutes from a lined box. And before she knew it they were in the cool dimness of the barn, where Blossom and Don Quixote observed them idly as they sank down together on the cement step that led to the tack room.

Rhett popped the cork, and several more equine noses popped out of the stalls to see what was happening. Inquiring minds.

He poured the pale liquid gold into the glasses, bubbles rushing euphorically to the surface. "To your indoor riding ring, Jules." He handed her a glass.

Don Qui tossed his head and twitched his muzzle, displaying his toothy grin.

"I think he wants some," she said, inclining her head toward him.

"He's not getting fine champagne. He can have some beer, along with Frost."

"Yeah, so . . . it seems to me that if we get bubbles, they should *all* get suds. You know—a pony keg." She grinned at him.

Rhett groaned and clinked her glass against his.

"I had to," she said apologetically. Then she raised the flute to her lips. The champagne flirted its way across her tongue, bubbles sparkling and celebrating before slipping down her throat. One sip was like . . . a gala.

"And I have to do this," Rhett said. He kissed her again, champagne on his lips. "And this." He took her glass, and set both flutes down on the floor of the barn. Then he picked her up, ignoring her startled laughter, and took her into the tack room, where he set her down astride a western saddle on a stand.

"What are you—" she began, but his mouth stopped the question. His hands began to answer it, cupping her face, moving down her neck, over her shoulders, and then farther south. Unbuttoning and unzipping things that should have stayed buttoned and zipped.

Jules found herself not caring about *should*s at the moment. But—

"Rhett," she said against his mouth. "What if somebody . . . ?"

"I don't give a damn," he murmured, with a smile so full of wicked intimacy and tenderness that it arrested any further thought. "I need to see you on this saddle without any clothes on."

"You do?" she said breathlessly.

"Yes, ma'am." He took her into his arms and kicked the door to the tack room closed.

It was a good thing that horses—and donkeys—couldn't tell any tales.

They drank the rest of the champagne in the tack room as the sun set, Jules wearing his shirt and not much else besides beard-burn.

Rhett's dark hair was mussed and his eyes had gone a shade closer to navy in the encroaching shadows. "You're so beautiful," he murmured, reaching for her hand.

"You need glasses," she teased.

"Nope." His expression changed, darkened. He closed his eyes. "What I do need to do is talk to Grady. Somehow make this right with him . . ."

"Excuse me?" Jules set her flute down with a snap. "You need to leave Grady out of this. It's none of his business."

"He won't see it that way," Rhett said ruefully.

"I am not his property. I'm my own person."

She got to her feet, picking up her scattered clothing. She slipped out of Rhett's shirt and dropped it on the saddle. "Why can't you see me as separate from him?"

"Jules—"

"I'm sick of being treated as if I belong to my brother, or my dad, or anyone other than myself. It's so offensive."

"C'mon, don't be this way."

"We're done, here, Rhett. I've got to feed and water the horses, anyway."

"Jules."

"This is a complete repeat of Dallas! Where you almost chewed off your arm to get away from me."

"That's not true. Can we talk about this?"

"No," she said, her clothes now back on. "Sorry. I'm not in the mood to talk. I've said it before and I'll say it again, Rhett Braddock: Get out of my barn." She jammed her feet into her rubber boots.

He sighed heavily as she walked away.

CHAPTER 22

Rhett had a restless night. *Choose,* Jules had said. *Me or Grady?* Impossible choice.

Jules or Grady? Grady or Jules?

Both Grady *and* Jules. There had to be a way. He just had to figure out how to broach the subject with Grady.

Unfortunately, he was stuck in Sunny's Side Up waiting for Lila, who had called at the crack of dawn to demand a meeting. This couldn't be good.

Six thirty-five A.M. Rhett checked his watch again as he sat in a booth with his cup of coffee, the ceramic rooster planter that held silver and napkins, and the red-checked tablecloth for company. "Don't keep me waiting!" his sister had said.

Something was off: Sunny was looking more thunderous than anything else, and had been downright curt when he walked in. Where was her warm smile? Where was her cozy motherliness?

Finally, Lila, looking uncharacteristically disheveled, raced into Sunny's. If she hadn't already alarmed Rhett with her early-morning call and the clipped request—really an order—that he meet her at the diner for breakfast, "Now. ASAP. Pronto!" he'd certainly be concerned now.

She held the door open and peered inside. And then when she registered him at his table, her eyes widened and she beelined right to the open bench seat in front of him.

She slammed both hands on the table and leaned toward Rhett. "I need coffee."

Rhett pushed his own mug closer so she wouldn't have to wait, even though Sunny was already heading over with her carafe. "Okay," Rhett said calmly. "Now you're freaking me out."

"I'm freaking *you* out?" *Slurp.* "I'm freaking *you* out?" *Slurp.*

Sunny jingled her way over, several spangly bracelets knocking against the coffeepot as she poured Lila her own cup. "Mornin,' " she said to Lila, in a considerably more friendly voice than the one she'd used on Rhett earlier.

"Morning," Lila replied, and then took a swig of the fresh coffee with her right hand while still clutching Rhett's mug with her left. He gently disengaged her hand and took his coffee back.

Okay, well, something was up. *What's it gonna be, ladies? A speech about how I'm being too showy in town or a speech about how I should visit Declan more often or a speech about how I haven't been inside my own darn family house in all this time . . . ?*

Lila and Sunny seemed to be engaged in some nonverbal communication that involved Sunny raising her eyebrows in a questioning sort of way and Lila shrugging her shoulders in a worried sort of way.

Rhett sighed. "Lila, no offense, but why are we here? Is this about Declan?"

Sunny leaned forward just slightly; Lila cleared her throat and asked Sunny for an omelet with about seven different fillings. Rhett narrowed his eyes at Sunny's retreating back, something sinking inside.

With her hands cradling the coffee mug, Lila exhaled loudly and said, "At least ninety-eight percent of the stupid things *I* do are a complete accident."

Rhett blurted out a laugh, but his sister didn't join in.

"I got a call this morning," Lila said. "I got a call from a friend who got a call from a friend who got a call—"

"From a friend," Rhett said impatiently. "Are you okay?"

Bam! Bam! Bam! went Sunny's cleaver. From the corner of his eye Rhett watched Sunny cutting up the peppers and onions and all the other things Lila had asked for to make an overstuffed omelet clearly designed more for privacy than for taste. "I'm fine."

Bam! Bam! Bam! A scraping sound came next, and then the sizzling of something hitting hot butter.

There was a beat of silence. Staring at Lila's

face, Rhett's heartbeat quickened. "Why do you look like you're in some kind of agony right now?" he asked quietly.

"Tell me you're not that guy," Lila said.

Sizzle!

"Rhett, what did you do to Jules?" his sister blurted.

High-pressure deals with high-powered people tended to teach you a few things about how to react in surprising situations. Maybe it was the way she phrased it, as if she was too ready to believe the worst. Or maybe he was just so caught unawares by the prospect that Jules—knowing exactly what could happen—clearly hadn't kept her word about keeping what they'd had together a secret.

Rhett just stared at his sister; not saying a word.

"That came out horribly," Lila said, her panic manifesting in the form of removing napkin after napkin from the silver canister sitting next to the salt and pepper. "There seem to be a couple of different versions of a story that's creeping around town this morning."

Sunny surged out of the kitchen. "It ain't creepin', hon. It's flyin' like buzzards to a fresh carcass."

Rhett flinched as Sunny set down the biggest, cheesiest, most excessive omelet he'd ever seen in his life right between them. His eyes went back to Lila's face. Her stare hadn't faltered, and she kept her eyes on his even as she felt around the table for two forks and plunged them deep into the heart of the omelet between them. "Did you seduce Julianna Holt in Dallas?"

Sunny hadn't moved.

"Uh . . ." He glanced up at her. "Could we have a moment?"

Looking put out, she retreated to the kitchen.

Rhett leaned back in his seat. "*Seduce* Jules? She's smarter than that!" he repeated in outrage. "It wasn't like that!"

Lila's eyes widened. "Oh boy."

He leaned in close and whispered through gritted teeth, "It wasn't a *seduction*. It was like . . . it was like . . ."

Lila leaned in close, too, and whispered, "Like what, Rhett?"

"It was like we fell in love with each other for a night!" he blurted.

Lila sat bolt upright. She blinked rapidly, apparently processing her brother's words. And then she wrinkled her brow. And then she said, "Huh." And then her features softened as she looked into Rhett's eyes again. "That is so not what I expected you to say," she said.

I guess I know what you expected. The same thing everybody in my family expects. Rich big-city jerk swaggering around and damn the consequences. Rhett slumped back against the bench seat.

"You fell in love with her for a night," Lila murmured into her fork. "Ain't that a thing. That's about the nicest description of a one-night stand I've ever heard."

"Well, it's the best I can describe it." *It's true. I fell in love with her for a night. Why doesn't that sound all wrong?*

"You've got a huge problem, bro."

"She must have said something," Rhett muttered. *Darn it, Jules, why? Why would you do that? You said you wouldn't!*

"Er, I don't know. There are a couple of pretty wild versions out there."

"Like what?" Rhett braced himself.

Lila unstuck the fork nearest to her and pulled out a steaming glob of cheesy eggs. Through a very cheesy mouth she asked, "Did you promise her you wouldn't buy the ranch if she slept with you and then renege?"

"What?"

"I didn't think so. I'm just saying there're a couple of bizarre versions."

Rhett swore a blue streak. "Versions that paint me as a pretty terrible person! Holy—"

He couldn't even find the words.

"Don't worry. I'll help you with damage control. We're a family and we're going to take care of this," Lila said.

"That's sweet," Rhett said not very sweetly at all, as the likely repercussions of these rumors began to sink in. *I've got to get to Grady and explain.*

"I'll get the town phone tree," Lila said. "We can stop the rumors."

"A phone tree!" Rhett snapped, starting to lose his cool. "A *phone tree?* And where, exactly does Grady Holt fall on the phone tree, Lila? Do you think if you call Mrs. Lundgren and she calls Dottie at the Grab n' Go and she calls Maggie Cooper and so on, maybe someone can tell Grady not to hate me by noon?" He stood up. "This can't wait. I need to talk to him before he hears the wrong story from someone else."

Lila's eyes narrowed. "Shouldn't you also be worried about where Jules falls?"

"She's the one who told somebody, Lila. I can choose not to be mad at her for that, but I don't have to worry about her feelings right now, either." Rhett pulled his car keys from his pocket. He ran for the exit, realizing that Sunny was holding the door open for him. He half expected the darn thing to swing shut and hit him on the way out. He jumped into Scarlett and turned on the ignition.

In the passenger seat was the silk-lined box containing the champagne flutes, and on the floor rested the silver ice bucket. He would never forget that interlude between them, and how happy he'd been to make her so happy. Rhett took his hand off the keys and sat very still for a moment, pulling himself together. *I fell in love with her for a night* . . . What if they had more than just one night?

What if he came clean with Grady and told him the truth. That, yeah, there was a moment. And he shouldn't have done it. But he did, and what he'd discovered . . . what he'd discovered was that he'd like to make a go of it with her.

And maybe, just maybe . . . that's how Jules felt, too. Why else would she have said something? If she didn't want this to happen . . . ? Maybe she *did* want this to happen. It was bass-ackward and she should have known better, but maybe she wasn't thinking clearly. He smiled to himself, reliving the scene in the barn yesterday. Chemistry like that might well cause a person to rethink a policy on second chances.

An immense sense of relief came over Rhett as he sat in his car. Yeah, Grady was going to be mad. But he'd see that Rhett cared about Jules. And Jules, maybe Jules had prepped him, maybe he was expecting Rhett to come ask permission to date her, and then all would be forgiven. Yeah, that was a completely reasonable scenario.

If he could just get to Grady before someone told him about the stupid rumors that he and Jules slept together in Dallas, everything would be fine.

CHAPTER 23

Jules awoke on Aunt Sue's sofa, exhausted and unmotivated to move at all. She had fed the horses last night after Rhett's departure and tried to sort through her feelings about what had happened between them. She'd put aside her fear; her vulnerability—she'd opened herself to Rhett—only to have the specter of Grady ruin everything for the second time.

She'd ignored the peculiar, knowing gaze of Don Qui, who'd clearly been either a sage or a therapist in another lifetime. *Just tell him yourself,* Don Qui seemed to say. *Yeah, so easy.*

Still in a foul mood, she'd taken a pizza to Aunt Sue's, refused to talk about what was bothering her, and crashed on the sofa fully dressed.

She'd always been a high-energy person, in almost constant, restless movement. So the constant fatigue she'd been battling recently was foreign and unwelcome. No matter how many cups of coffee she drank, she couldn't seem to shake it off. And the coffee made her feel sick.

Once again, she sprinted for the bathroom, wondering what kind of flu lasted forever.

Denial was a powerful thing. So it took a personality like Aunt Sue's to whack Jules over the head with the truth.

Jules was curled in a ball in front of the fireplace, on Sue's quilt-covered sofa with Sue's fat gray cat, Stinky, when her aunt delivered the blow.

"You're pregnant," she said matter-of-factly.

Jules bolted upright, dislodging Stinky, who almost fell to the floor. "*What?* No." She shook her head, which sloshed her brain from side to side.

"Yep."

A disgruntled Stinky reestablished his position against her thigh, plopping down with a disgusted yellow stare.

"Why would you say that, Aunt Sue? That's ridiculous . . ." Jules felt a blush starting to spread over her chest, then creep up her neck.

"You're tired, greenish in the face, and feeling sick all the time. My guess is that it wasn't an immaculate conception, and that it took place about eight weeks ago, right around the time you took that hunter-jumper up to Dallas."

Jules opened and then closed her mouth, like a guppy.

"So you know who the daddy is."

The blush warmed Jules's cheeks.

"Don't you, darlin'? And I know who the daddy is, too . . . Last name rhymes with *paddock*. First name: I-don't-give-a-damn."

"Uh," said Jules eloquently.

"I knew it. As I've already pointed out, you've had a crush on that boy since you were a kid," Aunt Sue declared.

"That's not true!"

"Do not even *try* your lies on me, girl."

Jules stayed silent.

"By the way, Sunny called me and the entire town thinks you slept with Rhett in Dallas. Wild rumors are flying."

"What? *How?* Oh my God . . . my parents? Do they know?"

"I don't think anyone would dare call your mother. My guess is that your parents are still in the dark. Now, have you been to a doctor? Have you gotten a test? Are you taking prenatal vitamins?"

Jules pulled her guppy maneuver again.

"Talk to me, honey. You done any of that?"

Wordlessly, Jules shook her head. "And I cannot go to our family doctor. *He* would tell Mom, patient rights notwithstanding."

"All right, then. Finish that tea and we'll go see your friend Mia at Mercy Hospital. I'll call ahead. I'm sure she'll slip you a test stick. If it's a yes, she'll take it from there."

"Now?"

"Is there a better time? You want to lie to yourself until the baby crowns?"

"Crowns?"

"Oh, dear Lord, girl." Sue shook her head. "We are gonna have to get you a book."

"I could just get a pregnancy test at the pharmacy."

"Sure you could. And Bert Phelps would tell everyone from the mayor to the vet to the butcher."

Too true. Jules mechanically raised her mug to her lips and swallowed some of the tepid peppermint tea it held. Then she sprang to her feet and fled for the bathroom as the tea decided to come up again and not go down.

As they sped off in Aunt Sue's turquoise Karmann Ghia, Jules held a Tupperware bowl in her lap in case of more nausea and tried not to give in to the tears that threatened.

"Did you not take sex ed in high school?" Sue asked. "Ever heard of birth control?"

"We used a condom," Jules retorted.

"Did you put it on the right part of him?"

"Yes!"

"Not on his nose?"

"Why are you heckling me?"

"You call this heckling? This is affectionate teasing. When it happened to *me,* I got called a little whore, was stuffed into a borrowed wedding gown that I hated, and was married off by a sour-puss pastor to a prize pig. You know the rest of the story."

"Yes, Aunt Sue, I know it."

"Don't do any of that. Do not accept the label, the white wedding, *or* the pig. Especially not the pig. Got it?"

"Yeah," Jules said wretchedly. "Got it."

• • •

Our Lady of Mercy Hospital loomed in front of them as they drove into the parking lot, Jules feeling that she should arrive, sirens blaring, in an ambulance for emotional emergencies, rather than a funky turquoise Karmann Ghia. But Aunt Sue was more likely to slap her upside the head with a wet trout than coddle her and put her in a wheelchair and ask about her feelings.

She marched her inside, down the depressing, beige-tiled hallway and into an elevator, Jules feeling as sickly green as the walls. The hospital always hummed with a variety of technology and smelled of bleach, illness, and, weirdly, Band-Aids.

Mia was on the second floor at the nurses' station, and quickly ushered her into an examination room. She pulled a pharmacy pregnancy stick from the pocket of her scrubs and pointed Jules toward the bathroom across the hall.

Jules walked in, feeling as if she were underwater. Everything had slowed down, details and sounds were muted, and her own thoughts felt mired in molasses. She stared at the face reflected in the bathroom mirror and found it difficult to connect it with her own. Then she stared at her belly in the mirror, lifting up her shirt in an aghast sort of wonder. She knew Aunt Sue was right. She knew without doing the test. But she took it anyway.

When Jules emerged with it, she refused to look. She just handed it to her friend, her lips moving in a silent prayer that she was wrong.

"It's positive," said Mia, a little blankly. "I'll draw blood and we'll test that way, too. But there's not a doubt in my mind, Jules." Mia set a hand on her shoulder and squeezed. "You're pregnant."

Jules stared at her dear friend. Mia's warm cinnamon brown eyes held empathy . . . and something else. Something she seemed ashamed of.

Jules couldn't quite put her finger on it until she realized it was envy. Longing.

Oh God. She was an idiot. Friend or not—of all the nurses to let Sue drag her to, Mia was the very last one . . . Mia and Rob had tried to conceive for more than five years, before he'd filed for divorce and run off to South America.

"Will you excuse me for a moment?" Mia's lips were trembling almost imperceptibly. But as her friend, Jules saw it.

"Mia, I'm . . . I'm so sorry," Jules blurted. "I didn't think. I should have—"

"Be right back!" Mia said in overly bright tones. And she vanished behind the door in a blur of green scrubs.

"Oh Lord," Sue closed her eyes. "I s'pose I should have driven you to Austin or San Antone.

Didn't think, in the heat of the moment. That poor girl."

Jules hadn't thought she could feel worse. She stared at her feet in their battered blue flip-flops. A normal woman would have on some pretty toenail polish, but she hardly ever wore anything but those knee-length rubber barn boots, and nobody saw her feet. Besides, she was more likely to give a horse a pedicure than get one herself.

"Well," Sue reflected, "in a perfect world, you'd have the baby and hand it over to Mia."

Jules gaped at her, processing her words. "That's . . . that's a brilliant idea."

"Is it?" Sue peered at her.

"Yes," Jules said slowly. "I think it is. How am I going to raise this baby? How am I going to take care of it?"

"Money won't be an issue," Sue said, a bit acerbically. "Rhett can sell his flashy car and set you up for the next twenty years."

"That's not what I mean. What do I have to offer anyone as a parent? I forget to take care of my own self—and Mom takes any excuse to remind me."

Sue rubbed at her eyes. "You know your mother isn't going to react well to this news."

Jules wanted to hurl all over again at the idea of having to tell her very conservative, Southern Baptist parents that she'd gotten "nekked" with Rhett Braddock. And that they hadn't even been dating. That it had been a sleazy one-night stand.

"Aunt Sue, I don't even know how to tell them. Will *you* tell Mom and Dad for me?"

Her aunt paused for a moment, then shook her head. She leaned forward and took Jules's hand in both of hers. "No, honey. That is one conversation that you have to have face-to-face with them. I can't do it for you, and you know it. This is about their daughter and their grandchild. You'll have to break the news on your own. Maybe Grady can stand beside you."

"Grady," Jules moaned. "He's going to kill Rhett with his bare hands! I can't tell Grady."

"Well, now. That is another wrinkle," Aunt Sue said.

"Wrinkle? It's an entire, wadded-up sheet!" Jules buried her face in her hands.

"All right, calm down. First things first. You'll have a conversation with Ever-Rhett. How he handles this will most likely determine how Grady handles him."

"Okay, okay." Jules shifted her weight, crackling the paper on the padded examination table. She stood up, slid off it, and paced the small room. "How do I tell him? Invite him for coffee? Or just tell him in the tack room and watch him fall off his chair?"

The door opened and Mia came bustling back in. Her nose was pink under the freckles, and her eyes suspiciously watery. Her mouth was set in a determined smile, though—and it was the smile that broke Jules's heart.

"Here's a starter package of neonatal vitamins. Get some more at the pharmacy. And—"

"Ugh—what's that glass tube for?"

"Jules, I know you're not a fan of needles, but I have to draw blood in order to do the official test. So just shut your eyes and take your mind somewhere else, okay?"

Jules looked at the vial again, at the little rubber hose, at the hypodermic needle and the alcohol wipe in Mia's hands. "I'm gonna be sick again," she said to nobody in particular.

"Back up on the table," Mia said, patting it. Then she slipped on thin rubber gloves. "Come on."

"If I even see that needle, I will faint."

"That's why you're going to keep your eyes closed. It's an order, Holt. Now, get back up here and stop being a chicken." Mia smiled to soften the words.

Jules gulped and climbed back onto the padded examination table.

"Give me your arm. And look at that diagram on the wall."

"The one with all the intestines and organs and whatnot?"

"Yes. Look at the human stomach. Imagine it's yours, with an entire Chocolate-Cherry Cake from Kristina's inside. Ganache frosting. Extra whipped cream."

"Yum."

"Now close your eyes . . ."

Jules did.

Mia swabbed her with the alcohol wipe.

"Chocolate-Cherry Cake," Jules repeated. And then there was the barest pinch.

"Good. Keep those eyes closed."

Jules did.

"There's vanilla ice cream, too. Also Kristina's, from Piece A Cake. The soft, creamy kind with real particles of vanilla bean in it."

"Mmm."

A pause came, then another pinch, then pressure. "Hold this on."

Jules did. Then she made the mistake of opening her eyes, saw a large vial of her own blood in Mia's gloved hands, and got woozy. "I'm gonna—"

"You're fine. Look at me. Did I say you could open those peepers?"

"No."

"So shut them again, if you need to. But you're fine," Mia repeated, marking *Holt, J.* on the vial.

"Mia, *you* should have this baby," Jules blurted.

Her friend froze. "That's not an option," she said crisply, stowing the vial in her shirt pocket and stripping off the gloves.

"What if it is?"

Mia, her face utterly blank, dropped the gloves in a waste-disposal unit. "Jules, you cannot say things like that to me unless you really, truly mean them."

"What if I do?"

"You haven't had a chance to think this through. And there's the question of the baby's father. Rhett's got rights here. He gets a say. So you can't just . . . just . . ." Mia looked at the ceiling, blinking rapidly.

"But—" Jules felt even worse than she had earlier, if that was possible.

"You *cannot* get my hopes up like this. It's not fair. It's actually cruel." Mia headed for the door again and pulled it open. "Take those prenatals. I have another patient to see now."

"Mia—"

"Gotta go." And her friend, valiantly holding back tears, shut the door behind her.

"That went well," said Aunt Sue.

"I am a human train wreck," Jules wailed. "Why does everything I touch go to—"

"Shh," Sue said soothingly.

"*It!?*" Jules moaned.

CHAPTER 24

Jules had never before regarded her mother's blue and white kitchen as a cross between a courtroom and a guillotine. Today was different, though. Today, she could practically see Judge Judy about to spring out of the fridge in black robes, wielding a gavel and a pithy opinion. And she'd swear that the French Revolution's Madame Defarge and her knitting lurked in the pie safe, waiting to collect one more head in a basket: Jules's own.

She considered quick options for offing herself in order to avoid this conversation. No time for the head-in-the-oven routine. There was hara-kiri by electric carving knife. Or drinking anti-bacterial spray. Perhaps death by stand mixer?

Billy and Helen Holt sat at the kitchen table across from Jules, looking bewildered.

"What's this about, honey?" Dad asked.

P is for *pregnant*.

R is for *ruh-roh*, as Scooby would say.

E is for *embarrassed*.

G is for *Grady* and *gun*.

N is for *not good*.

A is for *awful*.

N is also for *naked*.

T is for *time to speak*: unfortunately, NOW.

"Julianna?" Her mother raised her eyebrows.

Jules fidgeted. Flexed her foot against the leg of the oak table, as she used to do when in trouble as a child. "I'm, uh . . . There's no easy way to say this. Mom and Dad, I'm pregnant."

"What?" Billy said, stunned.

"But you're not married!" Helen exclaimed.

"Who's the father?" Dad demanded.

Mom's expression conveyed pure horror. "We brought you up better than this, Julianna."

"I'm going to have the baby," she said.

"We're going to be grandparents," Dad said, wonder in his tone.

"I'm not *old enough* to be a grandmother." Mom sounded flabbergasted.

"I'm only at around two months, so don't go telling a bunch of people—especially not Grady. I'll tell him. You two are the first to know." *Besides Sue and Mia and pretty much all of Silverlake now.*

"What about the father?" Dad asked again.

"Who *is* the father?" Mom pushed for the answer again.

Jules took a deep breath. "That's not really important—"

"The heck it's not!" Dad stood up, looking furious all of a sudden.

"Billy, calm down, honey." Mom turned from him to her daughter, smoothing her hair reflexively. "Has the father asked you to—"

Jules cut Mom off. "He's not really a part of my life." *First blatant lie.* "So he doesn't know, yet. I just found out myself."

"Not a part of your life," Mom repeated, freshly scandalized. "Who—what—what are people going to think? How did this happen if he's *not a part of your life?*"

Jules took another deep breath. "The usual way."

Billy Holt squeezed his eyes tightly shut. "I'm gonna kill 'im."

No, Grady will take care of that for you.

"I knew I shouldn't have let her outta the house until she was fifty," Dad said. "I'll kill 'im."

"Dad, I hate to break it to you," Jules said, "but I *have* had sex before now."

There was a horrified silence.

"Don't you talk to me about that," he said through gritted teeth.

"You know what?" Jules asked. "It disgusts me to think about you and Mom doing it, too."

Her father reared back. "We are married folks."

"Billy! Hush *up*," snapped Mom, turning fuchsia.

"You are *not*," Dad said pointedly to Jules.

"And I don't want to be. All I'm saying is that you'd have . . . um . . . more than one guy to kill. So don't bother killing this particular one. Okay?"

It was Dad's turn to change colors. His shade was more purple.

Mom announced, "I'm taking you to see Pastor Hines."

"No. I'd rather talk to Duncan Hines."

"How dare you joke at a time like this?"

"Who said I was joking? Look, I know you two still think I'm five years old, but, Guess what? I've drunk alcohol before, too. I even tried a little—"

Her father yelled, "I don't want to know!"

Jules blinked at him. He never shouted at anyone. "Okay. But my point is: I vote. I drive. I manage the barn. I'm an adult."

"Well, you don't manage your affairs like one," Mom said.

"It's the new millennium, Mom. Single women do have children. Nobody locks them up for it."

Billy Holt went quiet all of a sudden. "Here it is, Jules: If you do not tell us who the father is, right now, then you are adult enough to move off our property and find your own place. Is that clear?"

"Crystal," said Jules.

Dad slammed out the door and Mom burst into tears and ran to the bedroom. Jules stood for a moment in the silence of the kitchen and then went to pack a bag, preparing for a long stay at Aunt Sue's. Nobody was around when she left the house and headed out in a kind of daze to the stables for work. An immense feeling of relief swept over her when she stepped inside her refuge. She greeted Don Qui with a carrot and a kiss and began to trundle the wheelbarrow full of hay down the length of the barn, stopping to pitch some into each stall. But halfway down, something about the smell of the hay hit her wrong, and she gagged. Then, feeling dizzy, she braced herself on the low door to Blossom's stall.

The big chestnut eyed her curiously and came over to nose her.

"Hey, girl," she said weakly. She put out a hand to stroke her. And then she caught a whiff of the pile in the corner of her stall and dropped to her knees, her stomach heaving and her face suddenly slick with sweat. She heard steps behind her.

When she turned around, her brother was standing there, all six foot six inches of him. "Jules? What are you doing . . . and why?" Grady, the biggest, smartest teddy bear of a brother—and the very last person she could confide in.

"Nothing!" she said brightly. "Aren't you supposed to be at work?"

"Yeah, but I heard some—"

She swayed as another wave of nausea hit her due to the smell of the manure. "Excuse me." She got to her feet and tried to pass her brother.

Grady put a gentle hand on her shoulder to stop her, but on his face was an expression like thunder. "You're sweating, you're close to fainting . . . you're scaring me," he said through gritted teeth. "Do you need a doctor? Want me to call Mia?"

The truth just sat there on her tongue.

"Jules," he said, his voice cracking slightly. "Is something wrong with you? You gotta tell me. With Dad battling a tumor . . ."

Oh God. She couldn't have Grady worrying that it was something that bad. "No, it's not like that. It's not bad. I mean, it's not *good* . . . not exactly. Not that it's *not,* if you really think about it . . ." *Huh.* "It's just bad in almost every way . . . but not *every* way . . ." Okay, that did not go a long way toward putting Grady at ease. Jules closed her eyes, shook her head, and tried to pull herself together. "I'm going to be fine. My stomach is very upset. I haven't been eating enough." All true things.

"You think I'm an idiot," Grady said.

"I do not think you're an idiot."

"You must think I'm *some* kind of an idiot." His eyes narrowed.

"I do not," Jules said, desperately attempting to edge down the side of the wall to get away from her brother. Then she thought better of it, because that awful feeling was coming back and the bathroom was the opposite way. She stopped moving. "You're especially good at math."

"I *am* very good at math." Grady had a funny look on his face and there was no way she was asking why.

"Can we finish this conversation later?" Jules asked desperately.

"You saw Rhett in early March. I asked you to go check on him, and you saw him. Last month in Dallas."

Oh no. "Yep. And can I just say that the top of March can be a terrible month for visiting Dallas? It was super chilly. Makes you just want to stay in bed all day under . . . the . . . blankets . . ."

A muscle in Grady's jaw flinched. "The boys told me a kind of funny story this morning. Figured it was a mistake. Small-town gossip and all that. But it made me want to come by and see how you were doing, just the same," he said pointedly. There was a long pause.

Jules started to sweat again. "I don't feel good," she whispered.

"You and Rhett've been awful close since he's been in town," Grady said.

"Well, you may have heard we sold our family business to him." Jules tried to laugh. She sounded like a cat with a hairball.

"Jules," Grady said very, very quietly. "Tell me nothing happened with Rhett while you were in Dallas."

"Nothing happened." She glanced up to see if he'd bought it. Not a chance.

"Did Rhett . . ." Grady couldn't finish his own sentence at first. "Did Rhett . . . ?"

Jules's head was swimming; she felt dizzy. She couldn't think. So she shrugged.

"That's what happened? It's worse than I

thought!" Suddenly, it was Grady who looked like he wanted to throw up. "That sack of—" he said, in a voice full of anguish. "He's my *best friend*. You're my *sister*." He focused back on Jules, who was seriously considering just sitting down on the ground.

"Jules, look at me," her brother said. "Are you pregnant?"

Jules's eyes filled with tears.

"I'm going to kill him," Grady said. "With my bare hands." Grady punched the wall between the tack room and the bathroom. Hard. "Doing this to you. Keeping this from me."

"You're not killing anyone. He doesn't know, Grady."

"What? How can he not know?"

"We weren't in touch after," she said miserably. "And I only found out recently."

"Let me get this straight," Grady said in dangerous tones. "When you say you 'weren't in touch after,' are you saying that he didn't even call you afterward?"

Jules's stomach lurched. "It doesn't matter." Jules threw up her hands. "We all know he's going back to Dallas."

"The hell it doesn't matter!"

"Grady, stop. I have to work with him. And I don't want to talk about this. Just leave it alone, okay?"

"Are you kidding me? It's not like you had a

bad day. You're pregnant, and it's Rhett's doin'!"

"Keep it *down,* will you? I'm not ready to tell anyone."

"The whole town is sure ready to listen!" Grady ran his hand down his face. "Okay, right. Not helpful. Forget the whole town for a sec. What're you planning to do?"

She raised her chin defiantly. "What do you think? I'm having the baby."

Relief, shock, and concern filled Grady's eyes in equal measure. He took a deep breath, like he was settling himself. And then he nodded. "Okay."

Her brother's easy acceptance made her want to cry. "I know it's a big deal," she said, waiting for more Mom-and-Dad-style fireworks.

"I know it, too," he said, his voice gentle now. "But if you say you wanna do this, we're gonna do this."

Oh, Grady. Thank *you.*

"You're great with animals," he continued, "so I figure you'll be a natural mother."

Jules gulped. She had her doubts.

Grady gestured to the land, looked over to the main house. "Do Mom and Dad know?"

"I just told them."

"I'm sure that was a fun conversation."

"Not exactly."

"All right. Well. No matter how upset they are, we've got a tight family and everything you need. So, c'mere, sis. You look like you could use a hug."

Absolutely true. She went to him and laid her head on his broad chest while his arms encircled her. And then she knew; the reason he was so calm for her was because he was saving all the rest of it up for Rhett.

"It's all gonna be okay," Grady murmured as he patted her back.

"Let me talk to Rhett first," she mumbled into his chest.

"It's all gonna be okay," her brother said in the same soothing voice. But she could feel the tension, the rage in the bunched muscles of his arms. "It's all gonna be okay."

"Yeah," she breathed.

If only she could believe that. Alarmed, she pulled her head up. "You gotta let me talk to Rhett first," she repeated.

Grady just smiled. And that's when Jules threw up all over his boots.

CHAPTER 25

Rhett felt like he'd been driving around Silverlake forever. Grady wasn't at the firehouse. Rafi said he'd swapped shifts with him. This didn't give Rhett pause until Rafi narrowed his eyes and added something in Spanish that Rhett couldn't understand. The tone was enough to make him take advantage of Scarlett's acceleration on his way up to the Holt Stables.

It was a relief when Rhett'd taken maybe six steps toward the barn and Grady appeared out of nowhere. Rhett relaxed a little when he saw that his best friend looked calm, though it was odd that he was still in his uniform even though he'd swapped shifts with Rafi.

Rhett gave him a wave. "Hey, man, I've been looking for you." *Okay, this was going to be hard, but at least—*

"And I've been looking for you," Grady said.

The blow came out of nowhere. It slammed like a wrecking ball into Rhett's jaw and felled him to the dirt. Rhett had always appreciated the deep blue of a Texas Hill Country sky, but he couldn't recall ever seeing it from behind stars—or from a supine position on his back in the dirt with the thunderous expression of his best friend looming over him.

"Give me one reason I shouldn't kill you right now," Grady growled.

Grady had somehow found out about the one-night stand in Dallas.

"One reason!" roared Grady.

Rhett rubbed at his jaw. He couldn't think of one. What he'd done had broken the guy code. It had broken his own moral code. He truly hadn't meant to go there.

Jules. Sweet, hot, bourbon-laced handfuls of Jules . . . What had he been thinking?

He hadn't been. It had all been primal instinct: *Want. Mine. Now.*

"Get up!" Grady ordered. "Back on your feet. I am going to friggin' take you apart."

Rhett struggled up onto his elbows. "I'm sorry, man. It wasn't—"

"You're sorry?!" Grady erupted into a blue streak of cussing. "Get up!"

Rhett stood up, wincing. He didn't even brush the dust off his clothes. He just braced himself for the next blow.

All six foot six inches of Grady was shaking with rage. "You knock up my sister, and you kick her to the curb? *No,* man—" He drew his enormous fist back again.

Knock up? Rhett stared at him blankly. "What did you say?"

And then another wrecking ball hit his left eye and he went flying backward yet again, ass over teakettle.

The deep blue country sky turned black.

Grady had fists like granite. Rhett opened his eyes. Well, one of them. And from it he saw Jules hovering over him with bloody gauze in her hand, rhythmically dabbing around the eye that wouldn't open. To his surprise, Beast was seated next to him, whining and occasionally shoving her nose into his neck, which involved a lot of slobber.

Behind Jules stood her brother, looking like a massive, mean old hound himself, his arms crossed over his chest, his lip curled.

Beast turned and growled at Grady, then subsided under his glare.

Rhett couldn't quite put the pieces together but Jules's eyes looked red, as if she'd been crying. And that fist Grady was flexing . . . those were bloody knuckles.

"Jules," Rhett said weakly.

"You got about fifteen minutes before Declan gets here to pick up his trash," Grady's voice said.

Oh no. Not Declan. "Call Jake . . ." Rhett croaked.

"Jake's on duty. Looks like you're getting only tough love today, because I'm not bugging Lila with this BS." Grady stepped out of view and a door slammed.

Jules cupped Rhett's face tenderly. "I'm so sorry," she whispered. "I tried to stop him."

She looked like an angel. An angel with rooster feathers sprouting from her head.

Rhett closed his eye again because when she moved, the sun hit it full force. He put a hand to his jaw and winced. It was very possibly broken.

Jules carefully settled a bag of ice onto his busted-up jaw, and he hissed with the pain.

"Thank you." He opened his eye again, and got a heavenly scoop of cleavage as her T-shirt gaped open. *Thanks for that, too.*

"Poor Rhett," she said, leaning forward even more.

Lucky Rhett. He tried to grin again.

"I'm so sorry," Jules said again. "I tried to stop him. But he guessed. And he reacted."

"Ha. Can't blame him. I'da done the same. I kinda deserve it."

"No. You don't. I mean, you did . . . but you don't, now. If that makes any sense."

"Not really." Rhett sighed. Put up his hand again to wipe away a trickle of blood that ran from his mouth down onto his neck.

"I just mean—" Jules began again.

Rhett groaned. "I should have told him. I should have found a way." And then it all came roaring back into his mind. *You knock up my sister . . .*

Rhett pulled his hand away from Jules's hair. "Jules?"

She moistened her lips but didn't say anything.

"You're *pregnant?* You should have told me." He cleared his throat but it was still gravel when he said, "You didn't see fit to tell me about my own baby?"

"I . . . I haven't known that long. Maybe. I've been in denial."

"When would you have told me?"

Jules swallowed and then shrugged.

She didn't want him for more than she'd already gotten. She didn't care if he even stayed in Silverlake. Story of his life.

"Right," Rhett said, doing his best to keep the bitterness inside, along with the shock. "I don't really understand what sort of man you think I am, Julianna Holt."

She swallowed but didn't say a word. Did she notice she'd pressed her hand to her belly? Rhett watched her splayed fingers, shook up by the intense joy rocking through him. Jules's face, though, didn't look joyous.

He ducked his head so she wouldn't see how hurt he was. Not the cuts and bruises that Grady had left behind. His heart.

Silverlake was nothing but pain for him. He'd fooled himself into thinking he could belong again, be part of what was special about this place and the people. And once again, what he had to offer wasn't what anybody wanted, beyond what his wallet could provide.

Rhett sighed. If Jules was pregnant with his child, she could have his wallet and anything else that would help her in this situation. He would do the right thing, here. Right now, in fact.

"You don't need to worry about how things are going to be," Rhett said, forcing his voice to steady. "I'm offering you my name and my hand. I'll do right by you and this baby. You'll want for nothing. Send you as much money as you need. I can go back to Dallas, come out on the weekends. It's more than I got from my dad for the last part of my life. And no reason to wait on getting married. I don't like to think of you fielding all those looks and rumors you're gonna get . . ."

Jules was looking at him as if he'd sprouted three horns in the middle of his forehead. But he kept on talking. "Julianna Holt, will you marry me?"

After a moment of shocked silence, she said, "That's . . . that's very . . . um, appreciated. But you're not yourself right now, Rhett. You've taken some big blows to the head."

She doesn't get it. I've got to make her understand.

Declan chose that moment to drive up in his Silverado and Grady came out of the barn to meet him, his body language tense and towering.

Great *timing, bro.* "I'm serious, Jules." Rhett struggled to sit up and finally succeeded in propping himself up against the garbage can that stood outside the barn.

"Rhett—" She shook her head. "Don't."

"But, Jules—" Rhett said desperately.

Grady and Declan headed toward them. "Jules, get lost," Grady called out. "Declan's got this."

"Jules, *Will you marry me?*" Rhett asked again.

"Shut up," she said, just as desperately. *"Please."*

His brother picked up the pace and suddenly he was beside Rhett, taking quick inventory of the mess of his face. "Aw, hell," Deck muttered.

"Jules!" Grady barked, catching up and placing one proprietary hand on his sister's shoulder. "Let's go inside."

Rhett reached out for her. She had one hand pressed against her temple, the other on her stomach. She looked completely stunned. "Jules," he whispered.

"No, Rhett!"

Rhett slumped back as Grady led a dazed Jules away. Ironically, he wished again for the sweet oblivion of Grady's fist.

CHAPTER 26

Jules desperately needed to be alone. She pulled away from Grady and ran around the barn, the heels of her rubber boots thudding dully against the earth, more sharply on the flagstones that formed the path back to the trailer that was no longer hers now. She hurtled through the door anyway and threw herself on the single bed without bothering to take off the boots. Beast, who'd followed her, lay down beside the bed and whined.

Rhett had asked her to marry him. Unbelievable.

He'd looked horrific. Eye swollen shut and turning a dark plum color. Blood in his mouth, between his teeth, as if he'd just ripped into some kind of prey.

My fantasy zombie proposal.

She closed her eyes and tried to swallow a rising hysteria. How many times, as a preteen girl, had she imagined Rhett proposing to her? On a mountaintop, or with a banner flying out behind a private plane? In front of millions of people at a Super Bowl game?

And instead of a ring on her finger at that moment, she'd had a Ziploc bag of ice held to his jaw. *God, you certainly do work in mysterious ways . . .*

How many times as a teenager had she imagined

330

marrying Rhett Braddock? And here he was, proposing to her for real.

Except in those fantasy proposals, at those fantasy weddings, he'd always dropped to one knee and told her how much he loved her. He hadn't suggested a business deal in response to an accidental pregnancy.

Jules placed her hand on her belly only half consciously. Would this baby have Rhett's blue eyes and dark hair? His stubborn chin? His genius brain?

Would the baby be a boy? Or an adorable little girl that she could dress in frilly pink things that she wouldn't touch with a barge pole for herself? She couldn't help but smile at that.

She saw Rhett's grin again as he'd asked her, showing his gruesome, bloody teeth again, not understanding that his usual megawatt smile wasn't doing him any favors.

The hysteria at the sheer awfulness of the situation, the wrongness of it, the irony of it— the hysteria could no longer be denied. Horrible giggles burst from her throat as tears streamed down her cheeks.

She stared at the wall opposite her, in disbelief that she found herself in this situation. The very same situation that Sue had been in, all those years ago. Feeling that she had to marry someone who didn't love her. Because of an accidental pregnancy.

And it had ended in total disaster.

Jules stared more closely at the wall. This was the very same space her aunt had occupied when she'd made the decision to protect herself and her child. The wall, obviously, had been rebuilt after the tragedy.

A lot of people probably wouldn't have wanted to live here. But Jules hadn't thought much about it. Or about how she'd always gone to Aunt Sue's, and Sue had never come here over the years. Not once.

Sue, too, had rebuilt herself. But at what cost? She didn't really talk about it, aside from vague references. She'd never gotten married again. Why not?

Jules rolled off the bed, grabbed her keys and backpack, and headed out to ask her. It was time she and her aunt had a real talk.

She found Aunt Sue on her knees in the vegetable patch behind her little house. Her white hair hung in a braid down her back, and a cowboy hat sat on her head. She wore a denim skirt with a long-sleeved, pale blue T-shirt and a western suede vest over that. Nothing on her feet. As usual, Aunt Sue was barefoot when at home.

"Hi, hon." She shot Jules an appraising glance. "You seem . . . rattled."

"Go figure. Grady just punched out Rhett, who regained consciousness and proposed to me."

Sue put down her trowel and set her dirty hands on her knees. "Tell me you said no."

"I said no." Jules met her gaze miserably. "Of course I said no."

"Good girl. The last thing you need on top of everything else is an unhappy marriage." She got ponderously to her feet and brushed the dirt off her hands, then wiped them on an old hand towel lying on a wooden bench. "It makes things worse, not better."

"Do you ever wish you'd said no, back then?" Jules ventured.

Sue's head snapped back. "Of course I do. I wish I'd told everyone to go to hell. Wish I'd run for the hills." She took off the hat and turned it in her hands.

"But you didn't."

"I was a coward. If I had said one simple, two-letter word, none of what followed would have happened." Sue stepped into the kitchen and set the hat down on the table. "None of it."

Jules followed her.

"He wouldn't have felt trapped and desperate. He wouldn't have been drinking so much to drown his emotions. Wouldn't have felt the urge to take his fear and rage out on me. It all could have been averted—if I'd just said no."

Jules put a hand on her arm. "He could have said no, too, Aunt Sue."

Sue laughed bitterly and shook her head. "He

was on the wrong end of a shotgun. That's how it all started. And ended. Same gun."

Jules sucked in a breath.

"So it really did come down to me," Sue repeated. "If I'd just said no . . ."

"You're not being fair to yourself. You were a teenager being ganged up on by your family and a pastor, and it was a different time."

Her aunt was silent. Headed for the coffee-maker. Turned her back on Jules.

"You also weren't responsible for his actions; you weren't responsible for his temper or his violence. His abuse."

"I know. Coffee, hon?"

"No, thanks."

"Yeah, I think I'll go straight for the Baileys myself." Her hands shook as she retrieved the bottle, poured some into a glass over ice, then added a touch of milk.

"What happened to all of that guilt-is-a-useless-emotion stuff?" Jules asked.

"This isn't guilt. It's pragmatism."

"Sure sounds a lot like guilt to me." Jules struggled with her next question. She shouldn't ask it. "Would you do it again?"

Sue took a gulp of her Baileys and went quiet. "With that shotgun in my hands," she said, "I felt powerful for the first time. Able to control the situation. I was . . . exultant. Loving the power. I felt strong." She took another gulp of the Baileys.

"I told him to stay away from me. To get back. To leave."

"Good for you."

"But I also took the opportunity to tell him exactly what I thought of him. That he was a lowlife, a coward, a drunk. I made him even angrier. Called him a fool, too." Sue upended the Baileys and poured another.

"So . . ."

"So." Sue's mouth worked. "I was stupid. And I was right. Only a fool grabs the wrong end of a shotgun. Happened so fast. And then . . ." Tears filled her eyes. "Then he was . . . in pieces. The wall shattered. Blood . . . everywhere." The ice in her glass rattled as her hands shook.

"Oh, Aunt Sue." Jules wrapped her arms around her, squeezed her, rubbed her back.

"Would I do it again, you ask?" Sue choked on a dry sob. "The answer to that question is that I should have said no to the marriage. And I have to take responsibility for that."

"Okay, but you were a pregnant teenager from a conservative, religious family. And he'd knocked you around, he'd kicked you in the stomach while you were pregnant! He'd tried to hurt the baby."

Sue nodded. "Yes. But what I did—it didn't save her. If I had just said no to the marriage, if I'd just gone off somewhere on my own . . . then she'd be alive today." She broke down. "So promise me, Julianna, promise me. You will not get married under these circumstances. I know you have feelings for Rhett. But marriage is a big decision, a complicated one. It's not a Band-Aid, and nobody should pressure you into it."

CHAPTER 27

He still couldn't quite believe it. Nobody said no to him, not anymore.

Rhett stared into space as now Declan instead of Jules held the bag of ice to his face.

She was really turning down everything he offered. Rhett told himself he was too numb to care, anyway. A lie. But lies were better than the truth right now. That she didn't want him, didn't need him, didn't love him. Did anybody?

"Ready to go yet?" Deck asked gruffly. "I'm feeling motivated to get off Holt land at the moment."

Rhett nodded. He struggled to his feet, Declan suddenly at his side, propping him up.

"I messed up but good," Rhett whispered.

"Grady doesn't have a scratch on him—did you miss?" Declan asked.

Rhett shook his head. "I let him do it. Didn't take a swing at him."

Deck stared at him as if he'd sprouted antennae. "You *what?*"

"I deserved it. I'd let him do it again."

"Well, hell, Rhett," Declan said, leading him out to his Silverado. "There is clearly some story here that you may want to share with me."

"Not hardly."

Declan got him settled in the passenger seat; Rhett let his head loll back against the headrest. Grady's left hook was legendary for a reason, and Rhett's head ached even more than his jaw or the cuts on his face.

Deck shook his head and shut the door for him.

Rhett didn't want to talk, and Declan seemed to understand. The ride was a lot of jostling and bumping, courtesy of some sections of road that needed repaving. All the while Rhett got to enjoy a soundtrack of Declan muttering a string of barely intelligible words and phrases. The ones Rhett could decipher were all swear words.

"It's not Grady's fault," Rhett finally muttered.

Declan turned, his face full of fury. "I try not to act without thinking, Rhett, I really do. Try not to say things without thinking . . ."

Rhett braced himself to take whatever Declan was about to dish out.

"But I swear to you"—Declan's hands tightened on the steering wheel—"Grady better steer clear for a while, 'cause I'd like to show *him* what you get when you treat my brother the way he's treated you."

Rhett's mouth dropped open and then slowly closed as he managed a smile through his bloody teeth and busted lip. Declan looked like a ball of righteous indignation spoiling for a fight. For *him*.

What would he say when he found out why

Grady was mad or how Rhett had messed up with Jules?

"What are you looking at?" Deck asked gruffly. "I don't know why everybody thinks I'm such an angel."

"Aw, give me a break," Rhett said. "You're Silverlake's patron saint of neighborly kindness."

"No wonder I'm single," Declan said. "Sounds boring as hell."

They'd reached the crossroads where the road to the Holt Stables split off with the main road toward town and Silverlake Ranch after that. Declan slowed down, and then came to a stop, the truck idling at the Y. Rhett looked over in confusion, because, dear Lord, all he wanted was to lie down, close his eyes, and make everything go away.

"Where do you want to go?" Declan asked.

"To bed."

Declan sighed, staring straight out the windshield. "Firehouse or the ranch."

"Ranch," Rhett said.

"Probably a good call. Grady might have gone to the firehouse," Declan said, nudging the accelerator.

That's not why I picked it.

That said, if Rhett thought he was looking at some peace and quiet, the better call might have been a noisy, crowded firehouse full of people who wanted to punch his lights out. There were two new vehicles in the parking area by the main house and two more Braddocks standing on the porch waiting as Declan's SUV pulled in. *Oh, no.* Lila kept her own hours, but Jake must have traded shifts to come home. Both of them looked serious.

Small town, serious faces. They knew.

Wonderful.

"Looks like the cavalry's here," Declan said.

"You *know*," Rhett said to Declan. "You knew about Jules when you said you'd stand up for me."

"I'll always stand up for you," Declan said. "You're my brother." He got out of the car before Rhett could answer and opened the door. His head still swam as he awkwardly lowered himself out of the vehicle and then suddenly there was Jake on one side and Declan on the other and Lila holding open the heavy double oak doors to their home.

Their *home.*

The old wagon wheel still hung to the right of the doors, and Pop's old bootjack nestled under a rustic bench that Deck had probably made, stained, and sealed himself.

His brothers got him arranged on the brown leather couch in the great room, where Rhett drank in the gold and green vista of the land before he turned to stare into the massive field-stone fireplace. The logs in it blazed; the flames full of heartache, rejection, and memories of better times.

Over the mantel hung that same wedding portrait of Mama and Pop; Mama with that mysterious, secretive little smile of hers and Pop looking proud and challenging—as if saying to the world, *This woman is mine, from this day forward. Mine alone.*

Rhett swallowed a lump in his throat. How he still missed them both. They'd all been in denial after the head-on accident that killed them both. Rhett had "seen" both his parents in crowds for months afterward. Mama—he'd sworn he'd seen her in Griggs' Grocers, picking through the apples one morning. And Pop—at the old Sinclair gas station, where Rhett, as a kid, had always loved the green dinosaur on the sign.

He'd "seen" them on the old porch swing, too, where they'd liked to sit on spring evenings, before it got hotter than the devil's own pitchfork in the Texas summers.

The last he'd talked to Mama before that fateful day, he'd been in trouble. For eating one of the banana cream parfaits she'd prepared for her Bible study group the next evening. But there'd been *eight* of them . . . and often times a lady or two would have to take a rain check, and so there'd be extras left over. Which sneaky Ace would steal before anyone else could make a move.

• • •

"Everett Steven Braddock!" Mama's last words to him. "For shame. Give me that parfait glass, this instant."

She'd caught him red-handed. With whipped cream still on his upper lip.

"You are on dish duty for the rest of this week, young man. Understand?"

Rhett had nodded. Tried not to laugh at the overly severe expression on her face that told him she was trying not to laugh.

She shook a finger at him. "Do you have something to say to me?"

He'd hung his head. Fingered the yellow banana stain on his T-shirt. "Sorry, Mama. But they looked so good . . . You're such an amazing cook—"

"Don't you try to sweet-talk me."

"But it works." And then he had grinned.

"Out! Get out of my kitchen. And don't come back until all of your homework is done . . ."

Rhett stared out of the plate glass window to the left of the massive oak double front doors. The Braddock land had woken for spring and stretched for miles until it greeted the sky in a sunlit purple-rose as the day drew to a close. The land was a patchwork of different pastures and crops.

There were white-fenced paddocks with a few

horses grazing in them. There were neat furrows marching in orderly battalions toward the gully that fed the stock pond where he could see cattle grazing.

Rhett took in the improvements that Deck had made to the house. The weathered pier-and-beam architecture, the apex of the ceiling soaring twenty-five feet, at least. His brother had left either side of the house an open expanse of glass framed in by the rough cedar walls. Oaks shaded the house to both the left and the right. It was almost like sitting outside, in an elaborate tree house. He felt that he could climb right into the cradling oaks, as they'd done when they were kids.

He remembered the time they'd convinced Lila to climb into a mesh laundry sack, and then hung her from a branch, swinging, for a little too long . . . incredible that Lila would speak to any of them today, really.

Something fuzzy and wet nosed under his palm as he lay there: Declan had acquired a dog named Grouchy, who'd escorted him in with a lot of sniffing and tail-wagging. The critter looked like Oscar the Grouch from *Sesame Street*, and Lila had sewn him a "trash can" with a pillow lid. It lay on its side in front of the fireplace.

Rhett scratched Grouchy behind the ears and then with his foot rubbed the dog's belly when Grouchy flopped over and exposed it. And then a cat with a mangy-looking tail walked into the room, walked up to Rhett, and stepped on Grouchy in order to lean over and sniff Rhett's fingers.

Declan, Jake, and Lila came into the room; they'd been talking in low voices in the kitchen.

"Whose cat is this?" Rhett asked.

"Mine," Deck said.

"You have a cat?" Rhett asked in disbelief.

Lila and Jake appeared to suppress smiles.

Declan did not look amused.

"Who is this man and what has he done with my brother?" Rhett asked.

Declan rolled his eyes.

"Want some coffee?" Lila asked.

"Beer?" offered Jake.

"Bourbon?" Deck suggested. "A double?"

"Yeah," Rhett said to Deck. "Thanks. Got that Angel's Envy I sent?"

"Sure thing."

Lila put her hands on her hips. "The prodigal son returns to be a papa?"

Rhett sighed. Trust Lila to be subtle: not. "I'm not prodigal—or if I am, I've earned the right to be. I've made plenty of dough."

Jake eased himself into an armchair and eyed him. "Let's forget about money. Let's go ahead and talk about this elephant in the room, okay?"

"The pregnant one," Deck said, handing Rhett a tumbler full of bourbon and ice.

"Way too much ice, man. Wrong way to serve a high-end bourbon." But he took it.

"Shut up and drink it, Fancy."

"And I doubt that Jules would like being referred to as an elephant." The bourbon slid down his throat like the good Lord in velvet slippers, as Pop would have said. Rhett took another large swallow.

"I meant the topic, not the girl, and you know it."

"She refuses to marry me," Rhett said to nobody in particular. "I did ask."

"Was that before or after Grady pulverized you like a steak?"

"I didn't *know* before he hit me. She hadn't even told me."

Jake folded his arms across his chest and swore softly. "Grady's little sister. How did this happen?"

Rhett looked at him caustically, out of his good eye. The one that Lila hadn't covered with a bag of frozen peas. "The usual way."

"What were you *thinking?*"

"I wasn't. Leastways, not with the big head."

"Idiot," said Lila, but with compassion in her voice. Actual empathy.

Huh.

"What are you going to do?" Declan had returned with two Zilker Parks & Rec pale ales for himself and Jake, and a glass of wine for Lila.

Rhett didn't answer.

Grouchy sniffed the air with great hope, but it got dashed.

"No Hound-Hefeweizen for you, Grouch." Lila scratched him with the toe of her spike-heeled purple boot. "Sorry."

Grouchy looked devastated for all of two seconds and then crawled into his "trash can" headfirst, leaving them all to behold his magnificent hindquarters.

Funny, Rhett felt like doing the same thing. Mooning all of his siblings might feel better than facing them in this situation. Gone was his high-and-mighty stance as their financial benefactor and occasional bully. He was here as the knave of hearts.

He'd gone and knocked up a local girl. Done what Pop had told them all he'd tan their hides for doing. The irony of it just about choked him. So he swallowed more Angel's Envy with too much ice, because there really wasn't much else he could do.

You've taken some big blows to the head . . . Shut up. Please.

He'd asked the girl to marry him and she'd told him to shut up. Really?

That didn't happen to a billionaire every day.

In fact, it was quite possible that he was the one and only billionaire it had *ever* happened to.

An old Southern expression popped into his

mind. *One day a rooster; a feather duster the next.* "All right, everyone. Let's just sit down and talk this through." Declan took charge, since Rhett sure wasn't going to.

"Is Grady ever going to forgive me?" Rhett asked Jake.

Jake cracked his neck and eyed him dubiously.

"Tell him, will you? Tell him I asked Jules to marry me. She said no."

"Yeah. I'll tell him," said Jake. "Do keep in mind, though, that this is your former best friend, a firefighter who owns an ax and has a friend who owns a distillery full of whiskey barrels."

Rhett winced.

"Not helpful, Jake," Lila told him. She sat down on the end of the couch where Rhett's feet were and with strange tenderness pulled off his new Lucchese boots. She set them on the floor and pulled his feet into her lap.

Rhett tried to process that his feet were now actually being *rubbed* by his little sister. Who did, frankly, give a damn. He closed his good eye because it stung with unexpected moisture, and that was unacceptable, unmanly, and virtually un-Texan. They'd all been raised via the John Wayne model of masculinity, and that wasn't going to change no matter how politically incorrect it got. It just was what it was, and they were proud of it. Always would be.

"Who are you, and what have you done with

my little sister?" he asked her, swirling the bourbon in his glass. "The one we hung from the live oak in the laundry bag?"

She grinned. "I'll get you, my pretties, all of you. I will. One day. Just not today."

"Good Lord, how you screeched when the neighbor's dog started nosing your behind through the bag," Declan mused.

"And how *our* behinds burned after Pop got through with us!" Jake put in. "I couldn't sit down for a week."

"I got chocolate pudding," Lila said dreamily. "It was almost worth it."

"Focus, Braddocks," Declan said. "Let's review the situation: Rhett and Julianna Holt are having a baby, God help the poor critter."

"Hey, I resent that," Rhett said.

"Quiet. You're not in charge. We are all four of us going to figure this out. First question: Do you think she'll change her mind about marrying you?"

Rhett thought about that, bitterly. "No. She's made her answer pretty clear."

"All right. Second question: Do you need to see a lawyer?"

Rhett stared at him. "What for?"

"She may sue you for child support."

"I can promise you, Deck, that she will never have to! What are you saying, that I'm some kind of scab? A deadbeat dad? I don't think so.

Jules and the baby will want for *nothing*. Ever."

"No need to be so prickly about it. Third question: Will you stay in Dallas? Would she consider moving there, if so?"

"Jules is no city girl."

"And you've got a company to run there."

"Yeah . . . I can come home—" Rhett stopped. Had he really just referred to Silverlake, Texas, as home? "I can come home every weekend, though."

"Fourth question: Does she *want* to see you every weekend?"

Rhett stared at him.

Declan stared right back. "Valid thing to ask. Will she let you be part of her life?"

"I . . . I don't . . . know."

"Will she sue for full custody? Will you have to sue for part custody?"

Rhett upended his bourbon and set down the tumbler with a snap. He opened and closed his mouth.

"Jake, get him another, will you?" Deck gestured to the glass. "Looks like he needs it."

"I want to be a part of my baby's life," Rhett said. "From the very first second."

"Will she even let you be present at the delivery?"

Rhett's mouth fell open. "Can she stop me?"

"You need to consult a lawyer, Everett." Declan looked as serious as Rhett had ever seen him.

"You may be a big shot, but trust me: On this, you are in over your head. You are a mushroom in the dark, buried in—"

"Got it. Thanks, bro, for pointing that out."

Jake returned and handed Rhett another hefty tumbler of Angel's Envy.

"Thanks."

"You're cut off after that one. You need to figure out all of this," Jake informed him.

"Duly noted," Rhett said wryly.

"He probably shouldn't be drinking at all with a possible concussion, you morons." Lila got up, her wineglass now empty.

"There's nothing wrong with me," Rhett groused.

"Seriously debatable." Jake grinned.

"I'm going to be an auntie!" Lila twirled in a giddy circle. "So I'm going to trade this wine in for a Tito's, rocks."

"Got Deep Eddy," Deck said.

"Okay, that works."

"Hey, do you remember when Pop took us to swim there, at Deep Eddy Pool in Austin?" Jake asked. "That pool was freezing . . . colder than Barton Springs."

"I remember you feeding my Barbie's head into the mouth of your big plastic shark," Lila said, with a dark look at Rhett.

"Was that me?"

"Yes. That was you. And now I will get my

revenge. Can you imagine the fun I'll have with your *baby?*"

Rhett shuddered. "Please, Lila. No matter what we did to you when we were younger . . . please don't do any of it to my kid."

"Mwah ha ha ha!" Her eyes gleamed. "No promises."

"Great. I think I'm going to need another drink," Rhett said.

"Have you even eaten anything?" Lila asked. "I could make you—"

"No!" Jake and Declan said urgently.

"Jeez, you'd think there was something wrong with my cooking." She looked at Jake. "I'm not eating anything Declan could make, so you're it."

"Lucky you. I swapped some fresh eggs and honey for one of Dottie's lasagnas the other day. It's in the fridge," Deck said.

Rhett watched as he lay on the couch while his family went into high gear setting up the meal. Despite the circumstances, the troubling aspects of his situation, the disrespect, and the mock threats, Rhett found himself grateful. He was comfortable and comforted and at home.

Here at Silverlake Ranch . . . which he'd left behind so long ago. Go figure.

"Why do you think Jules said no?" Lila asked Rhett once they were seated and served at the dinner table. That was weird enough in itself: four of the Braddock siblings eating dinner together at the massive walnut table that had been around since Mama and Pop's time. With actual place mats. And napkins—though they were paper, and not the cloth that Mama had always insisted upon.

True, there wasn't anything besides the lasagna, but at least the current crisis had broken the ice among all of them. The lasagna was still cold in the middle, but Rhett felt the warmth of his brothers and sister . . . and marveled at it. Only Ace was missing.

"Why?" Rhett repeated. "Because I acted like an a-hole in Dallas and ran out on her? Because she thinks I'm only proposing because of the baby?"

"But there's more to it?" Lila prodded.

Jake popped a forkful of lasagna into his mouth, eyeing Rhett intently.

He looked back at his brother and nodded in silence.

"How much more?" She was relentless. "Like . . . Charlie-and-Jake more?"

"Maybe," he said cautiously.

Jake's face split into a grin. "That's so awesome."

"It's not at all awesome," Rhett growled. "She turned me down."

Lila jumped back in. "I wonder if it's because her aunt Sue's shotgun wedding—"

"Can you please not use that term?" Rhett said.

"Nobody is holding a gun to my head. I *want* to marry her."

"Why?" Declan asked. "To do the right thing?"

"No. Because I . . . I . . . care for her. And I know we can make it work."

"Anyway," butted in Lila again. "I wonder if it's because Sue Holt's instant marriage ended so badly. And Jules is really close to her aunt."

"The thought had occurred to me," muttered Rhett. "And I don't think Sue cares much for me."

"She sold you boots," Deck pointed out. "She wouldn't have sold you Luccheses if she hated you. She'd have tossed a saddle at your head or chased you out of the shop with one of her jewelry hammers."

Rhett grunted.

"Maybe you should ask her father's permission to marry her," Declan suggested.

"Why?" Lila asked. "That's so old-fashioned."

"It's traditional and classic," Deck said. "Not old-fashioned."

"It's patriarchal," Lila said. "Asking a man for his daughter's hand—as though she's property."

"I think it'd be a nice touch," Jake said. "Talk to Billy. Get him on your side. I'll work on Grady."

Grady. Maybe Grady would speak to him again, if he talked Jules into marrying him.

"How did you end up asking her?" Lila wanted to know.

Rhett shrugged. "Words came out of my mouth. Along with blood."

She stared at him. "Well, maybe that's it. She thinks you only asked because you hit your head, and Grady was standing over you, ready to kill you. Why don't you buy a ring—a really nice one—and do it right? Go down on one knee? The way every girl dreams about?"

Rhett thought about it: Subtract angry, blood-thirsty brother. Try a top-notch restaurant. Produce massive diamond. Make pretty speech while balancing on one knee like a supplicant at the throne of a queen. It could work . . . assuming that he could get her to the restaurant.

"Yes!" Lila jumped to her feet. "And I get to help pick out the ring. I'm thinking emerald cut, at least five carats, with baguettes on either side. That'll tell her you're serious."

CHAPTER 28

How was it that Rhett had noticed almost every new business on Main Street except Stoned?

"You've got to be kidding me," he said, as an over-eager Lila dragged him to the door. "I thought we were in Texas, not Colorado."

She laughed. "Do you know just how upset the town council was over the name? They begged, pleaded, and threatened Monty Bates to change the name . . .

"Monty? The same Monty from grade school?"

Lila nodded. "So he offered 'The Full Monty' instead, and they finally backed down. Then people started coming from as far away as Austin and San Antonio because they loved the name and it made them laugh, which brought more tourism and tax dollars to Silverlake, and the council stopped complaining."

The cannabis references stopped with the shop name, Rhett had to admit. In the windows, and in the expansive glass cases, gemstones of all types winked and sparkled.

Inside the store, one of the most spectacular pieces was a wide, triangular collar in black and white diamonds, which happened to adorn the neck of a tall, elegant, and deeply tanned woman in a dalmatian-print silk blouse. She was probably in her early seventies, and on her finger was a diamond solitaire, the likes of which Rhett had seen only on actresses like Elizabeth Taylor or Kim Kardashian.

But the most astonishing thing about her was her matching dog. Next to the white velvet stool she sat upon was an extremely fat, shiny dalmatian that looked so bored that it didn't even bother to wag its tail when Rhett and Lila walked in. It just yawned.

"That's Cruella," Lila said under her breath. "They grossly overfeed her so she won't eat the neighbor's cats."

"Is that a dog or a cow?"

"Shh. Sophia!" his sister called. "How are you? I've brought you and Monty another customer. This is my brother—"

"Everett," Sophia finished, sliding her derriere off the stool and gliding over like a gazelle. "My word. You look exactly like your mama." She extended her hand.

Blinded by the ice cube on her finger, he nevertheless extended his own hand. "I go by Rhett, ma'am. Have we met before?"

Her mouth quirked. "Indeed we have. I'm Monty's mother. Do you remember a certain soiree that your mama gave at which there was a large and luscious lemon rosemary cake with vanilla cream frost—"

"Oh no. That was yours?" Rhett felt a flush creeping up his neck.

"Yes. That was mine. You and young Andrew thought that since it was in a corner, you could slice off the back quarter of it, pull the vase of flowers closer, and nobody'd be the wiser."

Rhett coughed, the heat reaching his cheeks.

A blond, muscular man in gray slacks and a designer black T-shirt stepped out of the back and eyed him mock-severely. "You also tried to blame it on me, if you recall."

"Monty!" Rhett said, chuckling. "How've you been, man?"

"A lot better than high school . . ."

Monty had had an extremely rough time coming out.

"Thank God it passes," Rhett said fervently. "I didn't have such a great time, either. How's life treating you now?"

"Good, good. Especially since I have a good reason—revenge—to gouge you on a ring." He rubbed his hands together evilly and laughed. "What goes around comes around."

"I'm not sure I like the sound of that," Rhett said, but shrugged.

"So. Julianna Holt, huh?" Monty looked quizzical and all but scratched his head.

"This town," Rhett muttered. "Did someone put it on a billboard somewhere?"

"Dude, between Grady's knuckles and the

grapevine: Sunny, Sue, Dottie, unnamed sources at Mercy—no billboard needed." Monty looked him up and down. "Still sporting the shiner and the chipmunk cheek, I see."

"Yeah."

"Sexy. I'd stay away from Grady for a while. Word is, he's still mad as a rattlesnake in a sack."

Rhett sighed. "Look, that's why I'm here."

Monty raised an eyebrow. "Diamond tennis bracelet for Grady? He's not the type."

"Ha, ha. I need a ring. A really beautiful one. For Jules."

"Yeah. Lila's already briefed me. At least five carats, emerald cut, baguettes on either side. Hang on a sec—"

"I'm really not sure what French bread has to do with anything," Rhett grumbled to Lila.

"A baguette is also a cut of diamond, you moron," she told her brother.

"Would you two care for a glass of wine? Something stronger?" asked Sophia.

"Maker's Mark? The entire bottle?" suggested Rhett.

"He's kidding," said Lila.

"Not so much," he said darkly, as Monty brought out a black velvet tray festooned with ten different rings.

"Ohhhh," Lila breathed. She pounced on one and slid it onto her own finger: a round stone the size of a pearl onion, surrounded by smaller ones.

"That doesn't look like Jules," Rhett said.

"It's fabulous on *moi*, though." She grinned.

He glowered. "Focus, sis."

Monty pushed a different ring toward them: a massive rectangular stone set in platinum with smaller rectangular stones flanking it. "That's what Lila ordered."

Rhett stared at it. The stone was stunning, blazing with fire in the overhead lighting of the jewelry store. "You think Jules would like it?" he asked.

"Trust me," said Lila. "There is no woman on the planet who wouldn't like it. It's *gorgeous*."

He tried to picture Jules digging out a horse stall while wearing a ring like that and couldn't quite manage the visual. But Lila was a girl. She knew the female mind much better than him, that was for sure.

"Let's look at the rest," Monty suggested. "Here's another round stone, brilliant cut. It's spectacular, F in color, flawless."

Rhett shook his head. "Jules is . . . different. I don't see her with a round stone."

"Okay. Here's a marquis cut, three carats, H in color."

"It's nice, but . . ." Rhett waved it away.

Lila tried it on, too. "Stunning," she breathed.

"Put it back," Rhett ordered.

They looked at several more: a pear-shaped stone, a cushion-cut yellow diamond, a princess cut that was flawless in every aspect except that Jules wasn't a princess kind of girl.

"Well, what kind of girl is she?" Lila asked, finally, exasperated.

"She's . . . just Jules," he said. "Unique. Quirky. Unexpected. Prickly. Beautiful without having a clue that she is."

"Why not bring her in to choose a ring herself?" Monty suggested.

"No, no, no, no, no." Lila overrode that. "He needs it for tomorrow evening. He's going to pop the question then, at Jean-Paul's, and—"

"Lila, is it necessary to tell everyone all of my personal business?" Rhett asked.

"Of course it is. We need this to be perfect," she said. "So Jean-Paul needs to know how she likes her steak cooked, and what champagne you want to have, and—"

"What if she orders scallops?"

"You know what I mean! Yes, it's necessary to tell people so that we have all the details right."

"Fine," Rhett said tightly.

"The most important detail here," Monty said, "is what ring size you need?"

"Huh?" Lila and Rhett both looked at him blankly.

"I don't have a clue," Rhett finally said.

"Medium?" Lila guessed.

Monty shook his head. "I'm guessing I'm going to have to give you the idiot discount," he said, trying not to laugh.

"Lila." Rhett squinted at her. "If you can deviously and immediately find out this crucial piece of information, I will buy you any ring in here that you want."

Her eyes gleamed. "Done!"

"Within reason," he amended.

"Uh-uh. No way. No reason. We had a deal. Excuse me. I need to make a call." And with that, Lila stepped out of the shop, her brow knit, clearly motivated to accomplish her mission.

Cruella looked after her and yawned.

Rhett looked at Monty.

Monty looked at Sophia.

"I'd go with the one Lila chose initially," Sophia instructed. "It's truly impossible for any girl not to like that ring."

"Sold, then," said Rhett, without bothering to ask the price. He fished out his Black Card. "Can you size it by tomorrow?"

"For you?" Monty nodded. "I won't even charge you a rush fee . . . since you'll probably already be crying when you see the Amex charge."

Rhett grinned. "Well, at least this should finally make up for that quarter cake you got blamed for, all those years ago."

Sophia slid back up onto her white velvet stool. "Honey, I'm taking a cherry cobbler to the church potluck. How about you go for two thirds of that and feel so guilty you come back for this necklace?"

"I'll think about it," Rhett promised.

He completed the transaction and stepped out of the shop, surprised to see Lila just ending a call on her cell phone. "Hi, bro!" she sang. Highly suspicious.

"What are you up to?" Rhett asked.

"Well. I came up with a surefire way to get Jules's ring size. But there's a small string attached."

"Lila, what—"

"Look, I thought about dragging her bowling and trying to get the size from the holes in the ball. I thought about sneaking in while she was sleeping and tying fishing line around her finger and then cutting it off to measure. But I thought there was a chance Mia would know her size so I called her first, and she didn't know her size but she did tell me that Jules is staying at Sue's because—"

"Lila—what string is attached?"

"—her mom and dad kicked her out because she wouldn't tell them who the father was, so—"

"They what? She wouldn't?"

"—I finally just decided to bite the bullet and call and ask her mom for her ring size. Well, Jules's dad answered the phone, and he'd like you to, uh, pay them a visit. Right. Now."

Stunned, Rhett stared at his sister. He'd rather take fifty more blows to the jaw from Grady than go see Jules's parents right now. "Lila, I'm going to kill you."

"Okay," she said. "But if I were you? I'd ask Mr. Holt for permission to marry his daughter first. Just a suggestion. Anyway, I have every confidence in you, which means that I've got a ton to do to get ready for the proposal."

"How would you like to die?" Rhett asked Lila as she got into her car.

"If you're giving me a choice, then probably with that other, very large diamond ring through my nose," she said.

"I cannot believe that you did this," he said, shaking his head.

"It was the most direct way to address the problem, you left it up to me, and you are going to have to face them sooner or later," Lila reasoned. "Besides, they're old-fashioned, and because of that I changed my mind about the patriarchy. It *is* nice to ask the bride's father for permission to marry her."

"I'd have preferred to choose the time and place myself!" Rhett slammed a hand onto Scarlett's roof.

"Well, sorry: I chose it for you. If you're going to come home and be my brother again, then you need to accept me for who I am. I meddle, and I'm very effective at it. For example, I got Jake

363

and Charlie back together again." She said this proudly and affectionately.

"Congratulations, little sister. But your meddling is making a hash out of *my* life, thank you very much."

"I'll fix it," Lila said cheerfully. "I promise! Now, you go ask permission. I'll handle Jean-Paul's. You call Monty with the ring size. And you get Jules to the restaurant at seven P.M."

"How am I supposed to do that?"

"Well, you can start by asking her to come, you moron."

"Oh, now I'm a moron?"

"Haven't you heard? Most geniuses are morons in their personal lives. So you're not alone."

"Good to know," Rhett muttered. "Good to know."

Rhett's collar felt instantly tighter. He sat in Scarlett with the engine running and aimed the air-conditioning vents right at his face, cranking the temperature down to sixty-two degrees. *You got this. You have negotiated multimillion-dollar deals before breakfast. You have chatted with heads of state and C-suite guys all over the globe. You are not intimidated by one simple Texas rancher.*

Rhett swallowed, redirected the AC vents, and aimed Scarlett toward the Holt place. God help him . . . he'd almost rather go back to prep school again in his pearl-snap shirt than face Helen and Billy under these circumstances.

He got there all too soon, and instead of stopping at the barn as usual, he passed it and rumbled all the way up to the little blue house. He shut off the engine, climbed out, and tried not to feel all of fifteen years old and headed to the principal's office.

Billy Holt met him at the door, his face dark with anger. "Did you buy this place out of guilt, Rhett Braddock? For tangling with my daughter?"

"No, sir—"

"I'd like to knock you down!"

"Grady's already done that, sir."

"Good for him. Now, about the last darn thing I'd like to do is invite you inside. But get on in here, because we surely do have some private business to discuss." He held open the door, a look of disgust on his face. As if he were inviting in a cockroach.

This was going well, so far.

Rhett took a deep breath and walked into the kitchen where he'd felt so welcome only a little while ago. It hadn't changed; everything else had, though.

Billy Holt didn't ask him to sit. "You have disrespected me, my wife, my daughter, and our values, Braddock. Not to mention your friendship with my son. And only the sorry past with my sister Sue keeps me from meeting you at the end of a shotgun."

Helen Holt sat in the chair opposite, her face calm, her mouth a straight, uncompromising line.

"Mrs. H," Rhett said. "Good morning."

"Is it?" she replied. She got up. "Coffee? Blueberry muffin?"

But the way she said it, she may as well have offered him arsenic.

He wasn't going to stall. "Mr. and Mrs. Holt. I'm here to ask your permission to marry Julianna."

Helen's mouth softened. She gave a nod and turned toward the coffeepot, getting a mug down for him and pouring some.

But all Billy said was, "I don't know that she'll have you."

Ouch.

"I'm sorry about the circumstances," Rhett added. "We didn't . . . plan . . . any of this. It just happened."

Billy's eyebrows snapped together. "We are not going to talk about how any of it happened," he said darkly. "We are only going to talk about what happens next."

Rhett nodded. "I want to marry your daughter."

"Why?" Billy asked baldly.

"Well, uh . . . among other things," Rhett stammered, "I want the baby to have a father."

"What other things?"

"Because I—" he blurted. Did he love Jules? It was . . . possible. He loved being with her. He loved the way she had of staring right into him, as if she could see everything inside and how it ticked. Why it ticked.

He loved her rooster-tail hair. The way she threw back her head when she laughed. The passion she had for animals. How she kept her wallet in her boot. The way she looked buck naked on a saddle . . .

That sounded a lot like love.

Rhett realized he'd gone too long without saying anything. "I—"

Billy's mouth tightened, and he exchanged a meaningful glance with his wife.

"I care very much about Jules," he said at last. "I want to take care of her. I want—"

"Your sister told Billy you had enough forethought to buy our daughter a ring," Helen said. She looked at her husband.

"Yes, I did."

"Maybe he's given this more thought than we realized, Billy."

Thank you, Lila. "Yes, well, yes . . . I just need to know what size—"

"It's a six," Helen said.

Billy shook his head and sat down heavily.

"Sir?" Rhett flailed. "May I have your permission?"

His would-be father-in-law looked upward

toward the heavens. "Again?" he asked softly.

"It won't be like that," Rhett said. "I can promise you. There will never, ever be a need for Jules to defend herself from me."

Helen made a soft noise of distress.

Billy folded his arms across his chest and stared at him. "I know. I do know that."

"Sir," Rhett said yet again to Billy. "May I please have permission to marry your daughter?"

The older man looked at Helen again and sighed. "You can ask. But of course what she says in reply is up to her."

CHAPTER 29

Jules stood in Don Qui's stall the next day, absently rubbing his furry ears as he listened to her rave like a madwoman. She *was* a madwoman. She had told Rhett Braddock to shut up when he'd asked her to marry him. "Even for me, Don Qui, that's a new low of gracelessness."

Don Qui rubbed his face on her shirt, nodding his head up and down.

"Thanks for agreeing," she told him, frowning.

He nibbled at her hair.

"Dude, it may not have conditioner in it, but it's not *hay*."

He snorted.

Rhett Braddock asked me to marry him. And I said no. What woman in her right mind turns down Rhett Braddock?

Me.

"He doesn't love me, Don Qui," she said, blinking furiously to keep tears at bay. "He's just doing the 'right' thing, which is *wrong*."

Don Qui eyed her with sympathy.

"It sucks," Jules added, eloquently. "And what kind of man would ask me for a date after this? Huh? Ugh. He's going to want to talk baby logistics . . . This is horrible. Can you and I just run away together? Sell apples or tamales from a cart?"

Beast gave a woof from outside the stall.

"Of course you can come, too," she told her. "Of course."

Rhett had asked her to meet him this evening at Jean-Paul's, and Jules didn't even own a dress. Well, not a nice one. She did have a floral polyester item that advertised itself as a dress, but looked like '80s wallpaper gone terribly wrong. Her mother had bought it, of course. She'd said thanks and hung it in solitary confinement in the closet.

She really didn't want to wear it to Jean-Paul's. But she couldn't go in jeans. Which left her two alternatives: Slime out of the date altogether, since it was bound to be uncomfortable and filled with emotional and conversational landmines. Or go see Amelie.

Mia wasn't good with clothes; Sue wouldn't want Jules to go on any dates with Rhett. Amelie was her only hope.

So at lunchtime, Jules got into her wreck on wheels, inhaled its familiar animal scents, peered out the drool-smeared windows, and puttered over to Main Street.

She looked left and then right to make sure nobody saw her going in, and then slunk through the door like a thief. Well, she tried, but the darn bells on the door jingled to announce her presence.

Amelie came out of the back right away, her

incredible hair twisted up and falling from the knot on her head in an elegant spray that danced around her ears. *"Jules?"* Her dark eyebrows climbed almost to her hairline. She was a vision in a pale yellow lace minidress that set off her flawless dark skin to perfection.

Jules scuffed the toe of her rubber barn boot on the polished wood floor. "Yeah, I know. I'm about the last person you'd expect to see in your dress shop."

"Definitely." But her smile was wide and warm. "How can I help you, *chérie*?"

Amelie had gone to fashion design school in Paris. Jules still wasn't sure how she'd ended up in Silverlake, with Jean-Paul the only other French speaker in town. But here she was.

"I have a dinner date at Jean-Paul's tonight," Jules said darkly, as if she were going to jail. "So, I need . . . like, a skirt. I don't think I can afford a whole dress."

Amelie's beautiful sculpted lips quivered as if she was trying not to laugh. But there was nothing mean or judgmental about the amusement. "I see. Well, I do have some skirts. But I also happen to have a sale going. Technically it starts tomorrow, but . . . I own the place, so I can make an exception for you."

"Really? That'd be great. Thank you."

"So I'm quite sure that we can find a whole dress for you. In fact"—Amelie took in her figure

371

with a professional glance—"I have something that will be stunning."

Jules dug down into her boot, trying to reach her wallet.

"Do you . . . have an itch?" Amelie seemed mystified.

"No, no. I just need my wallet," Jules reassured her.

"Ah. Of course. Julianna, come to a dressing room. We will need to slip those boots off anyway. They will ruin the lines of the frock . . ."

"Can I wear flip-flops with it?" Jules wanted to know.

"Let's start with the dress," Amelie said diplomatically. "Then we will get to the trimmings."

Trimmings? As if she were a Christmas tree . . . Jules wasn't sure she liked the sound of that.

Half an hour later, Amelie looked at her watch, hung up the dress they'd selected, and said simply, "It is time."

"It is time for what?" Jules looked at the criminally expensive navy silk sheath that Amelie had tucked and gathered and then somehow gotten her out of. She also didn't quite believe the story that it was 75 percent off.

"For your salon appointment. While you are being coiffed, I will make these alterations. Then I'll meet you at—"

"Coiffed?" Jules repeated. "What is that?"

Amelie smiled good-naturedly. "It means someone does your hair. In your case, Edwynna at A Cut Above."

Jules was confused. "But I didn't make an appointment."

"I know. I made it for you. And Edwynna made another: Right after you see her, you'll go to Glam Gal for your mani and pedi."

"My what?" Jules asked. "No way. I don't do my nails . . . and I can't afford all of this stuff!"

"It's taken care of."

"By whom? Why?"

"You've been selected by the Silverlake Sirens for a makeover, darling."

"Who are they?"

"An anonymous group of ladies here in Silverlake who stage fashion interventions."

"Since when? I've never heard of them. This feels like a setup," muttered Jules. "I think the entire town somehow knows about this date at Jean-Paul's with Rhett."

"Do you think so? What a theory." Amelie shepherded her to the door and pointed down Main Street at A Cut Above. "There. Run along now."

"Just because I've never set foot in there doesn't mean I don't know where it is," Jules grumbled. Then, feeling strange and awkward and deeply grateful, she gave Amelie a hug. "Thank you."

"You're very welcome. I'll catch up with you at Glam Gal, yes? When I'm done with the alterations."

Edwynna, with her blue-violet eyes and cascading black waves of hair, looked like a plus-sized young Elizabeth Taylor with hair extensions. She hustled Jules into a chair, trapped her in a black cape, and took her hair out of its rubber-banded knot on top of her head. "Please lose this look. It's a crime against humanity and nature, too."

Jules gulped. "Why?"

"Because you are way, way too pretty to look like Olive Oyl got put in a blender with a rooster."

Jules wasn't sure whether to laugh or cry. "It's that bad?"

"It's not good," Edwynna said cryptically. "Now, I'm not tryin' to be mean, here . . ."

It just comes naturally?

"If it's all right by you, I'll trim the ends and shape your hair all over, leaving it long but tapering it so that it's sleek and falls naturally."

"Uh. Okay. That sounds good. Because I won't do a lot of messing with my hair. The horses and Don Quixote don't care. Neither do I."

"Didn't you get *any* Southern girl genes from your mama?"

"Not one."

Edwynna, who wore black platform sandals

374

with triangles cut out of the wedges, took in Jules's rubber riding boots, without saying a word. But her face said it all. *U-G-L-Y.*

Jules tried to look at them through Edwynna's eyes. Okay, so they weren't so lovely. Maybe she should go by the saddlery and see if Sue had any cowboy boots on sale. Though she'd just put the dress and accessories from Amelie on her credit card . . .

Edwynna hauled Jules into the back, tipped her backward into a chair, and stuck her head in a sink to shampoo her hair.

"Thank you for taking me on such short notice," Jules said. "Amelie probably told you it's a date or something, but it's not. Rhett and I are just meeting to discuss some stuff."

Had Edwynna just rolled her eyes?

No. Jules was just upside down and had misread her expression. That was it.

"Oh no. Of *course* it's not a date. Especially with Rhett being so gruesome and backward and all." Edwynna smiled.

Gruesome? "Oh, you're kidding around," said Jules.

"I never kid around," Edwynna said, doing something heavenly to Jules's scalp. "It wouldn't be prudent."

"Wow . . . if you keep massaging my head like this, I'm not going anywhere. I'll just stay here all night."

Jules had been worried about feeling sick, and anticipated that going through all these motions might make her feel worse, but the coddling was actually having the opposite effect. Particularly when she wasn't staring at herself in a mirror, noticing that her face was slightly fuller than she recalled it being the last time she'd bothered looking.

But all too soon, it was over, and Edwynna hauled Jules back to her station. Then, in a flurry of combing and snipping, she transformed her. And then aimed some product and a blow-dryer at her hair and transformed her some more.

Suddenly, Jules had bangs and tapered layers and a flowy sort of mane. Her eyes looked huge framed by the new look. She gaped at herself.

"Oh, my stars," Edwynna exclaimed when she finally holstered her blow-dryer. "I have outdone myself! You look gorgeous." She bent forward, grabbed a can of hair spray, and asphyxiated Jules with it.

When Jules could breathe again, she opened her eyes to see the stylist rummaging in a drawer. "Okay, I did promise GiGi at Glam Girl that she could do your makeup, but I cannot resist . . . I'll just do your eyes and she can do the rest."

Before Jules could yell for help, Edwynna swooped down upon her with an eyeliner pencil. "Hold still."

She made some mysterious moves with it and

then produced a palette of eyeshadow and a tube of mascara.

"I don't really wear makeup," Jules protested.

"Tonight you do."

"But I don't want to look like a clown—and this is just a meeting . . ."

Edwynna grabbed her chin, which made it difficult to speak. She clearly wasn't listening, anyway, so Jules gave up.

"Voilà," the stylist said at last. She clapped a hand to her heart, a neon pink tube of mascara trapped beneath her palm.

Jules stared at herself in the mirror. She closed her eyes, opened them, and stared again. "Who *is* that? It's not me."

Edwynna laughed and then looked at her watch. "You got two minutes to get to Glam Gal. So scram."

"But—I must owe you some money—"

"No money. You are a walking advertisement for my services. The other half of Silverlake will be here within a week." And Edwynna used her phone's camera to take several pictures of Jules. "The girls are not going to believe this transformation!"

Jules wasn't sure whether to be pleased or offended by this statement. But she "scrammed," as directed, and found herself next in Glam Girl, surrounded by curious stares and bottles of nail polish.

CHAPTER 30

Rhett sat with his new Pet Rock at the best corner table in Jean-Paul's, nervous as the proverbial long-tailed cat in a room full of rocking chairs. He opened the black velvet box for what had to be the hundredth time and looked at the rock, which winked coldly back up at him.

"Hi," he said.

Of course it didn't answer back.

Was it too rectangular? Was it too big? Would she rather have a yellow gold setting than a platinum one? He didn't know. The rock seemed offended that he wasn't sure it was right. Its sparkle seemed a little malicious.

He snapped shut the box and shoved it back into his pocket. He checked the time: 6:57. Would Jules be early? Or on time? Would she be late? There were only those three mathematical possibilities, unless he wanted to get into seconds or minutes.

A horrifying thought hit him: There actually was a fourth possibility. Jules might not show up at all. He looked around the restaurant, at what seemed like miles of white tablecloth and silver and glowing candlelight. At the greenery studded with more upscale, Venetian jesters that was woven through the banister that led to the private room upstairs, tiny lights gleaming from it. It wasn't just limited to the stair rail—there was greenery strung everywhere human beings could string it, studded with other types of Venetian masks. It looked beautiful.

Then he had another horrifying thought: What if this place was too fancy for Jules? What if she'd have preferred Whataburger? What if—

And then a stunning stranger walked gingerly into Jean-Paul's on a pair of skyscraper heels. She wobbled a little as she approached the maître d' stand and grabbed on to it for support. If the woman hadn't had her hair swept into an elegant updo with tendrils of hair trailing romantically past her ears; if she weren't wearing a navy silk sheath that showcased her curvy little body; if a diamond solitaire on a slim chain hadn't been lucky enough to encircle her lovely throat . . . he'd have sworn that the woman was Julianna Holt. But Jules would never be dressed like that.

Not-Jules turned his way when Jean-Paul himself beckoned her, and tottered a few steps before lurching toward his arm. Jean-Paul caught her and braced her, murmured something.

And Rhett sat back in his chair with his mouth falling open, like some kind of yokel. A hummingbird could have flown in and built a nest before he closed it again, remembered his manners, and got to his feet.

"Jules?" he said as she slowly, proudly, put

379

one foot in front of the other without a single wobble all the way to the table.

"Thank you," she muttered to Jean-Paul.

"But of course," he said, beaming. He and Rhett engaged in a brief struggle over who would pull out her chair and Rhett won.

Jules sank into it gratefully, and Rhett realized that she'd been in excruciating pain from the shoes.

Jean-Paul consoled himself by putting her napkin into her lap, handing them each a menu, and dubiously giving up the wine list to Rhett, as if he wouldn't remember which champagne to order.

"Amelie says these instruments of torture on my feet were invented *by* men *for* men," Jules groused. "You idiots can have 'em back, if you ask me."

Rhett couldn't help it. He threw back his head and laughed. This vision was, indeed, his very own Jules. At least, he hoped she would be, with a little help from his friend the Pet Rock.

"All this"—Jules gestured to herself—"and you laugh at me?"

"You're *gorgeous,*" Rhett said.

She blinked and then went pink in the face.

"You just happen to be funny, as well," he said, charmed. "It's a winning combination, I promise you."

"Huh."

"Champagne, please, Jean-Paul. The Bollinger Vieilles Vignes Françaises."

"Of course, sir. Right away."

"I probably shouldn't—" began Jules.

"One glass will do no harm," Jean-Paul reassured her.

She was clearly mortified. The entire town knew their business and probably knew what was about to unfold here as well. He wouldn't be surprised if noses started pressing up against the front windows. "Uh—well," she said, at last. "Maybe just a sip."

Once Jean-Paul had departed for the cellar, she looked at Rhett point-blank. "What are we celebrating?"

"We'll get to that," he said, trotting out his most blinding smile . . . and then winced because it hurt his face so much.

She definitely noticed, and he retired the smile immediately.

"Is something wrong?" she asked.

"No, no, not at all." He couldn't stop drinking her in. "You look incredible."

"But not like *me*," she said, fidgeting with her silverware.

"You look like you with a lot of frosting on top," Rhett said. There, that was a good line, wasn't it?

"Frosting," Jules repeated darkly. "You mean hair gel and hair spray and hair dryers and hair torment? Amelie dressed me and then dragged me to A Cut Above. And then to Glam Gal." She pronounced the last two words as if they were the names of revolting insects. "Where GiGi also spackled me with a bunch of makeup. And for some weird reason, Monty ran over and draped this borrowed ice around my neck at the last possible second."

"Interesting," Rhett said. "I like it. Do you?"

"I think it's . . . really sparkly. Way too sparkly."

"Hmm." Rhett shrugged. "Monty will be disappointed."

"Don't tell him!" she said, scandalized. "It'll hurt his feelings. He was being nice."

"I won't say a word." Rhett didn't have the heart to tell her that Monty was angling for another high-dollar sale and wasn't just being nice. "Do you like your hair, at least?"

Jules frowned. She put a hand up and felt around. "It's *crunchy*," she said.

"Crunchy like lettuce, or crunchy like walnuts?"

"You're laughing at me again." Jules squinted at him.

"Not at all."

"It's like . . . they all ganged up on me to glam me up. So weird."

Jean-Paul appeared with the champagne, a white cloth napkin draped over his arm, and a silver ice bucket on a stand.

"That would make such a great horse feeder if it were a little bigger," Jules mused.

"*Oui, vraiment,*" Jean-Paul agreed, with an utterly straight face. He got down to the serious business of opening and pouring the champagne.

Rhett tried not to fidget while he did so. He wished him gone, and then when he was, wished for him to come back again. Because he, the billionaire deal maker, had no idea what to say next or how to transition the conversation into a proposal of marriage.

So he just dove in. "Jules, among other things that I'm hoping we celebrate, I'd like to raise a toast to our baby."

"Okay . . ." she said cautiously. "But it's kind of weird and unexpected."

"So is your turning up pregnant. But it's also a beautiful, wonderful thing. So can we drink to it?"

She looked away from him and at the bubbles rising and popping in her glass. "Okay."

He raised his glass.

She raised hers.

They clinked them together and drank.

From across the restaurant, Jean-Paul beamed and then picked up the phone at the maître d' stand.

Jules savored the taste and then set down her flute. "I have no clue what exactly that is, but it does taste like liquid gold. Too bad, since that's my last sip."

He hoped not. "I'm glad you like it."

"So . . . things are going to get complicated," she said.

"They don't have to. Jules—" Rhett got up and then dropped to one knee.

She looked alarmed. "What are you—"

He fished the box out of his pocket with his left hand and attempted to take hers in his right one. But the box caught on his pocket lining, which threw him off-balance, and suddenly Rhett had to brace himself on the table. *This is going all wrong* . . .

"Will you marry me?" He succeeded in getting the box out of his pocket and regained his balance.

Only then did he realize that his proposal had landed in the middle of the table like a stale ham sandwich.

Jules stared at Rhett. Carefully, she said, "That's . . . that's very . . . um. Appreciated. But . . ."

But? She wasn't supposed to say *but*. That was a word that didn't belong anywhere in this carefully orchestrated evening. Half the town had helped him stage it. They were probably all ready to cheer . . .

"Rhett." She smoothed her napkin. "This isn't . . . necessary."

"Necessary," he repeated, a yawning pit growing in his stomach.

"It's not the eighteenth century, and I'm not

'ruined' or 'spoiled goods' because I'm going to have a baby without being married—despite what my mom may think."

Her words hurt more than Grady's fist had. How to recover? "She's on board with this, just so you know."

"You talked to my mother first? That's not a point in your favor."

"No—not exactly. I asked your father for permission. It seemed like the right thing to do."

"And here you are, trying to do another right thing," she said in mechanical tones.

This was not going well.

"Because you think you've wronged me," she added.

He'd forgotten to even open the box. He was making such a hash out of this. He flipped the lid open and slid the box toward her while she examined the ring, her face now completely blank.

Rhett got to his feet.

"Wow," she said. "Wow. That is . . . that's huge."

"You like it?" he asked cautiously.

"It's beautiful. How could a girl not like it?" She fidgeted with her napkin again.

She didn't pounce on the ring, crying out with delight, or throw herself into his arms.

This was killing him. Just killing him. And he couldn't let her see it.

"So we'll get married," he said. "Right away."

"Rhett. Listen to me. We are not going to get

married. It's a really bad idea. We will handle this another way."

He just blinked at her. "You're turning me down? No, no, no . . . you can't do that, Jules. You've gotta let me make this right."

"Make it right for whom? Your guilty conscience? Grady? My parents? The town gossips?"

"For you," he said. "*You,* Jules."

"I don't need you to do that," she said gently. "Thank you, though."

"Thank you? Thank you?! Are you kidding me?"

"Marriage is hard enough," Jules said carefully, "when two people love each other. That's not the case here."

"Julianna. I—I care deeply about you. We've known each other since we were little kids, and—"

"Stop." She squeezed her eyes shut and held up a hand.

"I even own the stables now. We're practically family!"

She shook her head. "Family members don't usually sleep with each other and then scram in the morning so fast that they leave tire tracks."

"You're still angry about that, and I can't blame you. But please don't let a grudge stand in the way of giving our baby a home and two parents under the same roof."

"Rhett, this isn't about some grudge! If I ever get married, it will be for love. Not for any other reason. Not for a pregnancy, not for security, not for money. Love."

"We can learn to love each other," he insisted.

She gave him the saddest look he'd ever seen. In fact, she looked like a kicked puppy.

It wrenched something deep inside him; it physically hurt.

Jules shook her head.

Jean-Paul set down the phone, rubbed his hands, and turned toward them. His face fell when he took in the less-than-joyous tableau. He picked up the phone again. *Really?*

Rhett leaned on the table with both hands, partly to catch his breath; recover his equilibrium. He pushed the box toward her. "Please . . . would you just try it on?"

She hesitated.

And he took advantage of that. He plucked the ring from its black velvet nest and slid it onto her finger. It was a little tight, and he realized with a pang that it was probably because of the pregnancy. Once on her finger, it sparkled madly, overcompensating for something—he didn't know what.

Her lips trembled.

"Think about it?" he asked.

Reluctantly she nodded, and he felt a tiny, dishonest spark of triumph. "Keep the ring. Let's talk again in a few days."

"Okay," Jules whispered. "Will you . . . I'm

sorry, Rhett, I really am. But will you excuse me?" And she ran for the ladies' room.

He knew she wouldn't return to the table.

Teetering on the stupid heels, Jules careened into the ladies' room at Jean-Paul's, didn't even recognize herself in the candlelit, gilt-edged mirror, and hurtled into a stall. She braced herself with a hand on either side of it, hanging over the toilet and panting.

The diamond around her neck glittered weirdly in the water below her, which made her turn and look at the colossus on her left hand. It was gorgeous. It was stunning. It was perfect . . . too perfect for someone as imperfect as she was.

This was a ring for someone like Bridget. Bridget could wear this, and wear it well. But not Jules.

And yet there it was, winking back at the glamour lighting in the ladies' room.

It was hard not to be mesmerized by the diamond and its two sidekicks.

Harder still not to be mesmerized by Rhett, trying to pull off her dream proposal and absolutely crashing and burning. He had tried so hard to salvage it, over and over again—as if he couldn't believe that he, Rhett Braddock, big shot, was flailing and floundering so miserably.

She knew he wasn't used to that, and it was oddly and horribly endearing.

He still looked pretty rough, thanks to Grady. She had scanned his poor, battered face for signs of confusion or insanity. All she saw was the fierceness of intent in his one Bimini blue eye, and the squareness of his jaw—well, the side that hadn't swelled to the size of a watermelon. He was lucky Grady hadn't broken his nose.

Will you marry me? The words she'd waited to hear from him since she was eleven years old.

But there was no joy in his face. No joy in the words.

Awful enough without him reminding her of her ridiculous crush on him, the silly torch she'd carried since childhood. Still did, if she stopped lying to herself. Which made it all so much worse.

She'd tried to keep her voice gentle and swallow the rising hysteria that had started that now-familiar spiral in her stomach. She'd done her very best to stick with a pragmatic *no*. And yet somehow she found herself now bent over the barrel of *maybe*. How?

This felt wrong on every level.

Jules stood upright and left the stall. She walked to the oval gold mirror and took in her reflection with a mixture of amusement and disgust. What had they all thought this was, prom night? They'd all known or guessed or checked in with one another—Amelie, Edwynna, GiGi at Glam Girl . . . and she'd known they knew, deep

389

down. But she'd not only been in denial, she'd needed the help. Needed to pretend that she could get out of her Cinderella costume, her Cinderella life, and go to the ball. Dance with the prince.

Well, she was done playing dress-up like a little kid. Jules turned on the water faucet, bent forward, and splashed her face. She used the fragrant, French-milled, pear-scented soap that Jean-Paul ordered from Paris to scrub her face totally clean of the gunk that had lent itself to the fantasy.

And when she looked back into the mirror, dripping, she saw herself again. Mostly. She dried her face with one of the chichi hand towels provided, took off the diamond necklace, and dropped it into the evening bag that Amelie had loaned her.

A large clump of mascara adorned the monster rock on her finger. She rinsed it off, idly wondering what it had cost Rhett, and deciding she didn't want to know.

A soft knock came at the door. "Mademoiselle Julianna?" Jean-Paul made her name sound so exotic. *Zhulyanna.*

And she was about as exotic as a cactus in a ceramic cowboy boot planter. "Yes?"

"Ah . . . M'sieur Rhett . . . he wish to know you are okay?"

"I'm fine. Thank you, Jean-Paul."

"There is, ah, anysing I may get for you?"

She thought for a moment. "If you have a take-out bag, that would be great."

"Tout de suite, mademoiselle."

When she stepped out of the ladies' room a couple of minutes later, he handed it to her, looking almost comically mournful that the evening had been such a debacle.

The bag held something solid. "What's in here?"

"Gâteau au chocolat," he said with a small bow. "Sometimes *chocolat* is better than man, eh?"

"Thank you," Jules said. She leaned forward and kissed him on the cheek. Then she pulled the box of cake out of the bag, slipped off her high heels, and tossed them inside instead.

He eyed the ring, clearly perplexed, and lifted an eyebrow.

She shrugged. "You know as much as I do," she said before slipping out the back door and padding barefoot to her familiar, beat-up truck. At least it wouldn't turn into a pumpkin on the way home.

CHAPTER 31

Fool Fest, directed by a manic Lila, was in full swing. Rhett felt the irony as he sat in Schweitz's, taking refuge from the chaos with his brother Jake and a whole lot of other townsfolk.

Outside, the little garden gnome did his very best to retain what dignity he'd ever had, holding his pint aloft like the Statue of Liberty held her torch. The problem was that someone had dressed him in a ballerina tutu and a yellow lace bra. That someone had also stuffed the bra full of succulents, which looked a lot like the ones from Aunt Sue's garden. They erupted, ridiculous, from the cleavage, and waved in the breeze. The gnome stood stoic, doing his best to ignore them even as they clustered at the bottom of his beard.

A band with limited talent was playing anything with *fool* in the title. "Fool for Love," "The Fool on the Hill," "Won't Get Fooled Again" . . . and similar songs played on a track inside Schweitz's.

Outside there was controlled pandemonium: kids with face paint running amok with turkey legs and cotton candy; adults with plastic cups of beer and wine; at least five identical jesters doing magic tricks, turning cartwheels, and playing jokes on people.

There was Kristina from Piece A Cake, her long, blond braid hanging over her shoulder as she deftly dished up her baked goods on paper plates while her cousin took people's money. Ray Delgado, the butcher, did the same from his booth with smoked brisket and sausage and the turkey legs. Schweitzie himself was out there, slinging beer and wine. A group of church ladies sold cookies by the dozen.

"Looks like you just might beat me to the altar after all," Jake said, slapping Rhett on the back. "That's good, right? She didn't say no."

Rhett lifted a shoulder, let it drop, and poured some more beer down his throat. "Word has it that she's still wearing the ring, anyway."

His optimism had waned as time passed and there was no text, much less a phone call or the sight of Jules driving up next to him with her window rolled down and a smile on her face.

"Thinking about it" is a maybe on its way to a yes, isn't it?

Or no. Maybe it was a no. Maybe it was a I'm-gonna-let-you-down-easy-by-pretending-this-is-a-tough-choice no.

Or maybe it means I'm overthinking this whole thing.

"That's good, man. She's just getting used to it, that's all." Jake clinked his Shiner against Rhett's.

Rhett managed a smile. "I thought if I ever proposed to a girl, she'd look a sight happier than Julianna Holt did." He was feeling a little shell-shocked. Even if she did get to *yes,* the look on her face made him wonder if it would stick.

"Let's get you another beer," Jake said, waving Otto over.

"To the Braddock boys!" a girlish voice called from across the bar. Bridget stood up, hoisting what appeared to be a water glass. "Never boring!" She made her way over, leaving behind a table with her laptop and a hot pink leather portfolio full of papers, to come say hi.

"You're working in the bar?" Jake asked.

"It's just the billing. I wanted a good view for the Fool Fest parade, and I'm not a coffee shop girl," she said. "Otto says he put in Wi-Fi just for me." She batted her eyelashes and they all had a laugh.

"Nice to run into you again," Rhett said. "Although I see you more in Dallas than I do my own family here."

"That's on you, buddy," she said. Her mani-cured hand slipped over Jake's shoulder. Jake smiled but stiffened slightly and Rhett shot him a commiserating look. She wasn't over him yet? How long would it take?

You're one to talk. Mooning over Jules all this time after one night. Begging her to marry you. Begging. Rhett pressed the heel of his hand to his pounding temple. He thought it would feel better than this. He thought he'd feel relief, hope for the future . . . happiness.

He gulped back his drink. *I should be happier. Jules and I are gonna get married and have a baby and she's going to learn to love me and I'll have a home in Silverlake again and it's all gonna be okay . . .*

"Rhett!"

Rhett focused on his brother. Jake and Bridget exchanged glances. "You all right?" Bridget asked. "I never pegged you for one to give a crap about what other people say about you. But I guess it turned out well for everybody. I'll expect to be a bridesmaid at the wedding, of course, ha ha."

It was Rhett's and Jake's turn to share a look. "Where'd you get this from?" Jake asked.

"Oh, come on, your little soap opera has been playing twenty-four/seven on the channels in this town. Do you not know how many people came together to give Jules a makeover before you popped the question?"

"Uh . . . no. She did look incredible."

"That's what I hear. I'm so happy for you two! And I can't help feeling a little responsible," Bridget added playfully. "Without my advice, I bet Jules would still be turning the hose on you instead of picking out a dress."

The sinking feeling that was already mixing badly with the beer in Rhett's stomach got worse. *Advice? What is she talking about?*

"What advice did you give Jules?" Jake asked in clipped tones.

"The same advice I give to all my nonpaying clients: Make nice. Make the best of a bad situation. Keep your friends close and your enemies closer."

Something deep inside Rhett went cold.

"Getting pregnant is about as close as you can get!" Bridget blathered on. "Seriously, congratulations!" She grinned.

Rhett stared at her, acid spreading through his gut.

To her credit, the smile died out quickly when she registered their faces. "Okay, why does this feel weird?" she said. She was completely serious now, the professional lawyer in her kicking in.

A long, terrible pause ensued.

"Just when exactly did you give Jules this advice, Bridget?" Rhett asked, struggling to keep his voice low and even.

"Oh, I don't know . . . I guess it was here in Schweitz's, early on. When you'd just gotten back into town. Yeah. Because she turned right around and bought you a drink. Remember?"

Yeah. He sure did remember. And he also remembered not understanding how or why she'd gone from raging lioness to friendly kitten.

Bridget.

"I need to go," Rhett said, stumbling to his feet.

Make nice. Make the best of a bad situation. As in, I'd like to buy this guy a beer!

He had known there was something off about that. It had been too quick a switch . . . and then she'd stopped doing things like throwing his flowers into a horse stall and started being reasonable. Friendly. And worse . . .

Keep your friends close and your enemies closer.

She'd played him. Jules had . . .

He felt gut-shot.

"Rhett," Jake said, standing likewise and then looking desperately around for Otto so he could pay the bill.

"I'll get it," Bridget said. "I'm so sorry. I must've misunderstood something . . ."

Rhett pulled his wallet from his pocket, grabbed several bills, and slammed the money down on the bar table so hard Bridget flinched and finally ceased talking.

Which was fine, because Rhett didn't want to hear any more.

With Jake on his heels, he pushed out of the bar, grateful for the slap in the face provided by the cool air.

It sure was time to wake up.

He ignored his brother saying his name and pushed into the crowd. Scarlett was parked in an alley several streets away, since they always roped off Main Street for Fool Fest. He had a hike in front of him.

Sunny was helping behind an ice cream stand, and waved a cone in his face. "Want one, hon?" she called.

He waved her away, along with Ray's proffered turkey leg, and out of the corner of his eye, he glimpsed them both frowning after him. Someone else called his name—Was it Lila? He didn't care. He pushed through mothers with strollers, toddlers and teenagers, moms and dads, old folks in wheelchairs, and even a clown on a pogo stick. They washed over him in waves of T-shirts and sneakers, their scents of sunscreen and corn dogs and sticky candy making him nauseous.

He threw five bucks at another vendor, snagged a cold Miller Lite from him, and veered left on Elm as he popped the top. His head swam with images of Jules, snippets of conversations, her hot-and-cold treatment of him . . . he couldn't make sense of it all. Except now it *did* make an awful sense. Her inconsistent behavior toward him—she'd been slipping up. Veering off a deliberate strategy. He was such a fool that he couldn't even grasp the enormity of it.

Lila careened around the corner. "There you are! I have been looking for you everywhere. Come with me. Now."

"Lila, leave me alone—"

"No! You owe me this, bro. This is my Fool Fest, my first-ever production of this size, and

I need your help. No foolin'." She grabbed his hand and tugged him along.

Beyond annoyed, he shotgunned the rest of the beer as if he were still in college. Before he knew it, they were weaving through alleys until they got to the very end of Main Street, where the Silverlake High marching band was striking up "Fool to Cry" by the Stones. The Stones did it better. A lot better.

But Lila blithely yanked him around the corner, almost smack into the big float for the parade: A sparkling, crazy-painted ship with a big jester decorating the prow. It had tall masts made out of plastic piping and big paper sails that advertised all of the Silverlake businesses that had contributed funds, finery, or fellowship to the festivities. On the side it said in huge block letters: SHIP OF FOOLS.

"Get in," Lila ordered.

Rhett balked. "Oh, very funny. Not."

"Rhett Braddock, get your wayward, prodigal butt into the seat of that float before I tell the whole town that you have . . . a harem . . . or herpes . . . or something really, really BAD," threatened Lila. "And if you won't be blackmailed, then do it out of guilt for being missing, or just do it out of the kindness of your heart for your little sister. *Get. In.*"

Rhett whipped his sunglasses out of his shirt pocket, settled them gloomily on his nose, and grudgingly did as he was told. Then, to his horror, someone shoved none other than Julianna Holt in beside him, from the other side.

She looked just as happy to see him as he did her. That is to say, petrified.

The whole crowd around them began to whoop and holler, and the engine of the truck under the float started up. They were about to be paraded through town.

"No, Lila, really—" Rhett tried to get up.

Things couldn't possibly get worse.

Except they could. His sister plopped an awful, gold-painted, faux-jewel-encrusted crown on his head, and another one got dropped onto Jules's head, her rooster-tail hair sprouting through it.

The marching band in front of them struck up "Ship of Fools," and they were off, rumbling down Main Street. Behind them rode Mayor Gloria Fisk and her husband, and behind *them* grumbled old Progress, Kingston Nash's ancient green pickup. Charlie rode by his side, and the entire bed of the truck had been planted with bluebonnets. It was a sight to behold.

A troupe of jesters followed behind, dancing and shaking the bells in their caps, banging on tambourines.

Crowds lined Main Street, laughing and cheering. Little kids sat on their daddies' shoulders, pointing and dripping ice cream.

"And may I introduce to you," boomed Lila's voice from her handheld microphone, "Silverlake's new King and Queen of Fools! Congratulations, you two!"

More cheering, yelling, and whistling.

"Can we get a wave, Royalty? Huh? C'mon, greet your loyal subjects. Give 'em some sugar!"

Jules looked at Rhett and swallowed.

Rhett looked at Jules. *I'm gonna kill my sister. And not gently.*

Jules lifted her right hand and weakly waggled her fingers.

He forced himself to do likewise.

The cheering and whistling rose in decibels.

"Guess what, folks? It gets better . . . these two are engaged to be MARRIED!"

The crowd erupted into even more whooping and hollering.

Rhett turned to stone.

Jules turned redder than a poppy.

"Show off thaaaaaat RING, girlfriend!" Lila shouted, beside herself with pride and glee.

Rhett stewed silently. *Gonna skin her like a carrot. Gonna boil her in oil. Gonna feed her to some bears. Gonna snap the bones afterward . . .*

"*RING!*" Lila yelled again, since Jules, clearly mortified, had sat on her hand.

"You'd better do it," Rhett muttered. "She's not going to give up."

Looking as if she wanted to burst into tears,

Jules flashed the giant Pet Rock at the crowd, which went crazy.

"That's right, folks! And it's from Monty's place, right here on Main Street, for any of you who had a doubt. Anyone else ready to pop the question?" Lila hollered.

Rhett could barely bring himself to look at Jules as they made agonizingly slow progress down Main Street in the float. *King of Fools, huh? Yeah. That about sums me up.*

As for Jules, she seemed embarrassed, but also confused. She kept stealing looks in his direction. She turned the ring again and again on her finger. At one point she slid closer to him, and then, when he didn't respond in any way, she slid away again.

Let her be confused. She sure confused me.

Finally, they got to the end, and Jake, who'd been following, waited for Rhett to disengage himself.

Rhett had worked himself into quite a rage by then. Jules had made an April Fool of him all month, and now he'd been crowned the king of them. Wonderful.

He brusquely said goodbye to her and climbed out of the float, while she looked after him as if he'd kicked a bunny.

"Speech! Speech!" yelled Lila.

He glared at her, shook his head, and forced himself to produce a big, fake grin for the crowd.

"I'm honored," he called. "Thank you very much. I am certainly Silverlake's biggest fool."

After some applause, he made his way to Jake. "I need something from the firehouse," he said.

"From the—Are you crazy? Grady's there. It's not exactly safe terrain for you."

"I don't care. You with me, or not?"

Jake nodded, and they made their way back to their vehicles.

Rhett had Jake follow behind Scarlett in his truck on his path back to the firehouse for his laptop and papers. The deed to the Holt property would be there. A stupid, simple piece of paper that had created a whole mess.

Was it possible for Jules to be so cold and calculating? Had that been the plan, to twist him around her little finger in some revenge scheme for how he'd left her in Dallas? Her way to manipulate him to do what she wanted with the stables?

No wonder she doesn't want to marry me. She never had feelings for me in the first place. The things he'd pointed to in his mind as evidence that her feelings could grow into something meaningful . . . were they all part of an act?

The few beers weren't even close to numbing Rhett's senses, as he wished they would. Instead, they had a steadying effect, allowing him to be fully conscious of his anger and his need to control it, particularly now that he was heading back to Grady's territory. And if Grady came at him again, so be it. Truth to tell, Rhett was spoiling for a fight.

CHAPTER 32

Rafi and Mick were polishing the chrome on Big Red in the open garage when Rhett pulled up in Scarlett with Jake behind him, and . . . *Oh, look, there's Declan now, too. Huh.*

"What are you doing here?" Rhett asked his eldest brother.

"I called him on my way over," Jake said. "Just, you know, I wasn't sure what you had in mind, coming over here."

Something pinged deep in Rhett's soul where the loneliness had always lived.

"*¡Oye, Grady! Rhett está aquí.*" Rafi yelled into the stairwell. "*Amigo tiene cojones, ¿no?*" He and Mick had put aside their cleaning supplies. "Jake," Mick said in a warning tone. "This could get ugly." Jake swore quietly as Mick ran upstairs; Rafi was just standing there next to the vintage fire truck, noticeably frostier than the last time Rhett had stopped by.

"I just came to get my stuff," Rhett growled. Beside him, he heard Jake sigh.

And then Mick came back down from the upper floor into the garage. "He told me to tell you to get the hell out of here."

Rafi held out his arms and shrugged. "There you go."

"Tell him I said no, let's talk about this like mature adults," Rhett said.

"Do I look like your cabana boy, *guapo*?" Rafi snarled.

Jake stepped forward, his brows knit. "Hey, Rafi, look—"

Suddenly, Tommy burst through the back door, knocking the pool octopus out of his path. The kid was a few years younger than the rest of the squad and spoiling for a fight. "Just got the call."

Declan had been leaning on his car. Now he stood up.

"Why don't *I* go up and get his stuff?" Jake said. Mick shrugged and stepped back. Rafi followed suit. Tommy stepped forward and flexed his muscles.

"Seriously?" Rhett muttered.

Jake walked right up to Tommy, using his extra foot to tower over the kid. "He's my *brother,* Tommy."

"So's Grady," Tommy said.

And that's when Rhett realized even if the guys themselves didn't, that the firefighters were standing in formation, now, more or less lined up across the garage. Squaring off against the Braddocks. This wasn't what he was used to, not since he was a kid, but he'd learned how to fight at Deerville, and he'd always commanded a boardroom. Some combination of the two could surely get him out of this mess.

He sighed heavily. And what a mess it was. Rhett wanted to throw up. No way was he going to mess up Jake's hard-won life because of his own stupid mistakes.

"Jake," Rhett said, without looking at his brother. "Do what you need to do. I'll understand. I'm going back to Dallas anyway." But nobody moved. Rhett looked over in surprise.

Jake stood, straddling the line, shaking his head. In a too-cheerful voice, tense around the edges, he said, "How 'bout nobody does anything except get your stuff? That way, Grady gets what he wants, which is Rhett gone, and Rhett gets what he wants, which is his stuff!"

"Jake," Rhett hissed. "Don't screw up what you have here over this. It's not worth it. This is your life here."

Jake looked like he was in real pain as he surveyed the faces of his team. "If they give a damn, they won't make me choose."

Rhett dragged a hand down his face. How was it possible this just kept getting worse? Declan hadn't said a word. Rhett looked over and found him pulling off his long-sleeved flannel shirt. "What are you *doing?*"

"What does it look like I'm doing?" Declan asked.

"It looks like you've been watching *Road House* one too many times and are preparing for a brawl," Rhett said.

Deck gave him kind of a strange look. "Yeah. So?"

"This is ridiculous on several levels. One, the odds are terrible. Two, this has nothing to do with you. Three, if you get hurt, who's going to take care of duties at Silverlake? Four—"

"He always did like math," drawled a familiar voice.

Grady stood on the last step, just below Mick. His arms were full of Rhett's belongings. His suitcase. His laptop. His papers. That brand-new Stetson. On Grady's face was a look of scary self-control. The kind that could snap if a man wasn't careful.

In full view of everybody, Rhett crossed that line, walked up to Grady, and slid the deed to the Holt Stables out of the pile with a snap. Their eyes met and Rhett froze, his anger and pain overwhelmed by the sudden realization that he'd lost his oldest friend. "Grady . . ."

Grady's eyes flashed with hostility.

"Aw, fine. Just forget it," Rhett muttered, his pride taking over again. He turned, leaving Grady standing there with all his crap.

Boom!

Rhett looked over his shoulder just in time to see the suitcase, clothes on hangers, his laptop, the papers hit the floor and Grady launch himself at him. *"My baby sister?"*

This time Rhett was ready.

They grappled upright for a moment before falling backward onto the oil-stained garage floor. With Grady face-palming Rhett, nobody heard him say, "Can we not do this again?"

Too late. Eight men launched into a full-out hockey-style brawl for the public to view, just inside the open doors of the fire department for all of Silverlake to enjoy. Rhett was too busy with Grady to keep tabs on Jake and Declan, but he was all too aware that there were three Braddocks and five of everybody else.

And in a last flurry of curse words and thrown punches it was Mick's voice ringing out loud and clear. "Okay, that's enough, boys. Everybody got to have their say. Everybody got to draw a little blood." He clucked at them like they were children. "Did you get it out of your system? I sure hope so because that display was just pathetic. Really sad. We need to up our training, stat. How ya doin there, Tommy? Okay? Your nose broken?"

He continued checking on everybody all friendly-like. "Braddocks one, two, and three, y'all feelin' a little better? 'Cause you were about to get your butts kicked . . . too bad Ace wasn't here, what with his primo athletic conditioning, not to mention I think the only thing we were missing here was a baseball bat . . . and Jake, brother, I'm just going to say right now that I particularly feel for *you*, buddy, between a rock and a hard place and all." The big guy wearing his apron was pulling everybody apart, separating them carefully back on either side of the line.

Rhett and Grady sat across from each other, the garage door line between them. Grady's chest was heaving still and an angry welt across his forehead was dripping blood. More blood mixed in with oil formed a paste on his opposite cheek.

Weary beyond measure, Rhett looked at Jake as the other firefighters trooped back inside. This must be awful for him, caught between loyalty for his family and for his team. And then at Declan, who'd taken off his T-shirt to try and stop the blood seeping from his badly cut lip. He managed to grin around the wadded-up T-shirt and gave Rhett a thumbs-up sign. The Braddock boys together again, at last.

Rhett started to laugh. "I'm home," he said, feeling the bittersweet truth in his bones. "I am definitely home."

"It's not funny to me," Grady said softly.

Rhett shut up and looked his former best friend in the eye.

Grady swallowed hard. "Why didn't you just tell me to begin with?"

"Because I thought you would never find out, which meant I couldn't hurt you," Rhett said. "And . . . because telling you felt too hard.

Telling my best friend that I messed up in the worst way I ever could. Telling my best friend who'd stuck with me through all the years when I didn't have anybody else to call brother." In his peripheral vision, Declan lowered his head to stare at the ground. But Rhett had to stay with Grady. He owed this to him, especially before he confronted Jules with her own lie and then packed up Scarlett and went back to Dallas.

"I knew I'd lose you, and I was right. I'm sorry you feel I betrayed you. Thing is, I guess I did. Except that I'm in love with your sister."

He said the words without thinking, but as soon as they came out and hung there, in the air, in front of God and everybody, he knew they were true. Grady's eyes widened.

Rhett nodded. "I'm in love with Jules, even though she's made things impossible. So I didn't really betray you. But it doesn't matter now, anyway. It's going to take a long time to get over her, so I can understand how long it's going to take you to feel better about me. I hope you can get there." Rhett looked the other man in the eyes. "I'm sorry I didn't do what I should have done, and I'm sorry I didn't say what I should have said, when it mattered. I don't know what else to tell you."

One thing he wasn't going to do was tell Grady that his lil' baby sister had pulled the wool over both their eyes with her Bridget-influenced scheme to seduce Rhett into getting her way with the stables. Who was seducing whom now? If Grady couldn't believe that Rhett was in love with Jules for real, he'd never believe that Silverlake sweetheart Julianna Holt had coldly faked being in love with Rhett.

Which of them had the heart of a city slicker?

He was supposed to be the cold, hard businessperson here.

But he couldn't hold a candle to her con.

If he hadn't been so stunned and heartsick, he might even have admired it.

And if he hadn't heard Bridget define it out loud, he'd never have believed it of Jules.

He rewound his mental camera and recalled all of the times she'd clearly been forcing herself to be civil to him. And the sex? Had she been getting payback?

He just didn't know.

Rhett staggered a little as he got to his feet but steadied fast, with one hand braced against the inside of the garage.

Grady's eyes followed his. "You going back to Dallas?"

"Yup."

"You gonna throw in the towel on the baby?"

"Nope."

"Good. 'Cause you're going to be a great daddy," he said, grudgingly. Looking pretty pissed about it, though.

Rhett smiled and cautiously reached out to help Grady stand up.

Grady ignored the help and lurched upright, wincing a little.

Then he turned his back on Rhett and headed into the firehouse. With a sick feeling in his stomach, Rhett watched his best friend—his ex-best friend—walk out on him.

And then it was just the three Braddocks.

Rhett started collecting his belongings, Declan and Jake on either side, pitching in to make quick work of it. They dumped it all in the back seat of Rhett's car. Rhett stuck the deed on his dashboard and turned back to his brothers.

He just looked at them, couldn't find the words for how grateful he was to have them back in his life.

"Jake, I'm sorry about all this," Rhett said, gesturing to the garage. The space was still in disarray, boots knocked over, the pool octopus deflated, a length of unraveled hose.

Jake managed a smile, even as he examined the nasty scrape on his elbow. "Well," he said, "it's been a tough six months for the department; don't know why the rest of the year should be any different."

"Are you still taking heat for Charlie standing up against the squad at the council in October?" Declan asked.

"Yeah. And if I'm still taking heat for that,

413

might as well take some heat for standing up for you at the same time. Get it over with. I have faith that the boys'll come around eventually."

Rhett felt a lump in his throat. He put his hand on Jake's shoulder. "You could've stayed out of it."

"I don't think scattering to the winds did much for any of us," Jake said. "Maybe we should try sticking together?"

Rhett pulled his younger brother close, clapping him on the back. "Thanks," he whispered into Jake's ear. "That means a lot. How 'bout I give you a hand cleaning up?"

"We'll take care of it," Declan said, kicking the toe of his boot into the ground. "How about you take care of your business at Holt Stables? Then come home to the ranch before you head out." He finally looked up. "I'd love to have you stay for a final Fool Feast at Silverlake Ranch, if you have a mind. Aren't we all feeling a little foolish?"

Rhett nodded. He got into his car, looked out the windshield toward the road leading to Holt Stables, and forced himself—oh, he had to force himself—to harden his heart.

It was over. All of it. Jules. The ranch. His time in Silverlake was nearly up. It was all over.

At least he had another set of cuff links in his glove compartment, right? *Ha ha.*

Wearily, Rhett turned the key in the ignition, glancing at his vibrating phone. A text from Jules.

Please come ASAP. Frost needs you.
Jules.

One hand tightening on the steering wheel,
breath hitching in his chest, Rhett bowed his head
in surrender.

Chapter 33

Jules stood in the doorway of the barn with Beast at her side, dreading what was to come. Rhett sat in his car for an eternity before the door slowly opened and he got out. She gasped as Beast went to greet him and he absently stroked her head.

He looked okay, medically speaking—but his jeans and T-shirt were smeared with filth and oil. So the hot gossip about the firehouse brawl wasn't an exaggeration. She was going to kill Grady. Enough was enough.

There was a fresh cut over Rhett's left eye, and he probably had some nasty hidden bruises, but otherwise he seemed . . . intact.

The set of his shoulders told another story, though. He was broken up, and she'd certainly done her part to make him so. Saying yes didn't feel right. Jules stared at her left hand where she'd tried on that rock of a ring. *Why, then, did saying no feel even worse?*

The ring hung heavy in her pocket. She was pretty sure it had tried to crawl off her finger as soon as she'd started mucking out stalls. She could almost hear it shrieking that it was certainly not cut out for this . . .

But how did she give it back to a man who looked as down as she'd ever seen a man look?

A man who was about to lose a beloved part of his life? She might as well pour salt into a fresh gunshot wound.

Rhett had to know she was standing there, but he looked the other way, staring at the empty riding ring; you could still get a whiff of fresh paint from here.

Then he shaded his eyes and looked out over the grassy hill beyond the pasture, where Frost was standing in the wildflowers.

Her heart pounded in her chest as he walked toward Frost, while Beast returned to her. Rhett tucked some rolled-up paper into his back pocket as he strode up to his old rodeo horse and pressed his forehead to the old stallion's. Jules leaned heavily back against the weathered boards of the barn, a little breathless. She was going to have to tell him that Frost's time was up, on top of everything else.

The regret she'd been battling since his last proposal hit her like a truck. She and Beast walked toward the pasture, her steps quickening. Rhett was talking to Frost; Jules couldn't hear the words, but she could hear the soft rumble of his voice.

Shaking a little, Jules mustered up her courage. "You can't ignore me forever," she said.

"I know. I've tried before. The minute you walked through that door in Dallas, I was done. Didn't even know just how bad," Rhett said. "Couldn't ignore you after that. Couldn't stop thinking about you long after I walked out on you. Won't stop thinking about you long after I head back to Dallas." He gently stroked the length of Frost's nose and scratched behind the horse's ears.

The numbness in Rhett's voice shook Jules to her core. Something was way, way off. The words were everything she'd ever wanted to hear; the delivery scared her.

"It doesn't change the facts, though. You got me back good," he said bitterly.

What? Got you back?

Then he abruptly changed the subject. "He's not breathing right. He's not steady on his feet. You're right: I think he's in pain," Rhett said. He leaned toward the old Appaloosa and slipped both arms around his neck. "Aw, you waited for me, huh, boy? I'm right here. I'm sorry I was away for so long, but I'm right here now."

Frost snuffled weakly into Rhett's shoulder.

Jules blinked, a lump growing in her throat as she tried to keep up with Rhett's thought process. He was in a world of hurt. She could feel it. "I tried to take him back to the stables but he wants to stay out here in the wild. I called the vet. I guess you got my text."

Rhett didn't answer. He ran his hand slowly along Frost's spine, starting at the withers, as if his fingers were storing memories. Jules reached out to put her hand on his shoulder, to tell him very clearly that Frost was ready to go, and even though she wouldn't marry him, it didn't mean she didn't care about him—God, if he only understood just how much—and she was here for him if he needed—

But as soon as she touched him, he jerked away as if burned. "Don't," he said evenly.

O-kay . . . Jules stood there, at a loss. Beast whined, then shook her head and sent slobber flying everywhere.

"Frost," Rhett murmured. "I always felt like John Wayne on you."

She stood silent, hurting because he was hurting. Wishing he would let her comfort him. But he had to go and be . . . a man. Stoic and unreachable in his grief.

"He's going to die," Rhett said, suddenly angry. He took a step back, bumping into Jules, flinching, and turning away from her. He dashed tears from his eyes. "And now nothing in Silverlake matters anymore."

Oh, Rhett. Her heart ached for him.

He seemed to have forgotten that she was there. He buried his face in Frost's neck, his strong fingers twining in his horse's mane, almost as if he could keep Frost here on earth by sheer force of will.

Without even realizing it, she made a soft noise of distress.

He jolted. "Why don't you go and leave me and

Frost in some peace?" he asked bitterly. "Why don't you just leave us alone?

Beast gave a soft woof.

Jules looked between Rhett and Frost. *Was Rhett out of his mind?* Where was this hostility coming from? "No," she said. "I'm not leaving you alone at a time like this."

Rhett turned and looked at her with narrowed eyes that switched to confusion and then softened as she focused on his horse, patting softly, letting Frost know he was loved.

Jules stayed quiet as Rhett talked to Frost about the past.

"I wish I could have taken you to Connecticut, boy . . . I'm so sorry. But it's not that I left you . . . I got sent away. I missed you something fierce. And then, once the pain had faded, I was afraid to feel it again. I was so pissed at Deck that I stayed away—and that meant staying away from you, too."

He dashed away more tears.

It broke her heart to see this big, tough, hardened businessman crying. She touched his shoulder again, trying to offer comfort.

"Get away from me," Rhett growled. "Go on. *Go.*"

Beast woofed again, as if to say *ouch.*

Jules dropped her hand.

Grief makes some people mean. And they lash out.

420

Helpless, she stepped back. But she refused to leave him like this—not that he seemed to notice.

"So I didn't come back," he said to Frost. "That was wrong. You made my whole childhood, took me from boy to man. Riding you was my solace after Pop and Mama died . . ." His voice broke.

Across the field, Esme's van pulled up next to Scarlett. Jules waved both her arms to signal their location and got a wave back.

Rhett heard the door slam and looked up. "No. Please, no. Do you have to go *now?*" he asked Frost desperately, his voice clogged with sorrow.

Let him go, Jules thought to say to him.

But as Rhett put his arms around Frost's neck again and hugged him close, she saw for herself just how fiercely this man could love, how honest his feelings were below the surface. *Let him feel it all.*

The vet had walked over, quietly organized her equipment, and gave Jules a nod. They'd been down this road together before and there was no need for sterile words or explanations.

"Rhett, it's time to say goodbye," Jules said softly. "Do you remember how it goes?"

Rhett took a deep breath, shuddered, and in a controlled voice said, "I remember."

Jules stayed next to the vet, using her body to give Rhett a little privacy as the vet administered to Frost with quick, practiced movements.

Rhett spoke to Frost the entire time. "You're not alone. Feel my hand? See? It's me. You're not alone, Frost. We're right here . . . right here, boy . . . we'll ride again, you and I."

In a little while, Frost wheezed and went down, his legs giving out in a rush that had the old horse suddenly lying in the field of wildflowers.

Beast whined and laid down, too, her brown eyes giving away her distress.

Jules sucked in a quick breath. It never got easier. *Oh, sweet boy.*

As the light and the life faded from Frost's mismatched eyes, one brown, one blue, Rhett made an anguished sound. He didn't move, just knelt on the ground stroking Frost's side. He bent over him, his shoulders heaving as he gave way to his grief.

Jules knelt down on the other side of Frost, pressing her hand gently against his body. "Ssh, it's okay . . . it's okay, boy. It's okay . . ." she murmured, her fingers suddenly tangling with Rhett's.

Their eyes met. Jules surveyed Rhett's face, tear-streaked to match her own. "It's okay, Rhett," she said squeezing his hand. He squeezed back, lost in the moment, letting go only to brush back a lock of Frost's mane.

"It'll never be okay again," he said. And then: "I want him buried at Silverlake."

· · ·

Rhett sat out in the wildflowers with his hand on Frost, feeling his old friend's warmth give out little by little. The air was crisp on his skin, but that determined sun shone high in the sky, as if it didn't know today was a day for mourning things lost. Beast remained with him, settled about a yard away, her muzzle resting on her front paws. Rhett was grateful for her presence.

Staying for a final Fool Feast didn't seem like an option anymore. Lila would be so disappointed.

Jake, too, actually.

Come to think of it, Declan would be bothered by it more than anybody, though he wouldn't say a thing.

Why not *stay?*

Jules had gone to the parking area with the vet to make arrangements, out of earshot, for Frost. Rhett watched her from afar, one hand still stroking Frost.

Because she doesn't love me.

You still have your family.

It's a lot, but it's too hard being here knowing what I can't have.

You have a baby on the way. You're gonna be around here for that. Haven't figured it out, but you're definitely going to be there for that child.

A wave of resentment swept through Rhett as he thought about how simple things would have been if Jules had only said yes. But she'd have been deceiving him . . .

He reeled with bitterness. All these years, he'd been so careful to avoid getting tangled with a gold digger in Dallas. He'd been on his guard around women for a long time. Now, suddenly, Julianna Holt, with her tomboy ways, had blindsided him. He hadn't seen it coming. Because he hadn't wanted to see it.

Since the moment she'd bought him that beer in Schweitz's, he'd watched her struggle and strangle on her emotions right in front of him. Forcing herself to be nice. *Keep your friends close and your enemies closer* . . .

He wanted to throttle Bridget. One thing he knew for sure: Jules wouldn't have come up with the strategy on her own.

No . . . she'd just executed it. Along with any hopes Rhett had for a happy ending in his life.

"What do you think I should do now?" Rhett asked Frost.

A breeze riffled through Frost's mane.

"Well, I guess I know what you'd say," Rhett said softly. "You'd tell me to stay through our final family Fool Feast, in Mama's best tradition, and choke down Lila's cooking. You'd say you love Silverlake Ranch. And you love Lila and Jake and Declan most of all. You'd say that you'd never miss a chance for carrots though you'd appreciate it if yours were served raw, with a side of apples."

Goodbye, old friend.

Rhett mopped his face with his arm. "You'd tell me that if *you* had the chance, you'd go back one more time. You'd tell me not to leave with any regrets." *Love you, Frost. Go run free, and I'll see you again someday.*

Rhett pressed his forehead to Frost's for the last time, gently tugged his forelock, and headed back toward the barn as Beast trailed him.

With every step he forced himself to harden his heart, because he knew that if he didn't, that when he got close enough to Jules to look into those hazel eyes of hers, he might break down again.

And so by the time he got to the parking area and the vet was driving away, Rhett Braddock had armored up enough to make it to Scarlett without losing it.

Jules was right on his heels, though. "Rhett, wait!"

"Leave me alone, Jules. I can't take anymore. I just can't."

Jules caught up to him, grabbed his hand.

Rhett shook her off. He didn't want to see her face, didn't want her to see his, didn't want to share his grief with someone who thought so little of his love. He pulled the deed to the property out of his back pocket and threw it to the gravel. Beast looked perplexed and went over to sniff it.

"What is that?" She stared down, trying to make out the letters.

"You win," he said. "You can stop pretending. Frost is gone. The stables are yours. And I'm gone."

"What are you talking about? I know Frost is gone," she said, "but—"

"No. It's all gone. Any faith I had in you? Gone. You and me? *Gone.*"

Jules went white with shock and swayed in front of him.

He thought she might faint. So he reached out and braced her. But it was her turn to pull away. She picked up the deed and ripped it to shreds, letting them fall where they may. "We're not gone, Rhett Braddock. We're right here."

God, he wanted to believe her. *Jules, you're killin' me.*

"Keep your friends close," he said. "And your enemies closer."

She turned a shade whiter. "Wh-what?"

"You were pretending to care about me to get control of the stables. That's what Bridget told you to do, isn't it?"

"Bridget?" A look of sudden understanding lit up Jules's face. "That's what's turned you so cold? This is *so* messed up. I can see why you— okay. Yes, Bridget told me things would go easier if you and I were friends. And, yes, I took that advice."

426

He nodded. "So I'll FedEx you another copy of the deed. I don't want anything that reminds me of you—especially not your family property." He turned on his heel to get into Scarlett.

"You don't understand," Jules said. "And you'd *better* want your child—who will, I'm sorry to say, remind you of me."

He froze. She'd gotten his attention. He turned back around and glowered down at her.

She raised her chin.

"I do want my child. I'll have my lawyers get in touch."

She dug frantically into her pocket; held out the ring. "What about this?"

"Keep it."

"No—you don't get what I'm trying to say! What about your big proposal, asking my dad, going down on one knee? Didn't that mean anything to you?"

He shook his head and laughed softly. "A damn sight more than it meant to you. You can add 'Humiliating Rhett Braddock in Public' to your list of wins. Congratulations."

"*Oh!*" Her jaw worked; her rooster-tail hair quivered. She stamped her foot. "You are *so* stupid." She marched forward and smacked the ring into his chest.

"Ow!"

This time Beast woofed at Jules. The dog clearly didn't like the tension.

"Would you please shut up and *listen* to me?" Jules said to Rhett.

He stared at her.

"Yes, okay, Bridget did tell me to . . . cultivate . . . you. So I did. I'm sorry. But then you started doing all these nice things, and I started to like you again. I was okay being friends with you. But being friends with you wasn't enough."

Rhett scrubbed a hand through his hair. "Go on."

"I . . . wanted . . . more."

"More," he repeated.

"It wasn't even something I could control or wanted to control. I started to fall in love with you all over again. The way it was before Dallas. Even more than that, really . . . and then I got mad at myself and you for it. I felt really messed up. But I couldn't help myself."

"What are you saying?"

"I can't take your ring," she blurted.

And all the hope that had started to rise and spiral in him crashed.

"Fine." He shoved it into his pocket and turned again, feeling blindly for Scarlett's door handle.

"Stop!" she yelled. "What I mean is, the ring isn't me. But, Rhett, I've *been* in love with you. *So* in love with you that marrying you with anything less than that in *your* heart would devastate me."

"What?" he whispered. He turned again to face her. "You said no *twice*."

"Because I thought you were asking for the wrong reasons. And the history with my aunt Sue—"

"I thought you didn't care."

"I don't want to marry you for anything less than love. Do you understand that?"

He stared at the scraps of paper that littered the gravel and were supposed to represent everything that mattered to her; she'd ripped the deed apart as if it meant nothing. He met her gaze, really looked into her eyes and, by God, if she wasn't telling the truth.

"You're in love with me?" Rhett repeated.

"*So* in love with you, Rhett. Are you in love with *me*?"

"What do you think?" Rhett moved so fast he sent gravel flying into the air. And then Jules was in his arms again and his mouth was on hers.

Beast wagged her tail frantically before shaking her head again and spraying them with congratulatory slobber.

"Are you saying what I think you're saying?" Jules asked on a breath.

"What I'm saying," Rhett said, his mouth restless against her lips, "is that I love the way you won't change for anyone; you're Jules, take it or leave it. And I couldn't be happier about that because the woman you are is exactly the woman

I want. You're smart and beautiful and a little bit crazy. Just the way I like it. You dig in and go to the ends of the earth for the things and the people you care about. And I'm just wondering if I could be one of those people for the rest of our lives."

Jules kissed him back, this time snaking her empty hands up the muscled contours of Rhett's back.

"I am never letting go of you again," he whispered when they came up for air.

"Mmm . . . you might want to rethink that."

"Uh-uh."

"Might . . . want . . . to . . ."

"Nope."

She smiled against his lips. "Not even to meet little Frosty?"

Rhett stilled and then slowly pulled away. "Who?"

Jules pulled back, looked up, and rested her palm against Rhett's cheek. "Thing is, Mr. Braddock, I may not be the owner of these stables, but I have been and will continue to be the manager. And as such, I have the right to make certain purchases I deem important."

"What are you talking about, Jules?" Rhett asked softly.

Jules took Rhett's hand in hers and pulled him into the barn as Beast trotted happily after them. They walked down the wide center aisle, all the way to the last stall, where Don Qui, in his colorful harness, was playing nanny to a newcomer; welcoming him to the fold.

Rhett stared in disbelief as a young colt nosed up to him. A colt with a dappled gray coat, one blue eye and one brown eye. The spitting image of Frost, no doubt a member of the same bloodline.

His breath caught.

Rhett couldn't remember a time when someone had done something so perfect for him. "Little Frosty, huh?" He entered the stall and let the colt explore and snuffle him before placing a kiss on the baby's forehead and turning back to Jules.

"Circle of life, you know?" Jules said.

Rhett gently placed his hand against her stomach.

Circle of life.

Jules smiled. "I would be so happy if you'd stick around to see the little ones grow up," she said.

Rhett took her in his arms once more. "Is that you finally saying yes?"

"Yes," Jules said. "Yes, yes, yes!"

CHAPTER 34

The big house at Silverlake Ranch was teeming with people, courtesy of Lila's plans for a family-style grand finale to the Fool Fest mayhem. It was wonderful to be a part of the community again, but it also felt good to Rhett to step outside with only Declan, to walk up the grassy slope at the far end of the Braddock homestead. From there they could see the water sparkling in the lake in the sunlight.

Deck touched the leaves of a small sapling, appraising it with a rancher's eye.

It was still strange standing next to his older brother: a slightly rangier and older carbon copy of himself. Same jawline. Same cheekbones. Same build. Dark eyes, though.

Strange, but good not to have fancy technology and miles of disappointment separating them anymore.

"I wanted to say . . ." Declan began, and then stopped. He sighed and looked down at the bluebonnets peppering the grass at his boots. "You and me, Rhett . . . we were so close once. Messing around with engines and chasing each other down in the fields. I remember fishing next to you in Pop's boat for hours, no need to say a word. I remember you and me sitting on the corral fence, sussing out which horses would be the best rodeo mounts. And then I remember when . . . you stopped calling." His voice hitched slightly. "You stopped asking about the fishing and the horses and the land."

His gaze moved out to safer ground, locking somewhere on the horizon. "If I ever made it seem like I wanted you to stay away, Rhett, I'm sorry. Banishing you from Silverlake was not at all what I was trying to do."

"You told the others I didn't want to come home," Rhett said evenly, careful to keep the old hurt out of his voice.

But Deck was no fool. He heard it anyway. "It was wrong," his brother said. "I even convinced myself after a time that you wanted to be where you were. I mean, it's obvious why you stopped calling, but in my head I rationalized it. I took it to mean that you didn't care. That you'd settled into a different life—one that didn't include us. One that was more highbrow."

Rhett swore softly.

Deck shook his head. "Wish I could take back some of what I did." His gaze swung back to his brother. "But not all of it. I thought that school was where you were supposed to be. I know I was a hard-ass. But Mama and Pops would be so proud of what you've accomplished. I'm proud of you, too. I want you to know that."

The words hung between them for a long

moment before Rhett could absorb them. Then he drank them in, like a thirsty plant after a drought. *Declan is proud of me. Huh.* He cleared his throat, uncomfortable with how much that meant to him.

Declan was *proud* of him.

"I want you to know something else," Deck said.

The grass at their feet swayed in the chilly breeze. Deck looked back at the busy ranch house lit up with fairy lights. Someone shouted and a peal of laughter followed. The corner of Deck's mouth turned up slightly.

"What do you want me to know?" Rhett prompted, when Deck didn't continue.

"It was *so* hard for me to keep you there." Declan turned back and managed a bittersweet smile. "I wanted to put you on the first plane home when I heard what you were going through. Or come up and kick some preppy butt. But I also knew you could handle it. That it would form your character."

Rhett swore again.

"Sometimes I prayed to Mama and Pop for guidance. I'd tell them what you said on the phone to me. But I never got a sign from them. God never told me what to do, either—that's for sure. Which formed *my* character, Rhett. It was on me, barely a man myself, to raise you all. And fighting your battles, or helping you run from them—no. It didn't feel like something they'd want. What they wanted was for you to take advantage of your opportunities and make the most of them. And for their sake, as well as your own, I wanted to get at least one of you out the door right."

Rhett had to swallow hard again. Keep the emotion from rising to his eyes, where it would betray him.

Deck, as usual, saw it anyway. "All the things you've been through in life . . . I'm sorry if it's not the life that you imagined when we were kids. But it's still been a good life, right?"

Rhett looked into Declan's haunted eyes. "It's still been a good life." He instinctively looked back at the house for Jules. She was standing on the porch with Billy Holt and didn't see him, but just seeing her there, comfortable and happy on his family property, touched his soul. "And now, thanks to Jules, it's going to be great."

Deck smiled.

Rhett punched him in the shoulder. "So thanks, you a-hole, for selling off my rodeo horse and inciting me to make an epic *up yours* statement. This is all your fault!" He grinned. Then he added softly, "Thank you. Love you, big brother."

Deck started to punch him back. Then he changed his mind and wrapped him in a bear hug. "Same," he said, his voice gruff. It took a while before he pulled away.

"Declan, are you going to *cry?* Because we've got a football game to play."

"Be back in a minute. I gotta see a man about a horse," Deck muttered, and walked away.

"Be sure to look it in the mouth, you hear?" Rhett chuckled as his oldest brother flipped him the bird.

Jules stood on the screened porch next to her dad; her with an iced tea, him with a beer, in defiance of her mother. Mom was inside, deftly correcting a culinary disaster of Lila's but convincing her that it had been delicious to begin with. This operation took tact, skill, and kindness . . . and Jules's respect for Mom grew even as she hid her smile.

She had to love Lila for even trying to cook—it was not something Jules ever intended to do. When she'd informed Rhett, he'd grinned and tugged at her rooster feathers. "No problem, darlin'. We can hire that done." *We can also go to Walmart or the prepared foods section at Griggs' Grocers,* she'd retorted.

"How you doin', Dad?"

"I feel great, baby do—" He stopped short at her expression. "It really bothers you when I call you that."

Jules nodded.

"Okay, sweetheart, understood." He turned back to the action. "What are those clowns plotting out there?"

Declan had marked off a football field–sized rectangle in the grass and he was huddled at one end with the rest of the Braddocks while the opposing team, Silverlake's very own Pissed-Off Fire and Having-Trouble-Forgiving Rescue swarmed around on the other end.

It seemed the squad members were patching things up slowly, but Grady said he wanted another chance to take down Rhett and Jake before he had to go about the business of being friends again. It wouldn't feel done until he'd drawn Braddock blood at least one more time, Grady had said, scowling around a mouthful of steak and potatoes at last night's family dinner.

"Well, that's a sight you don't see every day," said a familiar voice, and Jules looked up to see Aunt Sue at her elbow, her bottle of Baileys peeking out of her purse. Mia and her dad, Silverlake High's baseball coach, walked up behind her.

"Hey, y'all! Glad you could make it." Jules hugged each of them in turn.

Mia still looked exhausted, and Coach looked his usual beefy self, though it appeared that he'd started dyeing his thinning hair. It was a peculiar shade of auburn.

Jules raised an eyebrow at Mia, who shook her head and shrugged.

"Come on in—drinks in the kitchen."

Coach pointed at the Braddock crew: Declan,

Rhett, Jake, and Lila huddled up, their arms around one another as they discussed a strategy to avoid getting their heads smashed in by a squad of angry firefighters. "Only one missing Braddock here: Ace," Coach said wistfully. "Wish he'd come home to Silverlake every once in a while. Miss that boy."

Mia's lips tightened almost imperceptibly, and she went into the house.

"Wish I could play," Dad said, gazing toward the field.

"Not me," Coach said, chuckling. "I'm glad to sit on the porch."

As if on cue, Rhett suddenly looked up to the porch and called out. "Hey, Billy. We're gonna' need a referee here. It could get ugly."

Jules's dad grinned and made his way down from the porch. Declan broke out of the huddle and set up a folding chair for him before jogging back to his family huddle.

Her dad settled in, stuck a couple fingers in his mouth, and blew a loud, shrill whistle. "No biting, grabbing testicles, no kicking a man or woman down! Oh, and try to get the ball over the other team's line. Y'all ready?"

Both teams hooted and hollered. Jules, with a wide smile, looked at Aunt Sue.

Aunt Sue winked at her. "I'm going to need me some iced coffee," she said.

Jules shook her head. "Spiked coffee, more like."

"Why, I have no idea what you're talking about, Julianna Holt."

Snort.

Dad called up the captains.

Declan and Grady came forward, managed a round of rock, paper, scissors without punching each other, and then jogged away. Based on the high-decibel swearing from Grady, Declan had emerged victorious.

Declan faked a pass out to Rhett and spiraled the ball to Lila, who took off like a shot. She made it twenty yards before the firefighters realized she had the ball and then Mick elbowed his own teammate Rafael aside and plastered her to the ground in a tackle.

Everybody on the porch sucked in a breath and the game paused as Mick stared down at Lila beneath him.

"Keep your hands to yourself, Mick!" Grady shouted. "Or they'll accuse us of cheating!"

"Well, that's no fun," Mick called back.

Suddenly Lila just pushed Mick off her, popped up, and shouted at everybody to get back in formation. And like that, it was on.

"I'm glad you came," Jules said to Sue as Declan threw another graceful spiral out to Jake, who collided with Grady as they both leaped for it. They came away with nothing but a handful of each other's shirts.

"I wasn't sure I'd be welcome. Wasn't sure at

all," Sue said frankly. She'd gone in for her iced coffee, and now she jiggled the cubes.

"Declan asked me to invite you, if I hadn't already."

"That's Declan. Don't know why that boy hasn't settled down." After a moment's hesitation she asked, "Does *Rhett* know I'm coming?"

"Yep. He said he appreciated your spirit."

Aunt Sue burst into peals of laughter. "Very politic."

Rhett had agreed that the Saddlery could stay in business, as long as her aunt took a fair cut of the consignment items, sold snacks and peach tea at a good markup, and worked to actively market her jewelry and leather goods so that the place started turning a profit.

"You gonna be okay with him, Aunt Sue? Treat him right?" She turned and caught her aunt's gaze square. "I'm in love with him, and we're having a baby. I want you on our side." Jules felt her face burn as she made the next confession: "We already got a license. I wanted to make up for turning him down so hard and the best way I could think of was taking him down to Dusty Hinckle at the city clerk's office, signing my name on his heart, and showing him my intentions."

A host of emotions flickered in Sue's eyes. She took a long draft of her coffee. "Well, I promise not to shoot him, anyways."

Startled, Jules choked on a laugh.

"So did Dusty read you his crusty lecture on how marriage is a sacred commitment and all? Not to be entered into lightly or for the wrong reasons."

"Yep," Jules said ruefully. "I told him everything was just fine. That I was marrying Rhett for his money."

Aunt Sue hooted. "You did not."

"I sure did. And then, when he looked shocked, I asked if there was a problem."

"I'll be by your side, come what may," said Aunt Sue, after she stopped laughing. "And maybe . . . maybe you'll let me babysit some." She stared into her coffee, her throat working.

Poor Aunt Sue. She would never forget her unborn child. Never stop wondering who she'd have grown up to be. Jules put an arm around Aunt Sue and squeezed her. "Some?" she asked, to lighten the moment. "We plan to take total advantage of you as our unpaid nanny."

Sue laughed. "Oh, is that how it's going to be?"

"Uh-huh. You'll see," Jules said, shading her eyes and turning back to watch Rhett happy, laughing, messing around in the mud with his brothers and sister.

Dad blew the whistle on a foul for Mick, and the game stopped for a moment.

Rhett looked up to the porch.

Jules waved.

He mouthed *I love you* and pressed his palm to his heart.

"What is this, a romance novel?" Aunt Sue called.

He turned back to the game to find everybody watching.

Jules laughed as they started hooting and hollering, messing up his hair, and pounding him on the back. He shot that mile-wide smile again, back up to her on the porch.

Dad whistled to start the next play. "Focus! Eyes on the ball, not my daughter, young man."

"You two are disgusting," yelled Grady. "Hike it, Lovesick!"

CHAPTER 35

The sun was already starting to go down when dinner was called. Rhett paused in the doorway to the great room as those he cared about most in the world streamed in around him with a smile, a kind word, or a shoulder squeeze. He stood with his hands shoved into his pockets and walked to the window, silently admiring everything Declan had done to the house. He couldn't get over the scores of memories: Ace drawing beneath the trees, Lila crawling up into one to read her *Anne of Green Gables* books. Jake hanging the tire swing from the big oak in back . . . which was still there. He and Declan had built a platform in another one off the side of the house and created a rope ladder that they pulled up so that nobody could enter their clubhouse. He smiled.

He ran a hand over the expansive old farm table that had been Mama and Pop's—had come down from Mama's own mama. Declan had sanded it down to bare wood and applied a beautiful new finish. It stood over a new, more modern rug that Lila had chosen.

"Here you go," his sister said, handing him a stack of plates. "You get to help."

Rhett nodded and followed her around the table as she set down place mats.

"Grab some silverware?" she asked as she added an absolutely horrific centerpiece of a jester reclining on a bunch of fake fruit.

"We have to look at that while we eat?" he protested.

"No—*it* has to look at *you,* nimrod."

He grinned. They'd always be siblings, no matter how many years went by, no matter how adult they were supposed to be.

"Of course we have to look at it while we eat: This is a Feast of Fools," Lila said.

Declan appeared with a couple of bottles of wine for the table and stopped short upon sight of the jester. "No. Really? That's just plain awful."

"Tackiest thing I've ever seen," agreed Lila cheerfully. "And it stays."

"Awfully bossy, aren't you?" Deck set the bottles down on either end of the table.

"You bet. Mama is up there laughing. She always did love creating the jesters for Fool Fest. So this is actually in her honor."

Jake and Charlie strolled in and winced. "Dear Lord," was Charlie's only comment.

Mrs. Holt emerged from the kitchen with a massive baked ham, took one look at the centerpiece, and surprised them all by laughing. "Oh my. Beverly would have loved it."

"Right?" Lila nodded.

Mia followed her with a huge pan of scalloped potatoes that had Rhett's mouth watering.

And Jules brought in a green bean casserole the size of a football field.

They set down the food and backed away from the jester.

"Does it bite?" asked Jules.

Lila shook a finger at her. "Only when it's disrespected and maligned."

"Tell me that there's a dessert that gets flambéed," suggested Jake. "So that it can accidentally catch on fire."

"That's really not funny," Declan said.

Soon the rest of the guests had arrived and they were all seated and helping themselves to food: Coach and Mia, Jake and Charlie, old Kingston Nash and Aunt Sue, the Holts, Rhett and Jules, Lila and Declan at each end of the table. Grady and Old George flanked Deck. Mick and Rafi flanked Lila.

Mrs. Holt asked her husband to say grace. Billy did so, garnering a great cheer when he added that he'd already been blessed: His treatment was working and his prognosis was excellent, a best-case scenario.

After order was restored, Lila asked everyone to think of something foolish they'd done and share it with the group.

They went around the table.

"Not bringing enough Baileys to drown out the sight of that hideous jester," said Aunt Sue.

"Letting my granddaughter plant my truck

bed full of bluebonnets," growled Kingston. "She won't take 'em out, and now Progress gets watered every day!"

Charlie shook with laughter.

"Trying to make mole," admitted Lila.

Everyone laughed—though Rafi made more of a choking noise.

And so it went.

Then Declan surprised everyone by clinking a fork against his wineglass. "That was great. But I'd like to propose next that we each come up with a toast. And here's mine: To all of you, for being here at Silverlake Ranch with this fool." He gestured to himself, and his mouth worked. "I can't even find the words to tell you how much it means to me."

"Hear! Hear!" They all raised their glasses.

Everyone had a say; some of the words were funny, some bittersweet, some downright mushy, and others deliberately trying to get a laugh.

At last it was Rhett's turn. He'd thought about making a joke and saving his words for a more private time. But everybody he loved in the world was in this room, at this table.

"I don't think there's a way for me to explain just how happy I am to be here with all of you," Rhett finally said. "This is a perfect day."

He looked around at each face, his eyes pausing on Declan, Jake, and Lila. "I'm home in Silverlake, and, no foolin', I've got my family back."

He found Grady's face, and the storm in his best friend's eyes had retreated. He smiled over the platters of food and got a smile back—with an eye roll, of course. "My best friend doesn't want to kill me anymore. At least not as much as he used to, and I like to think it's getting better all the time."

Soft laughter filled the room, with Grady joining in.

Rhett nodded at the rest of the crew scattered around the table. "You can't have too much family, and everybody here is here because . . . somebody at this table cares a whole helluva lot about you." He locked eyes with Aunt Sue. "I look forward to getting to know all of you better in the future."

She smiled gratefully, her eyes glistening with unshed tears.

Rhett finally looked to Jules sitting next to him, her hand in his. Her smile was radiant, her grip strong and sure. "And you, Jules. You remind me every day what sort of man I want to be. I couldn't be happier sitting here at a table next to you, surrounded by the fields and the lake, the livestock, and everything under the sun that I've loved all my life right here in Silverlake. I cherish you more than anything in this world."

Jules buried her face in Rhett's shoulder; he could feel the warmth of her breath, the shape of her smile before she pulled back. "I love you, too. I wish we could get married today, right here, right now."

"Do you, now?" Rhett asked softly. "Do you mean it?"

"Are you kidding?" Jules asked. "It's everything I could want. You know me. You know who I am." She opened her arms wide, taking in the beloved people sitting around the table. "What else do we need? We even have the license already."

"Holy moly, my heart is pounding," Lila squeaked from her place down at the far end of the table.

Coach cleared his throat. "You know I'm an ordained minister, right?"

The idea hung for a moment in the atmosphere, everyone collectively holding their breath.

Rhett looked down the table at Coach, and he smiled and inclined his head. He cupped Jules's face in the palms of his hands. "Well, then, Jules. What do you say? Right here, right now?"

Jules pursed her lips. "Well, maybe after a slice of Sue's pie."

Everyone around the table burst into peals of laughter. "Yes," Jules said with a grin. "Right here, right now. Actually, pie afterward, though. We don't have a wedding cake."

"Or a ring," Rhett said, frowning.

"We have a ring!" Lila said, holding up her hand. The Pet Rock he'd bought for Jules sparkled madly from her forefinger.

"Not that one," he said, shaking his head.

"Well, I *would* rather keep it," she conceded.

Everyone laughed.

"Okay, okay. I have an idea." She waved Rhett to her, then steered him away from the dinner table that had turned very suddenly into Wedding Planning Central; everybody was getting involved.

She led him to a closet and took out an old mahogany box that used to rest on Mama's vanity. Lila opened the box and Rhett sucked in a breath. He didn't recognize all of it, but among the pieces of jewelry there were some he distinctly recalled her wearing.

"Didn't this all go to you?" Rhett asked.

Lila shrugged. "Sometimes I come over and open the box and just look through it, but I've never worn it. I don't know. It makes me a little sad. I think it would be nice if you picked something out for Jules. Something Mama wore. Don't you?"

"That's generous of you," Rhett said softly, hugging his little sister.

"Least I can do," she said, waggling the Pet Rock again. "You sure I can keep this?"

"Yup. I want Monty to have the sale." He made his choice from Mama's jewelry and slipped the ring in his pocket. "And it's still nice of you, squirt."

"Maybe. Or maybe I'd do just about anything to make you want to come home, big brother."

The siblings shared a hug, which was interrupted by a ruckus coming from outside.

"What the—?" Rhett said, heading back out to the living room with Lila in tow.

He stopped short. Jules stood in the living room surrounded by Mia, Charlie, Aunt Sue, and Mrs. Holt, all of them putting the finishing touches on a wildflower bouquet and twining some blossoms in Jules's hair.

He must have made some sort of sound, because they took a step back, and then it was as if everyone else disappeared. Jules stood waiting for him in a pretty flowery dress and a pair of cowboy boots, holding a cluster of Mama's doorstep bluebonnets. He'd never seen anything lovelier.

"Your honeymoon suite is ready and waiting," Jake murmured, pressing the key to the fishing shack into Rhett's hand. He laughed. It was a perfect honeymoon suite for a girl like Jules.

And there was Coach on the porch, the good book in his hand. "We're ready when you are," he called.

Jules held out her hand and Rhett took it, his heart so full it felt like it could burst.

Coach led the two of them in a pair of short, simple vows, the kind the first settlers of Silverlake might have said. Rhett slipped his hand into his pocket and pulled out a simple gold band with a small horseshoe fashioned from diamond chips.

Jules sucked in a breath. Rhett looked at her, a worried expression flitting across his face.

"Rhett, it's *perfect*."

"It was my mama's," he said softly. "Oh, Jules, she would have just loved knowing we were together."

"She does," Jules said, blinking back tears. She looked up to the sky. "I know both your parents are watching right now."

Rhett met the eyes of each of his siblings, taking time to acknowledge that truth with Lila, Jake, and then Declan. He slid the sweet horseshoe ring onto Jules's finger, and then stared down at his boots for a moment, composing himself before he nodded for the coach to continue the ceremony.

"Oh," Jules said, flustered that in all the fuss to get her ready for the wedding, she hadn't thought of what to do about a ring for Rhett.

But suddenly Grady stepped forward, pulling off the white metal band he wore on his thumb. He handed it to her. He clapped Rhett on the shoulder, saying as he moved away, "I'll *always* have your back, knucklehead. Take good care of my sister."

Thank you, Jules mouthed to her brother. She slid the ring onto Rhett's left hand.

And then with Rhett smiling down on her, so

much like the image in her mind of that boy from long ago, Coach said, "I now pronounce you husband and wife."

Rhett's arms came around her and he dipped her low, his mouth on hers. Everyone cheered like crazy and they had to end their kiss, they were laughing so hard.

"I love you," Jules said, pressing her cheek to his heart.

Rhett brushed his lips softly against her ear, whispering, "I love you, too." Then he swept her up in his arms and walked to the porch steps.

The firefighters had formed a saber arch using equipment from the ranch: Mick with a rake and Rafi a hoe. Old George had a broom, while Jake and Grady had their arms slung over each other's shoulders, their free hands hoisting the end of a garden hose and a rolling pin.

Everyone cheered, and Aunt Sue, Mom, Charlie, Lila, and Mia tossed the extra wildflowers as Rhett carried Jules down the steps and headed toward the trail leading to the fishing shack.

As they passed Scarlett, Rhett burst into laughter; the boys had used shaving cream to write JUST MARRIED across the back windshield and used string to tie the empty beer cans to the bumper of his car.

The shack wasn't far from the main house, and in no time at all, Rhett had whisked Jules to the threshold. Pausing to take her mouth with his, Rhett kicked open the door with his boot, and carried her inside.

Jules pulled his head to hers and they kissed until they could hardly breathe. Rhett tossed her on the bed, quickly pulling off their boots and joining her on the homey quilt. He wrapped his arms around those new soft curves of her body. He pressed kisses into her neck as Jules smiled, running her fingers through his hair.

The fire glowed in the little cabin's fireplace. A plate of the homemade pie sat on the small table. Rhett's cowboy hat rested on the chair by the door.

"God, I love my family. My whole, big, old, and new extended family," Rhett whispered. "You know how they say you can never go home again?"

"Yeah," Jules managed to say as Rhett's fingers undid the buttons of her dress and found a new swath of skin to make his own.

He took her mouth, slowly and sensually releasing her only to press a kiss to her neck. "They were *so* wrong." He added a kiss to the underside of her wrist. And a kiss to her inner thigh. "I *am* home again—with you."

ACKNOWLEDGMENTS

Thanks to Megan Frampton, gifted and wise beta reader, for reading and vetting early drafts—without laughing too hard.

Thanks always to the editorial, production, art, marketing, and sales teams at Berkley/Jove. We couldn't do it without you!

Center Point Large Print
600 Brooks Road / PO Box 1
Thorndike, ME 04986-0001 USA

(207) 568-3717

US & Canada:
1 800 929-9108
www.centerpointlargeprint.com